LORENZO DE' MEDICI

By the same Author

THE SACK OF ROME
CHARLOTTE BRONTË'S SHIRLEY
(ed. with A. D. Hook)
THE BAROQUE AGE IN ENGLAND
SIENA:
A City and its History

LORENZO DE' MEDICI

An Historical Biography

by

JUDITH HOOK

HAMISH HAMILTON
London

First published in Great Britain 1984
by Hamish Hamilton Ltd
Garden House, 57–59 Long Acre, London WC2E 9JZ

Copyright © 1984 by Judith Hook

British Library Cataloguing in Publication Data
Hook, Judith
    Lorenzo de' Medici
    1. Medici, Lorenzo de'
    I. Title
    94 5'.51   DG737.G
    ISBN 0-241-11218-4

Typeset by Rowland Phototypesetting Ltd
Bury St Edmunds, Suffolk
Printed in Great Britain by
St Edmundsbury Press, Bury St Edmunds, Suffolk

For Peter and Priscilla

CONTENTS

ILLUSTRATIONS

PREFACE

Lorenzo de' Medici is one of those rare individuals who continues to arouse as much passionate controversy after his death as he did during his lifetime. None of his biographers has succeeded in remaining dispassionate in the face of his complicated personality for he has always tended to become a symbol of other people's hopes and fears. As they view the past and the present, so they interpret Lorenzo. Thus Florentine, Tuscan and Italian nationalists have praised him, without real justification, as the creator of the Florentine Renaissance, as the inventor of the idea of the balance of power, as an early protagonist of the idea of a united Italy, while those who deplore the demise of the Florentine republic in the sixteenth century, tend to portray Lorenzo as the opponent of 'democratic' values, as an advocate of arbitrary and centralised power, a tyrant or the prototype of Machiavelli's Prince.

He was, of course, none of these. Lorenzo was a man living and working within a specific historical context which had a greater determining effect on what he thought and did than he had upon the course of history on which, in fact, he had little impact. He is historically significant not so much because of what he did or did not do but because the combination of the situation in which he found himself and his own many faceted personality and wide interests meant that he was involved in virtually everything of significance which was happening in Italy at a critical period in the peninsula's development. In that sense he may be seen as the truly representative 'Renaissance man'.

This biography is unashamedly directed at that much maligned figure – the general reader. It grew out of my realisation that there no longer exists in English an up-to-date introduction to its subject which is readily accessible to the non-specialist. The problem lies in the fact that, as far as academic history is concerned, Florentine Renaissance history is a growth industry. The virtually unparalleled resources of the Florentine archives make that city a Mecca for scholars, particularly those who are exponents of *Annales*-inspired history. Scarcely a month passes without some new major work on Florentine history appearing in some language or another. Lorenzo, personally, also commands the attention of a whole army of dedicated scholars, including those who are now currently engaged in the massive task of editing his complete correspondence. All of these works are immensely erudite but tend to assume a considerable prior knowledge of their subject which sixth-formers and undergraduates, not to speak of the ordinary layman, do not possess. Nevertheless, the conclusions of such books have, inevitably, affected the way in which we regard Lorenzo de' Medici and have certainly modified my own approach to the subject of this book, which is designed not as a substitute for more specialised works but as an introduction to them.

Because of my interest in rendering Lorenzo accessible to the general reader I have, wherever possible, quoted from printed sources. This has not always proved feasible. The archival research which I found necessary was undertaken in Italy over a number of years and I am grateful to the British Academy, the Carnegie Trust for the Universities of Scotland and the University of Aberdeen who have shown their continued faith in the importance of the study of the humanities by funding my visits abroad.

I am also grateful to the staffs of the Archivio di Stato in Milan, Florence and Siena and to those of the inter-library loans departments in the Universities of Aberdeen and Glasgow. I also owe a considerable debt of gratitude to a generation of Scottish sixth-formers and their dedicated teachers who have not been afraid to tackle the difficult subject of Laurentian Florence in their Sixth-Year Studies course and who have frequently shared their enthusiasm for the topic with me. Finally, I would like to thank my husband who has had to live with Lorenzo during the past four years and who has managed to find time, within his own busy schedule, to read and correct my manuscript.

1

THE MEDICI 'PRINCE'

In the beginning, for Lorenzo di Piero di Cosimo de' Medici, whom historians would later erroneously call The Magnificent*, there was the family. In the end, that same family came to dominate his life to such an extent that everything he did was determined by the need to preserve its status and reputation, its business and political interests and, above all, its property. For the sake of it he would choose a bride, decide upon his own children's careers, and select their marriage partners. For it, he would sacrifice his feelings, his time, his peace of mind, would immerse himself in uncongenial tasks and squander effort in ways that brought little personal reward; would increase his political power and thus earn for himself the name of tyrant, and endeavour, by every possible means, to protect the Medici into the foreseeable future.

Any honest man among his Florentine contemporaries would have agreed that, in thus acting, Lorenzo had little choice. Although by the mid-fifteenth century the age of the great family-clans, when all that happened in Florence was determined by the feuding between her leading families, was long over, the family still remained the central political, social and economic fact of life for every Florentine patrician. There might be a growing fashion for living a more secluded life with one's own immediate relatives, rather than in power complexes made up of all of one's family, but family interests still reigned supreme over any other obligations, and the protection of relatives remained a primary moral concern of all Florentines. The vast majority of the city's ruling-class would have shared the sentiments of Giovanni Rucellai – Lorenzo's uncle-by-marriage – who told his sons, 'even if one of your own family does not know how to thank you or repay you, you still ought always to benefit your relatives, in preference to a stranger.'[1]

For the Medici it was even more important that the family should cling together, for, in Florentine terms, they were parvenus. The name of Medici was not entirely absent from the chronicles of Florence's glorious past, but it was not, on the whole, a name that evoked honourable or heroic qualities. Indeed, in so far as the Medici were mentioned in those chronicles, they tended to appear in some very doubtful company and in ambivalent roles. In the fourteenth century, they were never of the first

* The title derives from the courtesy form of address, used for any Italian of high rank in the fifteenth century.

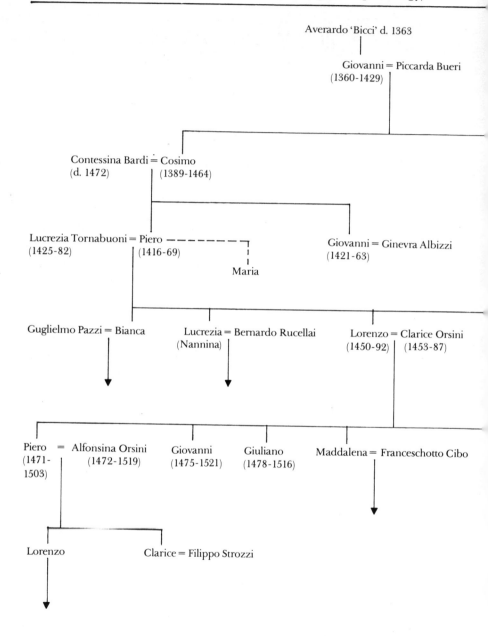

LORENZO'S FAMILY
(A simplified genealogy)

Averardo 'Bicci' d. 1363

Giovanni = Piccarda Bueri
(1360-1429)

Contessina Bardi = Cosimo
(d. 1472)   (1389-1464)

Lucrezia Tornabuoni = Piero – – – – – – – – ⌐
(1425-82)   (1416-69)   ⌐
                            Maria

Giovanni = Ginevra Albizzi
(1421-63)

Guglielmo Pazzi = Bianca

Lucrezia = Bernardo Rucellai
(Nannina)

Lorenzo = Clarice Orsini
(1450-92)   (1453-87)

Piero   = Alfonsina Orsini
(1471-   (1472-1519)
1503)

Giovanni
(1475-1521)

Giuliano
(1478-1516)

Maddalena = Franceschotto Cibo

Lorenzo

Clarice = Filippo Strozzi

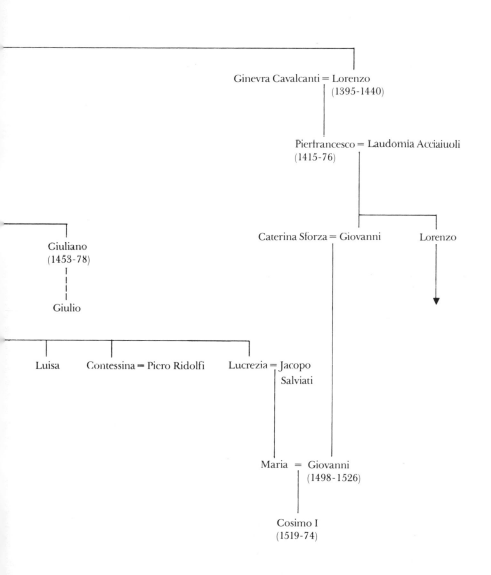

Ginevra Cavalcanti = Lorenzo
(1395-1440)

Pierfrancesco = Laudomia Acciaiuoli
(1415-76)

Caterina Sforza = Giovanni   Lorenzo

Giuliano
(1453-78)

Giulio

Luisa   Contessina = Piero Ridolfi   Lucrezia = Jacopo
                                                          Salviati

Maria   =   Giovanni
            (1498-1526)

Cosimo I
(1519-74)

rank, socially or politically, and even after 1434 when Lorenzo's grand-father, Cosimo, was the leading figure in Florentine affairs and a major statesman of European reputation, the Medici were still aware that there was something lacking in their background. For the next hundred years and more they would give themselves away by encouraging historians, chroniclers, genealogists and simple flatterers to manufacture, on their behalf, an obviously fictitious but suitably respectable background.

The simple truth was that the branch of the family into which Lorenzo was born was even more obscure than that which had played a part in the political life of Florence in the fourteenth century. The founder of the fortunes of that branch of the family which was to come to dominate Florence in the fifteenth century was Lorenzo's great-grandfather, Giovanni di Bicci de' Medici, whose ancestors came from the mountainous district of the Mugello to the east of Florence, where they owned the farm of Cafaggiolo. Giovanni was an exceptionally gifted merchant and banker, who, by the time of his death in 1429, was reputed to be one of the richest men in Italy.

During Giovanni's lifetime, the city of Florence, which ruled over a large area of northern Tuscany, was still a republic in name but the government of this city-state was actually dominated by a narrow oligarchy, led by the Albizzi family. It was wealth, wrested from commerce, which enabled Giovanni to build up a network of supporters to challenge the Albizzi monopoly of power and patronage. After Giovanni's death, his son Cosimo emerged, in turn, as the chief critic of the ruling faction. Just as astute as his father, Cosimo was able to survive the crisis of arrest and exile in 1433 to return to Florence in the following year, and lay the foundations of what was soon to become Medici supremacy in the city.

Once achieved, that supremacy would always be difficult to challenge, and Cosimo and, in their turn, his son and grandson, did much to ensure that no such challenge could succeed. Nevertheless, it remained true that the power of the Medici in Florence depended in the end on the consent of that establishment oligarchy, known to contemporaries as the *reggimento*, the small group of people who really mattered in Florentine political, social and economic life.

The support of the *reggimento* was essential because of the particular nature of the organisation of political life in Florence. Government, theoretically, lay in the hands of the whole citizen body, whose views were constitutionally expressed through the *Parlamento* – a mass-meeting in the Piazza della Signoria – and who were represented through the traditional communal councils. From these councils election was made to various executive and administrative boards of which the most important was the *Signoria*, composed of eight Priors and presided over by the Standard-Bearer of Justice, the theoretical head of the Florentine state. In order to prevent the seizure of power by any one family or faction, the composition of each of these boards changed frequently. The *Signoria*, for instance, was re-elected every two months. As a further safeguard, election to office was by lot, names being drawn from a series of purses which contained the names of all those qualified to hold office. Periodically, the names in these purses were revised by a group of officials – the *Accoppiatori* – who, for the purpose, held what was known as a scrutiny.

Long before the Medici came to predominate in the Florentine government, systems had already been evolved designed to manipulate this system in order to ensure the monopoly of power by one party, group or family. The Albizzi themselves had been masters at such manipulatory devices and thus, to some extent, the means used by the Medici to manage the city of Florence were inherited from their rivals. For example, the Medici maintained the tradition of influencing elections to government office in order to try to ensure that their own supporters would always be in a majority – a process made easier by the increasing resort to *Balìa*, another time-honoured Florentine institution, by which power was delegated to a nominated *ad hoc* committee for a specific purpose and for a limited period of time. Under the Medici, a *Balìa* was normally used to nominate the members of the *Signoria*.

For this system of management always to work, however, the Medici had to be certain of the support of a substantial majority of the *reggimento*. An upstart family, with jealous and powerful rivals always hovering in the wings, the Medici could never quite be certain of enjoying that support. Indeed, in 1459 opposition to them was, in fact, strong enough to force a brief return to the system of electing the *Signoria* by lot. This challenge the Medici met by the creation of a new council – the Council of One Hundred – made up of Medici supporters, which was given precedence over the old communal councils. It was from this council that the *Accoppiatori* were, thereafter, selected and, in this way, the Medici were able to ensure that only the names of their own nominees were placed in the election purses. Even then, with so many people still involved in the process of political management, the system was never completely foolproof. It depended entirely upon the continued loyalty of the supporters of the Medici, and neither Cosimo, nor his son Piero, nor even Lorenzo, could ever be absolutely certain that that loyalty would be forthcoming on any one particular issue.

Yet, if this situation bred a permanent insecurity into the Medici, manifested in a multitude of ways – not least in that sense of the transience of things which permeates Lorenzo's writings – they had, apparently, little real cause to fear. At the time of Lorenzo's birth, the Medici were at the apogee of their wealth and power, and, effectively, the first family of Florence. Their fabled riches were spoken of from London to Constantinople. In every major city there were branches of the Medici bank. Everywhere the heraldic device of the *palle* – the Medici roundels – was immediately recognisable. When, therefore non-Florentines thought of Florence, they inevitably thought of the Medici, and foreign rulers, who preferred dealing with individuals rather than committees, persisted in regarding them as the city's ruling dynasty. Such attitudes were strengthened by the fact that it had now become socially and morally possible for the Medici, not only to be, but actually to live in the style of, the first family of the city.

In former centuries, the stern application of Christian dogma, combined with Florentine republican mythology and a healthy distrust of the tax-collector, had discouraged the ostentatious display of wealth. Lorenzo's grandfather, Cosimo, continued to show an overt respect for traditional Florentine values, and, although he spent money, tended to do so circumspectly. By the 1450s, however, a new ethos had grown up which positively encouraged the spending of money. Wealth was now seen as an expression of nobility and a source of power and reputation. Failure to spend money, if one possessed it, was regarded as a manifestation of avarice, and avariciousness as the worst of all sins. Conspicuous expenditure on dress, entertainments, on public and private events, became accepted and positively valued as manifestations of the wealth and power of Florence. In such an ambience, there were few moral restraints upon Lorenzo's enjoyment of a way of life which was the envy and admiration of his contemporaries and which has frequently provoked the disapproval of subsequent historians.

By contemporary standards, it was thus into a world of considerable luxury and comfort that Lorenzo was born on 1 January 1450 to Piero di Cosimo de' Medici and Lucrezia Tornabuoni. Piero and Lucrezia already had two daughters of their own, besides Maria, the fruit of a most uncharacteristic liaison of Piero's father. Bianca, four years older than Lorenzo, seems to have been particularly close to her brother, and, despite the many difficulties which eventually beset their relationship, their mutual affection remained undimmed until Bianca's death in 1488. Less is known of Lorenzo's relationship with his other sister, Lucrezia or Nannina, who had been born in 1447, but it is clear that all of these children, who were joined in 1453 by a new brother, Giuliano, grew up together in an atmosphere of great warmth and affection in which the exchange of love was part of the daily currency of life. Theirs was a close-knit family, whose collective life centred on the Medici palace in the Via Larga, designed for Cosimo de' Medici by Michelozzo, begun in 1444, and almost completed by 1450. Although Cosimo liked the story which spread around that he had deliberately chosen an unostentatious design for his palace, the fact remains that twenty other dwellings had to be demolished to make room for it, and the completed building, built in the new Renaissance style, was an imposing structure, centring round an inner courtyard, from which a magnificent staircase swept up to the *piano nobile*. Furnished with every luxury available, it housed a collection of tapestries, hangings, gems, silver, antiques and works of art which was internationally famous, and it would be stretching human credulity to believe that this was seen merely as the unassuming little town-house of a careful merchant-banker. To contemporaries, in fact, the palace was a symbol of Medici predominance and of that magnificence which now attached to the family name.

In the Via Larga, Lorenzo was always surrounded by relatives. He lived, not only with his immediate family, but with his grandparents and his handsome, gifted and popular uncle, Giovanni, and, until his death in 1461, with a younger cousin. Also inhabited by Medici was the adjoining house in the Via Larga, for this was the home of Pierfrancesco de' Medici, son of Cosimo's brother. Relations between the two branches of the family were not always harmonious. There were several occasions for quarrelling over property, for Giovanni di Bicci had refused to make a will and, under Florentine law, his property had, therefore, passed to his two sons as joint-heirs. The property had, indeed, been jointly administered until Pierfrancesco came of age when it was divided, according to an arbitration award. From that time onwards there were difficulties, as we gather from Lorenzo himself, who claimed that Pierfrancesco got the best of the bargain. But, while relations between them were not always happy the two families still got on well enough to continue to administer the family home at Cafaggiolo jointly, and Pierfrancesco's two sons, Lorenzo and Giovanni, shared in the common life of the Medici clan.

The only flaw in the family happiness was its undue share of ill-health. All the Medici were, to a certain degree, chronic invalids and Lorenzo was no exception. From birth he suffered frequent, incapacitating attacks of asthma, associated with eczema, and, as he grew older, he suffered more and more from gout and arthritis which caused him great pain. He was always surrounded by doctors and bombarded by medical advice, while treatises on medicine rapidly became a staple of his reading matter. Doctors were regular inmates of, or visitors to, the Medici Palace and some of these were men of considerable eminence; Benedetto Riguardati, for example, doctor to the Dukes of Milan, who also attended the Medici, and Antonio Benivieni whose *De Regimine Sanitatis* is dedicated to Lorenzo. Inevitably, therefore, Lorenzo de' Medici grew up to become one of the leading experts on medicine in Italy. Rulers of other states or eminent Florentines would turn to him for advice on whom to hire in the case of serious illness, and Lorenzo would often act as an intermediary between doctors and patients.

Of all the varied treatments suggested to Lorenzo by this army of attendant medical specialists, the only one that proved effective was visits to one of the many curative baths which abounded in Tuscany and which, aside from the medical treatment they offered, provided a relaxed and convivial atmosphere and occasions for informal meetings with friends, family or fellow politicians. Throughout his life Lorenzo was a frequenter of such establishments, his favourites being the baths, owned by his mother, at Morba; Spedaletto, where he owned a villa; and Poretta in Bolognese territory.

The basis of Lorenzo's happy childhood was the loving marriage of his remarkable parents, Piero di Cosimo de' Medici and Lucrezia Torna-buoni. Well-matched in intellect and tastes, as well as by temperament they were genuinely devoted to each other. To many this was surprising for, on first encounter, Piero did not appear a lovable or even a likeable man. Although generous and affectionate to his children, to those outside the family circle he appeared stern. He was unpopular in Florence for he was often abrupt and brusque and lacked the easy-going manners and common touch of his father. That his manner did his position in Florence no good is confirmed by Lorenzo himself who complained that during the crisis of 1465–6, when Piero's role in the government of Florence was under attack, his father's forbidding exterior and lack of affability lost the Medici friends every day. Matters were not helped by the fact that Piero was frequently wracked by terrible pain from the gout which was his own personal share in the Medici inheritance of ill-health.

There was, however, another side to Piero, and it was this aspect of his personality which was more often seen by his family. He was both highly cultivated and genuinely good and, while cultivation could be found readily enough in fifteenth-century Florence, goodness was a rarer com-modity. Piero had enjoyed an excellent humanistic education and, like all his family, was an expert musician. An avid collector of manuscripts, coins and cameos, he was a great patron of the visual arts, well-known among Florence's lively community of practising artists. The first impor-tant patron to employ della Robbia, who decorated the ceiling of Piero's study in the Medici palace and made the tiles for the floor, it was also Piero who commissioned Benozzo Gozzoli to decorate the chapel in the same palace.

A sincere and devout Christian, Piero was imbued with a genuine piety, expressed through a series of acts of charity and disinterested kindness. Even his critics admitted that, in an age when pardoning one's enemies was something commonly talked of but rarely practised, Piero showed restraint in dealing with those who harmed him, politically and commercially, and exercised an unusual spirit of forgiveness. It was this aspect of his character which undoubtedly drew him closest to his wife, Lucrezia, who shared all of his deep religious commitment.

Lorenzo, it is clear, adored his mother who was, he said, 'the councillor who took many a burden off me', but then Lucrezia was adored by everyone. Even those who did not know her well were yet forced to

Piero di Cosimo by Mino
da Fiesole

admire her, for she possessed all the qualities which would endear a woman to the Florentines. Gentle and dignified, she was yet a shrewd businesswoman who not only continued to administer her own property and estates after her marriage, but also managed to transform the run-down baths at Morba into a fashionable and profitable health-resort. In an age which truly valued learning, she was no mean scholar and also a gifted writer of prose, displaying in her letters that wit and charm which endeared her to those who knew her best. There is always an immediacy about Lucrezia's letters which speaks meaningfully across the gulf of five centuries. An accomplished writer of religious poetry herself, she was yet broad-minded enough to act as a generous patron to other writers who did not share her exclusive concern with the sacred, and whose writings often bordered on the bawdy. Lucrezia was, in addition, if a somewhat scatter-brained housekeeper, a devoted wife, mother and, eventually, grandmother, who, with absolute enjoyment, played a full part in all aspects of the complicated life of her extended family. The only matters, in fact, that ever caused her real concern were the health of her husband and children and the recurring necessity of being separated from one or the other. Away from the children, she fretted for them, but absence from Piero was as bad, and she found herself writing that it seemed 'a thousand years since we saw you'.[2]

Another important influence in the life of the young Lorenzo was his grandmother, Contessina, the wife of Cosimo de' Medici. Lorenzo never seems to have known his grandfather very well but, with his grand-mother, he delighted to spend long hours chattering and playing. As he grew older, it might have been supposed that he would take less pleasure in the company of an old woman, but, in fact, such glimpses as we have of his life as an adolescent show that he and Contessina continued to enjoy a rare delight in each other's company. During a carefree holiday, for instance, they rode one day from Cafaggiolo in a happy cavalcade to hear mass at a nearby friary, with Contessina perched somewhat precariously on 'Lorenzo's mule, wondering at herself that she should be so much better at it than she had thought possible'.[3]

Contessina, sensible of the fact that her nineteen-year-old grandson might well have better ways of passing the time than dancing attendance on his grandmother, was duly grateful and told his father that: 'Lorenzo is a good lad and gladly spends time with me, every so often'.[4]

Lorenzo's closest companion in these years of childhood and adolesc-ence was his younger brother, Giuliano (born 1453). Giuliano was the fairy prince of the Medici family, all gold to Lorenzo's dross. Even as a child Lorenzo can never have been particularly attractive; a friend once remarked that, in regard to his appearance, nature had behaved to him as a step-mother. He had a dark and swarthy complexion, and a slightly twisted smile, while his nose was so flattened that he never had any sense of smell. Acutely short-sighted, plagued by asthma and eczema, he was an odd contrast to his enchanting younger brother who grew up, straight and tall, with robust good looks which belied his frequent ill-health. The dark hair and complexion which, to Lorenzo, gave a perpetual air of melancholy, merely accentuated Giuliano's handsome appearance. Lorenzo liked sport well enough and was 'second to none in agility'[5] but, for Giuliano, physical exercise of all kinds was a consuming passion. It is no wonder that he should have become 'the darling of the Florentine youth',[6] particularly when it was discovered that he had inherited all of his grandfather's famed abilities as a chess-player.

Yet, if nature had been less than fair in her distribution of good looks between the two brothers, she had compensated when it came to intelli-gence. Giuliano, who was certainly no fool, was an accomplished classical scholar, and, as he grew older, he became a shrewd collector of manu-scripts and books; but, in intellectual terms, he was completely outshone by Lorenzo. Lorenzo's many-faceted intelligence was not only analytical but truly creative. Everything he turned his mind or attention to he did well, and, if he had not had the fortune to be born a Medici, he would still have made a brilliant career as a scholar or artist. From his earliest youth his retentive memory, musical gifts, facility in expression, and capacity for deep feeling, had all been abundantly evident.

Lorenzo's education was therefore of crucial importance, for bad luck or bad teachers might have destroyed this talented, but highly-strung and strong-willed child. No doubt, as in most upper-class families in fifteenth-century Florence, he received his earliest lessons from his mother. Certainly it was she who took responsibility for his early religious instruction, and she who instilled into him those principles of Christian piety by which her own life was ordered.

These principles derived from that essentially civic devotion so characteristic of fifteenth-century Florentine culture. Religious practice in the city tended to be centred not on a local parish church but on one of a number of religious confraternities which had grown up in response to the spiritual needs of the Florentines. At least seventy existed, and most Florentines of any social standing belonged to one of them. Some were exclusively for children and adolescents, others for adults, and while some had a broadly popular base others were exclusively aristocratic.

As the confraternities varied in their composition, so they varied in functions. Thus, confraternities of the young tended to meet every Sunday and on other major feast-days; under the guidance of a superior they would say Vespers and all the other major offices of the Church. But the real purpose of these religious clubs was a festive one: to prepare to process the city as a corporate group in celebration of the feast of St John the Baptist, patron saint of Florence, and on other major feast-days. On such days the colourful banners of each confraternity were solemnly carried through the streets, and often the young men would also organise the performance of *tableaux*, or the singing of hymns and *laudi*.

As far as confraternities of adults were concerned, several engaged in the same kind of activity and played a major part in all the public festivities of Florence. Others acted as agencies of mutual insurance, and regularly provided charity for members who fell on hard times. Others were flagellant confraternities, while the so-called 'Companies of Night' were, essentially, religious secret societies. Whatever their nature, however, all the confraternities played a major role in the religious and social life of Florence. At their regular services, theological doctrines were examined and explored in the light of the needs of a commercial and industrial community and, for an essentially lay audience, the great themes of practical Christianity were treated in a popular fashion, shaping a devotion whose characteristic expression became an outflowing of charity.

The educational value of the confraternities should not be underestimated, and it is important in evaluating the various influences that were brought to bear on the young Lorenzo to remember that from his earliest youth he was accustomed, not only to beginning the day by hearing mass, but to being taken to the Confraternity of San Paolo where he distributed alms to the poor. As soon as he was old enough, he also joined the

Confraternity of the Magi which was already a major centre of the Medici patronage structure. This confraternity, originally founded in 1428, met every Tuesday in the sacristy of San Marco, a convent closely associated with the Medici name. As early as 1446, the Company of the Magi was organising an annual festivity – a play to honour the Magi, performed on the day of the Epiphany, whose splendours were designed to outshine those of any other confraternity in the city, and which was therefore organised by leading artists. Both Cosimo and after him Piero de' Medici served as Presidents of the Magi, a position to which Lorenzo himself automatically succeeded after Piero's death. Under Cosimo's influence, the Company of the Magi which numbered about seven hundred members had rapidly become the preferred meeting-place of pious humanists and Neo-Platonists, and here Lorenzo would have heard disquisitions on various learned themes by many distinguished men. We know, for instance, that in 1468, Donato Acciaiuoli delivered a famous oration on the Eucharist to the Company, and that, on other occasions, Cristoforo Landino expounded Hermetic Platonism and Marsilio Ficino spoke of the symbolism of the Star of the Magi.

By such means, Lorenzo came to absorb a straightforward, deep and lasting faith which stood him in good stead throughout his life. For this he had good reason to be grateful to his parents. He had equal reason for gratitude in that he was also brought up in a way that would enable him to play easily that public role in the life of Florence which was demanded of him. He was taught that he must make the welfare of Florence his first consideration and trained, almost from the cradle, to the kind of discipline which such service required. His first public appearance occurred as early as May 1454, when he was involved in the celebrations that surrounded the knighting of the Frenchman, Jean d'Anjou. The air of dignity that the little boy displayed on this occasion, and the fact that he had been dressed in the French fashion as a delicate compliment to the foreign visitors, were universally admired.

Five years later, even more was required when both Francesco Sforza, the Duke of Milan, and Pope Pius II visited Florence. On his arrival, the Duke was formally received by Cosimo in the chapel of the Medici palace, where two recitations were given in Sforza's honour, one by Lorenzo in verse and one by Giuliano in prose. This celebration was followed by numerous other entertainments but culminated in a glorious procession along the Via Larga. Thirty musicians at the head were followed by a standard, bearing Lorenzo's personal device, and by twelve young men of the noblest Florentine families, all accompanied by liveried servants. Behind them rode Lorenzo who was followed by an allegorical chariot on which was represented the *Triumph of Love*. Twice the procession passed in front of the Medici palace, before Lorenzo halted, inviting all the participants to enter and refresh themselves.

No doubt such exciting moments came as a welcome interlude to serious study, for Lorenzo's formal education began when he was about five years old. In line with fashionable ideas about education, he was entrusted to the care of a humanist tutor, Gentile Becchi. Becchi, who always remained a devoted friend and supporter of the Medici family, already had an international reputation as a classical scholar and was also an accomplished writer of witty vernacular prose. However, in the primary ambition of his life he was destined to permanent frustration. His one desire was to win fame as a poet, but it is impossible to pretend that even his best poetic endeavours were ever more than mediocre. However, if he could not write good poetry himself, he could teach others to like literature. He was an excellent teacher and rapidly engaged the interest and enthusiasm of his young pupil. A letter, written by Lucrezia, when Lorenzo was only six years old, describes him learning verses which Becchi had set for him and then teaching them to Giuliano. Four years later, Becchi, whose method of instruction involved alternating the study of Christian with classical texts, would report to Piero that his young charge was currently reading Ovid and Justinian and that, 'You need not ask how he delights in these studies. His conduct is excellent and he is very obedient.'

Like many of his young aristocratic contemporaries, Lorenzo probably attended Cristoforo Landino's course on poetry and eloquence at the Florentine *Studio* in 1458. Presumably Lorenzo enjoyed the spirited defence of vernacular poetry which was made on the occasion by that redoubtable humanist but also imbibed the useful knowledge that, in Landino's view, in order to write good Italian, one must first become a good Latinist.

In the Medici palace, where the children mixed freely with both the inmates and visitors, it was inevitable that Lorenzo would also come in contact with the many other scholars who were clients or friends of the Medici. Such contacts were of primary importance for a young man being raised in the humanistic tradition, for it is a characteristic of humanistic thought that its successes were achieved, not through treatises or essays, but through dialogue based on the conversational model. Every Renaissance humanist shared the belief that it was because of its very nature that dialogue could clarify even the most difficult of subjects. Such a belief indubitably reflects the actual cultural experience of this generation of thinkers, who, through conversations and discussions among themselves, had arrived at a new understanding of the nature of reality, just as much as it reflects a deliberate imitation of a Platonic model.

Certainly dialogue was a means of learning which Lorenzo used throughout his life, beginning with these early days in the Medici palace where he encountered the famous Greek scholar, Argyropoulous, who, under Medici patronage, taught Greek and philosophy in the *Studio* after

1456 and with whom Lorenzo began to study formally in 1461. Soon after that he appears to have begun to study Plato, in depth, with one of the most famous of all the Medici clients, Marsilio Ficino.

Ficino, beginning as Lorenzo's mentor, but becoming in time also his friend, had a profound effect on the shaping of the young man's mind. Ficino was one of a new generation of philosophers, one of those who came to be known as the Florentine Neo-Platonists, the truly creative and regenerative group in the cultural life of fifteenth-century Florence. Their fathers and grandfathers, it is true, had already rediscovered the ancient world, and had reasserted the relevance of a study of that world when dealing with contemporary problems. They had pored over their copies of Plato, Aristotle, Cicero and Livy in order to derive wisdom from ancient writings. But Ficino's generation was different. He and his fellow-scholars did not merely learn and read about the philosophy of the ancients. Living in accordance with it, they turned that philosophy into a new creative tool, making it a system for looking at the world and the puzzle of reality, creating a transcendental system of thought which enabled them to look beyond the immediate to what they saw as eternal truths. Typically, the key dogma of this group was the immortality and universality of the soul, a dogma which led them to see everything in the world as a symbol of what was believed to be the true reality beyond the apparent limits of human experience. Typically, also, their days were spent avidly speculating on the nature of beauty, on the purpose and meaning of harmony, on love, on friendship and on God. All of the intellectual vitality created by this ferment of ideas Ficino conveyed to Lorenzo who became a convinced and dedicated Neo-Platonist.

Other lessons Lorenzo also learned from Ficino, including the value of enjoying all experience. Ficino, for instance, loved the Tuscan country-side and some of his happiest hours were spent roaming the hills around Florence, where he learned, as he explained to Lorenzo, that such exercise was a remedy for melancholy, a necessity for a healthy life, and a useful opportunity for meditation. And Ficino also reinforced the lessons Lorenzo had already imbibed from Landino, that vernacular writing was valuable in itself, and not to be despised, but that it could best be approached through a prior understanding of and grounding in the classics.

Ficino also taught his young friend to respect the past and to value history, to use all human experience as a proper measure by which to judge his own actions. In doing so he both liberated Lorenzo by and imprisoned him within a myth. For the true model of perfect behaviour he consistently presented was the life of Lorenzo's own grandfather. Thus, after Cosimo's death, Ficino wrote much extolling his virtues, praising Cosimo's piety and his sense of justice. He described him as hard-working and careful, both in relation to his own business affairs and to

Botticelli's *Adoration of the Magi* includes idealised portraits of the Medici including the kneeling Cosimo who pays homage to the child, Giuliano (extreme left) and Lorenzo (centre right), as well as a self-portrait of the artist (extreme right)

those of Florence, a man as greedy of time as Midas was of gold, who counted the hours of each day with precision and yet who always had time for the study of philosophy. And so, he urged Lorenzo, '. . . as God fashioned Cosimo according to the idea of the world, do you continue as you have begun to fashion yourself according to the idea of Cosimo'.[7]

To have one's grandfather presented in godlike garb was, in a certain sense, liberating. For, if Cosimo was all that Ficino maintained he was, then he was a true aristocrat in terms of Neo-Platonic thought, which considered nobility of character, rather than nobility of birth, as the true justification of aristocracy. Thus, the taint was removed from that worrying family background. Other authors hastened to echo Ficino's sentiments; the young doctor, Antonio Benivieni, who, as we have seen, was a close intimate of the Medici, addressed to Lorenzo an *Encomium* in which he argued that, with Cosimo's death, the glory of the city had been extinguished. All, however, need not be lost provided Lorenzo would dedicate himself to imitating his grandfather's virtues and behave like those ancient heroes – Hannibal, Cornelius Scipio and Caesar who, even as young men, already gave promise of future achievement. Here we see the deliberate creation of a myth in which Lorenzo features as the true heir of his grandfather, both as a successful statesman and as a protector of the arts. The myth was positive and useful; but any myth can also become a mental straitjacket. Sometimes Lorenzo would act too carefully on the model of his grandfather, making an imitation of Cosimo a substitute for thought, ignoring the fact that both people and situations change.

Meanwhile, however, he continued to enjoy a happy life, protected by Piero's determination that the cares of business and politics should not weigh upon his sons' shoulders too early. Lorenzo and Giuliano were encouraged to establish their position as leaders of Florentine society by spending freely. Lorenzo was able to cultivate enduring friendships with men who shared his interests: the aristocrat, architect and art theorist, Leon Battista Alberti, the poet Luigi Pulci, a protégé of Lucrezia Torna-buoni, known as 'The Fifth Element' in the Medici household, Braccio Martelli and Sigismondo della Stufa, both constant companions, and a number of young patricians like Luigi Alamanni and Bernardo Rucellai. It was at this time, also, that Lorenzo began to develop his musical interests, emerging as an accomplished singer and performer on a number of instruments – but particularly the lyre, the instrument of Apollo, god of poetry.

Lighter interests were pursued with enthusiasm. There were frequent holidays and pleasure trips; in July 1463, for instance, in the company of Braccio Martelli and Sigismondo della Stufa, he travelled to Pistoia, Lucca and Pisa. Their time was divided between fishing, sightseeing, feasting and visiting the Medici properties in Pisa. In 1464 there was another trip to explore the hills of the Mugello, and Lorenzo also made regular visits to the villas at Cafaggiolo or Careggi, particularly during a plague epidemic or in the heat of the summer.

Lorenzo's life was a regular round of games, hunting, hawking, fishing, jousting and, inevitably, love. Courtly love, enhanced and en-riched by the new and fashionable theories of Neo-Platonism, was all the rage in Florence. In accordance with the oddly stylised set of attitudes embodied in this movement, love retained the quality with which it had been imbued by the *dolce stil nuovo* poets; it was the expression of true nobility of soul. The courtly love tradition virtually forced the sixteen-year-old Lorenzo to select one single lady as the object of his total devotion and his choice fell on Lucrezia Donati, still only eleven years old. The young Lorenzo proclaimed her the sole inspiration of his poetry and at tournaments wore her device. Given the conventions of courtly love, and of *dolce stil nuovo* poetry, it is virtually impossible to guess how seriously Lorenzo felt the emotions he claimed to feel in relation to Lucrezia, just as it is difficult to guess at the precise impact made on him by either of his subsequent loves Simonetta Vespucci and Bartolomea de'

Nasi. It seems, however, that underlying all the elaborate conventions in which the fashion of the day demanded that love be paraded, there was much genuine feeling. Certainly the evidence of Lorenzo's poetry suggests a soul and heart, touched by human passion, knowing all the moods, joys, torments and music of romantic attachment. Lorenzo wrote after the fashion of the *dolce stil nuovo* models, notably Dante and Petrarch, but his work is always less spiritual than theirs. It is clear that he had a deep longing for some physical consummation of his love in this world, while it is equally clear that this longing was largely unfulfilled.[8]

Much in Lorenzo's writing thus reflected the world of natural affection, but it was the artificial and the elaborate that were most obvious in the mock tournaments in which the Florentines took such delight in the fifteenth century, and which were an opportunity for public display of wealth and family power. One of these tournaments, immortalised in a poem by Luigi Pulci, marked the emergence of Lorenzo into young adulthood. Despite the fact that he was already betrothed to another woman, it was given, in honour of Lucrezia Donati, by Lorenzo in the piazza of Santa Croce on 7 February 1469. In this strange fifteenth-century rite of passage, the costumes, the allegories, the emblems were what counted, not the actual skill of the horseman. Lorenzo, himself, recognised this, remarking that, 'Although I was no champion in the use of weapons and the delivery of blows the first prize was awarded to me, a helmet inlaid with silver and a figure of Mars as the crest.'[9]

Giuliano's costume was rich enough, being made of brocade, encrusted with real pearls, but for sheer ostentation, pride of place went to Lorenzo. Dressed in black velvet, his cap was decorated with a gold filagree feather, set about with diamonds and rubies. His shield was emblazoned with the three gold lilies of France, on an azure ground, and in its centre shone the famous Medici diamond, known as *Il Libro*. Lorenzo was preceded into the lists by a knight who carried a standard which had been specially painted by Verrocchio for the occasion. It represented the sun above, a rainbow below, with a motto in pearls: '*Le tems revient*'. In the centre of the standard Lucrezia Donati was portrayed, wearing a dress embroidered with white and gold flowers. She was weaving a garland from a withered laurel tree which sprouted fresh leaves, the laurel being Lorenzo's own personal device. Other banners displayed nymphs, one in white with a garland of rose-leaves, another quenching the flaming darts of love in a fountain, and another breaking love's arrows and scattering their fragments in a field. All was lavish, costly, splendid. All had more than a touch of princely magnificence; the horse, on which Lorenzo made his entry, was a gift from the King of Naples; that on which he fought, from the Marquess of Ferrara; his armour was from the Duke of Milan. The whole tournament was thus a symbol of the particular relationship which the Medici, although merely citizens in Florence, enjoyed with the princely houses of Italy.

One possible consequence of that relationship, and certainly an indication of the fact that Lorenzo represented not merely a new generation of the Medici but also the changing relationship between his family and the society of Florence, was the missing element in his education. Until the very last years of his father's life, Lorenzo had no knowledge of the banking-house or workshop. This omission probably had something to do with a misplaced desire to provide Lorenzo with the education and lifestyle of a prince, although it may simply have been an oversight on Piero's part, who cannot have assumed that his life would be so early cut short. Whatever the reason, the fact remains that Lorenzo received no practical training in commerce, banking or business and this left him crucially unprepared to take over the commercial empire of the Medici in 1469.

The dangers of this situation must have begun to become apparent in 1464, when Lorenzo was first confronted with all the responsibilities which were by then inherent in bearing the Medici name. For some time Cosimo had been ailing. It was said that he spent much of his time lying with his eyes closed and that when Contessina dared to ask him why, he replied irritably that he was practising for when he would be in his grave. By the last weeks of July it was clear that he was in fact dying, and on 1 August the end came. His last thoughts were for the family, his last worries about its problems and obligations, his last efforts directed towards ensuring the continued survival of the Medici in the confusing whirlpool of Florentine politics:

> He spoke of the private possessions of our family [Piero told his sons] and of what concerns you two; taking comfort that you had good wits and bidding me educate you well so that you might be of help to me . . . Then he said he would make no will . . . seeing that we were always united in true love, amity and esteem.[10]

Cosimo's death was an event of major significance in Lorenzo's life, for it represented a direct threat to the position of the Medici. Even those who disliked the idea that any one family should hold a predominant position in the city had been able to stomach Cosimo's role, having persuaded themselves that his position was wholly exceptional. But they felt no loyalty to Piero or to his sons.

Part of the Medici power-base derived from the fact that they were the leaders of the pro-Milanese faction in the city, and had made the maintenance of a Florentine–Milanese alliance the corner-stone of foreign policy. But many prominent and powerful Florentines had always opposed this alliance, both on theoretical and practical grounds; hence, from the moment of Cosimo's death, Piero faced open attacks on his policies. In addition, a growing number of Florentines felt both concern at the increasingly 'undemocratic' quality of government and jealousy at the position of the Medici. Thus Cosimo's demise released a flood of opposition attacks and attempts to restore open elections to the *Signoria*. Piero was forced to turn to his sons to help him in the critical task of maintaining Medici supremacy in Florence. He knew that it would take all the resources of the family if he was to ensure that the position he had inherited from his father was to be passed on undiminished to his sons. Piero's health, in any case, was now deteriorating so fast that Lorenzo was forced to take a more active role. He was regularly being used as a means of contact between Piero and the vast network of Medici friends and supporters scattered throughout Tuscany. Information which could not be trusted to letters was passed on through Lorenzo by word of mouth. Official positions also began to come his way; despite being under age, he served in 1466 on the *Balìa* as a substitute for his father and, on the same basis, he was admitted to the Council of One Hundred.

More congenial to his personality were the ceremonial tasks he increasingly fulfilled, either entertaining distinguished visitors or making semi-official trips to foreign courts. The first such opportunity arose in 1465, when, in order to strengthen the alliance between Milan and Naples, Ippolita Sforza was married to Alfonso of Aragon, son of the King of Naples. Alfonso's brother, Federico, was sent to Milan to collect his brother's wife. On such an important occasion it was vital that a representative of the Medici family should attend the proxy wedding celebrations to reassert the Medici commitment to the Milanese–Florentine–Neapolitan alliance. Lorenzo was the obvious choice, particularly as Piero also saw this as a golden opportunity to make contact with other friends of the Medici. So Lorenzo was dispatched first to Bologna, where he was received with princely magnificence, then to Ferrara, where he was so cordially treated that he stayed much longer than was originally intended, finally to Venice. Here, he was treated more coolly by the government, but much enjoyed making contact with leading Venetian humanists.

In accordance with his over-anxious father's instructions, throughout the journey Lorenzo dressed, rode and behaved like a prince. Piero saw this occasion as a 'touchstone of Lorenzo's abilities'[11] and was concerned that his son should openly manifest all the wealth and power of the Medici. Accordingly he told Lorenzo that, '. . . whatever is settled do with splendour and in honourable fashion . . . whatever is decided will please me, only, as I said, do not stint money, but do thyself honour.'[12] A week later, he was still worrying that Lorenzo might not be spending enough money to cut a figure within the aristocratic circles he was now frequenting. He need not have worried. Lorenzo always had a strong instinct for what was appropriate behaviour in any setting, and in the

Medici palace at Milan he entertained a vast range of important guests in a series of spectacular parties, before playing a prominent role in the proxy-wedding celebrations of 19 May.

The parties, festivals and entertainments that followed went on for days but long before they came to an end, Lorenzo had already taken his leave and ridden back to Florence. Ippolita Sforza was to travel to Naples through Tuscany and would include a visit to Florence in her itinerary, so Lorenzo was needed to prepare for her arrival. On 22 June she rode into Florence, with her two brothers and her brother-in-law, and alighted at the Medici palace which was to house the royal party during their stay. It was a delightful time. Lorenzo forged important new links of friendship which ultimately stood him in good stead. He and Federico had common interests in literature and sport while in Ippolita he found an enchanting companion. So close did they become that, in future years, she always turned first to Lorenzo when, as so often happened at the glamorous but chronically impecunious Neapolitan court, she found herself short of ready money.

The opportunity to renew this friendship came in the following year. Lorenzo was sent on an embassy to Rome and Naples, accompanied by the ever-faithful Gentile Becchi and Roberto Malatesta. The purpose of the visit to Rome was to negotiate with the new pope, Paul II, a contract relating to the recently discovered alum mines at Tolfa which lay within papal territory. Alum was a substance vital to Florence, both for her textile and other industries, but the supply had always presented difficulties, since, previously, the only source had lain in the Levant. Now the discovery of a new source, so close at hand, opened up tantalising prospects of quick profit-making to anyone who could gain a monopoly or controlling interest in the mines.

At the same time, in his dealings with the pope, Lorenzo was to try out his abilities as a diplomat. In the unstable world of fifteenth-century Italian politics, Paul II was still an unknown quantity and Piero wanted Lorenzo to discover what the pope's attitude would be to the Italian League, whose pivot was the Milanese–Florentine–Neapolitan alliance. Lorenzo was thus instructed to persuade the pope that the League represented no threat to him, but was, rather, the only means of ensuring the continued stability of Italy.

Leaving Florence at the beginning of March, Lorenzo passed through Siena, whence he sent some of the famous local cakes to his friends. Arriving in Rome, on or about 8 March, he proceeded to stay in the city for a month, taking the opportunity to visit the city's antiquities in the company of Alberti, and enjoying himself so openly and enthusiastically as to earn a testy reproach from Piero, who felt that Lorenzo might, more honourably, have gone into mourning for Francesco Sforza, the Duke of Milan, who had just died. Lorenzo might have justifiably regarded this reproach as a little unfair, for, however he may have chosen to spend his spare time, he did manage to conduct a series of valuable negotiations with the pope, including winning the valuable alum contract for the Medici bank.

In any case, on 7 April he was off on his travels once more, and reached Sessa on 12 April where he had his first interview with the King of Naples. Two days later he was in Naples itself, to begin a two-month stay which perfectly blended business and pleasure. Solid political bargaining had certainly to be undertaken; Lorenzo's primary task was to counter the influence of the Acciaiuoli, a rival Florentine family, who were working to undermine the commercial and political influence of the Medici within the Kingdom of Naples. King Ferrante, for his part, renewed efforts he had been making on behalf of the exiled Florentine family of the Strozzi. As a result of these negotiations the sentence of exile, first imposed in 1434, was lifted in September.

Negotiation and hard bargaining therefore occupied much of Lorenzo's time, but there were also ample opportunities for him to relax in totally congenial surroundings. He could enjoy a constant round of court festivities and delight in the opportunity to discuss philosophy and literature with cultivated friends.

All too soon, however, worrying news began to reach Naples from Florence and it became clear that Lorenzo must speedily return home. Travelling by way of Ancona, he arrived back on 10 May to find the city in turmoil.

In 1465 and 1466 Florence was gripped by financial panic. A Turkish–Venetian war brought the Levantine trade of the Mediterranean to a virtual standstill, and this brought heavy losses and bankruptcy to some Florentine firms. Even the Medici bank had had to take its share of the losses and Piero, recognising that the firm was seriously over-extended, began retrenching and calling in debts. Inevitably this action caused widespread resentment and finally led to an overt attack on the Medici regime.

As usual in Florence, the leaders of the malcontents were a motley crew, united only by a common hostility to a Medici monopoly of patronage, prestige and power. Their only clearly articulated aim was to get rid of the Council of One Hundred, the foundation of Medici electoral control. They included the rich patrician, Luca Pitti, who, during Cosimo's lifetime, had played a prominent part in the political life of Florence, and whose self-image as the social equal of the Medici was taking concrete form in the building of a sumptuous palace on the south bank of the Arno. The leaders also included Agnolo Acciaiuoli, who had been disappointed in hopes of a Medici bride, and whose family were, as we have seen, commercial rivals of the Medici; Dietisalvi Neroni the brother of the Archbishop of Florence; and Niccolò Soderini, whose constant, public, celebration of the virtues of the traditional republican constitution of Florence successfully obscured the fact that he headed a family whose power-base and organisation was so strong as to make them the most likely successors to power, should the Medici be successfully ousted from Florence.

These opponents of Piero, who were joined in May 1466 by Pierfrancesco de' Medici, kept up pressure on the regime from the autumn of 1465, trying to oust the Medici by constitutional means. By September, the move to abolish the *Accoppiatori* and restore election by lot to the *Signoria* had been passed, not only with large majorities in the traditional communal councils, but also with a sizeable one in the Council of One Hundred. After this restoration of the traditional system, the first elections fell on 1 November and it was, perhaps, inevitable that Niccolò Soderini should have been drawn as Standard-Bearer of Justice. The popular enthusiasm for this election was tremendous; asserting their new-found control over the city, a cheering crowd of his supporters flowed out into the streets and accompanied Soderini to the Palazzo della Signoria where, as the 'restorer of liberty', he was publicly acclaimed and crowned with an olive wreath. But, as so often happened in the volatile world of Florentine politics, even before the end of his two-month period in office, power had swung away from Soderini and his friends and back towards the Medici and their supporters. And so matters continued for week after week, political power shifting backwards and forwards between the parties, and public passions running so high that it seemed fighting must inevitably break out in the streets. An explosive situation was made all the more dangerous by the offers of military support that both Piero and his opponents received from foreign powers; Piero from Milan, his adversaries from Ferrara and Venice.

Total disaster or civil war was only averted at the last moment when Luca Pitti panicked and made a dramatic change of allegiance. Convinced that the political tide was flowing against him, and without consulting his allies, he suddenly declared his unswerving loyalty to the Medici regime. At the same time he called for a *parlamento* to settle the political crisis. This time-honoured means of forcing through revolutionary change in Florence involved summoning all citizens to assemble in the Piazza della Signoria to endorse any proposed changes in the constitution.

The Medici acted swiftly. When, on 2 September 1466, the citizens of Florence assembled for the *parlamento*, they found the Piazza della Signoria already ringed by three thousand troops. Lorenzo, in full armour and mounted on horseback, was among them. Naturally enough, in the circumstances, no opposition was offered to the creation of a *Balìa* with full powers to amend the constitution. Agnolo Acciaiuoli and Dietisalvi Neroni were exiled for twenty years, while Luca Pitti was allowed to live out the rest of his life in political disgrace and social oblivion in Florence.

The constitution was restored to the form of 1434, but with one additional safeguard for the Medici regime: the system of election by lot was suspended for twenty years. On the whole, however, what impressed contemporaries about the whole episode was the gentleness and spirit of forgiveness which Piero displayed towards those who had injured him, and the deliberate policy of conciliation he employed in order 'to console the citizens as much as is possible by observing justice and custom'.[13]

After this crisis, Lorenzo was drawn more and more into the decision-making process. Piero found it increasingly difficult to resist the overwhelming pain of his disease and turned to his elder son, declaring that, without him, he was like a man with no hands. Now, even the complicated affairs of the Medici bank had to be dealt with as much by Lorenzo and Giuliano as by Piero.

Yet, the political problems of the Medici remained undiminished. Defeated in Florence, the conspirators of 1465–6 simply moved their activities and opposition into a different sphere. With Venetian connivance, they hired mercenary troops and conducted an indecisive, slow-moving campaign in Florentine territory which brought no permanent advantage to either side. In such a situation there could be no question of Lorenzo leaving Florence again, and so, when it came to the question of choosing him a bride in Rome, it was his mother who was dispatched to make the match.

Historians have often puzzled over the fact that two such conscientious, loving and intelligent parents, themselves united by great marital tenderness and affection, could have chosen Clarice Orsini as a bride for their brilliant son. They were never under any illusions about her. With the best will in the world, it is impossible to read Lucrezia's disarmingly frank remarks without sensing that she was lukewarm on the subject. Clarice, Lucrezia reported, although by no means as pretty as her own daughters,

> is reasonably tall and fair-skinned. She is gentle in manner without the ease we are used to, but she is biddable and will soon conform to our ways. Her hair is not blonde – they are not blonde here – but it is reddish and plentiful. Her face is on the round side, but I find it pleasant. Her neck is slender, almost perhaps on the thin side, but graceful. We didn't see her breasts – the women cover them here – but they gave the impression of being well-formed.[14]

So, Clarice, while not exactly ugly was certainly no great beauty. She was distinctly foreign, dull and unforthcoming. Nor can it have taken the intelligent Lucrezia long to establish that, although dutiful and endowed with commonsense, Clarice was unintellectual, totally lacking in individuality, and irritatingly pious in a very conventional manner. On the other hand, her uncle was Cardinal Latino, one of the most influential men in the Curia, and she was an Orsini, daughter of one of the most powerful families of the Church State. It was this qualification which made her a fitting Medici bride, for the Medici were increasingly interested in acquiring influence at Rome and within the Church State. The Roman branch of their bank was the most profitable part of their commercial empire, and they were also anxious to acquire power in the papal Curia, the greatest source of patronage in the western world, as well as to maintain and encourage the favourable balance of trade between Florence and Rome. In addition, Piero must have reflected, the Orsini were famous as *condottieri* and might, in future years, be able to provide military assistance were the position of the Medici in Florence to be threatened.

So it was agreed, and the betrothal finally took place in November 1468. Clarice was to be Lorenzo's wife, bringing with her to Florence a dowry of 6,000 *scudi* and the support of the vast Orsini connection. Her letters to her future husband, during their betrothal, are shy, simple, and entirely conventional, although touching in their evident desire to please Lorenzo and his family.

Piero's continuing ill-health made it imperative that the marriage should take place in Florence, and accordingly it was to Florence that Clarice came as a bride. On 4 June, preceded by a group of musicians, and surrounded by a mob of laughing young Florentine aristocrats, she rode through the city from the house of Benedetto degl' Alessandri to the Via Larga. Her dress was of magnificent white and gold brocade, and she was mounted on the horse which Lorenzo himself had ridden during the famous joust of February 1469. In front of the Medici palace, a vast platform, decorated with tapestries, had been erected to provide a public stage for dancing and feasting. Over all stretched an awning of purple, green and white cloth, decorated with the arms of the Medici and the Orsini. In the inner courtyard of the palace stood the centre-piece of Donatello's *David*, and around it were set out tables, covered in fine white damask. In each corner of the courtyard stood a great copper basin in which to rinse out the wine-glasses. Further into the palace, in the garden were more tables, this time set around a fountain.

This was the elaborate setting for the celebration of the marriage of Lorenzo. For three days the festivities continued, festivities which included five banquets, to which at least four hundred prominent Florentines were invited, daily dancing, and plenty of good wine. No one could complain that it was not a most splendid affair, and yet there was also a deliberate absence of ostentation. Thus, it is clear that little of the famous Medici silver was on display on this occasion, and there is no mention of the great carved sideboards which were increasingly popular during this period and which would have been familiar to Clarice from Rome. And, if the food and wine were plentiful, the menu was not

Medici – now the Riccardi – palace in the Via Larga

Courtyard of the Medici palace

ostentatious as one of the organisers of the celebrations, Cosimo Bartoli, was swift to point out:

> There was never more than one roast. In the morning a small dish, then some boiled meat, then a roast, after that wafers, marzipan and sugared almonds and pine-nuts, then jars of preserved pine-nuts and sweet-meats. In the evening jelly, a roast, fritters, wafers, almonds and jars of sweetmeats.[15]

The revels ended on Tuesday 6 June, and the couple adjourned to the church most closely associated with the Medici name, San Lorenzo. Here they celebrated their nuptial mass, Clarice rather ostentatiously carrying one of her hundreds of wedding gifts, 'a little book of Our Lady, most marvellous, written in letters of gold upon blue paper, the binding decorated with designs in crystal and silver'.

Such is our public knowledge of the marriage of Lorenzo. Of his own feelings we know no more than his own laconic comment that a 'bride was given to me', and what we may deduce from the fact that marriage appeared to make little difference to a way of life at this time which, if anything, is characterised by a new intensity of experience. Although Clarice grew to love her rather awesome husband with a deep affection, she must rapidly have recognised that she would always play second fiddle to his other interests and friends. And, in fact, in the early months of their marriage, she can have seen little of him, for he was often away from Florence.

Only a few weeks after his marriage, for instance, on 14 July he left for Milan to deputise for his father as godfather to the newly-born son of the Duke. Up to the last minute Piero had dithered about whether or not Lorenzo was the suitable person to send. Not until 12 July did he finally give permission, and even then he could not let Lorenzo go without giving him a last minute warning. His son was to be sure to obey all instructions; and not get involved in any diplomatic matters since, on this trip, he was not going as an ambassador, and, as he explained in a letter to Lucrezia, 'I don't think it is proper that the ducklings should teach the old ducks to swim.'[16]

Accompanied by a dozen other young Florentines, including his brother-in-law Guglielmo Pazzi, Bernardo Rucellai, Bartolomeo Scala, Gentile Becchi and Francesco Nori, Lorenzo travelled through Prato, Pistoia, Lucca, Pietrasanta, Sarzana and Pontremoli, finally finding time to write to Clarice from Milan on 22 July to announce his safe arrival and ask if there was anything she wanted from Milan. In the same letter he expressed a longing to return to his new wife, but he does not in fact seem to have been over-anxious to get back. After standing proxy at the baptism, and presenting the Duchess with a gold necklace and a diamond worth 2,000 ducats, he left Lombardy but not to return directly to

Florence. First he stayed a few days in Genoa, which he had always wanted to visit, then a few days in Pisa, so that it was not until the middle of August that he was reunited with Clarice at Careggi.

Piero was visibly weakening by the day, yet Lorenzo seemed never to be still. He was always on the move, either between Florence and one of the Medici villas, or off to Pisa to supervise Medici interests there. His days were filled with his normal multiplicity of activities, as if he wished to cram the whole of human experience into each twenty-four hours; hunting, writing, talking about poetry or philosophy among congenial friends. It was a cheerful, happy, laughing ambience in which he moved, and yet it also had moments of melancholy and profound seriousness. As the pressures of life increased, Lorenzo moved closer to Ficino than ever before. In these months, their relationship deepened and became more complex, as they sparked off ideas in each other and debated subjects of mutual literary and philosophical interest. In a series of letters, Ficino, aware of the imminent accession of his friend to a position of supremacy in Florence, but clearly alive to Lorenzo's weaknesses, especially his arrogance, tendency to melancholy, and rashness, urged the young man to use their friendship to his own advantage by allowing Ficino to teach him how to avoid the dangers of power, and how to keep alive the ideals of truth and beauty to which he professed commitment.

How necessary Ficino's veiled warnings and advice would be in restraining Lorenzo would become apparent before the end of the year. On 2 December 1469 Piero di Cosimo de' Medici died, stoically bearing to the end all the dreadful sufferings of his disease. He was buried in the Church of San Lorenzo while Lorenzo gave himself up to an agony of grief which made his friends and family fear for his health.

2

THE MEDICI INHERITANCE

Piero left no will. Recalling his father's death, Lorenzo was to comment, '. . . we drew up an inventory and found we possessed 237,988 *scudi* as is recorded by me in a large green book bound in kid.'[1] It was a fine inheritance. Lorenzo was now the recognised leader of the young Florentine aristocrats. He embodied their aspirations and attracted the attention of an army of sycophants. He had charm as well as wealth. He had inherited the immense prestige of the Medici name. His position in Florence seemed assured.

Lorenzo's wealth, power and prestige all derived from his family's fortune-building. But Piero had also bequeathed problems. The Medici bank was central to the family's wealth – and to those problems. It was to create Lorenzo's gravest difficulties, and yet it was the aspect of his life in which he took least interest. In 1469, in addition to the main branch in Florence, which controlled two industrial concerns producing woollen cloth and one producing silk, there was a network of foreign branches. In Italy such branches existed at Milan, Pisa, Venice and Rome, the last controlling concerns in Naples and the alum company which exploited the Tolfa mines. Outside Italy there were branches at Avignon, Lyons, Geneva, Bruges and London. Representatives of the Medici bank were also scattered around the Mediterranean, from Spain to the Levant. From its centre in Florence, it had spread like a spider's web across the whole of Europe.

Lorenzo had neither the experience, nor the inclination, nor, indeed, the time, to supervise this vast commercial empire in detail. Like his predecessors, he was obliged to delegate power. He inherited as general manager of the bank, Francesco Sassetti, who had always served his father, but whose power to determine the general policy of the Medici business seems to have been increased by Lorenzo's reluctance to get too deeply embroiled in the day-to-day running of the bank. It was therefore unfortunate that, at precisely the same period, Sassetti should have been so overcome by admiration for Lorenzo's cultural activities, that he too should have devoted more and more time to humanistic pursuits and less and less to business. To what extent, however, the delegation of power to Sassetti explains the subsequent decline in the bank's efficiency remains a matter of debate, although all would agree that Lorenzo was unlucky in inheriting at a critical moment. Since its foundation in 1397, the bank had expanded continuously until 1455, but, after Cosimo's death, there began a period of gradual, inexorable decline, which gathered momentum after 1478, and which appears to have been caused by a combination of poor management, rash policies, structural weaknesses and unfavourable business conditions, against a background of shrinking international trade.

Lorenzo's political role in Florence could only exacerbate the situation. Two axioms were always preached by Florentine businessmen. The first was to retain direct personal supervision over all of their enterprises and, in particular, over their representatives abroad. Purists, indeed, argued that it was essential to visit any overseas branch at least once a year. The second was never, under any circumstances, to lend money to princes or courtiers. Ineradicably embedded in the Florentine collective memory were the crashes of the Bardi and Peruzzi companies, which had been directly caused by a failure to observe this second axiom. But Lorenzo's political position made it impossible for him to observe either principle. Since his other commitments made day to day personal supervision of the bank out of the question, he was forced to leave the running of the business to subordinates and could not check regularly on either their methods or their balances. As for lending to princes, this was a political necessity, for, as we shall see, Lorenzo needed the support of foreign princes in order to bolster his position in Florence; and, paradoxically, the weaker the bank became, the more he needed that support.

In the early years after Piero's death, the inherited banking empire created problems in a variety of locations. For example, Lorenzo had constant trouble with the difficult and touchy Tommaso Portinari, manager of the bank at Bruges. Here, particularly by making loans to the Duke of Burgundy, the credit of the bank had been over-extended to a point that Lorenzo thought undesirable. He complained bitterly of Portinari that 'in order to court the Duke's favour and make himself important, he did not care that it was at our expense'.[2] Even more difficult was the associated problem of the London branch of which Lorenzo remarked frankly that:

> I have at present no matter or affair of weight that causes me more worry than this of London for it seems to me that neither here nor there does our firm have any more urgent concern.[3]

The problem arose from the fact that the Medici had been caught up in the events of the English Wars of the Roses, for the local manager, Gherardo Canigiani, had made massive loans to Edward IV which, after Edward's deposition in 1470, could not be recovered.

Simultaneously, the Milan branch of the bank ran into difficulty, as a result of a long-standing debt which the Duke of Milan was constantly promising to honour but for which he conspicuously failed to produce any ready cash. In this situation there were, as Lorenzo realised, clear political implications. His enemies were only too ready to point out that the Duke was reneging on his commercial obligations in order to bind Lorenzo, and, through him, Florence, to a Milanese alliance.

Lorenzo, however, while recognising the dangers inherent in such situations, appears to have been prepared to cut his losses and to use the Medici bank largely for political purposes, as a means of buying allies and friends for the Medici. Certainly, he continued the tradition which dated back to the time of Giovanni di Bicci of employing only trusted Medici supporters to staff the bank, and he appears to have placed greater dependence on their political fidelity than on their commercial abilities. After 1478, for instance, he toyed with the idea of liquidating the Milan branch of the bank and breaking his association with the manager there, Tommaso Portinari's brother, Accerito, who he claimed was losing thousands of florins through sheer incompetence, but, when it came to the crunch, Portinari's political support was deemed to outweigh his lack of business sense.

The predominance of political over commercial interests may also be seen in the history of the Neapolitan branch. There had been no Medici bank in Naples since 1426 and, when Lorenzo established a new branch in 1471, it was not for commercial reasons but in order to foster the Florentine–Neapolitan alliance. The new bank never really made a profit and, after 1479, its political nature became even more evident since almost all the loans it made were to the Neapolitan crown and to Neapolitan noblemen who were notorious, throughout Europe, for their inability to repay debts.

Contemporaries were quick to recognise the increased political function of the Medici bank and, indeed, to take advantage of the situation. Those who wished to curry favour with Lorenzo not only banked solely with him but persistently reminded him that they did so, and political friends of the Medici made it quite clear that they expected the bank to treat them favourably when it was a question of extending credit or paying interest.

The Medici bank, therefore, although the foundation of the Medici fortune, now played a different role in the family's complex of interests. If it *could* be used to make money, then Lorenzo was not one to let slip an opportunity, but his real financial assets lay elsewhere. These included a priceless collection of highly portable antiques, works of art, manuscripts and books. The family jewels alone amounted to an immense fortune. In 1465 Piero had estimated the women's jewellery was worth 12,205 florins. To this had to be added rings worth 1,972 florins, pearls worth 3,512 florins, medals and cameos to a value of 2,579 florins, vases in *pietra dura* worth 4,580 florins, silver to the value of 6,702 florins, and various curiosities like the 'horn of a unicorn' whose estimated value was 3,000 florins.[4]

Lorenzo's inheritance, however, included much more than the bank and a priceless assortment of art treasures and jewels. He was also heir to a network of landed properties in and near Florence. He lacked for residences neither in the city, where he was now master of the Via Larga palace, furnished with 'tapestries and household ornaments of gold and silk, silverware and bookcases that are endless and without number',[5] nor in the country. An hour or two's ride away in the hills to the north of Florence lay the villa of Careggi, which, in 1457, had been restructured for Cosimo by Michelozzi, and which rapidly became the setting for gatherings of intellectual friends and acquaintances of the Medici who liked to meet together in this congenial setting to discuss poetry and philosophy. It was to Careggi that Lorenzo most frequently invited Angelo Poliziano, Pico della Mirandola and Marsilio Ficino to whom he also gave the adjoining farm of La Fontanella. It was at Careggi, too, that Lorenzo worked most successfully, writing and revising his poems and literary criticism; and in the end it was to Careggi that he retired to die. Yet it was never his favourite country house. His preference was for the superb hunting country and ample hill pastures of the Mugello, further to the north. Here was situated the Medici villa of Cafaggiolo, where Lorenzo spent so many happy days as a young boy and growing adolescent. Built like a fortified farm-house, complete with its own towers, moat and drawbridge, Cafaggiolo symbolised Medici power within the Mugello, where, as early as the eleventh century, they had been an important family.

Together with the Medici property at Trebbio, Cafaggiolo was the

The villa of Cafaggiolo as it was portrayed by Utens in 1599

major centre for the organisation of the vast agricultural production of the
Mugello, particularly of grain, hay and wine, which was supplied to the
ever-hungry population of Florence. Attached to the Medici estate there
were over sixty peasant holdings, many houses and cottages, three
water-mills and extensive woods and pastures. Here, therefore, was an
important centre of Medici power, but here also was a perfect base for all
the country pursuits, beloved of Lorenzo – hunting, fowling, fishing. For
him it was the ideal place in which to combine business and pleasure.
There is no doubt that Lorenzo loved Cafaggiolo dearly and bitterly
regretted the fact that, in 1485, he was forced to surrender it to his two
young cousins to meet their legal claim against him.

Fortunately, by that date, a substitute already existed on the edge of the
Mugello, in the shape of Lorenzo's villa of Ambra at Poggio a Caiano.
From 1470 onwards Lorenzo was acquiring property at Poggio with a
view to building his own house, after his own ideas. To Giuliano da San
Gallo he entrusted the task of designing what was, in effect, the first
purpose-built Renaissance villa, but, while San Gallo was the architect,
Poggio a Caiano, created in the Hellenising spirit of Neo-Platonic philosophy as an environment for that relaxation with nature which was the
dream of the Florentine humanists, and built under Lorenzo's direct
supervision, was essentially Lorenzo's creation.

Poggio a Caiano today

It took remarkable vision to build Poggio. Before any construction work could begin, the hill on which the villa was to be built had first to be flattened, and the course of the river Ombrone had to be diverted in order to create space for the planting of gardens and the setting out of the park. The scheme also involved the building of a wall around the whole estate to emphasise the villa's exclusion from the rest of the world.

Major work on the building of Poggio was therefore not begun until 1485, and Lorenzo did not live to see it completed. But, even in its unfinished state, Poggio became the delight of his later years, a constant source of interest, a perfect centre for relaxation, an attractive hunting-lodge, but also a highly profitable agricultural estate.

Poggio a Caiano, is, in fact, a good example of Lorenzo's tendency to transfer money out of commercial and industrial enterprises and into agricultural investment. Such behaviour was by no means uncommon. Ever since the late fourteenth century, agriculture had increasingly been developed on a capitalist basis in Tuscany, with the peasantry being transformed into a rural proletariat of day-labourers, wage-earners and share-croppers, as the major Florentine familes – the Albizzi, Strozzi, Pazzi, Rucellai, Guicciardini, Ricasoli and Salviati – bought up vast agricultural estates and farmed them intensively. Land did not bring such spectacular profits as were possible in business and commerce but, on the other hand, it did not bring such spectacular losses, was a permanent investment, provided a rural power-base, and was a defence against that most dreaded of Tuscan spectres – famine. In Lorenzo's own case, indeed, the produce from the Medici estates was vitally important, being used to maintain the Medici household, both in the city and in the country, and providing gifts for friends, allies, leading politicians, and all members of the Medici clan.

The importance of land in providing a firm and reliable power-base for the Medici outside Florence should not be overlooked. It is true that Lorenzo's father, grandfather and great-grandfather had also made a habit of investing in land, but their purchases had been concentrated in the Mugello, which, as we have seen, had always been the traditional area of Medici territorial control. Lorenzo, by contrast, made very few acquisitions there. At first he concentrated on land-purchase in the area around Careggi where, by 1480, he owned twenty-seven farms, an oil-press, other uncultivated land and several woods. Increasingly, however, he began to acquire property throughout the entire Florentine state and particularly in the area between Florence and Pistoia. He inherited and continued to acquire extensive properties in and around Pisa and in the Casentino. Here he made himself the invaluable patron of the monastery of Camaldoli whose abbot, Mariotto Allegri, was an enthusiastic Platonist. At Bibbiena, also, by a careful purchase of property, he acquired a devoted body of Medici clients who would serve his family well in the future. Thus, Lorenzo seems consciously to have aimed at spreading the area of territorial influence exercised by the Medici throughout the entire Florentine state even though such a plan meant breaking completely with the more cautious policies of his predecessors.

It was not, however, solely the increase in territorial and political power that inevitably accompanied the purchase of land in fifteenth-century Tuscany which made land an attractive investment for Lorenzo. Personal preference must also have played a part, for Lorenzo had a genuine interest in farming and delighted in country-living for its own sake. He may have been neglectful in his supervision of the Medici bank, but he ran his own estates with care and supervised *them* down to the minutest detail. His poetry is famous for reflecting this interest, and so emerges as one of the earliest expressions in the Italian vernacular of a love of the countryside and an informed and accurate knowledge of the natural world. Moreover, Lorenzo's lyrical response to the Tuscan landscape was matched by other interests, including some of those dearest to his heart, which could only be pursued in the country.

From earliest childhood he had always delighted in horses and this early interest developed into a passion for specialised horse-breeding and the training of horses to run in races throughout Italy and Tuscany, in particular. Lorenzo regularly imported horses in order to improve his stock. In 1470, for instance, he purchased four 'more than beautiful'[6] horses in Sicily, which were soon joined by another pair, the gift of King Ferrante of Naples. Four years later more horses were imported from Rimini and Perugia. In the spring of 1477 Lorenzo again purchased stock in Naples and, in the autumn of the same year, he dispatched his trusted groom, Martin da Rezzo, further afield, to buy horses in Sicily and Tunisia. Many horses were given him throughout his life; in 1482, for instance, he was pleased by the gift of a Turkish war-horse which was sent by King Ferrante from the spoils taken during the recapture of Otranto from the Ottomans, and, in the same year, another war-horse came from the Duke of Urbino.

Such gifts show how, as with most aspects of Lorenzo's life, personal interest brought political advantage. Just as the Medici bank could be used for political purposes, so could the most private of Lorenzo's interests. A passion for all things equine was shared by most of Italy's rulers – a passion reaching the point of obsession in the case of Alfonso, Duke of Calabria – and the ritual exchange of horses, in the form of gifts, could thus often form part of complicated diplomatic manoeuvring. Thus, for instance, in 1477, at a time when his personal relationship with King Ferrante was deteriorating, Lorenzo sent the king two of his favourite stallions, *Il Sardo* and *Il Gentile* and, subsequently, in the following April, the king was sent another favourite grey. Similarly, the recognition of the value of the support of his Orsini relatives, in the critical years after 1478, took the form of gifts of horses to Niccolò and Giulio Orsini. Even when horses were not exchanged or gifted, they could still be important pawns in the complicated manoeuvring for position which was the chequered world of fifteenth-century Italian diplomacy. Thus Lorenzo's request for a loan of jousting-horses, made to the rulers of Piombino and Forlì in 1478, had little to do with any real need of horses, but everything to do with a desire to test the attitudes of Piombino and Forlì towards the Medici and Florence.

Hunting-dogs and hawks played similar ritual roles. In December 1470, for example, Lorenzo received a gift of hunting-dogs from the Marquess of Mantua, while, only a month later, the Duke of Milan wrote asking Lorenzo to find him some good bloodhounds. Hawks and falcons of all kinds were constant subjects of correspondence and instruments of ritual gift-giving, and, while there is substantial evidence that Lorenzo, whose falconers always accompanied him wherever he travelled, had a passion for hawking, such gifts counted mostly as a means of easing diplomatic exchange.

Nor were political considerations absent from other favoured country pursuits which tended to increase the reputation of the Medici name. Thus Lorenzo's interest in formal gardens was internationally known, especially his work on the gardens of the Medici villas which were deliberately created to form part of a total artistic environment. The botanic garden and herbiary at Poggio, on which Lorenzo lavished great care, was thus always an object of interest to visitors to Florence, as were the many curious and exotic animals which played an integral part in Lorenzo's country life. As Careggi he reared Calabrian pigs; at Poggio golden pheasants, imported from Sicily, gazelles and rare hares, imported from Tunis, and a number of gifts sent by the Sultan of Babylon: apes, parrots and the famous Medici giraffe: 'so gentle that it will take an apple from the hands of a child'.[7]

Lands, estates, villas – these were among the more appealing aspects of the Medici inheritance. But the Medici bank was not the only part of his inheritance to give Lorenzo problems. Indeed, every asset brought with it associated problems and burdensome obligations. Simply to be the leader of the Medici clan created difficulties. Of course, the existence of that clan was not without its advantages. It was a truism in fifteenth-century Florence to say that a large number of relatives was politically desirable and part of the success of the Medici can be explained by the fact that they were among the largest of Florentine families, numbering, at the time of the 1427 *catasto*, thirty-two separate households.

Lorenzo's own household was a focus of love and warmth and always provided him with a haven of peace and goodwill. Clarice might be dull and, on occasion, obstinate and irritating, but she was Lorenzo's wife and he always loved her. Historians have tended to suggest the opposite, arguing that there is no evidence of affection between the pair but such arguments have been based on little more than knowledge of one spectacular and well-documented quarrel and the assumption that, because they were intellectually ill-matched, Clarice and Lorenzo must have been unhappy together. More solid evidence of a warm and close relationship would seem to exist in the regular annual production, interrupted only by miscarriages, of new inmates for the Medici nursery, and in the concern shown for each other in the correspondence of husband and wife. When Lorenzo was away, Clarice worried ceaselessly about his health and his state of mind, and regularly dispatched presents, food and comforts to him. He, for his part, wrote to her regularly and, no matter how tired he was, normally with his own hand, always addressing these letters to 'my very dear wife'.

This warm and close relationship could only be strengthened by the common delight which both parents took in their seven offspring. Lorenzo was at his happiest among his children. A devoted, although by no means uncritical father, in his dealings with them he revealed a gentleness which rarely otherwise found expression. Lucrezia, the first-born, arrived in August 1470 and was swiftly followed by Piero, Maddalena, Giovanni, Luisa, Contessina and Giuliano, and to the upbringing and education of them all, Lorenzo devoted close attention.

Lorenzo's brother, Giuliano, also remained an important member of the Medici inner circle. The continued deep affection, ease of intercourse and familial closeness of the two brothers is apparent throughout their correspondence, and it is clear they worked well together as a team. Indeed, it is impossible to determine in any accurate way, the precise allocation of the familial, economic, commercial or political responsibilities of the two brothers, who were certainly co-heirs in fact, as well as in law. While Lorenzo was always the acknowledged senior and the accepted leader, this cannot be said to have diminished Giuliano's importance. Whenever Lorenzo was away from Florence, Giuliano simply took over the running of all the Medici affairs, as, for instance, in July 1469, when Lorenzo was hunting partridges at Cafaggiolo and Giuliano dealt with the Duke of Milan directly. Conversely, if Lorenzo had to be in Florence, Giuliano would be the one to entertain visiting dignitaries at Cafaggiolo or Careggi. Each brother was thus mutually dependent upon the other, as both were dependent on the Medici family as a whole, and particularly on their much-loved mother.

The nuclear family was, therefore, a positive and beneficial force, the central core of Lorenzo's existence, giving him the love, affection and opportunities for relaxation vital to his mental well-being. But the wider family also brought with it problems on a massive scale, for Lorenzo's political inheritance was a vast sphere of influence, carefully nurtured by his predecessors, designed solely to ensure the predominance of the

Medici in Florence. The predominance was necessary, for it was only by being able to control the policies of the republic and, in a state which habitually used taxation as a means of social and political control, fiscal policies in particular, that the economic empire of the Medici could be preserved. But, if political power was necessary to ensure continuing economic power, economic power, as Lorenzo's enemies realised, was necessary to continuing Medici political dominance. That political dominance could not be openly exercised. Lorenzo had no permanent position in the Florentine government and was officially regarded as no more than a private citizen. During his adult life he held very few public offices, was never even a member of the *Signoria*, and for frequent periods he had virtually no official standing. Thus, his control over Florentine affairs had to be exercised indirectly by means of friends, clients or supporters who held key positions in the republic.

While, therefore, political parties, in a twentieth-century sense, did not exist in fifteenth-century Florence, it is legitimate to speak of a Medici party, whose purpose was the maintenance of Medici power. Contemporaries knew such groupings and factions existed and used the word 'party' to describe a political association of men, created through ties of marriage and baptismal sponsorship, through local churches, confraternities, charities, religious orders, guilds and through particular cultural groups or events. Typical of such cultural groups were the Florentine *brigate* or brigades, groups of young men who joined together to elect a Lord as their leader during carnival each year. The characteristic expression of these brigades was the *armeggiara* – a public cavalcade through the streets of Florence designed to demonstrate the power and prestige of each brigade. Essentially, the brigades were public assertions of power, made through the youth of the great families of Florence.

By the time of Lorenzo, such brigades played an important part in binding together the Medici party, for it was normal for the creator of such a brigade to feed and clothe its members in return for their public honouring of him, and, while the brigade itself was normally limited to a membership of twelve, it would be accompanied by a host of additional attendants and servants, all wearing a common livery. The brigade thus both brought together a group of young men in a system of mutual obligation and also created vital clientage relationships, central to the structure of the Medici party. For this reason, throughout his adolescence, Lorenzo played his part as the leader of such brigades, the most famous being that of 1459, when the function of the *armeggiara* was faithfully spelt out:

> He for many reasons has great power
> Since his family can do much,
> Son of Piero and grandson of Cosimo.

Thus these genteel (youth) made him Lord. . . .
Whence he wanted to show everyone
That they were all subjected to one Lord.
Now that genuine youth moves
Upon a horse marvellously ornate,
Everyone watches what he does. . . .
His dress surpasses easily that of
All those of whom we've spoken
And well shows that he is Lord . . .
And no one found fault with him. . . .[8]

As we have already seen in the case of the Company of the Magi, a similar role was played by the Medici-controlled confraternities, and it is evident that the Company of the Magi in fact also continued to play a central role in Lorenzo's political calculations. By 1468 it was being run by a governor, who held office for four months, whose post was regarded as one of the greatest honour and responsibility, and was universally assumed to be in Lorenzo's gift. Lorenzo also had a considerable influence over who was elected to the confraternity, in itself a matter of prestige and honour, as Luigi Pulci suggested when, in a letter to Lorenzo, he spoke of being elected to the 'rank of the Magi'.[9] Centred as it was on the convent which Lorenzo always referred to as 'our San Marco',[10] the spiritual heart of the Medici regime, the Company of the Magi was not, however, merely a source of honour and prestige but also of substantial spiritual benefits, for, in 1467, the Company had been granted by the pope the truly unusual benefit of conceding one hundred days' indulgence to all who attended any of its regular meetings. Thus, Medici supporters depended on their patrons not just for their material, but also for their spiritual well-being.

Lorenzo's interests could not, however, be limited to the Magi if he wished to extend his power-base to the whole of Florence. From 1469 he was also a member of the Company of Santa Maria della Laude and Sant'Agnese and, in 1470, he joined the flagellant confraternity of San Paolo. That same year, in association with Gentile Becchi, he drew up new constitutions for San Paolo, but, although these regulations specifically forbade any member to join another flagellant confraternity, Lorenzo belonged to at least two others for they were too valuable as instruments of social control for his interests to be restricted to only one.

Many such structures underpinned the network of relationships which, combined together, made up the Medici party. The Medici were not, of course, the only Florentine family to have such a patronal extension, nor, indeed, were they the inventors of the system, but the basis of their power in Florence did rest on the fact that theirs was the largest such faction and that, in consequence, at critical moments they could call on more support than could any of their rivals.

Who, then, were the members of this Medici party? First, as we have seen, came the family, composed of the Medici and their more immediate relatives. Secondly, there were other families to whom the Medici were loosely related, usually through marriage-bonds, but also through baptismal sponsorship. Thirdly, there were the friends, friends of friends, allies, clients and dependents, tied by a multiplicity of interests to the fortunes of the Medici family. All these groups together made up the Medici party whose 'conservation' Lorenzo gave as the specific reason for accepting a leading role in the regime after his father's death.[11]

Two weaknesses in the party were already evident which would considerably add to Lorenzo's burdens when he became its head. The first was that, even within Florence, the party was very locally based, its most consistent and loyal supporters being concentrated in the districts of San Giovanni and San Marco. For the rest of his life Lorenzo would have to struggle to extend his influence through the city, as a whole, if he hoped to preserve Medici hegemony permanently.

The second disadvantage was the enormous power wielded by the leading patricians within the Medici party. These were a group of powerful Florentines, typified by Lorenzo's uncle, Tommaso Soderini, who came from families whose fortunes had traditionally been linked with those of the Medici, but who were quite wealthy and powerful enough to withdraw their support if they chose to do so. They included the Tornabuoni, Rucellai and Soderini, linked to the Medici by marriage ties, the Acciaiuoli, probably the most loyal of the Medici families, the Ridolfi and the Guicciardini. To what extent Lorenzo would be able to dominate Florentine politics would always depend on his ability to influence this group. Opponents of the Medici might argue that the family drew their support from new men, but while there is some substance in the view that upward social mobility was easier during periods of Medici dominance in Florence, all the evidence suggests that those who actually participated in politics remained, for the most part, the traditional patriciate. It was thus the support of this group that Lorenzo had to win, and this he could do only by operating an effective patronage system, perpetually biased in their favour.

This was the maze from which Lorenzo could never hope to escape. In order to protect the position he had inherited, he was forced to maintain an army of supporters and clients. But supporters and clients in fifteenth-century Florence were not in the habit of giving their services for nothing. The whole system depended on granting reciprocal favours, benefits and gifts in order to further, not only the interests of the Medici party as a whole, but also the interests of each member of the party as an individual. Supporters must be rewarded, cajoled, flattered, managed, courted or

simply bought. They must be found public office, given favourable
tax-assessments, protected in the law-courts and from the city's police-
officials. And each client brought in his train another set of supporters –
the friends of friends – who had, in turn, to be placated and on whom
further time, energy and money must be spent.

The whole system was inherently corrupt, encouraging sycophancy
and dissimulation. It perpetually favoured the greatest flatterer or the
most shameless beggar since the assumption that it was such men who
would reap the richest reward was the assumption on which the Medici
power-structure was built. For what it came to mean in terms of actual
day-to-day life in Florence we have the evidence not only of anti-
Medicean critics but also of the closest supporters of Lorenzo, like
Giovanni Rucellai who advised his sons against participation in public life
since:

> What use will it be to you? You will say: I can lord it over others, steal
> and rob with complete liberty. I can ensure that my tax burden from the
> commune is lightened . . . but you will always be inundated with
> claims, complaints, accusations, reproofs and attacks and surrounded
> by men who are unjust, avaricious, litigious and importunate, who will
> fill your ears with suspicions, your soul with greed, your mind with
> doubts, fear, hatred and enmity.[12]

Florentine political instincts were always sound. Rucellai could see well
enough what was wrong with the system and so could Lorenzo. Yet it was
the system he had inherited, one, indeed, to which he had been exposed
since childhood for, by the age of fifteen, he was already accustomed to
soliciting political support by bestowing favours; equally one must admit
that he rarely showed any moral aversion to this means of exercising
power. What he recoiled from was the sheer volume of hard work
involved in constant political manipulation.

After his father's death, in fact, the first thing Lorenzo realised was
that, for the rest of his life, he could look forward to little more than
unremitting toil. It was a life, for instance, which inevitably entailed a
mountain of correspondence. When he was in Florence his letters were
always dealt with by Lorenzo personally, assisted by a band of secretaries
who, by the nature of their occupation, became also his daily counsellors
and probably his closest friends. Between them, every day, they had to
cope with a whole range of topics, ranging from the conduct of diplomacy
to the state of the fences at Poggio a Caiano. His secretaries might take
some of the burden off Lorenzo and it is clear that many replies to letters
were merely sketched out by him and then actually drafted by the
secretariat. But, equally clearly, a very large number of letters had either
to be dictated in their entirety or actually handwritten by Lorenzo.
Diplomatic reasons, for instance, frequently required Lorenzo to write

autograph letters, but humane considerations also played a part, as, for instance, in writing letters of condolence. For the same kind of reason, Lorenzo normally preferred to write letters to his immediate relatives himself, and it is typical of his courtesy and tact towards those closest to him that, if it were late at night, he would choose to write a letter himself rather than waken one of the secretaries.

Revealingly, such letters make frequent reference to how tired Lorenzo is or apologise for brevity or confusion. Thus, during one of his periods of greatest stress, in January 1479, he told one correspondent, 'If what I am writing seems confused and without order, you must excuse me. I have been writing all morning . . . and I still haven't eaten.'[13] Again, in June 1488, he explained the confusion of another letter by saying, 'If I have left anything out, I will have to write again . . . for now I am exhausted . . .'[14] While to Pietro Alamanni, his representative in Rome, he remarked simply in September 1489: 'I have written all day and I am tired.'[15]

Only ill-health ever interrupted the constant flow of letters. Church holidays went unrecognised by Lorenzo's secretariat, as did family holidays, for, even when he retreated to the country, there was no relaxation of the discipline of daily letterwriting. Although his secretaries would open the mail and sort it in Florence, most letters were still sent on for Lorenzo to deal with, for this correspondence was the life-blood of the system of Medicean rule. It was essential to that constant management of men, family, friends and allies in which Cosimo had been so skilled and which Piero had had less time for.

That management, of course, also involved numerous daily contacts. Day after day a new procession of clients or supplicants found their way to the Via Larga to be interviewed, talked to, bought. A benefice must be found somewhere for some Medici adherent, a schoolmastership for another. The Marquess of Mantua must be approached about the possibility of a job for one of the Strozzi. Thanks must be rendered for gifts received, and appropriate gifts dispatched by way of return. The records remain full of the tasks undertaken for the numerous, often anonymous, supporters of the Medici like 'Ser Carlo di Berto da Firenzuola' for whom a post was solicited in 1468, the 'friend of Messer Bartolomeo Scala'[16] for whom a letter must be written to the Podestà of San Gimignano in April 1478, 'the ancient friends and creatures of our house' on whose behalf letters must go off to Siena,[17] or 'at the request of Francesco Sassetti, for one who is his friend'[18] to the ruler of Piombino in January 1483.

In addition to all this personal activity, Lorenzo's position involved him in taking a great deal more than the normal share in Florentine government expected of a young patrician. He had to learn to dominate and control every committee on which he sat, and that in itself might involve hours of preparatory work. He was also perpetually involved in the organisation of festivals, the entertainment of visitors, the daily obligation of public religious observance and of generous alms-giving. Worst of all, there remained always, as we have seen, somewhere in the background, the organisation and running of all aspects of the Medici business. For a young man of vitality and creativity it must all, on occasion, have seemed exhausting and perhaps pointlessly time-consuming.

Yet there could be no escape from this Medici system, and its pattern of mutual obligation and the exchange of favours preserving a power structure based on patron–client relationships. Lorenzo must daily be involved in a constant search for offices and benefices inside and outside Florence with which to reward his supporters. He must use his political position to interfere with the due process of the law, to get sentences reduced or commuted. A loyal Medici client did, after all, assume that provided his behaviour was not too outrageous, he could rely on protection from the attentions of Florence's law-officers and often this protection extended far beyond the boundaries of Florence.

Allied to such habitual interference with the operation of the law was Lorenzo's practice of purchasing supporters by getting bans of exile rescinded. Thus, in 1471, his mere promise to try to get the sentence of exile on the Albizzi lifted produced an abject and effusive promise of future political devotion. Fulsomely thanking Lorenzo, Maso degli Albizzi declared that it seemed as if his whole family had been 'lifted from hell into paradise' and promised that the Medici might henceforth dispose of the Albizzi, 'as your faithful friends, servants and slaves'.[19]

One of the commonest favours to be begged of Lorenzo was that he ensure a family's eligibility for public office, for, in Florentine eyes, such eligibility was essential to high social standing. Thus, even the rumour of a new scrutiny would produce an endless stream of begging-letters, imploring Lorenzo to use his influence on the supplicant's behalf.

Subsequently, Donato Giannotti, one of the sternest critics of the Medici, claimed that Lorenzo's ability to control the scrutiny was responsible for the introduction of sycophancy, practised as an art-form, into Florentine politics. He vividly described how men who had sons 'manoeuvred to have them extracted from the purses . . . this consequently gave the tyrants a golden opportunity to buy men and gain them for their clients.'[20] Such behaviour could only be encouraged by three regular features of Medici political management; first, the legal requirement that a scrutiny be held every five years, second that a deceased man's electoral standing might be allowed to devolve upon his son, even if the latter had not yet reached the minimum age for office-holding, and, third, the Medici habit of appointing prominent supporters to office by decree, regardless of age.

Another valuable source of benefits for his supporters Lorenzo found in the Church, whose vast international network of benefices could be used to reward faithful clients. The necessity of tapping this store of patronage became a life-long obsession. It explains Lorenzo's relentless search for a cardinal's hat for one of his immediate family, since it was generally recognised that to have a member of the family in the Sacred College made it easier to gain access to the clerical patronage of the Curia. It explains the careful courting of cardinals and prominent ecclesiastics, the obsequiousness shown to members of the ruling pontiff's family, and, eventually, the virtual seduction of Innocent VIII into the Medici party. Here, the family link with the Orsini was important because of the power which that family enjoyed in Rome. But, even with their influence on his side, Lorenzo had still to devote many hours to writing letters in a ceaseless search for benefices for his friends, his relatives and his family.

Lorenzo also appreciated, to a degree that his father and grandfather had not, that for the Medici to retain power permanently in Florence, they must have the crowd on their side. Hence, the importance Lorenzo attached to popular festivals. In this courting of the populace, he found himself in a typically paradoxical position. The humanism, cultivated within Medici circles, was imbued with an aristocratic and anti-proletarian ethos, and its 'high' culture was deliberately set against the 'popular' culture of the masses. Lorenzo's answer was to foster and to manipulate that popular culture as a valuable thing in itself, and also to set it apart from the traditional Florentine festivals, patronised by the commune, most notably the patronal festival of San Giovanni which became downgraded in favour of the popular festival of Carnival of which Lorenzo was a dedicated patron. Thus communal patronage was gradually frozen out and all culture in Florence, whether of the aristocracy or of the people, became imbued with a pro-Medici bias.

Lorenzo thus deliberately discouraged associations of people which were city-wide or reflected communal values and instead encouraged neighbourhood associations. In consequence, it is from the time of Lorenzo that the populace of Florence are first found in organised groups, known as 'powers', who were patronised by the Medici. Lorenzo also encouraged the emerging plebeian neighbourhood confraternities. In 1488, for instance, the wool-beaters were allowed to form their own confraternity and the silk-weavers were permitted to build their own hospital. Significantly, both these occupational groups had their meeting-places in the Medici parish of San Lorenzo and could be used as instruments of political power by Lorenzo.

A power-base within Florence, then, Lorenzo had inherited, maintained, and greatly extended, but to concentrate solely on Florence would seriously distort the picture. From a study of Lorenzo's correspondence, it is clear that another mainstay of his position lay in the whole Florentine state, for his political survival was dependent on his ability to find posts for clients in the subject-cities, like Pisa, Arezzo, San Gimignano, Pistoia and Volterra. Yet Lorenzo's ability to influence such appointments was always limited, being dependent on a number of factors. Each of the subject-towns was, itself, divided between a pro-Medicean and an anti-Medicean faction, with power constantly oscillating between the two. It was always in Lorenzo's interest, of course, to maintain his own supporters as the ruling faction in these towns, but this involved further complicated political bargaining, wheeling and dealing, as he tried to oblige his clients with a constant stream of favours.

Often he was successful. The Medici had never shown any of the traditional prejudice of the Florentines towards the subject-towns, and Lorenzo was as ready as his Medici predecessors to employ non-Florentines in his service. In addition, he occasionally made the favouring of a subject-town a deliberate act of policy. This was conspicuously the case with Pisa where, at the expense of Florence, he recreated and nurtured the University. So substantial was support at Pisa, whose governors assured Lorenzo that, 'without your Magnificence [we] neither wish nor can obtain anything'[21] that Lorenzo frequently treated that city as if he were, indeed, its ruler. We find him, for instance, in December 1477, writing to the Captain of Pisa directly and ordering him, 'to take every care to preserve Pisa from the plague',[22] or in 1478, ordering him to ensure 'that the soldiers who are harming the corn shall be kept in their lodgings',[23] or bringing his personal influence to bear to expedite cases through the Pisan law courts.

Careful nurturing of the subject-towns, therefore, brought substantial political benefits and most of them, at some time or another would have echoed the sentiments of Arezzo which described Lorenzo as, 'the sole refuge, safe remedy and security for any wish or desire of ours'.[24] Effectively, Lorenzo was normally in a position to nominate to a vast range of offices and this opened up a whole new area of patronage which could provide for the friends and clients of the Medici. Such offices ranged from the humble to the really important – from the schoolmastership of Colle Val d'Elsa to the judges of Pistoia, and requests made for such posts were usually treated as demands. In fact, the respect accorded to Lorenzo in some of the subject-towns might even, on occasion, prove embarrassing, as in January 1478 when he had to write to the Podestà of Prato and order him to ensure that: 'justice is done by everyone and our workmen are not given preferential treatment',[25] or October 1485, when he wrote to assure a client, 'that I neither desire nor seek the pasture-rights of Bibbiena . . . which are [yours] to rent.'[26]

Yet, as with everything to do with Lorenzo, we should beware of taking too static a view of his relations with the dependent communes. Just as his power in Florence waxed and waned, changed and developed in relation to changing circumstances, so did his relations with the subject-towns. As in his dealings with the official Florentine governmental agencies, he could only request, never order. Eventually, as we have seen, Prato became loyal but this was certainly not always the case. At first, so estranged was the city from the Medici that a precious silver vase, offered by Prato as a wedding-gift to Lorenzo and Clarice was refused and, in consequence, in both 1469 and 1470 when relations between Florence and Prato were peculiarly strained, Prato several times refused to appoint Medici nominees to local offices.

Lorenzo disliked such refusals for they reflected on his honour and, therefore, affected his power. The refusal in 1471 by the commune of San Gimignano to accept his nominee as their chancellor, was met by an irritated, arrogant and tactless outburst. San Gimignano hardly improved matters by pointing out that Lorenzo's previous nominee had been a total disaster and the squabble, thus provoked, grumbled on for months. Thus, all one can truthfully say, in broad terms of Lorenzo's relationship with the Florentine state as a whole, is that the Medici regime was sometimes more popular outside Florence than it was inside the city and that the subject-cities did provide many patronage openings for Lorenzo.

More stable support for Lorenzo came from a different source, from rulers of other states, all of whom at Piero's death, 'sent letters and envoys to condole with us and offer us help for our defence'.[27] Ever since the time of Giovanni di Bicci, the Medici had deliberately built up such friendships, as a means of preserving their position in Florence, and Cosimo, in particular, had been outstandingly gifted in his ability to analyse the potential utility of such relationships. In this area, Lorenzo inherited all the talent of his grandfather, as both his critics and his admirers agreed. Poliziano, for instance, thought that the fact that Lorenzo was treated as an equal by foreign powers, gave him increased power, because this recognition of his prince-like status reflected glory on Florence and, essentially, authenticated its republican regime. For Poliziano, therefore, it was a positive good that:

> The Medici family were splendid and magnificent in all their undertakings, especially in receiving foreign personages. No famous man either came to Florence or Florentine territory whom that household did not treat with this sort of magnificence.[28]

And, Alamanno Rinuccini, although among the severest of Lorenzo's critics, recognised the same phenomenon, even while regarding it with severe displeasure:

> An immense ambition and vainglory induced Lorenzo de' Medici to never say 'no' to any foreigner, no matter if even of the lowest quality, as long as he believed he would speak well of him.[29]

The most important of Lorenzo's relationships with foreign rulers always remained that with the rulers of Milan, a relationship which derived from the days when Cosimo used his position to give a radical new direction to Florence's foreign policy by allying with Milan, her traditional enemy, and with Naples. The fruits of that alliance had been the general Italian Peace of Lodi of 1454 and the Italian League of 1455, designed to prevent members threatening the general peace by attacking their neighbours, and also to provide a united front against any ultramontane aggressor. The Sforza–Medici alliance was of fundamental importance to both parties. Lorenzo needed Sforza in order to preserve his position in Florence, but, equally, Sforza needed Lorenzo to preserve the Milan/Florence alliance, for there were many in Florence who would have liked to break with Milan. And Lorenzo, therefore, remained the channel through which those who needed favours or help from the Duke of Milan or who looked for advancement in his service were bound to pass.

Centrally important as the Sforza friendship was, Lorenzo also inherited other prestigious foreign friendships. The one in which he took most pride was that with the King of France who regularly addressed him as 'cousin' and called Lorenzo his 'most dear and trusted friend',[30], but equally valuable were his personal relationships with Ferrante of Naples and his son Alfonso, Duke of Calabria. Prestige also attached to the fact that Lorenzo was regarded as the arbiter of good taste by the celebrated Matthias Corvinus, King of Hungary, and was also the recipient of gifts and letters from the Sultans of Egypt and Turkey. Within Italy, he was also known personally by Giovanni Bentivoglio, ruler of Bologna, by the Marquess of Mantua and the Dukes of Ferrara and Urbino, and Iacopo Appiano, Lord of Piombino.

In addition, Lorenzo, as the new head of the Medici family and party, could count on the support of many of the rulers of the small, semi-independent states of the Church State and the friendship of a number of prominent *condottieri* and Italian noblemen. By his marriage, he had, of course, become a part of the Orsini complex of familial relationships which stretched from Venice to the Kingdom of Naples. The Orsini were extremely valuable since they could provide Florence with the mercenary troops she needed in time of war. Strategic considerations were also important for one of the leading Orsini, the Count of Pitigliano, ruled a little independent state, on the border between Siena and the Church State and was, therefore, a useful buffer against papal expansion into Tuscany. Closely allied with the Orsini were also the Vitelli of Città di Castello who declared themselves to Lorenzo as 'completely yours, and so we will be unto death, always following the course of action which seems reasonable to your Magnificence.'[31] Other noble supporters of importance included the Marquess of Malaspina who looked to Lorenzo to get him military contracts from Florence and the great mercenary captain, Roberto da Sanseverino.

In the neighbouring republic of Siena, too, were to be found loyal partisans of the Medici, particularly among the Bellanti, Petrucci, Luti and Buoninsegni families. This Medici 'party' within Siena had been carefully nurtured by Cosimo and Piero, and Lorenzo followed faithfully in their footsteps, intervening on behalf of Sienese 'friends' with the Sienese government or in the Sienese law courts, entertaining them at the Medici villas, and even going so far as to provide exiled Sienese in Florence, 'with sufficient maintenance to enable them to live honourably as befitted their state'.[32] In return these Sienese friends loyally advocated Medici policies in their own civic councils.

In both political and material terms, therefore, Lorenzo inherited considerable power from his father. Many contemporaries would have assumed that the Medicean hegemony in Florentine life must, in consequence, be unassailable, that the city would be unable to extricate itself from domination by the Medici family, or pursue policies other than those determined by Medicean interests. So a great many contemporaries assumed, but even in the hours which followed Piero's death, there could be found men in Florence, even within the Medicean circle, who believed that Lorenzo's youth and relative inexperience provided an opportunity to overthrow the Medici family, and return to what they saw as the golden days when power in their city rested not in the hands of one family or one individual but in the hands of all the *reggimento*. It was to the problem of these potential enemies that, for the next ten years, Lorenzo would have to address his mind, and it would be their ambitions, as much as his own desires, which would determine his policies.

3

THE MAKING OF A STATESMAN, 1469–72

Respect for maturity and old age was built into every political and social structure of fifteenth-century Florence, where it appeared self-evident that young men were too unstable, too lacking in gravity, to be able to participate in public life. As far as his contemporaries were concerned, Lorenzo, in 1469, was merely a youth. It would be another ten years before he could qualify for major political office or emerge with a fully-formed character. This contemporary view explains the curious fact that only by studying Lorenzo in the years immediately after his father's death, can biographers hope to glimpse his true character, for, subsequently, in response to social and political pressures, he learned to hide behind a mask, deliberately designed to conceal his true feelings and responses. So successful did the disguise become that Lorenzo managed to baffle, not only his fellow Florentines, but all subsequent biographers, struggling with the task of unravelling the enigma of his personality.

That personality, faithfully reflecting all the contradictions of the age, was a bundle of paradoxes which found resolution only in transient moments of stasis. It is, therefore, significant that forms of evasion should have become the hall-mark of his character. Many commented on his method of 'responding shortly and ambiguously, so that you have to understand him by the merest sign'.[1] This evasive quality in Lorenzo's conversation was much more than a pose; it reflected a genuinely contradictory personality.

Arrogant, cruel, on occasion positively vindictive, impatient with those who differed from him or who lacked his penetrating intelligence, Lorenzo was also kind, charming, polite and totally generous in all his human responses. Attacked for pride by all his critics, he was lavishly praised by his friends for his humility and humanity. Acutely aware of his family's inferior social position, and insecure because of it, Lorenzo yet behaved in public like a born prince. He kept high-ranking Florentines kicking their heels for hours in the courtyard of the Medici palace in the hope of an audience. He walked the streets of Florence, with an armed body-guard, and he was obsessed by the concept of his own honour which he said he esteemed and prized 'above all things'.[2] He was, indeed, as the Milanese ambassador commented in October 1472, 'astute and able; but thinks too highly of himself and raises his sails too high for any good to come of it'.[3]

Vasari's posthumous portrait of Lorenzo emphasises Lorenzo's melancholic temperament and the ambivalence of his character

Family, household and friends, alike, were victims of bewildering changes of mood. Generosity and irritability often seemed equally mixed in Lorenzo. Wherever credit was due, he gave that credit quickly, praising his representatives and servants on every available occasion. 'I have written what I think at great length' he once told Bernardo Buongirolami, 'because the loyalty you show me, deserves it.'[4] Yet, just as frequently, Lorenzo's ready and sardonic wit would be turned against those selfsame servants. His generosity of character flowed freely within the context of his family life, although he could be terrifying when angry. His children knew that any special effort on their part was sure to be rewarded by their father. They were secure in Lorenzo's love and, from babyhood, were completely devoted to him; and yet there were occasions when he seemed totally detached from them, so aware of their failings as to seem scarcely a relative.

His friends, meanwhile, also found his character confusing. In consequence, with the possible exception of Poliziano, they never found a satisfactory formula by which to describe his impact on them. Ficino, for instance, knew Lorenzo very well, was aware of his faults and weaknesses, and was by no means uncritical of his behaviour. Yet, when it came to describing Lorenzo's virtues, Ficino was at a loss, forced to take refuge in hyperbole, myth and classical allusion. Lorenzo, he wrote, possessed all three of the endowments Orpheus had called Graces – splendour of intellect, joy in decision-making, and vigour of body. 'Those Graces', he continued, 'now inspire [Lorenzo] from on high, and they will do so as long as he only acknowledges that he freely received these favours from God alone.'[5]

The note of obsequious flattery, struck here by Ficino, is present in every one of Lorenzo's friendships and yet those friendships were genuine enough. They were based on that humanity which all emphasize as one of Lorenzo's virtues. And, by humanity, contemporaries meant naturalness and ease of manner as well as a ready identification with another's concerns or interest: 'having compassion on the afflicted, and, particularly, on those who are afflicted in a way that we also are afflicted'.[6]

On this basis of shared humanity, Lorenzo maintained his close relationship with those young men, like Bernardo Rucellai, and Donato Acciaiuoli, 'one of [his] most intimate friends'[7] with whom he had grown up. After Piero's death, they continued to participate in all of Lorenzo's artistic and intellectual pursuits; they shared his passion for hawking and hunting; they accompanied him on jaunts into the countryside; they participated in all the courtly and artificial joys and sorrows of Lorenzo's relationship with the beautiful Simonetta Vespucci. With such friends, Lorenzo laid aside formality and found the relaxation vital to his well-being. Riding, walking, talking, writing poetry, improvising on the lyre, discussing every topic under the sun, they all were ready to go on sharing every aspect of their experience. We are fortunate to possess, from Poliziano's pen, a description of one of their holiday trips in 1476, when:

> . . . after leaving Florence, we came as far as San Miniato al Tedesco, singing all the way and occasionally of holy things, so as not to forget Lent. At Lastra we drank *Zappolina* which tasted much better than I had been told. Lorenzo is brilliant and makes the company gay – yesterday I

counted twenty-six horses of those who are with him. When we reached San Miniato yesterday evening we began to read a little of St Augustine; then the reading resolved itself into music and watching and giving directions to a well-known dancer who is here. Lorenzo is just going to mass . . .[8]

Such swift changes of mood and interest were as genuine as the close friendships which are implied. Yet, even such relationships exacted a price, and Lorenzo was not unambivalent about them. In order to maintain his position as the acknowledged leader of this group of young men, he could not only rely on wealth and prestige. He had, in addition, to make himself constantly agreeable, constantly available, constantly ready to participate. That he sometimes resented this is suggested by his own description of his first meeting with Lucrezia Donati. Despite the literary convention involved in the description and, indeed, the political necessity to emphasise his distaste for youthful pursuits, a genuine sense of being forced into social postures, against his will, lies behind Lorenzo's account of how:

. . . a public celebration was being held in our city in which many participated, including most of the handsome young aristocrats. It was almost against my will . . . that I betook myself to this festival with certain of my companions and friends, since, for some time, I had been indifferent to such affairs, and, if they pleased me at one time or another, this was rather because I wanted to behave like other young men than because of any great enjoyment I derived from them.[9]

Social necessity, however, and the role of the Medici in Florence, ensured that Lorenzo's life in the city would be one of constant, public, participation in a perpetual round of festivities, feasts, formal receptions and religious celebrations. He was always in the public eye. Understandably, then, whenever he could, Lorenzo would escape, if only for the day, to one of his villas. Here, in odd moments of leisure, he continued to write poetry or to compose songs, as a means of refinding himself and coping with the pressures of public life. Only through such creativity could his true self survive and its importance for him is vividly expressed in a letter to Niccolò Michelozzi of 28 August 1472, written from Cafaggiolo in which Lorenzo urged his secretary to return 'as quickly as you can, since I have hourly need of you. I am waiting for the lyre and the other things, and, whatever you do, be sure to bring them with you.'[10]

Universally regarded as prudent and perspicacious, Lorenzo was a man whose life was consciously governed by reason and tolerance. He was remarkable, among fifteenth-century Florentines, for having no truck with astrology or astrologers, an attitude he may have derived from his careful study of Dante. He is equally remarkable, among fifteenth-century Europeans, in his unswervingly tolerant attitude to Jews. The Jewish community of Florence enjoyed a rare period of genuine security in Lorenzo's lifetime, but he was also known as the friend and protector of Jews throughout Italy. In 1477, alone, for instance, he interceded with the papal governor of the Patrimony of St Peter on behalf of a certain 'Abraham, a Jew of Viterbo',[11] with Giovanni Bentivoglio on behalf of a Bolognese Jew, and with Siena for 'certain Jews from Montalcino'.[12] On other occasions, he took action on behalf of Jews in Lombardy, Ferrara and several other parts of the Church State.

Tolerant, unprejudiced and committed to reason, Lorenzo certainly was; yet, on occasion, he could act impulsively and find himself the victim of his own emotions. While he might reject the inherent irrationality of astrology, at critical moments of his life he surrendered to an equally irrational fatalism. Up to a certain point he would plot a reasoned course, only at the last moment to surrender to near-despair. 'Let what will happen, happen', he told Girolamo Morelli at a critical moment in 1479, 'no more can be done.'[13] His poetry is suffused by a pessimistic assessment of the power of fortune over the individual and man's ability to change his destiny, as in the celebrated description of the power of death:

> How vain, indeed, is every hope of ours,
> How falsely-based each plan,
> How full the world of ignorance,
> Death, master of all, shows us.

Lorenzo has always been portrayed as prone to melancholy. Were the sole evidence of such melancholia to be found in the writings of Medici clients, we might suspect that we were dealing with little more than a rather subtle form of flattery, since the Platonic tradition associated genius, and especially the genius of poetry, with melancholy. But Lorenzo's life and his own writing confirm such descriptions. So overcome by despair was he, at times, that he feared for his own mental stability and, on at least one occasion, sought Ficino's aid in preserving his sanity. In periods of intense introspection Lorenzo was sometimes led to feel alienated from the whole world. At such times he felt profound spiritual disquiet, reaching the stage indeed where he saw the hand of God raised against him. Then, even his sincere religious faith could not entirely suppress his unfulfilled longings, nor preserve him from the temptation to despair:

> O God, O Highest God, now what do you do?
> That I search only for you and never find you.

Time passes too swiftly for man to be able to achieve anything; 'Soon the flower of our life fades!' Only Death comes quickly. This neurotic fear of the passage of time could, then, only be furthered by Ficino's warning to

'Spend the most precious moments of time, short as it is, cautiously and wisely, lest you ever have cause to repent in vain your prodigality and irreparable waste,'[14] and his bringing up, once again, the example of Cosimo, who, even when over seventy, would 'sigh deeply'[15] at the thought of all the precious hours he had squandered in his youth.

Yet, it was the same Lorenzo, on occasion brought to a condition of physical collapse by the depth of his depression, who is to be found, just as frequently, surrounded by laughter and gaiety, as Poliziano portrayed him, a man with a wit so irrepressible that humour breaks incongruously into even his most solemn diplomatic correspondence. Lorenzo's sense of the vanity of human desires might lead to despair but, just as often, it issued in a positive assertion of the value of love, laughter and pleasure; the Lorenzo of 'False life! The vanity of our preoccupations!', is also the Lorenzo of:

> While this brief life endures
> Let each man be happy, each man fall in love.

Like all depressives, he was a victim of occasion, weather and climate. Sunshine simply made him happy, while the winter invariably depressed him so that he dreaded its advent, trying to banish the cold and the gloom from the Medici palace by blazing fires in every room.

All of Lorenzo's paradoxical qualities and humours need to be borne in mind when considering the four years that followed Piero's death for each was to play a part in the evolution of a young statesman. These years were particularly important in Lorenzo's career, marked, as they were, by his emergence as the dominating figure in the ruling oligarchy, by a number of near-catastrophic misjudgments, but, above all, by his increasing mastery of diplomacy, as he came to understand that, both his position in Florence and his ability to control Florentine foreign policy were, essentially, inseparable.

From the beginning ambivalence served, as usual, to confuse the issue. On the day following Piero's death, a delegation from a large meeting of leading citizens which had determined to preserve Lorenzo and Giuliano 'in prestige and greatness'[16] came, according to Lorenzo:

> to us in our house, to condole with us on our loss and to encourage me to take care of the city and the regime as my grandfather and my father had done. This I did, though, on account of my youth and the great peril and responsibility arising therefrom, with great reluctance, solely for the safety of our friends and of our possessions. For it is ill living in Florence for the rich unless they rule.[17]

It is typical of Lorenzo that, even in this, a private memoir, he should have been unable to resolve the ambivalence of his life. For a man who claimed to be reluctant to succeed to his father's position in the state, he had been remarkably active in the previous weeks. Piero had fallen ill at a moment of considerable strain in the Florentine–Milanese alliance, when, distrustful of the activities of the Duke of Milan, the Florentines, by the end of October 1469, had been brought to the point where they were threatening to break off the alliance. One consequence had been an increase in Lorenzo's importance for the Duke, who, from September onwards, had been wooing the Medici heir-apparent.

Lorenzo responded readily to these overtures, becoming, in a sense, the Duke's 'man', in a way his father had never been, and it was, naturally, to the Duke he turned for assistance as Piero lay dying. On 1 December he wrote:

> declaring to your Excellency that, even though I am certain to have the good support of friends here, yet I do not think I shall be able to be successful, unless Your Illustrious Lordship deigns to intervene, in my favour, to help me.[18]

On the following day, an even more urgent letter was dispatched:

> Yesterday, I wrote to your Excellency concerning the illness of Piero, my father. Since then his condition has worsened so that I have little reason to hope for his recovery and, once again, I want to confirm to Your Illustrious Lordship that all my hope lies only in you. I ask you, as I asked in my other letter, that you would give thought to my preservation, which can proceed only from your Excellency, to whom I humbly recommend myself.[19]

Sforza responded swiftly to this plea for aid. Only four days after Piero's death he wrote to the *Signoria* recommending to them: 'Lorenzo and Guiliano . . . whom, owing to the love we have always nourished for that house, we hold . . . dear as if they were our own sons.'[20] To add strength to his argument, he added that although he was sure they would not actually be needed, he had already ordered his troops in the territories of Bologna and Parma to be ready to come to Florence's aid and that 'we are ready, in such a case, to come in person with the rest of our troops'.[21]

Meanwhile, within Florence, Lorenzo had been taking other measures to protect his position and the whole Medici party machinery had been put into action to ensure the smooth transfer of power from Piero to Lorenzo and Giuliano. Throughout the city, displays of support for the Medici were organised, while Tommaso Soderini summoned a meeting of all the leading Mediceans to discuss the future.

As we have seen, that meeting, in the convent of San Antonio, took place on the evening of Piero's death. More than seven hundred pro-Mediceans participated and agreed to accord to Lorenzo and Giuliano the position of supremacy previously enjoyed by Piero. On the following day, 'a crowd of these leading men, knights and citizens'[22] met in the

Medici palace in order to devise proposals for new taxes that were approved by the Council of One Hundred on 9 December. Considering that controversy over taxation had been tearing the city apart throughout the previous twelve months, Lorenzo was right to regard the passage of this measure as a vote of confidence in the new regime, for, as he wrote to Otto Niccolini in Rome:

> This was done so that if anyone had said that there would surely be disunion in our city after Piero's death, they will now be able to observe that quite the contrary effect has resulted.[23]

This is a key remark, if we are to understand the role which Lorenzo played in Florence, and his attitude towards that role. There has always been a tendency to over-estimate the power of Lorenzo, and to speak of the making of Florentine policy as if decision-making was Lorenzo's alone. Contemporaries were often as guilty as subsequent historians, in this respect, for observers from monarchical or princely states found it difficult to conceptualise a situation in which, inherently, all political decision-making was collective. Instinctively, they treated Lorenzo as if he were the ruler of Florence, and historians have followed their lead, for it is easier to think and write of decision-making when actual decisions appear to be those of the one, rather than the many. It is only the increasingly sophisticated understanding of the political process that has developed in the twentieth century, and our own experience of collective decision-making, which has created some genuine understanding of the nature of political life in fifteenth-century Florence which was both intensely patriarchal and passionately corporate in its nature.

Lorenzo de' Medici was never a tyrant, although his enemies accused him of being one. He was well aware of the danger that he might be so perceived, but tried to take every precaution against it. Within Florence he was elaborately careful in his deportment. He always dressed in the manner of other citizens and, when in the company of older men, he accorded them the place of honour on his right. He was as careful to observe every formality of the Florentine constitution as his father and grandfather had been – in constitutional terms, the Medici regime was always scrupulously legal.

On the other hand, there is no doubt that Lorenzo was accustomed to getting his own way and disliked being thwarted in any of his undertakings, nor that he could be both arrogant and obstinate. He had a decided preference for good and efficient government, and a pronounced distaste for chaos. His lifetime did see an increasing concentration of power within Florence, but it is worth remembering that there was nothing new about this. It was, in fact, a process which had been going on since the end of the fourteenth century. Increasingly, administrative law had come to be exercised by magistracies rather than by the traditional communal officers; increasingly, the power of the executive had grown. Both these processes were definitely accelerated by Lorenzo, but he was always an instinctive Florentine, and during his lifetime Florence remained a self-governing, citizen-republic not just in theory but also in reality. Lorenzo had a profound respect for his city's traditions, which provided the framework for policy making, and he was not just paying lip-service to a worn-out ideal when, in 1477, he reminded the citizens of the neighbouring republic of Lucca that they must work with the Florentines to preserve peace, 'which, both you and we, according to the nature of free peoples have always been anxious to preserve'.[24] Like all Florentines, he gloried in the idea of 'liberty' which was conceived as being essentially bound up with the city's republican constitution. To destroy that constitution would be to lose Florence that quality which made her so distinctive and distinguished an element in the world. Lorenzo, therefore, proposed 'to follow the method of his grandfather which was to do things as much as possible by constitutional means'.[25]

Such, at least, was the view of the Milanese ambassador, but one might well ask whether, at this stage, Lorenzo had very much choice. Although the Florentine people, as a whole, were probably willing enough to consent to Medici rule, provided that the consequences of that rule did not involve them facing any major threat to their lives or livelihoods, it was not the Florentine people, as a whole, who mattered. Like every other Italian state, whatever its nominal constitution, Florence, as we have seen, was managed by a ruling élite whose first commitment was to its own values. It was to this group of about 3,000 families that Lorenzo must address his mind and, in particular, to that one per cent of families – about 100 – who possessed between them one-quarter of the total wealth of Florence and one-sixth of the wealth of the whole Florentine state. Among this group were to be found many members of the *reggimento*. It was the *reggimento* which believed it had put Lorenzo into a position of pre-eminence in which it had no intention of keeping him unless he manifestly served their interests.

Lorenzo, in consequence, found that he could not always get what he wanted, even from the most immediate Medici partisans, who particularly disliked, for example, his constant requests for benefits for his Orsini relatives. As far as the Mediceans were concerned, Lorenzo's role was clear-cut. He was to be a chairman, whose chief value lay in holding the balance between contending parties, and exercising, if necessary, 'a casting-vote in public affairs'.[26] Lorenzo, therefore, rapidly discovered that the decision-making process always involved constant consultation. He came to make a virtue of necessity, declaring that he asked advice frequently since, in that way, he could use other people's brains as well as his own, but he did find the whole business distinctly irksome.

At first, Lorenzo was very dependent on leading members of the

Medici party to guide him through the labyrinth of affairs. It is difficult, in fact, in the early years of the regime, ever to be certain whether initiatives or policies originated with Lorenzo at all. Thus, despite considerable differences over policy and very great difficulties in their relationship, Lorenzo had to rely on his uncle, Tommaso Soderini, simply because the latter's position in Florence was so important that he was bound to play a prominent part in government. Lorenzo, however, found useful counter-weights to Soderini in the pro-Milanese, Luigi Guicciardini, who had been an energetic partisan of the Medici since the time of Cosimo, and in Luigi's younger brother, Iacopo, who played an increasingly prominent role in government. Iacopo was genuinely fond of Lorenzo, although considerably older than him. A highly astute politician, of great standing within the *reggimento*, Iacopo gave Lorenzo excellent advice about the management of the Medici party. It was important that, alone among the Medici partisans, he was never afraid to speak his mind and, since the advice he proffered was consistently good, he became one of the few men in Florence who could restrain Lorenzo in a headstrong mood.

Another good friend was Angelo della Stufa, also a devotee of the Milanese alliance, and a member of one of the most loyal of the Medici families. His influence over Lorenzo derived, in part, from the fact that he had been one of the best of Piero's friends and so appears to have helped fill the emotional vacuum left in Lorenzo's life after his father's death. Revealingly, Lorenzo wrote to Angelo in June 1470, apologising for his youthful impetuosity and protesting his love and sincerity:

> which, together with our common interest, have perhaps made me say too much . . . and I have said more to you than I would to others, because writing to you is like writing to Piero my father, or talking to myself.[27]

'It is not without great difficulty that Lorenzo's position can be maintained,'[28] warned the Milanese ambassador. On two major counts Lorenzo was, indeed, faced with formidable opposition. The first was his youth. As we have seen, like other Italians, the Florentines allowed only the most marginal role in political life to young men, and, from the moment that it became clear that Piero was a dying man, Lorenzo's youth and comparative lack of experience had been a matter of concern at Milan. Two years later Lorenzo's friends were still preoccupied by the problem and the Cardinal of Rouen, writing to Becchi, expressed the wish that he could give Lorenzo twenty of his many years, as a protection against his political enemies. 'Act grave', Becchi, for his part, warned Lorenzo, 'if you want to be taken seriously by foreign rulers.'[29]

Lorenzo was always quick to learn. He began to cultivate a graver and more mature demeanour and to show an overt disinterest in the tradition-al concerns of young men – in *brigate*, in jousting, in games and even in public festivities. Some of his friends were somewhat taken aback by this change, particularly by the withdrawal of support from the communal festival of San Giovanni; 'I am a little surprised that you have diminished this *festa* as much as you have,'[30] wrote Luigi Pulci in 1472.

It was fortunate that Lorenzo's friends all tended to be older than he was. Of those closest to him, at this period, only Bernardo Rucellai was his contemporary. The rest were all from seven to seventeen years older and this lent Lorenzo some reflected gravity. The birth of his eldest child, Lucrezia, in 1470 may also have aided his reputation for increasing maturity and have convinced the anxious Lorenzo-watchers that his youth need not necessarily be a disadvantage. Nevertheless it was with an obvious sigh of relief, in June 1470, that the Milanese ambassador reported that Lorenzo had spoken in the *Pratica* – an *ad hoc* advisory board to the *Signoria* – 'not as a youth or as a timid man but as a man of wisdom'.[31]

The other main source of opposition to Lorenzo came from those who disliked the Milanese alliance. As we have seen, even before Piero's death, support for that alliance had been waning, and opposition to it continued to mount in the following months, weakening the Medici party by dividing it at its very heart. Tommaso Soderini, who should have been Lorenzo's chief support, in fact favoured abandoning Milan and allying with Venice. He thus, inevitably, became the focus of the anti-Milanese lobby and, in consequence, relations between Lorenzo and Soderini became so strained that, by August 1470, their friendship was said to have turned to enmity, 'to their own harm and danger, and to the grief of the wives of the men who love them and of their true friends'.[32]

Led by Soderini, members of the *reggimento* were clearly out to take advantage of Lorenzo's youth and to wrest political power away from the Via Larga, in order to pursue their own favoured policies. A deliberate and conscious power-struggle was being waged in which Lorenzo faced formidable and experienced opponents. But not all the cards were stacked against the young Medici who held a number of aces which had not yet been played.

Probably his most valuable asset, in these years, was his personal gift for loyalty and friendship. To a real degree, Lorenzo's success came from his ability to challenge some of the older-established members of the *reggimento*, making use of the loyalty of a number of men, from humbler origins, whose rise in the world was related to their devotion to the Medici family. Lorenzo turned out to be an excellent judge of men, able to discern genuine talent wherever it was to be found. He proved to be as good at selecting administrators, ambassadors and servants as he was at uncovering the talents of scholars, humanists, poets or artists. Here, that humanity, so universally admired, stood him in excellent stead. Perhaps the best key to Lorenzo's character, and the greatest tribute to his abilities, is the fact that he chose to surround himself not with mediocre time-servers or mere nonentities but with a group of remarkable men, most of whom would have a place in history, even had they not enjoyed the patronage of Lorenzo.

Over the years, one of his most useful servants proved to be Giovanni Lanfredini, whose family had only recently moved to Florence from Ferrara, and to whom, in consequence, a political career would have been barred had it not been for Medicean patronage. It was Lorenzo who first recognised Giovanni's abilities and drew him into the Medici orbit, employing him in a variety of capacities. For four years, from 1476 to 1480, for instance, Lanfredini managed the Venetian branch of the Medici bank, but he also enjoyed a highly successful career as a Florentine politician and diplomat. It was to prove much to Lorenzo's advantage when Lanfredini was elected to the *Signoria* in 1471.

Another key-figure was the Chancellor of Florence, the famous human-ist Bartolomeo Scala, whose obscure birth was constantly recalled by his enemies, but who, through three generations, proved a loyal friend of the Medici. Scala, who, like Lorenzo, tended to take his mind off problems by writing poetry, shared Lorenzo's literary interests, and his approach to politics. Both were interested in transforming the chaotic institutions of Florence into a more efficient governmental machine, in transforming a state of corporate, medieval quality into a recognisably modern adminis-tration. Although Lorenzo clearly found Scala, on occasion, a tedious old bore, he was well aware that he could not dispense with his political talents for Scala was the essential link between Lorenzo and the official Florentine government. They worked closely together and Scala was prepared to use his position in the Florentine Chancery to transmit information to Lorenzo about affairs of state and the contents of public correspondence. As Lorenzo had, as yet, no official position in Florence, he had no automatic access to public documents and it was thus essential that he have private sources of information. These Scala provided.

Scala proved to be particularly useful when Lorenzo was away in the country, for he would either visit him personally, to bring him up to date on Florentine affairs, or send him important letters. Alternatively, Scala might be dispatched by the *Signoria* or by some other government body in order to seek Lorenzo's advice. In 1474, for instance, he was sent, 'with the book in which all the letters from here and there are copied',[33] to seek Lorenzo's opinion on possible courses of action. He was also vigilant over Lorenzo's own interests within Florence. In 1473, for instance, when he was a member of the *Signoria* as well as Chancellor, Scala wrote to remind Lorenzo that the new Eight of Security was about to be elected and reported that:

It seems to the Gonfalonier, on whose behalf I am writing to you, that you should be informed of this, and he wants you to be here for this and other matters. If you don't think you need to be here, he begs you – as I do – to give us some idea of what you want done.[34]

Above all Scala was helpful in allaying Lorenzo's conscience, reinforcing the conviction that the interests of the Medici family could not be separated from the public interest. Scala had 'often said as much' and was convinced that the political objectives of peace and security, pursued by Lorenzo, were as important for the Medici as 'for the regime which is joined to you and for the city which is joined to the regime'.[35] He also bolstered Lorenzo's international reputation in a series of fulsome dedications to his books. In this, however, he was by no means unique for Lorenzo surrounded himself with a group of *literati* whose sole aim in life seemed, on occasion, to be to praise their patron and to raise his reputation to the skies. The value of such praise was that it increased the patron's fame and, therefore, his power, a direct connection specifically made by Ficino in a letter congratulating Lorenzo for having taken under his wing Angelo Poliziano, the poor boy from Montepulciano:

> Almost all other men support servants of pleasure, but you support priests of the Muses. . . . It was due to you that Homer, the high priest of the Muses, came into Italy, and someone who was till now a wanderer and a beggar has at last found with you sweet hospitality. You are supporting in your home that young Homeric scholar, Angelo Poliziano, so that he may put the Greek face of Homer into Latin colours. . . . Continue to attract such artists, Medici, for other painters adorn the walls for a time, but these render their inhabitants illustrious for ever.[36]

Poliziano proved to be one of the most successful of Lorenzo's protégés, and one of the few pleasures his patron enjoyed in 1470 was the completion of Poliziano's translation of Book II of the *Iliad* into Latin hexameters. Other scholars and writers also enhanced the Medici reputation or worked loyally for Lorenzo in other capacities; Niccolò Michelozzi, his Chancellor and Secretary, Luigi Pulci, who entertained the Medici household in the evening by reading his poems aloud, Luigi's brother, Bernardo, whose love sonnets were dedicated to Lorenzo, Sforza Bettini, Braccio Martelli, Dionigi Pucci, Matteo Franco, Bernardo Buongirolami, Baccio Ugolini and Bernardo del Nero, in whom Ficino saw the incarnation of the ideal Platonic citizen. All played an important role in creating a public image of their patron as magnanimous, powerful and, most pleasing of all, noble. To this extent they helped to preserve Lorenzo's position in Florence.

Lorenzo's greatest advantage, however, was the invaluable role he could play in foreign policy. Effectively, he came to fill a hidden vacuum

Presumed portrait of Lorenzo's son Giuliano with Poliziano in the fresco
painted by Ghirlandaio in 1485 for the Church of the S. Trinità

in the Florentine state. For centuries, Florence had experienced serious
diplomatic difficulties when negotiating with foreign princes. Rightly or
wrongly, such princes always saw a dual problem about having any
dealings with Florence. In the first place, how could they, royal or noble
as they were, negotiate, as equals, with a republic whose citizens and
policy-makers were, by definition, ignoble? Secondly, they experienced

the problem of instability which arose in Florence because of the rapid turn-over in office. In a city which changed the personnel of its ruling magistracy every two months, a foreign prince might justifiably ask what guarantee there was that Florence would maintain her alliances or honour her agreements. In such a situation, the value of the Medici was that they provided an element of continuity in an inherently unstable situation.

Lorenzo could also supply the missing ingredient of nobility. He had, as a result of Piero's careful forethought, married into a noble family, and he had been received by many rulers abroad as if he were a prince. He was a godparent to the children of the Duke of Milan. He had long-established relationships and contacts abroad. The King of France had granted his family the right to wear the *fleur-de-lys* in its armorial bearings. In addition, what appeared to be a major problem – the ambiguous nature of Lorenzo's position in the Florentine state – turned out to be an advantage, for that ambiguous position allowed him to conduct a diplomacy which was genuinely secret, to explore policy options which might or might not succeed, and yet leave Florence officially uncompromised.

In the long run, this all proved to be to Florence's advantage. Like Scala, Lorenzo was convinced that the interests of the Medici family and the interests of Florence were identical. In a basic sense, this was true, since the economic interests of the Medici were shared by other leading Florentines. It was also true that every inhabitant of Florence could only benefit from a period of peace and the stabilisation of Italian politics which, as Lorenzo explained to the Milanese in 1477, was always his objective:

> We know that Your Excellencies will not need much persuasion to realise how committed we are to universal quiet and peace, and how adverse to any disturbance, for you have seen many proofs which must be known to the whole of Italy. We are what we have always been.[37]

Foreign policy-making would never, of course, be Lorenzo's responsibility alone, and it would be a foolish historian who identified the foreign policy of Florence with that of Lorenzo. Constitutionally, diplomatic affairs fell within the competence of the *Signoria* in time of peace, and of the Ten in time of war, while all treaties and agreements were subject to ratification by the Councils who also voted the taxes to pay for troops. In addition, all decisions were group decisions in the sense that Lorenzo consulted regularly with the powerful leaders of the Medicean party, like Luigi Guicciardini, Angelo della Stufa, Antonio Ridolfi, Buongianni Gianfigliazzi, Pietro Minerbetti and Bernardo Buongirolami. Yet, the rapidity with which Lorenzo mastered the intricate world of diplomacy, the encyclopaedic knowledge he acquired in relation to all foreign affairs, as well as the efficiency with which he ran his own network of information gatherers, soon ensured that he was listened to. Within a few years, as a result, his had become a dominant voice in the framing of Florentine foreign policy, usually able to persuade the Florentines to follow his suggestions even when these, sometimes, conflicted with their most deep-seated prejudices.

All this, however, lay in the future. In the meantime, Lorenzo's foreign contacts proved most useful in preserving his predominance in Florence. We have already seen how critical the friendship of Sforza was in ensuring the peaceful transfer of power in 1469, and this friendship remained the key element in guaranteeing Lorenzo's position in the *reggimento*. It was by no means an easy relationship. Sforza, at first, did not fully trust Lorenzo nor believe in his capacity to survive. In the summer of 1470, he began looking for other friends within Florence while his agents in Rome entered into negotiations with a number of prominent Florentine exiles. Still, success bred success and, as Lorenzo's survival in Florence became more certain with every month that passed, so Sforza's support became less equivocal.

Lorenzo's success had not, however, come easily. He was perpetually irritated by the inability of Sforza and other rulers to accommodate to the fact that he had by no means complete freedom of action. Differences over foreign policy continued to tear the *reggimento* apart. Each *Signoria* was of a different political complexion from every other and, in devising policies, Lorenzo had to take account of such differences. Every negotiation had to be pursued and nurtured through the cumbersome machinery of the Florentine government, and, all the time, friends had to be flattered and rewarded, opponents placated. Indeed, given the difficulties, it is scarcely surprising that Lorenzo should have often reacted against the obligations which had devolved on him, and should frequently have shown himself bored, fed-up and thoroughly ill-tempered. By the spring of 1470, the mildest political threat could throw him into a towering rage and this irritability can scarcely have assisted him in combating the first serious threats to the Medici regime.

After Piero's death many Florentine exiles tried to engineer their return to Florence. In April 1470, their attempts came to a head when a group, backed by Borso, Duke of Ferrara, entered Prato secretly, seized the *podestà*, and called on the city to rebel against Florentine rule. Fortunately, in the person of Giorgio Ginori, Lorenzo proved to have a good friend in Prato. Ginori managed to gather together a scratch force, made up of other Florentines, and defeated the rebels. Several were taken to Florence to be beheaded, the rest being executed in Prato, reputedly by Ginori in person. The extreme severity with which these rebels were punished is indicative of the general insecurity of Florence in the spring of 1470, and probably reflects Lorenzo's own uncertainties about his position in the regime.

The crisis that engulfed Florence, in the wake of the Prato revolt, shows that Lorenzo was right to be concerned. Certain members of the oligarchy took the occasion to suggest to Lorenzo that the time was ripe to make various constitutional changes in Florence. These, it was argued, would ensure the continued supremacy of the Medici. The proposal was to form a permanent commission of *Accoppiatori* composed solely of forty-five known Medici supporters. There would be an additional limitation on the composition of this body. Only citizens from families who had occupied the office of *Accoppiatore* since 1434 would be eligible. In other words, the *Accoppiatori* would henceforth, be drawn solely from the leading families of the *reggimento*.

From Lorenzo's point of view, the scheme had a certain spurious attractiveness, but more experienced observers of the Florentine scene were quick to point out that the effect of the proposed reform would not be to strengthen the Medici but to concentrate power in the hands of a few powerful families. It was, in fact, an attempt, on the part of a few 'leading men' to create a situation in which 'Lorenzo would not be so powerful . . . with the aim of being able to manipulate him to their purposes'.[38] It was, in other words, to be a trial of strength between Lorenzo and other members of the regime. Significantly, the keenest advocates of the reform were the grandest of the oligarchs; Giovanozzo Pitti and Tommaso Soderini.

How far Lorenzo, himself, recognised the dangers is dubious. He appeared to be giving the project enthusiastic endorsement and was both surprised and annoyed when the scheme was put to the Council of One Hundred on 5 July and rejected, although, according to the Milanese ambassador, this rejection was regarded with satisfaction by all the 'good and true . . . friends of Lorenzo',[39] including Angelo della Stufa who warned Lorenzo to open his eyes to what was going on.

Lorenzo may, indeed, have been too busy in the previous months to realise to what an extent he was being manipulated. Only three days after the rejection of the reform scheme, he scored a notable diplomatic success, when extensive and complicated negotiations, in which he had played a prominent part and which served as his apprenticeship in diplomacy, bore fruit in the renewal of the League between Milan, Naples and Florence. The news was greeted at Florence by the ringing of bells, the lighting of bonfires and so much enthusiasm that, 'if they had had news of the capture of four Pisas they could not have done more'.[40]

Lorenzo was delighted by this diplomatic triumph, for he believed that he had staked his whole future and reputation on the outcome of these negotiations. He said as much in a letter to that unworthy henchman, Tommaso Portinari, whose continued business incompetence had merely added to Lorenzo's worries in these months. 'The complicated and continuous demands of public affairs', Lorenzo told him, 'have not permitted me to be as diligent about my own affairs, as is probably

necessary. I find myself at the moment with a great weight of business –
both public and private – on my shoulders. Yet I hope, by means of God's
grace and the aid of friends, to shed some of the burden and bring things
to a satisfactory conclusion, so that I am confident and willing to act,
particularly for the increase of the dignity of our family, towards which I
find all the citizens united in good-will. You will have heard of the
renewal . . . of our League, between His Majesty King Ferrante, the Duke
and ourselves . . . which gives firm assurance of peace and tranquillity
and of the strengthening of the regime and of our position.'[41]

Lorenzo was being over-optimistic. Far from the following months
revealing all the citizens united in good-will towards the Medici, uproar
broke out in the city as open rivalry between Lorenzo and Soderini
became public. One certainty in the Florentine political world was that
economic difficulties brought political conflict in their train, and, at this
period, Lorenzo's position was weakened by an economic slump and a
financial crisis in the state. Those who suffered blamed the Medici and,
since the Medici bank was also under pressure, there was little that
Lorenzo could do to alleviate the situation. Naturally enough, Soderini
seized every opportunity to make political capital out of the crisis. Power
fluctuated backwards and forwards between the parties, Soderini even,
at one point, being appointed ambassador to Naples against Lorenzo's
express wishes. The economic slump deepened and a decision to tax the
Florentine clergy brought a quarrel with Pope Paul II and a threat of
excommunication.

The tide, however, was turning against Soderini. The election of a
pro-Medici *Signoria*, headed by Angelo della Stufa, heralded victory for
Lorenzo and, in January 1471, by a majority, it is true, of only two votes,
the Hundred passed a law by which, for five years, the *Accoppiatori* were
permitted to nominate their successors. This reform, ensuring a succession of favourable *Signorie*, the birth of a male heir, Piero, on 15 February,
and the death of Paul II in July, lifting the threat of excommunication, all
contributed to an increase in Lorenzo's authority within the state.

In March, Lorenzo's prestige was further enhanced by a visit to
Florence by the Duke of Milan and his wife, Bona of Savoy. The ducal
couple were lodged at the Medici palace while their vast retinue of over
two thousand were housed at the expense of the Florentine government.
The visit was throughout a glittering occasion, long-remembered by the
Florentines, who correctly perceived it as honouring their city in general
and Lorenzo in particular. Sforza travelled like an Emperor. For his solemn entrance into the city, the ladies of his court were borne in litters of
gold brocade, the gentlemen's costumes bedecked with jewelled chains.
There were fifty grooms in silver livery, numerous richly caparisoned
war-horses, five hundred pairs of hounds, with attendant huntsmen and
falconers, and a guard of one hundred knights and five hundred infantry.

A train of some seventy mules carried the ducal treasure-chests, while a caravan of silk-covered wagons brought up the rear of the procession.

This display was meant to dazzle and impress, and dazzle and impress it did, although Florence being Florence, it did not pass without a note of criticism. The expense of the whole visit, in itself, was enough to provoke considerable vocal opposition even at the heart of the regime, and this opposition was fuelled by Sforza's own behaviour. It was suggested that, considering the season was Lent and the ostensible reason for this visit was to fulfil a vow to visit the shrine of the Annunziata, in thanksgiving for the birth of his son and heir, the Duke and his courtiers should have been a little less open about the way they guzzled meat. There were even those who held that, when the Church of Santo Spirito caught fire during the performance of a play in Sforza's honour, this was divine retribution, despite the fact that the Duke had not actually been present. And, as usual, among the more sedate Florentines there were worries that the young and flighty might be corrupted and begin to copy Milanese fashions or, even worse, Milanese morals.

Since, under Lorenzo's direction and at Lorenzo's expense, lavish decorations and ceremonies at the Medici palace had been devised by Andrea Verrocchio, much of the criticism directed at the Duke must also, by implication, have been directed at Lorenzo. But he ignored it all and concentrated on basking in Sforza's graciousness. Nothing in Milan, the Duke declared, could equal the Medici collections of art. According to the sixteenth-century historian, Ammirato, Sforza 'marvelled greatly at the numerous paintings by superlative masters, whereof he swears he has seen more examples in the one palace of the Medici than in all the rest of Italy. Likewise', he added, 'their drawings and their sculpture, and the marbles wrought by the ancients are as wondrous as the craft of today, the jewellery, the books, and the other objects of exceeding rarity and value, looking upon which he deemed that any quantity of gold and silver would seem as mere dross in comparison.'[42]

This rather elaborate and courtly flattery was not without a purpose. Sforza's opinion of Lorenzo's abilities was growing higher daily and he had a real political need of Lorenzo. One purpose of this visit was to seek Lorenzo's services as a mediator with Ferrante of Naples who had recently made a separate alliance with Venice, which seemed to threaten the unity of the Italian League. In addition, Sforza feared that Ferrante's action might reactivate the Florentine enthusiasts for a Florentine–Venetian alliance. He therefore needed to reinforce Lorenzo's position within Florence, since this remained the surest guarantee of the continuation of the Florentine–Milanese alliance.

That Lorenzo's position was strengthened by the visit does seem likely for, in July, he was able to proceed to a further constitutional reform designed to ensure the perpetual loyalty of the Council of One Hundred and to avoid any further fiascos like that of the previous year. A permanent body of forty men, chosen by the *Signoria* and the *Accoppiatori*, was introduced into the Hundred, while the rest of its personnel would change twice a year. In addition, at the expense of the traditional communal councils, the legislative powers of the Hundred were considerably increased.

This reform marks the end of Lorenzo's apprenticeship in the intricate world of Florentine politics. His triumph over his opponents was recognised by the Milanese ambassador who commented on the fact that, 'While before other citizens were honoured and flattered just like him, now everyone goes to him to recommend himself for election.'[43] Further consolidation of the Medici power structure continued. In September, the political world of Florence was narrowed even further by the reduction in the number of lesser guilds from fourteen to five, and by December it could be said that 'the affairs of this city have reached the point where everything is decided by a sign from Lorenzo, and no one else is worth a zero'.[44] Lorenzo was now proposing to abolish the Judge of Appeals and to restrict the authority of the Eight of Security, having already used property belonging to the two great corporate institutions of Florence – the Guelph Party and the *Mercanzia* to pay for governors and garrisons in the Florentine State. His increasing authority was further manifested in a continuing decline in communal expenditure on the feast of San Giovanni, coupled with a corresponding increase in the popularity of and expenditure on Carnival, as the Medici-related or Medici-inspired festivals were deliberately fostered. Most offensive of all to traditionalists, was the introduction in 1473 of a set of sumptuary laws which effectively attacked the right of any family, other than the Medici, to make public display of their power, wealth, prestige or honour. 'Lorenzo', wrote the bitterly critical Rinuccini, 'eliminated all those things that had traditionally won support and reputation for the citizens, like marriage feasts and dances, *feste*, ornate dress. He damned them all.'[45]

The Medici triumph, within the *reggimento*, seemed complete. The well-worn path taken by suitors to the Via Larga was thronged once more. The begging letters, the gifts, the promises of support were daily more numerous. Every leading oligarch, from Soderini downwards, would increasingly be forced to recognise that the *reggimento* and Medicean domination went together, that if Lorenzo fell, they would fall with him. From this period onwards the majority of the Medicean aristocrats would cause Lorenzo little concern.

They had, however, saddened him. In these months, a new note of caution creeps into his correspondence, and he developed a mania for secret negotiations. He found it difficult to come to terms with the fact that his very position ensured that many people would never like him, that insincerity would become an enforced element in the majority of his relationships. It was surely on the basis of his own bitter experience that he tried to comfort Angelo della Stufa who also faced much animosity in consequence of his staunch loyalty to Lorenzo:

> Persuade yourself to be patient, [Lorenzo told him] for patience you needs must have, since we know that this opposition has not arisen as a result of any ill conduct or defect on your part, but rather out of envy, a vice which you know is very prevalent and which is all the greater if a person's behaviour is good or honourable. Both ancient and modern history show more examples of ingratitude than of reward.[46]

One consequence of Lorenzo's increasingly powerful position was that the leading members of the Medici party were more and more dependent on him and on his presence. Unfortunately, since the King of Naples and the Duke of Milan had still failed to resolve their differences, despite Lorenzo's good offices as a mediator, the international situation continued to give grave cause for concern. Opponents of Lorenzo naturally tended to side with Ferrante and made their views so public that the Neapolitan ambassador, Bartolomeo da Recanati, was even ready to boast that 'Lorenzo's authority in that city is not what it once was'.[47] Although the *Signoria*, elected in May and June, did not, in fact, contain a majority of Medicean supporters, this was but a temporary set-back for Lorenzo, and Recanati was wrong in his assessment. There is no doubt, however, that the situation was serious enough for the Mediceans to have grave reservations about the departure of Lorenzo for Rome in the late summer of 1471.

Paul II had been succeeded by the able and learned, but ambitious, Francesco della Rovere who had taken the title of Sixtus IV. It was vital to Lorenzo's interests, particularly his business interests at Rome, that he should be on good terms with the new pope and, in consequence, he was determined to be part of the customary delegation from Florence to offer congratulations. The other ambassadors were Angelo della Stufa, Donato Acciaiuoli, Buongianni Gianfigliazzi, Domenico Martelli and Pietro Minerbetti. Lorenzo, therefore, was assured of congenial company, but it did mean that several of the leading Mediceans would be absent from the city at a critical juncture. Lorenzo, however, judged that, were the mission successful, it could only enhance his international prestige and his authority at home. Medicean concerns in Florence could be safely left in Giuliano's hands, so that the risk involved in leaving the city was well worth taking.

On this, his first major public undertaking on behalf of the Florentine republic, Lorenzo considered it proper to outshine his companions. For once personal display was not out of place for it reflected honour not just on the Medici, but on the state of Florence. And, indeed, eye-witnesses of his departure from the city on 23 September, do not suggest any contemporary criticism of Lorenzo's magnificence. They were, rather, deeply impressed by his deportment and by the splendour of his train. 'Thirty-five horses pulling wagons travelled with him,' according to one admiring observer, 'and he carried four hundred pounds of silver – which I saw packed – basins, various things, plates, saucers and other silver vases.'[48]

In many ways the visit to Rome proved to be all Lorenzo had hoped. His reception by the new pope could not have been more gracious, nor his person marked by more obvious attention. 'From all that I have seen', Lorenzo reported on 10 October, 'this pope is well disposed towards the Duke of Milan and to our city.'[49] Sixtus granted the account of the Papal See to the Medici bank, and made a personal – and much-cherished – gift to Lorenzo of two classical busts. Throughout Florence, the Pope's favourable reception was regarded as conferring 'honour and fame on our Republic',[50] and Lorenzo's reputation in his own city could, therefore, only be enhanced. He might, with justification, have looked forward to increasingly close and cordial relations with the Holy See, had not the visit been marred by one small cloud. Recently, the future of Giuliano and the precise role that he might play in the Medici power complex had begun to concern Lorenzo. One possibility, which had been mooted, was that of an ecclesiastical career to be crowned by the conferment of a cardinal's hat, which would give to Giuliano the status of a Prince of the Church. But when the possibility was raised, Sixtus IV responded with a firm refusal. Giuliano would not be made a cardinal.

All in all, however, the visit had to be accounted as one more success for Lorenzo, and it must have been with some regret that he returned to Florence in November to face a variety of problems: a new flood of begging letters, provoked by the imminence of a new scrutiny, continued difficulties in the Medici business empire, a worsening international situation, and the incident, known to history as the affair of Volterra, in which, for the first time, there appeared a possible conflict between the affairs of Lorenzo as a private individual and the concerns of the Florentine state.

Volterra was a city which, although falling within the Florentine sphere of interest, remained an independent commune. Her relationship with Florence was always turbulent. The Volterrans never willingly accepted Florentine dominion, were fiercely intransigent in defence of their own customs, and frequently provided a refuge for Florence's political exiles. As recently as 1427, they had been involved in a long-drawn out struggle with Florence over the imposition of Florentine taxation on Volterran territory, a struggle in which as it happened they had been supported by the Medici. A further rebellion against Florence was always likely.

When that rebellion came, the occasion appeared to be a trivial matter which could readily have been settled by negotiation, although modern historians would do well to remember the remark made by Gentile

Becchi, at the time: 'This affair of the alum – it makes me think of the Trinity: I don't understand it.' In 1470, a private company, in which the Medici bank had some kind of interest, was granted a lease to mine for alum at Sasso in the territory of Volterra. The head of the company was a Sienese, Benuccio Capacci, and among his Florentine and Volterran partners, the Volterran, Paolo Inghirami, was a well-known Medici supporter. Given the importance of alum for their textile industry, this project could not fail to interest the Florentines. And, given that, as we have seen, since 1466 the Medici had enjoyed a virtual monopoly of the output and sale of alum in Europe, nor could it fail to interest Lorenzo. It did not need commercial acumen of the highest order to recognise that he had a vested interest in keeping the price of alum high.

The subsequent actions of the Volterrans, however, seem to have had less to do with any economic threat to their city than with a power-struggle, within Volterra, between pro- and anti-Medici factions. The temporary decline of Lorenzo's authority in Florence in May and June 1471 was mirrored in Volterra by the seizure of power by the anti-Medici faction. Alleging that the original lease of the Sasso mine had been illegal, they seized it by force. Naturally enough, the dispossessed company appealed to the *Signoria* of Florence and to Lorenzo for assistance in recovering their rights.

It was unfortunate that, at this juncture, Lorenzo's influence in Florence had temporarily waned. Nothing was done about Volterra until July and even then the measures taken proved less than successful. Then in October, Bernardo Corbinelli, sent by the *Signoria* to resolve the situation, appeared to be siding with the Volterrans. He restricted his activity to sending twelve hostages for the good behaviour of Volterra to Florence. It seemed possible that he might even reach some kind of compromise agreement over the lease of the mine, on the basis of the total exclusion of Inghirami, but, after a series of incidents of increasing gravity, culminating on 23 February 1472 in a riot, in which Inghirami and his brother-in-law were murdered, the Volterrans declared a state of emergency and banished all known Medicean supporters from their city. It was a public attempt, backed by Lorenzo's political opponents in Florence, to suggest a divergence of interest between the Medici and the state of Florence. It was also, however, an act of overt defiance of Florence by a subject-town, which could not be ignored.

In Florence, even within the Medici party, opinion was definitely divided about what should be done. Tommaso Soderini led an influential group in arguing that, while the Volterrans should certainly be punished, they should not be driven into open rebellion, so giving grounds for interference in Florentine affairs on the part of the pope or of any other of Florence's neighbours. 'Better a lean peace', he is said to have remarked, quoting an old Florentine proverb, 'than a fat victory.'[51] Lorenzo, who now let his emotions run ahead of his reason, would have none of it. As far as he was concerned action was imperative. He had already made a personal request to the Count of Urbino for troops to subdue Volterra, as well as asking Naples, Milan and the papacy to send token forces of support. Arguing forcefully that the revolt of Volterra might well trigger rebellion in other Florentine subject-towns, he wrung grudging support from the *Signoria*. On 30 April 1472 war was declared, and a *Balìa* of twenty, including Lorenzo, was created to direct the military operations, for which 100,000 gold florins were allocated. The troops which included, as Lorenzo had hoped, reinforcements from Milan and from Sixtus IV, were placed under the command of the Count of Urbino, with Buongianni Gianfigliazzi and Iacopo Guicciardini being appointed commissioners to the army.

Urbino rapidly overran the Volterran *contado* where he met virtually no resistance, but was then brought to an abrupt halt before the walls of Volterra to which he was forced to lay siege. From the beginning of the campaign, Lorenzo took a strong personal interest in what, inevitably, was seen by many as a war to protect the honour of the Medici family. As soon as Volterra was invested he began to attempt to reach an agreement, taking upon himself the responsibility for deciding the acceptability of the terms of surrender. He wrote to Urbino 'recommending the Volterrans, making many representations on their behalf',[52] and wanted to go to the Florentine camp himself 'so that agreement might be reached through his intervention'.[53] Finally, the *Balìa* in which he was, presumably, the dominant figure, requested Volterra to surrender to Urbino, effectively promising the city good treatment if it did so. On 16 June emissaries sent out from Volterra finally agreed to a complete capitulation, and, in exchange for a definite promise that their possessions and property would be protected, to accept Florentine rule.

At this point, the divisions within Volterra played a tragic role. Many Volterrans were opposed to the agreement which had been entered into, and they managed to delay the surrender of the city. During the delay, Volterra's own hired mercenaries mutinied and began to sack the city, an activity in which they were swiftly joined by the Milanese troops from the Florentine army whom Sforza had failed to pay. Before long they had been joined by the rest of the Florentine army, and neither Urbino nor the Florentine commissioners were able to bring their troops back under their control until the evening of 18 June, by which time Volterra had been thoroughly ransacked.

As sacks of cities go, that of Volterra was comparatively mild, but in the later fifteenth century a sack was a rare phenomenon, and that of Volterra rapidly entered the mythology of warfare as an horrendous event that should not have occurred. It became the only blot on the reputation of that famous soldier, Urbino, who was held to be a model of chivalry. It further blackened the already bad reputation of Milanese troops and, in some way, it affected Lorenzo's reputation. The suspicion remained that he had been personally responsible for the sack, and that he did, indeed, accept some responsibility is suggested by the fact that, after visiting Volterra and seeing the damage that had been inflicted on it, he gave two thousand gold florins, from his own fortune, in an attempt at reparation.

From the historian's point of view there seems little about the Volterran incident in which Lorenzo could take pride. The autonomous institutions of the city were abolished and the once proud city subjected to direct Florentine rule, its continued loyalty guaranteed by the fortress which still dominates Volterra's sky-line and in whose design Lorenzo played an active part. This subjection of Volterra pleased the Florentines whose attitudes were always aggressively imperialistic and whose fear of revolt by their subject-towns bordered on the paranoid. However, it is not clear that Lorenzo profited personally from the war. The responsibility for the disputed alum mines was handed over to the wool-guild of Florence who were obligated to pay the commune an annual rent and to indemnify the original investors. Thus, it is difficult to argue that anybody, other than Florentine industry as a whole, benefited from the war, and impossible to suggest that only the private interests of the Medici had been served. Nevertheless there still remained a lingering feeling that Lorenzo had put his family interests before those of the Florentine state, and that he had shown himself to be rash and impetuous, even emotional, in his judgements. Not just in 1472 but for ever after, the affair of Volterra would remain a blot on Lorenzo's personal reputation and on what he would have called his 'honour'.

4

THE LULL BEFORE THE STORM, 1472–77

Lorenzo now entered on some of the most successful and creative years of his life. Despite the shadow which the Volterran incident cast over his reputation, it had the positive effect of showing he was a force to be reckoned with, a man determined to master events and to maintain his authority against all comers. Since, simultaneously, he managed to suggest that, in relation to Volterra, he had acted as a true patriot and his enemies had been motivated by nothing more than a selfish and sectional interest, his authority in Florence increased. To members of the *reggimento*, indeed, Lorenzo was now indispensable. Without his presence the Florentine state did not function well, since no one was anxious to take decisions without him. As he was often absent from Florence, couriers were constantly sent after him to ask his opinion on all matters of state, while, particularly on diplomatic questions, a paralysis of will seemed to enter the government whenever Lorenzo, patron of all, was not there. Thus, in a sense, the ultimate success of the patriarchal Medicean regime had been achieved in that, rather than appearing to seek power, Lorenzo often seemed now to have power thrust upon him.

In Florence, therefore, Lorenzo could hope for stability and, within the Florentine state as a whole, an increased authority. Volterra now lay securely within the Medici patronage empire and other subject-towns would think twice before opposing Lorenzo's known wishes. For his part, Lorenzo had learnt the value of tact in dealing with those same subject-towns and would take pains to ensure that there would be no more Volterras. Another consequence was that he found it increasingly easy to find posts, benefices and jobs for Medici clients within the Florentine state, his most successful *coup* being the appointment of that most loyal of Mediceans, Gentile Becchi, to the bishopric of Arezzo in 1473, despite the officially stated preference of the Florentine government for Girolamo Guigni, and considerable pressure at Rome on behalf of Luca Carducci. Friends and enemies alike could read the meaning of such appointments – to be a Medici supporter brought little risk and much hope of material reward.

Abroad, Lorenzo's reputation was also growing. Within Italy, one clear manifestation of this was the increasing frequency with which he was asked to act as an independent arbiter in the resolution of minor disputes, and, particularly the many border-disputes and arguments over cattle-raiding to which the much-divided Italian peninsula was prone. Since there was always a genuine danger that minor incidents might flare up into major conflict, Lorenzo's regular success in resolving such issues was a positive contribution towards preserving the fragile peace of Italy. This was widely recognised by his contemporaries but subsequent historians have rarely given him the credit he deserves for it.

As the increasingly thick files of the Medici archive make clear, outside Italy Lorenzo's credit was also mounting. That archive is full of letters of recommendation, or of request, on behalf of clients, from contemporary rulers: the King of Portugal, Matthias Corvinus of Hungary, and, above all, Louis XI of France. Louis XI, indeed, went out of his way to make public close ties with Lorenzo. In 1473, he asked Lorenzo to act as an intermediary to try to arrange a marriage between the Dauphin and a Neapolitan princess, thus paying tribute to Lorenzo's skills as a negotiator. He flattered Lorenzo by asking him to send his own personal agent to the French court. Ritual exchanges of gifts also emphasised the value Louis attached to Lorenzo personally, as did the visit he made in 1476 to dine at the Medici bank at Lyons, an event interpreted as a sign of great 'love and honour' towards Lorenzo.

The key ingredient in Lorenzo's success was not, as his political enemies claimed, that he was peculiarly favoured by fortune, for, in fact, fortune rarely proved to be on his side. What counted was his boundless energy. As in the case of Volterra, the manifestations of that energy could be dangerous, finding expression in impulsive action. But one effect of the Volterra incident was to teach Lorenzo to restrain his first reactions and to act or write or speak only after due reflection. In consequence, his energy became, normally, a positive force, working for the good of his family, friends and clients, of Florence, and of all Italy. Whether, on the other hand, it was a force working to Lorenzo's own personal benefit is another question. As we have seen, he had always been dogged by illness, but from 1474 onwards, his health became a matter of obsessive concern to his friends and one explanation for his recurrent nervous and physical complaints must be that he perpetually drove himself to the limit of his emotional and physical resources.

Yet, in doing so, he continued to demonstrate, daily, his gift for living, for extracting the maximum from every situation, from every moment. Still attacked, from time to time, by feelings of acute melancholia, he fought back with the resources of his intellect and his artistic sensibility. Deliberately, consciously, he tried to hold all aspects of experience in an ideal Platonic balance, harmonising art and life in pursuit of perfection. His pleasure in beautiful things was an expression of this outlook, his collection of finely-worked goblets, chalices and flasks, studded with semi-precious stones – jade, lapis lazuli, amethyst, pink quartz – not merely an insurance against hard times but a metaphor for Lorenzo's life, with all its deliberate style and overt creativity.

In these years, he returned, with a new enthusiasm, to the pursuit of knowledge and intellectual experience. At a public level, he emerged as an innovative and major patron of learning for, in the latter part of 1472, he went on a prolonged visit to Pisa where he intended to revive the ancient university. This project was very much Lorenzo's own and the level of his commitment can be measured by the fact that, in order to realise it, he was prepared to pay out large sums from his personal fortune at a time when commercial prudence suggested that he could ill afford it.

The problems of the Medici bank were, in fact, now so acute that, despite his continued reluctance to get embroiled in business, Lorenzo was forced to intervene personally. Virtually every branch of the bank was in trouble – Bruges, Lyons, and Naples probably presenting the gravest causes for concern. Lorenzo, in consequence, was faced with the potentially embarrassing situation of finding it difficult to raise large sums or, indeed, to find any liquid funds at all and, throughout July and August 1472, when he would normally have expected to spend two months relaxing in the country, the Medici bank made daily demands on his attention. Why, given these financial difficulties, he should still have invested so heavily in the Pisan project is explained in a memorandum, written about this time, in which he recalled that:

> from 1434 till now we have spent large sums of money, as appear in a small quarto note-book of the said year to the end of 1471. Incredible are the sums written down. They amount to 663,755 florins for alms, buildings and taxes, let alone other expenses. But I do not regret this, for though many may think we might have better kept a part of the amount in our purses, I think the money well laid out in the promotion of great public objects.[1]

This, then, was the justification for expenditure on Pisa's university. It would enhance Lorenzo's reputation by bringing honour to the Florentine state. As it happened, it also increased the range of patronage openings available to Lorenzo. Promising, but impoverished, young men could be found a place in the university while academic posts could be offered to distinguished scholars whom Lorenzo wished to seduce into the Medici circle. That the supervisory board of the University of Pisa and its staff were, for the most part, Lorenzo's appointees, no one even bothered to try to disguise. 'On my return from the country,' Donato Acciaiuoli told him, in September 1473, 'I heard that you had gone to Pisa and that, on your instruction, I had been appointed one of the new governors of the University. I thank you for the post, for I am delighted to have it, particularly as I shall be serving in your company.'[2]

Lorenzo's commitment to the University of Pisa was real. No expenditure of effort was too great, if it meant attracting a new and distinguished professor to join its staff, and there is no doubt that Lorenzo was extremely influential in attracting academics to Pisa. In 1478, for instance, it was entirely through his influence that the distinguished lawyer, Bartolomeo Sozzini was seduced away from the University of Bologna. Each year Lorenzo returned to the University to see what progress was being made. In the autumn and winter of 1473–4, indeed, he became so involved that he was unable to join his famly for the feast of All Saints and, in consequence, his mother wrote to tell him: 'we are sending, by Maso de Ciave, your share of the feast so that you can enjoy it with your friends. We send geese, chestnuts and *ravioli* . . . we wish you would come home.'[3] But, on occasion, so involved was Lorenzo, that not only did he not rejoin his family, he was unable to find even the time to participate in the field-sports he normally enjoyed at Pisa. He could spare no more than a day out with his falcons in September and time for a wild-boar hunt in January.

To revive the dead bones of the University of Pisa, had, therefore, become the public face of Lorenzo's commitment to learning, but, at a personal level also, he became more involved in intellectual pursuits during these years. His relationship with Ficino developed a new intensity and creativity. Rather than as master and pupil, they met now as intellectual equals or even as patron and client. These were the years in which there developed, around the person of Ficino, at Careggi, the so-called Platonic academy. This was not in any sense a formal academy, of the type that was to become familiar in sixteenth-century Italy, but rather the setting for a series of informal discussions and meetings, where debates on the dominant themes of neo-platonism took place under the benign influence of Ficino and, as often as not, under a much-prized bust of Plato himself, which, reputedly, had been found in the ruins of the academy of Athens. The most famous of these discussions took place in November 1474 when Lorenzo asked Francesco Bandini to renew the custom of celebrating Plato's birthday by gathering nine Platonists together to hold a disputation at Careggi. In the name of Love, seen as the central moving-force of the universe, in which the divine and the human united, these intellectual fellow-travellers explored the known facts about and the presumed meanings of existence, the purposes of man, and the nature of God. By its very nature, however, this could never be a debate with an end, and, throughout his life, Lorenzo continued to engage in similar discussions with his circle of like-minded friends. New intimates were constantly being admitted to the group, the most important, at this period, being Poliziano who finally entered the Medici household as a permanent inmate in 1473. Here, he fulfilled a number of important functions, as secretary and travelling companion to Lorenzo and Clarice, as friend and confidant of Lorenzo, and, after 1475, as tutor to Lorenzo's children.

One fruit of all this intellectual activity is obvious – a renewed creativity on Lorenzo's part. Although he never stopped writing verse and prose or improvising on the lyre, Lorenzo did have periods of more sustained and intense creativity. This was one of them. The *Altercazione* – the most studiedly intellectual of his works – was certainly begun at this time and is a direct comment on many hours spent discussing the nature of happiness with Ficino. To this period, also, belongs the *Selva* as well as a number of Lorenzo's best-loved songs and sonnets. It was also in 1473, as far as one can tell, that he began an occupation to which he dedicated time throughout the rest of his life – collecting and commenting on his own sonnets. The range and the quality of all this work is surely sufficient to justify the remark, made by Ficino, that whatever Lorenzo chose to turn his mind to, he immediately mastered it.

Further evidence of energy expressing itself through creativity at this period, is provided by the fact that, as we have seen, it was in these very years that the idea of building a new kind of country house – a purpose-built villa whose form would be an expression of divine harmony – was crystallising in Lorenzo's mind. He was buying properties at and around Poggio a Caiano where, eventually, the architectural ideals of Alberti, of Ficino and indeed of Lorenzo himself, would take tangible form, at the hands of San Gallo. The fact that Lorenzo could conceive of such a project was itself a reflection of a growing sense of security about the position of the Medici in Florence. Whereas all previous Medicean land-purchases and villa-building had been undertaken either as an investment against political disaster or as a hedge against economic difficulties, Poggio a Caiano was a totally novel conception. It was neither defended nor readily defensible and, although it was the centre of a highly profitable agricultural estate, this was not the reason for its existence. From the first moment of its conception, in Lorenzo's mind, Poggio a Caiano was rather, a place, a setting in which to reflect on nature and on man's relationship with it. How, precisely, this might be achieved was clearly something Lorenzo must have discussed, at length, with his friends during this period, from which his reputation as an authority on architecture seems to date.

According to his own reckoning, another, or indeed theoretically the *only* spur to creativity was romantic love, that curious hybrid, born of the fusion of Neo-Platonic ideas with the still vital traditions of the worlds of the chivalric romance and the *dolce stil nuovo*. Considering that he wrote extensively and perceptively on the subject, and given that he produced some of the most delightful love poems in any language, the facts about Lorenzo's own experience of love are surprisingly elusive. We have seen how, in his youth, his name was linked with that of Lucrezia Donati.

Subsequently, he claimed to be in love with the beautiful Simonetta
Vespucci, whose untimely death in 1476 was mourned by all Florence
and, most eloquently, by Lorenzo in his *Comento*. But then most of the
young aristocrats of Florence were reputedly in love with Simonetta,
including Lorenzo's brother, Giuliano. Finally, gossip linked Lorenzo's
name with the shadowy figure of Bartolomea de' Nasi, but again no
evidence exists that his love for her was ever more than a conventional
literary posture.

   His writing, nevertheless, suggests that feeling was not alien to Lorenzo. As we have seen, he was not some cold-blooded intellectual who
denied emotion or its value. Equally, there is every evidence of genuine
delight in sensuality and the joys of physical love, as, for instance, in
Venus's explicit seduction of Mars:

> Come to my sweet nest, where I await you;
> Vulcan is away and will not disturb our love.
> Come, for naked I await you in the centre of my bed;
> Do not delay, for time passes and flies;
> I have covered my breasts with crimson flowers.
> Come Mars, come away, for I am alone.

Overt sexuality, sensual joy, emotion – Lorenzo knew their reality. On
the other hand, he was an intellectual, raised in the Florentine tradition
which valued reason above all things; also, the humanistic tradition to
which he belonged emphasised prudence and the search for moderation
and self-control. He was, in addition, by virtue of his public role, a man
who essentially had no recognised right to personal emotion, both
because the Medici were too insecure to risk having scandal attached to
their name, and because Lorenzo had always to act as if he put the good of
Florence before his own desires.

   While, therefore, Lorenzo did suffer all the emotions associated with
romantic passion, he consistently analysed and intellectualised those
emotions. In consequence, many of his writings about the experience of
love are handicapped, not only by the Neo-Platonic formulae in which
they were expressed, but by a certain self-conscious quality. Frequently it
is not feeling he writes about, but thought about feeling, in the method he
described in the *Comento*:

> The person who feels excessive sorrow, usually tries two means to
> relieve it, either something pleasant, sweet and enjoyable alleviates the
> sorrow, or some serious and significant idea drives it away.[4]

And we might add, in Lorenzo's case, that there was a third method,
which was to resolve the tensions between feeling and thought through
the act of writing about them.

   The well-publicised intellectual activities of Lorenzo were not, of course, solely an expression of his own interests. Those interests were indeed continuous and enduring. But the publicity accorded to them was intended to emphasise Lorenzo's deliberate donning of more adult ways and a more sober demeanour, in order to disarm those critics who were still prone to complain that Florence was being run by a mere youth. Another means of making the same point was to create a new distinction of role between Lorenzo and Giuliano. While Lorenzo appeared as the young statesman, Giuliano took over the role of Medici prince. Much glamour was deliberately attached to Giuliano who now became the leader of Florence's adolescent males, giver of the most expensive entertainments, patron of the most magnificent *armeggiara*. To Giuliano it fell to carry the prestige of the Medici abroad and to uphold the family's honour internationally. In pursuit of those objects, Lorenzo sent him off on visits to Genoa in 1471 and Venice in 1472, where he was received and honoured almost as if he had been a reigning prince.

All this found its apotheosis in Giuliano's joust of 1475, which, by all accounts, outshone even that of Lorenzo. Plans for it dated from at least December 1474 when Roberto Bettini was sent to scour the Romagna to purchase and borrow suitable mounts for Giuliano. He was highly successful and all appreciated the honour done to the Medici when the Duke of Urbino promised, in the most gracious manner imaginable, to lend a favoured horse, 'begging Giuliano to use it for himself, at his pleasure, but to lend it to none other'.[5] Horses and harness were also sought, purchased and borrowed in Naples while Verrocchio was employed to paint a standard of Alexandrine taffeta and to design helmets for both Lorenzo and Giuliano.

Giuliano's joust has been immortalised in the finest of all Poliziano's poems, the *Stanze della Giostra*, probably the most successful evocation of a golden age in which Florence is portrayed as peaceful, happy and content, basking under the protection of Lorenzo-the-laurel-tree. Dressed in silver armour, mounted on a horse covered in rich jewels and trappings, Giuliano was made the centre of attention. He was followed, as a contemporary observed, by 'many . . . leading citizens, especially Lorenzo his brother, the most worthy man of his age, who commended Giuliano to the people by his presence'.[6] Among Giuliano's supporters was a knight, bearing the Verrocchio standard, on which the artist had depicted, in the upper part, a sun with the figure of Pallas Athena below, dressed in a golden tunic and an undervestment of white and gold. Her right hand held a tilting-lance, the left the shield of Medusa. Around the goddess was a field of flowers, containing the stump of an olive tree to which Cupid had been bound by a golden cord. His bow, quiver and broken arrows lay at his feet. Here, therefore, in visual terms, the Florentines might read the message preached by Poliziano in words; the protection of Florence by the Medici meant defeat for the forces of disruption, and a golden age of peace, maintained by wisdom and reason.

There were, as we have seen, sound public reasons for Lorenzo to pay public honour to his brother in this way, and the popularity of Giuliano could only enhance the popularity of Lorenzo himself. It is also true that Giuliano remained invaluable to Lorenzo in running the Medici empire. There is little evidence that the brothers were ever on anything but the most cordial personal terms. There is however substantial evidence to suggest that Giuliano's future was, increasingly, regarded as a problem.

Giuliano himself was beginning to dislike always having to live in his brother's shadow, and nurtured ambitions to achieve fame in his own right. At about the time of the Volterra incident, he was even heard to complain that 'he knew perfectly well that Lorenzo did not want him known in the world, or for him to have any reputation at all'.[7] This remark was less than just. Lorenzo was by no means unwilling to promote his brother's fortunes. The visits to Genoa and Venice and the joust of 1475 are eloquent testimonials of this fact. The problem was to find a field in which Giuliano could shine in his own light. A princely marriage was one possibility which was being explored in the summer, but Lorenzo was fully aware that such a marriage would be deeply offensive to the Florentines who would regard it as both arrogance on the part of the Medici and a threat to their traditional liberty. In any case nothing came of the project.

Meanwhile, there remained the possibility which Lorenzo had already raised with the Pope, that of having Giuliano raised to the dignity of cardinal. It was a question that kept being raised, not just by Lorenzo, but by his friends. Recognising that Lorenzo's constant ill-health at least raised the possibility that he might die while his children were still very young, they debated whether, in such a case, it would be better for Giuliano to remain a layman so that he might succeed to his brother's position of pre-eminence in Florence, or whether he might not be able to protect Medici interests more effectively as a prince of the Church. Certainly, as Cardinal Ammanati pointed out to Lorenzo in May 1472 there would be considerable immediate advantages in that the elevation of Giuliano to the Sacred College would bring an increase in Lorenzo's reputation, 'through the honour done to Giuliano, a great strengthening of your position, and the certainty of having one faithful supporter' among the cardinals.[8] He went on to suggest that it might be advisable for Giuliano, not to take holy orders but to adopt the dress of an apostolic protonotary, but Lorenzo considered it would be hard on Giuliano 'to don clerical dress, when he is not sure that he will have to continue to wear it or not'.[9]

Although the worsening relations between Rome and Florence made it very unlikely that Sixtus IV would consider making a Florentine cardinal,

Portrait of Giuliano by Botticelli

the rumour in the autumn that he was about to create a number of new cardinals, coupled with a declaration by Giuliano himself that he was, after all, anxious to embark on an ecclesiastical career, prompted Lorenzo to raise the question with the Pope once more. On 15 November he wrote to Sixtus, reminding him of 'the long desire of our house to have a cardinal'.[10] He wrote again, to the same effect on 2 December, and also tried to enlist the support of the Pope's nephew, Giuliano della Rovere. Simultaneously, he dispatched a personal envoy, Francesco Nori, to Rome in order to press the case. Nori had returned by 23 February 1473 when Lorenzo expressed his satisfaction 'at what had transpired'[11] although, in truth, he was still unsure of his position and of the Pope's attitude. Hence, Lorenzo tried to enlist the support of yet another papal nephew, Cardinal Riario, and urged the director of the Roman branch of the Medici bank, his maternal uncle Giovanni Tornabuoni, to put forward Giuliano's claims.

Tornabuoni was not without success. When pressed, Sixtus IV finally confessed himself not ill-disposed to the idea of Giuliano's elevation. He warned, however, that there would be considerable opposition to such a proposal among the cardinals. He therefore suggested that, in order to cultivate a more appropriate image of himself, Giuliano 'should apply himself to study, leave off his brocades and comport himself soberly'.[12] All was to no avail. New cardinals were, indeed, named in May 1473, but Giuliano's name was not among them. For Lorenzo, therefore, the problem of his brother's future remained as difficult as ever.

The demands of the rest of his family were delightful but they also consumed time and energy and brought periods of great anxiety. Lorenzo was intimately involved with every aspect of his children's lives to a degree rare among Florentine aristocrats who were more prone to bombarding their children with well-meaning advice than to playing an active role in their upbringing. Perhaps because he was so much younger than the normal Florentine father, this was never true of Lorenzo. In the summer of 1472, for instance, little Piero fell ill and Lorenzo, on medical advice, was entrusted with the task of finding a new nurse for him, although, as he remarked, he did not care for the plan 'since it is always a bad idea to change nurses, but, if the doctors insist, it will have to be done'.[13] Not just the health but the education of his children was a constant worry. Piero, Giovanni and, eventually, Giuliano, were each to be given humanist educations even more concentrated than that which Lorenzo had experienced.

As we have seen, at the age of three, Piero was entrusted to the care of Poliziano. Subsequently, he was taught by Martino della Commedia and Bernardo Michelozzi. By 1479 his education was already sufficiently advanced for him to be able to write to his father in Latin, though he was still struggling to master a proper Italic script. Nothing could be more revealing of Lorenzo's intimacy with his children than the evidence of these letters. In one Piero artlessly tells his father that he and his sister, Lucrezia, are having a competition to see who is the better beggar. She will write to her grandmother, while he is writing to his father, and whoever gets what he or she asks for will be the winner. It was a request that could not be ignored and a subsequent letter thanks Lorenzo for a long-promised pony which is 'so handsome and perfect' as to be beyond praise. It is also from another letter of Piero's that we have a picture of Lorenzo's whole family at this time:

> . . . Giovanni is able to spell. You can see for yourself how my writing is getting on. As for Greek, I work at it . . . but do not get very far. Lucrezia sews, sings and reads. Maddalena knocks her head against the wall but does not hurt herself. Luigia can talk quite a lot. Contessina makes a great noise all over the house. Nothing is wanting to us but to have you here.[14]

The precocious Giovanni was even at this early stage destined for an ecclesiastical career. The cleverest of Lorenzo's children he was taught by various distinguished humanists including Bernardo Michelozzi, Sante di Lorenzo da Dicomano, Urbano Valeriano, Demetrios Chalcondylas and Gregorio da Spoleto; he completed his education by studying canon law at Pisa for three years.

All this lay in a brilliant future. Meanwhile, from the time he could first lisp 'Loencio'[15] and demand his father's presence, he proved adept at impressing his personality on all around him. The girls, too, were not backward in making demands for presents and attention, although their requests were more often addressed to their grandmother than to Lorenzo. By May 1477 little Lucrezia could write well enough to say:

> It seems a thousand years until the time of your return, and, every day, I say a *Pater Noster* and an *Ave Maria* so that you may return happy and well to us. And send me the basket of roses you promised.

Two years later it was the turn of Maddalena to beg her grandmother, 'to send a doll, if you could, because I, too, would like to have one like Lucrezia, and I will make it a beautiful dress. . . . Send us some sweets, too.'[16]

Personal interests and family demands had, of course, to be fitted into a relentless round of work. The demanding Medici business empire, the management of the Medici party, the reception of distinguished foreign visitors to Florence, and the needs of Florentine diplomacy all clamoured for Lorenzo's attention. The public entertainment of foreigners and diplomatic issues appear to have consumed most time. As during the visit of the Duke of Milan in 1471, Lorenzo was always at the forefront in entertaining foreign princes, while the Medici palace figured prominently as a setting for such receptions. Only four months after Sforza's visit, Cardinal Francesco Gonzaga visited Florence and was lavishly entertained. Two years later, in June 1473, Elinor of Aragon, Duchess of Ferrara and daughter of King Ferrante of Naples, passed through Florence to be honoured by a series of receptions, banquets and entertainments. When her father wrote to thank Lorenzo, in the warmest terms, his letter made it clear that Ferrante regarded Lorenzo, rather than the commune of Florence as the true host of his daughter.

'By a letter from our daughter, the Duchess of Ferrara,' he wrote, 'and from our ambassador, we have been well informed of the great and remarkable welcome, which she received, particularly from you, and about the displays and entertainments given with great affection, splendour and magnificence . . . we will remain eternally obliged to you.'[17]

Only a couple of months later, it was a visit of the papal nephew, Pietro Riario, which again called forth Lorenzo's abilities as a host and as an organiser of public festivities, and in the following spring came a more exotic visitor, King Christian of Denmark and Norway, who was on a pilgrimage to Jerusalem.

Such entertainments were, of course, a part of Florence's complicated diplomacy. The honouring of such visitors has to be seen against a background of mounting complexity in which the fragile Italian League was fractured both from within and from without. Two major factors were involved, the ambition of Sixtus IV and the insecurity of King Ferrante of Naples, who, throughout the 1470s, was to become increasingly estranged from other Italian powers. Obsessed by the possibility that the French might resurrect the Angevin claim to the Kingdom of Naples, he resented the pro-French policy of Florence and Lorenzo's personal links with Louis XI, and the conclusion of a defensive alliance between Florence, Venice and Milan in November 1474 did nothing to alleviate his fears. He determined to break up this triple alliance. It was unfortunate, therefore, that many opportunities presented themselves for him to do so, as a result of a series of power struggles in the Romagna and Florence's deteriorating relationship with the papacy. As the restless and ambitious Sixtus IV sought to bring the small lordships of the Romagna under direct papal control, so those lords looked for help to powers outside the Church State. The inevitable consequence was a constant jockeying for position between Milan, Venice, Naples and Florence and the destabilisation of the Italian political world.

Of course, the main outlines of Florentine foreign policy were long established and, even within the fluid framework of fifteenth-century Italian diplomacy, could not readily be abandoned. In bringing his influence to bear on the conduct of foreign affairs, therefore, Lorenzo operated within certain fixed parameters: friendship with France and the maintenance of a Milanese, Neapolitan, Florentine alliance as the means of preserving relative peace and stability in Italy. As far as the Pope was concerned the Florentine attitude was also long-established. Outward devotion barely concealed a fixed determination to prevent the emergency of the papacy as a strong secular power in central Italy. This meant, in particular, Florentine support for and protection of the many small lordships in the Romagna, an area vital to Florence's trading interests, and also in the adjoining and scarcely less vital province of Umbria.

Here, in fact, was an area of potential conflict between the interests of Florence and the interests of the Medici. It was very important for Lorenzo, personally, that he be on good terms with the Pope. He knew that the Roman branch of the Medici bank was always the most profitable part of his business, yet was also aware of its peculiar vulnerability to sudden shifts in papal policy. In addition, with the rapid decline in the Medici bank as a whole, there was a corresponding decline in the sources of patronage. If Medici friends and clients were, therefore, to be kept loyal and happy, Lorenzo needed a new source of favours, and we have seen that these were most likely to be found at Rome and through the papal Curia.

Given these facts, it is surprising that Medicean/papal relations should rarely have been cordial. From the time of Piero, whose opponents in 1466 were reputed to have papal backing, it had been apparent that any pope was likely to look unfavourably on the growing power of the Medici, since, by bringing stability to Florence, they strengthened the republic. On the death of Piero, the Curia not only anticipated the fall of the Medici regime but eagerly awaited it, and, as we have seen, Lorenzo's early years in power were much occupied by attempts to repair the quarrel between the Medici and Rome.

Matters, in consequence, had improved but, despite the initial cordiality between Lorenzo and Sixtus IV, their relationship was always beset by difficulties. Lorenzo rapidly discovered that, whatever policies might be dictated by the needs of the Medici family, his position within Florence would bring conflict with the papacy. The basic problem was that what was good for the Medici was bad for the families of Sixtus IV. While, for Lorenzo de' Medici, his family might be the most important thing in the world, for Sixtus IV the interests of his families – Riario and della Rovere – were an absorbing passion. His all-consuming ambition was to do well by his relatives, to provide for every last impecunious kinsman and to establish them in positions of unassailable wealth and power. Unfortunately, the very areas in which he could best serve his families' interests were precisely those where the Florentines had most at stake – the Romagna and Umbria. The inherent difficulty in this situation became obvious in 1472 when the Pope purchased for his worthless nephew, Girolamo Riario, the small town of Bosco, gave him the title of Count, and married him to Caterina Sforza, the illegitimate daughter of the Duke of

Milan. Rumours were already abroad that Riario was nourishing a 'grand design', threatening to Florence's interests and dependent on Lorenzo's assistance.[18]

Nor were the Pope's ambitions for his family the only problem. More serious was the fact that, within that family, was to be found one man whose ability and diplomatic skill were of the order of Lorenzo's own: Cardinal Giuliano della Rovere, the closest and most influential of papal advisers, was already pursuing, through his uncle, the policy he would ultimately bring to fruition as Pope Julius II. Willing enough to go along with the schemes of Sixtus IV to provide for his family, his own vision was, in fact, a far nobler one. It was nothing less than to bring that chaotic and loosely run area, known as the Church State, under the direct control of the papacy. In doing so, he would inevitably threaten many of the tyrants, *signori*, and barons of the Church State who were allies or clients of Florence.

It could have been any one of the towns of the Romagna which would bring the conflict out into the open. As it turned out it was Imola which, in 1473, the Duke of Milan offered to sell to Florence. Since there was no question that, however loosely the Church State was defined, Imola was part of it, Sixtus was certainly justified in immediately addressing a brief admonition and complaint to Duke Galeazzo, informing him that he would not permit the sale of Imola which, in any case, he intended to bestow on Girolamo Riario.

Lorenzo would have had difficulty in coping with this situation even if he had had a longer experience of the complexity of Italian politics. As it was, he was placed in an impossible situation when Duke Galeazzo agreed to restore Imola to the papal see, on payment of 40,000 ducats and the Pope approached the Medici bank to ask for a loan for the purpose. The bank was in no position to raise such a sum. Then Duke Galeazzo, himself, advised Lorenzo against the loan, while Lorenzo's position in Florence would have become untenable had he been the means of furthering papal power in such a delicate area of the Romagna. On the other hand, refusal would certainly not assist Lorenzo in his plans to obtain a cardinal's hat for Giuliano and would put the Medici bank at Rome at risk. In the end, recognising that the interests of Florence were paramount, Lorenzo, with as graceful an effort at an apology as was possible in the circumstances, turned down the request and thus pro-vided a golden opportunity for his commercial rivals, the Pazzi, to ingratiate themselves with Sixtus IV. Although fellow-Florentines, the Pazzi showed no hesitation in placing the interests of their bank before the interests of their city, and having lent Sixtus his money, they managed to make it known within papal circles that Lorenzo had tried to prevent them doing so.

Hard on the heels of the crisis over Imola, came that of Città di Castello.

Once again, an underlying problem was the series of special relationships which the Florentines maintained with smaller powers within the Church State. A campaign undertaken by Giuliano della Rovere to subject Umbria, where the Orsini were most powerful, to direct papal control, began with successful attacks on Todi and Spoleto. It is worth noting that, on this occasion, Spoleto was subjected to a sack every bit as brutal as that of Volterra, but Giuliano della Rovere has never in consequence suffered from the moral disapproval which historians have tended to heap on Lorenzo.

With the fall of Spoleto, the papal army threatened Città di Castello, whose ruler, Niccolò Vitelli, was the long-standing friend, *condottiere*, and ally of Florence. As della Rovere lay siege to Città di Castello, Florence therefore leapt to Vitelli's defence. Six thousand Florentine troops were dispatched to the border town of Borgo San Sepulcro, while Milan and Florence mounted a concerted diplomatic effort to dissuade the pope from continuing with his attack. Sixtus wrote directly to Lorenzo, ordering him to cease assisting Vitelli. Laying stress on his formal position in Florence, Lorenzo replied, stating that he was powerless to intervene since:

> he had not been the author of this action. If it had been a personal matter he would have done whatever the Pope wished, but the whole commune of Florence was determined to assist this castle, and even if he wanted to recall the troops he could not do so without putting his whole position at risk.[19]

It was probably an accurate enough analysis of the situation. Florence was committed to the assistance of Vitelli, but Sixtus IV was not impressed. By way of reprisal he removed the papal account from the Medici bank, thereby increasing Lorenzo's financial difficulties.

Meanwhile, against all the odds, Vitelli had managed to put up a vigorous resistance to the papal army, and had cost the papacy dear in money and lives before finally being forced to surrender. Sixtus IV heaped all the blame on Lorenzo for whom he was beginning to conceive a burning hatred. Both he and Giuliano della Rovere complained bitterly that they had believed Lorenzo would never act against them, because of 'the great foundation of friendship and understanding' which had been laid between them during Lorenzo's visit to Rome.[20]

Yet another issue brought further clashes between Sixtus and Lorenzo: the question of clerical patronage within the Florentine state. Although, in the honeymoon period of his relations with the Pope, Lorenzo had accepted the Pope's nephew, Cardinal Riario, as Archbishop of Florence, there was little hope of papal nominees being accepted, without question, in the new context of strained papal–Florentine relations. The sudden death of Riario created a major crisis as Sixtus promoted the claims to the vacancy of Francesco Salviati, while Lorenzo supported those of his brother-in-law, Rinaldo Orsini. Given the suspicion in which the Orsini were held at Florence, it was a remarkable triumph when Lorenzo was able to get his own way. Sixtus, however, was never a man to take defeat lying down and, when the archbishopric of Pisa fell vacant in 1474, he promoted Salviati to the see, without even consulting Florence.

The sharp reaction of Lorenzo and the Florentines to this news has never been satisfactorily explained. It was clearly tactless of the Pope to have made so controversial an appointment, without even consulting with Florence, but he was legally entitled to do so. There is no evidence to suggest that any deep-rooted hostility existed between the Medici and Salviati families, and, personally, there was much to be said for Francesco Salviati. Nevertheless, Florence was united in its hostility and Lorenzo was doing no more than accurately reflect public opinion when he told the Duke of Milan that to consent to recognise Salviati as Archbishop of Pisa would be to betray the honour of Florence. For three years, despite the constant threats which emanated from Rome, the Florentines steadfastly refused to allow Salviati to take possession of his see.

Florence, therefore, had successfully enraged the Pope and become estranged from Naples. Her one remaining secure ally was Milan, but in December 1476 there came a new blow when Galeazzo Maria Sforza, Duke of Milan, was assassinated, leaving only a minor as his heir. To Lorenzo, dependent as he was on the Duke personally, and recognising the importance of the Milanese alliance to Florence, the news came as a bitter disappointment. Yet, while working with remarkable speed to minimise the dangers, he kept his head. The news of Sforza's death reached Florence only on 29 December but by the following day the two prominent Mediceans, Tommaso Soderini and Luigi Guicciardini, were already on their way as ambassadors to Milan conveying official Florentine condolences to the Duke's widow and offering her any assistance she might require from Florence. Lorenzo also wrote, in his own hand, reiterating the offer of assistance, and promising to do all in his power for Milan 'as long as he had life in his body, and if that failed, he would leave instructions in his will for his sons to do the same'.[21] In the following months, both Lorenzo and Florence remained true to their word and this support was vital in preventing the collapse of the Duchy of Milan into anarchy.

Meanwhile, in 1477, a further deterioration in Lorenzo's relationship with the Pope was provoked by yet another Umbrian city, Perugia, where the Venetian *condottiere*, Carlo da Montone or Fortebraccio, attempted to recover the position of supremacy once enjoyed there by his father and brother. This would have been impossible without, at least, the tacit support of Florence for, in order to attack Perugia, Fortebraccio had to cross Florentine territory. The interests at stake for Florence were very clear since, as Lorenzo himself explained, the ties between the two cities had always been very close. As he said, in September 1477:

> It is very true that there has always been the closest possible friendship between the Perugians and ourselves, and that always we have shared our fortunes. And we are determined to persevere in the close love that joins us, indeed we can do no other, since we have been joined together for so long that it has effectively become a fact of nature.[22]

It was certainly a fact, though not a fact of nature, that Perugia was always regarded by the Florentines as an outward bastion of Florence's own defences against an aggressive papacy. It was thus always to Florence's advantage that Perugia remain effectively independent of the papacy, and that whoever happened to be in control of so notoriously a faction-ridden city, should be a friend of Florence.

Florence could not, therefore, risk alienating Fortebraccio, but equally, she could not ignore the fact that his activities were threatening the peace of Italy. Having failed in his attempt on Perugia, Fortebraccio retraced his steps into Tuscany and ravaged the *contado* of Siena. Naples immediately offered Siena assistance, and urged Florence to do the same. For Lorenzo the situation was exceptionally difficult. He, personally, was very anxious to avoid an overt breach with Naples and had always made it an act of conscious policy to remain on friendly terms with Siena, but the Florentine involvement with Fortebraccio left him relatively helpless. His only resource was diplomatic activity, making use of his own personal relationships with the rulers of Italy. So, in July, he took the opportunity to meet informally with the Duke of Calabria at Pisa. Here, on behalf of his father, the Duke urged the necessity of a formal renewal of the Neapolitan and Florentine alliance for the purpose of protecting Siena, and preserving the peace of Italy.

After careful reflection, on 13 July, Lorenzo replied, setting out his own objectives and emphasising his desire for peace:

> We praise and commend this desire and effort for peace made by His Majesty, because it is in our nature to want peace; and we will remain not only well content but greatly obliged to His Majesty for all that he says he will do to ensure that peace is not violated. But, having decided not to get involved in this affair, in which we have absolutely no interest at stake, and having maintained this position up until now, we do not see any reason for changing our minds at present, but we will continue to remain neutral, giving favour neither to one side nor the other, although every day we are being given some reason to behave otherwise . . .[23]

Florence, in other words, would stand idly by and watch while Sixtus IV and Ferrante of Naples intervened on behalf of the Sienese. Fortebraccio's own castle of Montone was invested by Neapolitan troops and forced to capitulate on 27 September. The ultimate consequences were dangerous in the extreme for Florence. At a time when her relationships with the papacy and with Naples were strained to breaking point, Siena too was drawn into the papal–Neapolitan orbit. In February 1478, Sixtus IV, Ferrante of Naples, and the Sienese republic entered into a formal defensive league. Florence's southern boundary was now totally unprotected, and the hatred of Sixtus IV for Lorenzo confirmed.

5

THE PAZZI CONSPIRACY

In the years between 1469 and 1477 we have seen Lorenzo's development as a man and as a politician following a particular direction. From the conviction that he must control Florentine politics in order to maintain the interests of the Medici family, he came to realise that, paradoxically, in order to defend his position and that of his family, he had to make his first priority the defence of Florentine interests, or, rather, the interests of Florence's ruling families. That this might not always be to the immediate advantage of either Lorenzo or the Medici clan had also become apparent. Pursuing Florentine interests abroad, for example, had alienated both King Ferrante of Naples and Pope Sixtus IV on whose friendships the prosperity of the Medici bank depended.

In addition, Lorenzo had found that the protection of Florentine interests in the world outside the city sometimes involved him in actions which appeared to be both arbitrary and authoritarian. He, himself, claimed that this was not so. 'God knows', he told the trusted Morelli in October 1478, 'that if I have spoken too much and involved myself with many things, I have not done it because I was ambitious, but because, there being no one else to do it, it seemed necessary.'[1] The need to expedite foreign policy as quickly as possible and to override the slow processes of traditional communal government seemed self-evident to Lorenzo, but was less frequently appreciated by members of Florence's ruling families whose whole sense of self and of family prestige was tied up in the role which they traditionally played in the Florentine government. Since Lorenzo's arrogation of power to himself could only be at the expense of Florence's traditional institutions, and her long established habits of self-government, such critics were, perhaps, justified in asking what precisely there was left of Florentine 'liberty' and 'honour' to be defended abroad.

Of course, it is essential never to exaggerate Lorenzo's power. In 1478, he held no regular position in government and his influence remained indirect. Of the thousands of posts that fell vacant in any one year, only a small percentage were filled by his nominees. Whenever he was absent from Florence, other members of the *reggimento*, however reluctantly, did have to fulfil their traditional role as decision-makers. In addition, even when he was in the city, Lorenzo, as contemporaries knew full well, rarely took decisions by himself. Normally he did so only after the fullest consultation with that close inner circle of advisers, of which we have already spoken and which was known to contemporaries as the *pratica segreta*; Luigi Guicciardini, Piero Minerbetti, Antonio Ridolfi, Angelo della Stufa, Buongianni Gianfigliazzi and Bernardo Buongirolami. In a very real sense Florence continued to be run by an oligarchy and not by one man.

Yet we should not make too much of all this either. Whatever the precise constitutional or legal niceties of the situation, it is quite clear that many influential Florentines had been alienated from the regime, since, throughout the summer of 1477, criticism of Lorenzo's style of political management was widespread. He was not helped by the political and economic climate. Italy, as we have seen, was disturbed and unstable; the Turks were menacing the traditional trade routes of the Mediterranean, and making advances against the Venetian empire; Florence which enjoyed a period of relative prosperity for most of Lorenzo's lifetime, accompanied by a steep rise in her population, was at this time economically depressed and threatened by famine, while the Medici bank was not the only Florentine business in danger of imminent collapse.

In such a context, it is not surprising that rumours began to circulate that Lorenzo's position in Florence was threatened, and that an attack might be made on his life. Soon the rumours became explicit warnings. In July Ferrante of Naples wrote, warning him

> to seek to preserve your position, by bringing peace and quiet, by pleasing your friends and reconciling yourself with your enemies of which there are always too many and never enough friends.[2]

It was doubtful, of course, which category, by this stage, Ferrante himself would fall into. On a personal level, his relations with Lorenzo remained flawlessly cordial. Courtly exchanges of letters, gifts and favours continued unabated. In October 1477, for instance, they exchanged falcons, and as late as the following March, Ferrante, 'desirous in all things to please you',[3] threw open his stables for Lorenzo's servants to select a pair of jousting horses to be borrowed for a tournament in Florence, while, the following month, Lorenzo returned the compliment by the gift of a fine mare.

All this was most gratifying but, as a Florentine, Lorenzo could not help being disturbed by Ferrante's frankly expansionist policies. Nor was his concern lessened when he read the letters of the ever-faithful Giovanni Tornabuoni who was convinced that Ferrante 'will endeavour to surround or hem in the Florentine state, or else he will try to provoke some change of regime in your city',[4] and who advised Lorenzo 'to keep your eyes open, for one hears many rumours of strange plots, though, perhaps, I am needlessly afraid'.[5]

Tornabuoni was not, in fact, being needlessly alarmist. Nor were his the only warnings. In January 1478 the Venetians reported that Florentine exiles in Ferrara were planning to kill Lorenzo and Giuliano and that they had been in contact with King Ferrante. Similar information also came from Milan. Within Florence, although Lorenzo had not lost control of events, a number of Florentine families were obviously alienated from the regime. Of these, the most self-seeking was that of the Pazzi. Their disaffection was brought about by a typically high-handed action on the part of Lorenzo, one which both his brother and Iacopo Guicciardini pointed out would be sure to lead to trouble. The issue involved the problems of family, clientage and straightforward bribery in the management of the Medici party, and arose when, on the death of her father, who had failed to make a will, Beatrice Borromeo, the wife of Giovanni de' Pazzi, claimed the whole of his vast inheritance. Borromeo's two nephews, close intimates and clients of Lorenzo, successfully contested her right to inherit. To bolster their case, a retrospective law was passed through the Florentine councils, setting aside the claims of females to the estate of a father who had died intestate, in favour of the nearest male relative. While this law, as it happens, reflected with some accuracy prevailing attitudes to women, property and inheritance, its passage, at this precise time, could not fail to suggest that Florence was now being ruled entirely in the interests of the Medici party and, particularly, in the interests of Lorenzo's closest friends. At any rate, it so enraged Francesco de' Pazzi, Giovanni's son, that he quitted Florence for Rome in order to run the family bank, while nursing his grievance against Lorenzo.

By 1476, therefore, despite the fact that Guglielmo de' Pazzi, a frequent companion of Lorenzo's and husband of his favourite sister, Bianca, remained within the Medici circle, the rest of the family was totally excluded from the magic ruling circle which centred around Lorenzo, and was thus cut off from the favours and patronage that flowed from him. The irony of this was that, to a major extent, the Pazzi owned their prominent position in Florence to the Medici. Although they might, with some justification, regard the Medici as upstarts, since the Pazzi had been prominent in the annals of Florentine history long before the Medici had even left the Mugello, their position in the city was an ambivalent one. One of the noble families whose knightly qualities and antiquity were prized because they brought honour to Florence, their constant unruly behaviour, and general lack of respect for the law, led to their being deprived of all political rights in the thirteenth and fourteenth centuries. Subsequently, it was entirely due to Medici patronage that they enjoyed a political rehabilitation. Astute enough to cultivate an alliance with the rising family, the Pazzi were rewarded when Cosimo obtained the lifting of all political disabilities against them, so qualifying them not only to hold government office but also to engage in banking.

Before long, the Medici and Pazzi banks had become fierce competi-

tors, and nowhere was their competition more obvious or more unprinci-
pled than at Rome, where the Pazzi worked relentlessly to undermine the
Medici bank. Their ultimate aim, of course, was to take over control of
papal finance and it was, as we have seen, the Pazzi who lent Sixtus IV
money for the purchase of Imola. Their reward was the appointment of
Francesco de' Pazzi as Treasurer to the Holy See, in place of Lorenzo.

Not content with this public humiliation of the Medici, with all of its
long-term commercial and financial implications, the Pazzi became involved in a widely-based conspiracy whose aim was the assassination of
Lorenzo and Giuliano. It was a plot which had no higher motivation than
that of a simple struggle for power. The conspirators included not only
the Pazzi, Jacopo Salviati, the Archbishop of Pisa, the papal nephew,
Girolamo Riario, who was convinced that his position in Imola would
remain precarious for as long as the Medici controlled Florence, and the
Duke of Urbino, but even the Pope himself. The plot also appears to have
had at least the tacit blessing of King Ferrante. Enthusiastic participants
were Poggio's son, Iacopo Bracciolini and Bernardo Bandini de' Baroncel-
li. Bracciolini, who was a friend of Ficino, had just published his commentary on Petrarch's *Triumph of Fame*, with a fulsome dedication to Lorenzo,
but, apart from the fact that he was disastrously in debt, he had recently
been drawn into the Riario circle by his appointment as secretary to the
seventeen-year-old Cardinal Raffaello Riario. Bandini, also, was bur-
dened with debt and had long been a close business associate of the Pazzi.

Not all those approached to join the conspiracy, however, were equally
enthusiastic. Francesco de' Pazzi's cousin, Renato, opposed the whole
idea on the grounds that Lorenzo's financial affairs were so seriously
embarrassed that he would soon be bankrupt, which would inevitably
lead to his fall from power in Florence. In Renato's view, therefore, if the
conspirators were really serious about getting rid of Lorenzo, their
obvious course was to hasten his ruin by lending him money at high
interest. Unenthusiastic, also, was Iacopo de' Pazzi, head of the family in
Florence, who declared himself unwilling to participate in a plot which,
he bluntly pointed out, was doomed to failure. Equally sceptical was
Giovanni Battista da Montesecco, a captain in Riario's pay, who, when
the plan of the conspirators was unfolded to him, frankly warned his
employers, 'Have a care, gentlemen, what you are undertaking. Florence
is no small matter, and Lorenzo, I hear, is very popular.'[6] The conspirators brushed aside his objection; 'We know more about the state of
Florence,' they told him, 'our success is as certain as our meeting here
today.' Montesecco, who remained unconvinced, insisted that he must
have proof of papal backing for the enterprise. This was partially forthcoming. In a private audience, Sixtus IV assured Montesecco that he was
in favour of a change of regime in Florence, but added the curious proviso
that:

Sixtus IV and his four nephews receiving Platina by Melozzo da Forli

I will have no bloodshed. It is not consistent with my office to cause the death of any man. Lorenzo has behaved shamefully, but I do not desire his death, though I do desire a change in government.[7]

If Sixtus IV really believed he could bring about a change of regime in Florence without bloodshed he was being astonishingly naive. Whether he had been so blinded by his hatred of Lorenzo, and the constant bullying of the conspirators who already in their mind's eye saw the Medici overthrown, and the Pazzi installed in their place in Florence, as to be able to delude himself, or whether he had been overcome by a genuine fit of conscience, will always remain unclear. What mattered was that he had said enough to convince Montesecco that he would support the conspiracy.

Montesecco agreed, therefore, to take charge of the military details of the plot. The confused state of Italy, and the continued disorders in the Romagna and Umbria, provided ideal circumstances in which to gather troops together at strategic points. Mercenaries were assembled to be held in readiness at Città di Castello and at Todi. These troops were to advance on Florence as the conspiracy came to fruition.

Meanwhile, new political complications arose in the Romagna when Carlo Manfredi, Lord of Faenza, fell ill, for Girolamo Riario was determined to add Faenza to his possessions, 'by agreement, force of arms, or treaty',[8] despite the inconvenient existence of Ottaviano, the young son and heir of Carlo Manfredi. It was, therefore, on a spurious mission of goodwill, that Carlo Martelli and Montesecco were sent to Lorenzo. They were to seek his support for Riario's ambitions in relation to Faenza. They found Lorenzo relaxing at Cafaggiolo, and Montesecco, for one, was completely disarmed by this supposed tyrant's friendly good nature. Promptly invited to dinner, he was shown round the home farm and the stables which housed the most loved of Lorenzo's horses. Lorenzo himself was in the happiest of moods, laughing and joking with the grooms and the household servants, and telling Montesecco how much he preferred living in the country to the city.

It was, in consequence, a somewhat pensive Montesecco who rode back into Florence for an interview with Iacopo Pazzi. He had been instructed to try, yet again, to win Iacopo round to the idea of the conspiracy, but he had no success. Old Iacopo remained firmly opposed to what he was still convinced was a lunatic scheme and warned that, 'They will break their necks. I understand our affairs much better than they do in Rome. I wish to hear no more about this business.'[9]

The conspirators remained unmoved. They were determined to press ahead. This time it was Salviati who agreed to set up a situation in which it might be possible to combine the assassination of Lorenzo with an attack on Florence by papal troops. On 16 September 1477, he arrived in Florence, in his capacity as papal legate, with the ostensible purpose of discussing the problem of Faenza and the siege of Montone. He stayed at the Pazzi villa of Montughi, just outside Florence, where he was joined by Montesecco. Montesecco had come directly from inspecting the papal troops at Imola, and he warned Salviati that no time must be lost in making the assassination attempt.

Something, however, persuaded the conspirators to draw back at this eleventh hour. It is probable that they suspected that Lorenzo himself had some idea of what they were up to. The Medici network of informants had been keeping an eye on Montesecco and, as we have seen, Lorenzo was warned often enough that he was in danger. Yet he took no real action to protect himself, surrendering, as so often at critical moments in his life, to an inherent fatalism. Constantly urged by the Milanese to increase his body-guard, he would only reply 'that such guards are not easy to provide, and that he needed rather the protection of God'.[10]

Given Lorenzo's probable awareness of their plans, the subsequent attempt of the conspirators to decoy him to Rome was disingenuous in the extreme. In January, Riario invited him to come to the Holy City in order to settle all the matters in dispute between them and assured Lorenzo that:

> I have not the slightest doubt the Holy Father will welcome you with open arms while I, owing to the affection inspired by our friendly relations, am entirely prepared to gratify your Magnificence and whatever grievances may have arisen will vanish.[11]

Lorenzo, sensibly, declined the invitation.

In the spring of 1478, therefore, the conspirators reverted to their original scheme; Lorenzo was to be attacked in Florence as papal troops converged on the city. Seven of the ringleaders assembled in Florence: Iacopo Pazzi, who was now so compromised by his intimate knowledge of the conspiracy that he went along with it against his better judgement, Francesco Pazzi, Archbishop Salviati, his brother Jacopo and his cousin, Francesco, Iacopo Bracciolini and Bernardo Bandini. On the pretext that plague was raging in Pisa, where he was a student, they invited the young Cardinal Raffaello Riario to join them at the Pazzi villa. They knew that the Medici could not fail to honour so distinguished a guest to Florence. Riario was first received at the Medici villa in Fiesole by Lorenzo and by Piero who, together with Poliziano, had accompanied his father. Since, however, Giuliano remained in Florence, there was no question of killing Lorenzo on this occasion. But Lorenzo could not ignore the publicly expressed desire of the young cardinal to visit the Medici palace and view its treasures. Courteous as ever, he invited him to dine on 25 April, extending the same invitation to the Archbishop, Iacopo de' Pazzi and many other leading citizens, 'in order to honour the Cardinal',[12] and, to this end, according to Poliziano:

> they prepared the house; they got out the ornaments, spread out the tapestries, arranged the silver, statues and paintings for public view, put out the gems in their cases, and had a most magnificent banquet prepared.[13]

It is obvious that the major problem which continually dogged the conspirators was that of getting Lorenzo and Giuliano together. The brothers seem to have taken the sensible precaution of avoiding, as far as possible, appearing in public at the same time. Now, again, Giuliano excused himself from the banquet on the grounds of ill-health. This threw the conspirators into a panic for they knew papal mercenaries were advancing on Florence and that it was, therefore, essential to act quickly. Cardinal Riario was to say a high mass, celebrating the Ascension, in the cathedral on the following day, and the conspirators decided to seize the opportunity to kill the Medici while, simultaneously, Archbishop Salviati was to capture the Palazzo della Signoria. Montesecco, it was agreed, was to kill Lorenzo while Francesco de' Pazzi and Bernardo Bandini would deal with Giuliano. To the consternation of his employers, however, Montesecco refused, saying that, 'he would never have the courage to commit such an enormity in church, thus accompanying treachery with sacrilege'.[14] No persuasions nor threats could persuade him to change his mind, and so his place was taken by two young priests who did not share his scruples, Antonio Maffei of Volterra and Stefano da Bagnone, 'although', as Machiavelli rightly points out, 'these two were by nature and experience wholly unfit for such an act'.[15] According to Poliziano, Maffei's motivation was one of revenge for the sack of Volterra and Bagnone was the parish priest of the Pazzi village of Montemurlo, as well as secretary to Iacopo de' Pazzi. Neither had much experience of murder or assassination and their substitution for the highly professional Montesecco may well have saved Lorenzo's life.

On the following morning, 26 April, Cardinal Riario was accompanied by Lorenzo to the crowded cathedral, but, even as the mass began, the conspirators suddenly realised that Giuliano was not there. Francesco de' Pazzi and Bernardo Bandini, therefore, raced across the square to persuade Giuliano to accompany them to the cathedral. Laughing and joking they made their way back, Francesco even seizing the opportunity to embrace Giuliano in order to check that he was not wearing a mail-shirt under his clothes.

Reports as to the exact moment at which the attack on the brothers occurred differ. According to the Milanese ambassadors, it was at 'about the time of the singing of the Agnus Dei'.[16] Landucci says that it was at about the time of the elevation of the host, as does the Prior of San Martino; Filippo Strozzi, who was present in the cathedral, was convinced that the words *ite missa est* were the signal to the conspirators, while Machiavelli says that the attack came at the time of the priest's communion. Probably, it occurred between the priest's communion and the *ite missa est*, when the congregation were getting ready to leave and their attention was diverted.

Giuliano and Lorenzo were standing at some distance from one another and this complicated matters for their assailants who were forced to attack the brothers separately. The attack on Giuliano was successful. He was stabbed to death by Francesco de' Pazzi and Bernardo Bandini, pierced, Poliziano tells us, with nineteen wounds. Lorenzo's attackers were less successful. He had been standing at the opposite side of the cathedral, near the old sacristy, when he was approached by the two priests, Maffei and Bagnone, supported by a band of Iacopo de' Pazzi's retainers and some Spaniards from Cardinal Riario's entourage. Maffei put a hand on Lorenzo's shoulder, hoping that this would make him turn round, in order to stab him in the chest. He had reckoned without Lorenzo's swift reactions. Whirling his cloak round his left arm to defend himself, Lorenzo drew his sword on his assailant. The priest's dagger missed its mark and Lorenzo received no more than a slight flesh wound in the neck before escaping through the choir and across the high altar. As he ran, Francesco de' Pazzi and Bandini tried to intercept him, but found their way barred by the faithful Francesco Nori and other Medici friends. In a brief struggle Nori was struck down, and Lorenzo Cavalcanti wounded in the arm.

Lorenzo, meanwhile, had escaped into the north sacristy whither the dying Francesco Nori was also carried. Poliziano slammed the bronze doors shut. Antonio Ridolfi sucked the wound in Lorenzo's neck in case it had been poisoned. Panic and confusion reigned. Shut up in the sacristy, Lorenzo and his friends had no means of knowing what was happening outside. Lorenzo, who was close to hysteria, kept asking, 'Is Giuliano safe?' and no one knew what to reply. Loud knocks sounded on the door and there were shouts of, 'We are friends, we are relations. Let Lorenzo come out before the enemy gains an advantage', but everyone was afraid that this was only a trick. Finally Sigismondo della Stufa scrambled up into the organ loft. From here he could look down into the cathedral, where he saw Giuliano's corpse lying in a pool of blood. He was also able to establish that there were few people left in the cathedral and that those that were were Medici supporters. The sacristy doors were therefore opened, and Lorenzo escorted home, his friends trying to shield his sight from Giuliano's mangled corpse.

The whole episode had taken so little time that no one seemed able to grasp what was happening. Many thought that those cynics who had doubted the wisdom of bridging the crossing with Brunelleschi's dome, had at last been proved right, and that the entire edifice of the cathedral was about to come crashing to the ground. In their panic they had rushed for the nearest open doors and in the confusion, Bandini, the two priests and Francesco de' Pazzi had also managed to escape. Meanwhile, Cardinal Riario had remained, throughout, kneeling in abject terror next to the high altar. Here, he was comforted by the canons of the cathedral until an armed guard came to arrest and take him, for his own safety, to the Palazzo della Signoria, lest he be lynched by the mob.

For, by this time, the city was in uproar. The Medici palace was surrounded by citizens, clamouring for vengeance on the conspirators, and here, about an hour after his return from the cathedral, Lorenzo addressed them from one of the balconies. His neck was bandaged and he looked deathly pale, but his voice was firm and strong and he told the people: 'I commend myself to you. Control yourselves and let justice take its course. Do not harm the innocent. My wound is not serious.'[17] But, by now, the centre of the action had shifted to the Piazza della Signoria. Archbishop Salviati had not been present during the attack on Giuliano and Lorenzo. Pleading the sudden excuse of a sick mother, he had left the cathedral accompanied by some thirty Perugian exiles, Iacopo Bracciolini and other accomplices, for the Palazzo della Signoria. He arrived as the priors were at dinner and sent in word to the Standard-Bearer of Justice, Cesare Petrucci, to say that he had a message from the Pope to deliver. Petrucci agreed to come out and meet the Archbishop in an ante-room, but his suspicions had already been aroused by this impromptu and unheralded visit.

Salviati began to stutter out something about the Pope intending to promote Petrucci's son, but his manner was so strange that Petrucci was increasingly alarmed. The Archbishop coughed, stammered, peered continuously at the door, where he expected to see his Perugians, and finally became totally incoherent. Now thoroughly convinced that something untoward was afoot, Petrucci summoned the palace guard while Salviati rushed out of the room, shouting for his retainers. Unfortunately, they had succeeded in shutting themselves into the Chancellery which could only be unlocked from the outside. As Petrucci pursued Salviati he ran straight into Bracciolini. Seizing him by the hair he flung him to the ground where he was promptly arrested by the guard.

Snatching up various bizarre impromptu weapons, Petrucci and the other priors now climbed the tower of the palace and fastened it with a heavy chain, while the doors on to the public square were all bolted. The tocsin was sounded to warn the citizens of danger and to summon them to the piazza, bearing arms for the defence of their city.

It was into the midst of the hostile crowd thus summoned, who were quickly joined by the *Podestà* with some thirty troops, that Iacopo Pazzi now forced his way, with some hundred of his own men, faithfully playing the part he had been allotted in the plot he had never wanted. It was he who was supposed to rouse the people against the Medici by the time-honoured Florentine appeal to 'People and Liberty'. Even had the conspirators succeeded in killing both of the Medici, and in seizing the palace, his would have been an unenviable task. As it was, so many missiles were hurled on his head from the tower of the Palazzo that he was forced to retreat, while the crowd, ignoring his appeal to traditional Florentine liberties, responded with their own shouts of, 'Down with the traitors! *Palle! Palle!*' As he stood, slightly bemused and uncertain what to do, he was approached by his own brother-in-law, Giovanni Serristori who urged him to flee 'asserting that the people and liberty were as much on the hearts of other citizens as on his'.[18] He retreated to his own palace, where Francesco, who had been wounded in the thigh, had taken refuge. For several hours the two men anxiously waited for the promised papal troops but, when it became apparent that no help was coming, Iacopo rode to the Santa Croce gate which had been seized and held by Montesecco and his band of mercenaries and took flight in the direction of the Mugello.

The revenge taken on the conspirators was harsh, cruel, swift and extremely popular. As soon as the news of the death of Giuliano was brought to the Palazzo della Signoria, the Perugians were dragged out of the Chancellery, slaughtered and hurled down into the square. Francesco de' Pazzi was pulled from his hiding-place in the Pazzi palace and 'naked as he was'[19] hanged from a window of the Palazzo della Signoria, having refused to utter one word by way of confession. Archbishop Salviati was hanged beside him. As he fell, he bit at the dead body of Francesco, the halter tightened round his neck and he was left, in death, hanging on to the corpse by his teeth. Further executions followed on 27 April; two other members of the Salviati family, Andrea Pazzi and certain of the Archbishop's staff, along with Iacopo Bracciolini. More than a hundred retainers of Iacopo Pazzi were hanged together.

Those not executed by the government were hacked to pieces and dragged through the streets by the mob. The innocent suffered along with the guilty. Renato de' Pazzi, although he had opposed the conspiracy all along, was hanged for failing to inform the authorities of its existence, and his equally innocent brothers were imprisoned in the dungeons of Volterra. Lorenzo's brother-in-law escaped only by taking refuge in the Medici palace where his wife, Bianca, pleaded with her brother on his behalf. His life was spared but, for his own safety, he was exiled from Florence.

On his way to the Romagna, Iacopo Pazzi was captured by peasants. He offered them money if they would kill him on the spot, but the offer was spurned and one of his captors struck him a blow so crippling that he had to be carried back to Florence in a litter. Here, he made a full confession of his crime in which he said he had counted on the luck of Francesco who had always been successful in business. 'Why did you fail to consider the superior luck of Lorenzo?' asked the examining magistrate. Iacopo, too, was led off to execution, hanged from the same window as the Archbishop, in a purple gown and stockings, his hands tied behind him with a leather strip.

Botticelli was paid to depict the ringleaders on the walls of the Bargello and the Palazzo della Signoria. The work took him twelve weeks and he was paid forty gold florins for it, while Lorenzo put his poetic talents to the macabre task of writing epitaphs to be painted under these portraits. Such a curious activity illustrates the fact that, after the Pazzi conspiracy,

Medal commemorating the Pazzi conspiracy showing Giuliano's head
above the choir enclosure

Lorenzo gave full vent to the vindictive streak in his nature. In his pursuit
of vengeance he showed no mercy and gave no respite. Gruesome
executions dragged on long after Giuliano's burial in San Lorenzo on 30
April. Montesecco was examined on 4 May, made the full confession from
which much of our detailed knowledge of the conspiracy derives, and
was beheaded in the courtyard of the Bargello on the same day. On that
day, too, Maffei and Bagnone were hanged. The wretched Bernardo
Bandini was even pursued as far as Constantinople where Lorenzo used
his influence with the Sultan to procure his arrest; he was returned in
irons to Florence for execution.

To carry the name of Pazzi became a crime. The family was exiled, their
property was confiscated. To be a Pazzi, even to be married to one of the
Pazzi women, meant total exclusion from civic office. The *Signoria* decreed the destruction of Pazzi coats-of-arms throughout the city, and the
renaming of streets which bore their name. Even their most cherished
right – that of kindling the fire to light the Paschal candle on Easter
Saturday with the stone which, according to legend, Pazzino de' Pazzi
brought back from the first crusade – was taken away.

The cruelty which Lorenzo displayed, so alien to the spirit of forgiveness and reconciliation which had characterised his father's treatment of
his enemies is, no doubt, unattractive and certainly alien to the Christian
tradition; but, in acting thus, Lorenzo showed his consummate ability to
identify with the popular prejudices of the Florentines. He himself was
well aware that his behaviour laid him open to criticism, and he swore
that were it merely a case of Giuliano's death and his own near-escape 'he
would seek no more revenge nor take more account of the matter than if it
had been a case of the murder of two porters'.[20] He argued, however, that
the very security of Florence had been shaken to its roots and that this was
the crime that was being punished. The Florentines, by and large, appear

The same medal shows Lorenzo with his emblem of the laurel branch

to have agreed with him. Much of the relentless horror which surrounded the punishment of the Pazzi took its origin in the tradition of the *vendetta*, which despite the best attempts of the government to suppress it, still permeated Florentine society. Certainly, as Poliziano points out, it was popular superstition which led to the disinterment of Iacopo de' Pazzi's body by a peasant mob, who, after a long period of rain which threatened their crops, entered the city, broke into Pazzi's grave, and reburied his corpse outside the city walls.

Nor was this the end of the matter for, on the following day, a group of youths dug the corpse up again and dragged it through the streets to the Pazzi palace where they battered the door with the dead man's head and demanded: 'Is there anyone home? Is there anyone to welcome the master returning with his great retinue?'[21] Then, forbidden to take the corpse into the Piazza della Signoria, they flung it unceremoniously into the Arno.

Lorenzo's passionate desire for vengeance was also the product of acute shock and great grief, untempered by reason. The confusion and fear that stalked the streets of Florence, in the aftermath of the assassination of Giuliano, were likewise to be found within the walls of the Medici palace, and are even reflected in the record of Lorenzo's correspondence where a gap of five days and two blank sheets are laconically explained by the fact that, 'Here and on the following page must be recorded the letters written about the tumult, when Giuliano de' Medici was killed in Santa Reparata,* may God have mercy on his soul.'[22] Even when the secretaries resumed work they were still in a state of shock. So also was Lorenzo who had, after all, lost a dearly loved brother as a result of a conspiracy in which there was at least the possibility that his own brother-in-law had been implicated; he himself had barely escaped with his life. He was, in

---

* The original dedication of the cathedral was to Santa Reparata.

addition, deeply hurt to discover to how great an extent the Duke of Urbino and the King of Naples appeared to have been implicated, and was bewildered by the hatred of Sixtus IV since, as he told Louis XI: 'I well know and God is my witness that I have committed no crime against the Pope save that I am alive and . . . have not allowed myself to be murdered.'[23]

Despite his state of mind, however, work, of necessity, claimed him. His secretary recalled that on 1 and 2 May Lorenzo wrote letters to fourteen different people 'and a great many more which I don't remember'.[24] Many important decisions had to be made. Although the immediate danger was past, neither Lorenzo, nor Florence, nor the numerous Florentines abroad, were safe. Both Sixtus IV and Ferrante of Naples were angered by the failure of the assassination attempt, while the fury of Count Girolamo Riario knew no bounds. Sixtus refused to consider any aspect of the affair other than the continued detention in Florence of his great-nephew, Cardinal Riario, and the sacrilege which had undoubtedly occurred when an Archbishop was summarily executed. So annoyed was the Pope that only the prompt intervention of the Venetian and Milanese ambassadors prevented Donato Acciaiuoli, Florentine ambassador to the Curia, being thrown into prison.

The most pressing problem for Lorenzo at this juncture was to decide what should be done with Cardinal Riario. Venice, Milan and Naples all urged him to appease the Pope by releasing him, but Lorenzo saw Riario as a vital hostage for the protection of Florentines and Florentine property in Rome. Moreover, he was convinced that his own life was still in extreme danger from the Pope for, as he said, quoting the old Tuscan proverb, 'he who offends, never forgives'.[25] No guard in the world, he declared, could protect him from papal enmity. Riario, meanwhile, was instructed to write to Rome, in his own hand, describing what had happened and explaining that his detention was for his own safety.

Despite Riario's honest compliance with this request, and even after his release, as the result of Milanese and Venetian pressure, in 'order that there should be no evidence of anything other than entire unity among the allies',[26] Sixtus was not to be appeased. He ordered the Florentines to banish Lorenzo and followed this order on 14 June with a bull excommunicating him. This was accompanied by the threat that, if the Florentines did not deliver up Lorenzo's person to him within a month, the whole city would be placed under interdict. Florence, however, was unimpressed by the Pope's contention that he had no quarrel with the Florentines as such, and that his only aim was to liberate them from tyrannical rule. The man Sixtus chose to call a tyrant was, they said, known to them as the 'defender of liberty' and they were determined 'to stake everything on the safety of Lorenzo de' Medici'.[27] Any action taken against Lorenzo would, therefore, be regarded as action taken against the republic.

The Pazzi conspiracy had, therefore, the paradoxical consequence of further welding together the interests of the Medici and those of Florence. Not only did it demonstrate, as the Milanese ambassadors emphasised and the Duke of Urbino ruefully noted, Lorenzo's personal popularity and the basic strength of the Medici regime, it also brought Lorenzo more authority. It both ensured a general acceptance of the central role played by Lorenzo in the political life of Florence, and led to a series of public endorsements of that role.

On 12 June, for instance, a meeting of prominent citizens, including Lorenzo, was called to discuss the bull of excommunication and interdict which Sixtus had now launched against the city. This was one of the first occasions, after the assassination attempt, on which Lorenzo could test the collective feeling of the ruling élite of Florence. That he was not certain what their reaction would be is suggested by the fact that, throughout May, he deliberately kept a low profile, restricting his political discussions to a small and intimate circle, and avoiding public notice of his consultations with the Milanese ambassador. He could not be certain that the city would support him against the Pope, and we should not doubt the sincerity of the offer, made during this meeting, to face exile and even death if this would avert a war. 'All citizens', he explained, reverting to one of his common themes, 'must place the common before the private good but I more than anyone else, as one who has received from you and from my country more and greater benefits,'[28] But, one by one, those who heard him, rose to thieir feet to express their support, assuring him that the safety of Florence was inseparable from the safety of his person. To prove their sincerity they would provide a public body-guard of twelve to protect Lorenzo. This was, indeed, an important outward manifestation of a new relationship between Lorenzo and Florence, for such a guard indicated that Lorenzo was no longer regarded as one among equals, but different to all other citizens. For this reason, Lorenzo himself, always sensitive to the nuances of Florentine political life, suspected that it would soon come to be disapproved of as 'too much of a novelty'.[29] It was yet one more step towards investing the Medici with the trappings of royal sovereignty.

As if to underline the fact that he now held a new position in the republic, Lorenzo began, for the first time, to hold office regularly on public committees and, when war broke out on 7 July, he was elected to the prestigious Ten of War which was composed entirely of the most loyal Mediceans. Although, over the ensuing months, he was immensely scrupulous in maintaining the constitutional niceties, in pointing out that he was only one citizen among many who made decisions, and that all communications relating to war and peace should go to the Ten or the

Signoria, in fact, from this point onwards, the Medici party's control of Florence became more overt. This stemmed, in part, from the fact that the Pazzi conspiracy had rendered Lorenzo psychologically even more insecure. He might, in public, put a good face on things and assure his allies that they need not fear on his behalf, but each reverse in Florence's fortunes, each murmur against the government, made him afraid of a revolution against the Medici. He feared for his own life, he feared for the safety of his wife and children. They also were now protected by a permanent guard. Scrupulously he followed the advice of the Milanese government that:

> daily, you should seek to win the Florentines to you, strengthening certain friendships, reconciling yourself with those you are not sure of so that they will favour and love you, since the more there are who are fond of you, the stronger will be your position and the republic.[30]

The obvious consequence of following this advice was that the loyallest Mediceans would become most prominent in government, notably Luigi Guicciardini, Antonio Pucci, Antonio Ridolfi, Buongiovanni Gianfigliazzi and Bernardo Buongirolami, all of whom became extremely close to Lorenzo at this time.

Fear dogged Lorenzo's footsteps and he was also surrounded by fearful friends. In August the Milanese reported that the Mediceans 'dread each new day, and particularly with this eclipse of the moon which is expected on Tuesday night which will last from the third to the sixth hour'.[31] Yet, in the face of such alarms, Lorenzo demonstrated great courage. Despite the plague epidemic which continued to ravage Florence throughout the summer, he would not leave the city. Rather he flung his energies into serving the state and assisting his political friends. His burden of work became overwhelming as he confessed to Girolamo Morelli, explaining that, 'if you do not receive news day by day the only reason is that I have so much to do that it is difficult'.[32]

For their own safety, however, he sent Clarice and the children away. They spent the summer of 1478 at Pistoia as guests of the Panciatichi, known to be devoted adherents of the Medici. Then, in November, they moved to Cafaggiolo, accompanied by Poliziano as tutor to the increasingly difficult and frequently bored Piero. Subsequently, following a suspected case of plague, the family moved to a villa at Trebbio which belonged to Lorenzo's cousins, then on to Gagliano in the Mugello where, as Clarice remarked to her mother-in-law, 'you know there is nothing but the bare walls'[33] not even any bed-linen. His wife and children wrote frequent concerned letters to Lorenzo, telling him to be careful of his health, for the news of the death-toll from the plague was a constant source of alarm. Clarice also bombarded him with gifts of food and worried about her husband's inability to relax. 'I would love you to come and spend a night here in order to rest',[34] she told him.

This evident concern for her husband's well-being was not, however, sufficient to prevent Clarice being the cause of yet another worry. Missing Lorenzo, frightened for his safety, unable to make confession or take communion because of the interdict, probably already in the early stages of consumption, for she was very ill in September, she allowed herself to become involved in a major personality clash with Poliziano. She disliked his influence over Piero and disapproved of the fact that Giovanni was being raised on a diet of the classics, which she considered unsuitable for one destined for the priesthood. In consequence, at the beginning of May 1479, she unilaterally changed Giovanni's reading to the Psalter and, when this led to an open rupture, sacked Poliziano, not permitting him to remove even his books and musical instruments. Trying to smooth over the rift between his closest friend and his 'most dear wife' Lorenzo begged Clarice to reinstate Poliziano and to treat him kindly, lest:

> Piero should lose all that he has gained with such great difficulty. Be content to do it, if not out of love for him, at least for love of me, for it would give me great pleasure, besides the fact that you know how much benefit Piero derives from him.[35]

He dispatched Niccolò Michelozzi to try to patch up the quarrel between the two but Clarice's temper was up, her dislike of Poliziano confirmed by the fact that her husband was, in her view, taking his part. Lorenzo, she said, employed and entertained Poliziano only to spite her. She continued to refuse to restore Poliziano's books until, finally, on 5 June Lorenzo's temper snapped and he wrote her a note of icy rebuke ordering her to return Poliziano's property forthwith.

Family squabbles were the last thing Lorenzo needed as the tide of disaster swept over him. In the war which Sixtus IV now launched against Florence, the Pope was supported by Naples, while Venice, Milan and Ferrara allied with Florence, on the publicly-stated grounds that their League 'was one body, with one mind, sincere and indissoluble, so that we are determined to share the fortunes of (Florence) and of the Magnificent Lorenzo'.[36] In many ways, Lorenzo's carefully nurtured diplomatic links now proved their worth as friends came to his assistance. By doing so, of course, they also helped to bolster his position in Florence and to build up his shaken confidence.

The Milanese, as usual, proved to be the most valuable friends, repaying Lorenzo for his support in 1476. Personally, Lorenzo was very close to the Milanese ambassador, Filippo Sacramori, with whom he was said to have 'great intimacy and understanding',[37] and who regularly showed Lorenzo letters from Milan before they went to the *Signoria*. This personal link, maintained by virtually daily meetings, helped the smooth working of the alliance between Florence and Milan.

Everything possible was done by the Milanese, 'to enhance the authority of Lorenzo'.[38] Immediately the news of the assassination of Giuliano reached Milan, the Milanese government ordered Giovanni Bentivoglio, ruler of Bologna, to go to the defence of the Medici but, even before he received this instruction, Bentivoglio had set out. Letters to Lorenzo and the *Signoria* from Milan, reporting this, were particularly welcomed. Lorenzo was so delighted with his that he kept showing it to his friends: 'praising so free and loving a demonstration of support not only in the words of the aforesaid letter, but also the speed and promptitude in sending troops'.[39] And this was only the beginning of military assistance. In the end, more than 3,000 Milanese cavalry were committed to Florence's aid.

For Lorenzo, personally, even more vital assistance from Milan was financial, staving off bankruptcy. The Pazzi conspiracy occurred at precisely the moment of greatest embarrassment in the Medici bank when it was making heavy losses in Apulia, Flanders, Milan and London where the branch was wound up with losses of more than 51,000 florins. Throughout 1478 and 1479 Lorenzo was struggling to sort out the legacy of mismanagement and debt which the Portinari brothers had left him, particularly in Milan. With the outbreak of hostilities all his assets in Rome and Naples were seized and the Pope repudiated the debts of the Holy See to the Medici. By April 1479 Lorenzo was, therefore, forced to admit that he was virtually bankrupt, and bitterly accused Tommaso Portinari of doing more harm to him personally than the Pope and the King of Naples together.

Lorenzo remained solvent only by resorting to a number of dubious financial expedients. He was forced to call in all major debts, including one of 11,198 ducats from the Marquess of Mantua. He misappropriated public funds and, between May and September 1478, took money from the estate of his wards Giovanni and Lorenzo di Pierfrancesco de' Medici. In this context, Milanese financial assistance must be seen as critical. In August 1478 Lorenzo asked Bona of Savoy for 12,000 ducats of which he received only half. By the following March, Lorenzo was again desperate for credit and asked Girolamo Morelli to arrange to borrow 60,000 ducats from Milan, agreeing that it would probably prove impossible but hoping for assistance, and in the end sufficient aid was forthcoming to preserve Lorenzo's credit.

After the Pazzi conspiracy, the personal connections Lorenzo had built up with the Lords of the Romagna also stood him in good stead. As we have seen, Giovanni Bentivoglio could not have come more promptly to his assistance. Throughout the succeeding hostilities, although Lorenzo frequently doubted his reliability, in fact he never wavered in his support, despite constant fulminations from Rome against him; Bologna provided passage for allied troops coming to the defence of Florence, as well as winter quarters for some of them. As always, Florence, faced by war, found that her major problem was to raise adequate and sufficient mercenaries. Here, again, Lorenzo's personal connections in the Romagna and with the Orsini proved vital.

Equally significant was the moral and diplomatic support proffered by Louis XI to Lorenzo. The French King's immediate response to the Pazzi conspiracy was unequivocal: 'We are much displeased', he informed Sixtus IV, 'at so abominable a sin which we regard as even more grave than if it had been done to our own person, or to the person of one nearly related to us, and we hold that your honour has been most deeply offended.'[40]

Two embassies were sent immediately to Italy; one, under Commynes, to Florence to deliver the King's condolences, and to make contact with various Italian princes in order to form a defensive alliance, and one to Rome. Louis showed his confidence in Lorenzo by granting him full powers to negotiate on his behalf and specifically forbade Commynes to take any action without the fullest possible consultation with Lorenzo. That he regarded this public endorsement by Louis XI as a vital bulwark of his position in Florence, Lorenzo made clear, in June 1479, when the French appeared to be prepared to give way to a papal demand that Florence surrender Borgo San Sepulcro. Knowing that nothing would be more insulting to Florentine pride, Lorenzo wrote immediately to the Florentine ambassador in France, telling him to explain to Louis that it was impossible to accede to such a demand. He continued:

> I have promised these citizens that the King would never consent to any diminution of our honour or state. Do all in your power to prevent it, lest I lose my reputation with these citizens.[41]

On the whole, however, Louis XI once again proved a good friend to the Medici.

Lorenzo saw overt support from such allies and friends as an important symbol of unity. Such unity became a positive obsession with him at this time. The keynote of his diplomacy was always the importance of united and collective action. Thus, again and again, in public debate within Florence, in private conversation, and in his correspondence, he reverted to the idea that 'our great object is to maintain the union of the League in appearance and in reality'.[42]

For this reason he found the position of the Venetians worrying. He was pleased when, in June, he learned that Bembo had been appointed ambassador to Florence for Bembo was, of course, an old friend, but even an old friendship could not disguise the fact that Venice was not wholly committed to supporting Florence or Lorenzo personally. Lorenzo confessed himself bewildered by the situation in a letter written to Giovanni Lanfredini in Venice at the end of June:

> I seem to have entered into a labyrinth with nothing to guide me save hope, and yet I do not know what hope I can have, when, even such grave injuries as we have suffered, cannot persuade (the Venetians) to move. I see that at Rome they understand the humour of Venice and speak sweet words in order to send to sleep him who sleeps already. To tell the truth our affairs could not be in a worse state. It is essential that (Venice) either does something or that it is made clear to us that she neither can nor will act. I see my life, my position, my honour and my property at stake, and from Venice we do not get even a reply.[43]

The reluctance, particularly on the part of Venice, to make too great a commitment to the war, led to constant bickering and haggling among the allies over the hiring and payment of mercenaries. The Venetians, in fact, made so many difficulties over the payment to be made to the Duke of Ferrara as Commander-in-Chief of the allied armies that it was not until September, and then only after a direct personal appeal by Lorenzo, that he could be persuaded to take the field, by which stage the war was already going badly. As Lorenzo, himself, put it: 'all the plans of our enemies succeed and none of ours'.[44] By the autumn, the Milanese also were involved in a major internal political crisis, caused partly by the revolt of Genoa, which had been engineered by Ferrante, and partly by the ambitions of the uncles of the young Duke of Milan, in particular Lodovico Sforza, which brought the Duchy to a state of virtual civil war and forced the Milanese government to withdraw its troops from Tuscany. It was not until September that the situation was resolved when, effectively, Lodovico Sforza became *de facto* ruler of Milan.

Lorenzo, therefore, became the lynch-pin of the war effort and of every diplomatic initiative for peace. There were many such initiatives but all foundered on the papal demand that Lorenzo go in person to Rome to ask forgiveness. Lorenzo had a sufficiently developed sense of humour to relish the fact that he was being asked to seek pardon for having lost a dearly loved brother and for having escaped the assassins himself, but he was convinced that to accede to Sixtus' outrageous demand would be such a blow to his prestige and honour that it would destroy his position within Florence. Nevertheless by February 1479, for the sake of the unity of the League, he was even prepared to accede to this demand:

> If God and the rulers (of Milan) so desire, since I do not want, by making too much of my own position, to destroy any good that can be done nor to place this state in peril. It is very reasonable that, having entered a war because of me, peace for the combatants should be bought at my expense.[45]

To another suggestion, however, he would not agree, and that was a marriage between Count Girolamo Riario and one of his daughters:

> which for many reasons I cannot countenance and particularly because it would not be pleasing to the people as a whole. It would be a burden and a danger to me if I were to contract a marriage, so contrary to custom, with great lords and men, whose condition of life is quite different from mine.[46]

However, one after another, each diplomatic move towards peace foundered. The war dragged on. Lorenzo had never worked so hard nor faced so many dangers as in the spring and summer of 1479. He described the pressures upon him in a letter to Girolamo Morelli from the abbey at Fiesole, where he was staying in an attempt to escape the heat of a Florentine June:

> The plague epidemic grows steadily worse . . . this morning a victim of the disease was buried in the cemetery here, and we, not knowing of it, walked up and down over the grave for more than an hour. But this is one of the least of the dangers we face. We must find means of paying the troops and raising money . . .[47]

Sometimes he did escape to the country or to the baths but he could not leave his problems behind. Even as he rode to Careggi he would be pondering what advice to give to the Ten about the conduct of the war, or wondering what instructions to give his secretaries, concerning the affairs of the Medici bank, or what to write to Florentine ambassadors abroad. Sometimes the only reason for such a trip was work, for Cafaggiolo proved an ideal place at which to hold secret and informal diplomatic talks. Thus, for instance, the Milanese ambassador, Giovanni Antonio Talenti, met Lorenzo on 13 June 1479 at Cafaggiolo on his way to Rome. And even when Lorenzo did get away, he might receive an urgent summons to return to Florence. More often he was simply unable to leave the city when he wanted to. Thus, he wrote, to Clarice at Cafaggiolo on 17 July:

> I had planned to come there this evening and had sent ahead to make the arrangements. Since then so much business has piled up that I will have to stay here. I'm scribbling this note so that you won't look for me.[48]

He must remain in the heat and the stench and the dust of the city, working long hours, often into the night, when he was the only person still at his desk in the Palazzo della Signoria. Many of his letters, in this period, were written in his own hand, for the simple reason that everyone else was too busy to do it for him. Frequently, he undertook to write the official letters of the Ten, as well as his own correspondence.

Predictably enough, he, therefore, fell ill. At the end of August he was attacked by tertian fever and took to his bed. Despite the best efforts of his two doctors, Moses the Jew and Stefano della Torre, the resident doctor to the Medici household, he found it difficult to shake off the fever which lingered on throughout September, making him weak and depressed. 'I have written you a long discourse', he told Morelli on 18 September, 'and since I still have a little fever, it isn't strange if I talk a little nonsense.'[49]

He knew that he was working too hard, yet the work must continue. By the end of the summer, Lorenzo was convinced that Florence's situation was desperate. She could no longer support the twin burdens of plague and warfare, particularly when the war was going badly. The strain was beginning to tell and, not least, on Lorenzo himself. He told Morelli in October:

> For the love of God, Girolamo, have compassion on the infinite problems I have, for it is a wonder that I have not lost what little sense I have. I have written to you only briefly for I know that with you there is no need of words and besides I am so exhausted that I can do no more.[50]

The autumn brought no relief. That Florence was not overwhelmingly defeated was due entirely to the mistakes of her enemies. The Duke of Calabria, commanding the papal and Neapolitan troops captured Poggio Imperiale, and drove the Florentine army in headlong retreat to San Casciano, a bare eight miles from Florence. There was little real obstacle to prevent Alfonso from taking Florence, and if he had shown any of his famed generalship at this moment, the war might well have ended. Fortunately, from Lorenzo's point of view, Alfonso allowed himself to be diverted into blockading Colle Val d'Elsa, one of the most loyal of the Medicean towns. Unexpectedly, Colle put up a spirited resistance, heavy rain hampered military operations, and Alfonso was delayed for two months until 12 November. With winter now upon him the Duke then offered the usual seasonal truce which Florence was only too grateful to accept.

For, as we have seen, it was not only military disaster which faced the city. The countryside had been ravaged by the armies, and the danger of famine was real. This was particularly dangerous for Lorenzo who had always made a point of providing cheap food for the Florentine poor, a policy which, to some extent, explains his popularity with the lower orders of Florentine society. As we have seen, a plague epidemic was raging. There was mounting impatience with the heavy taxation required to pay for a war which had brought Florence nothing but loss of territory, an impatience which, ominously, found expression in the common view that Lorenzo was personally responsible for every Florentine misfortune. Even more ominous was open rioting in the streets. Aware that the war was doing exactly what Sixtus IV had hoped by way of undermining his popularity, Lorenzo resolved to stake everything on one magnificent gesture. He had been toying with the idea since at least May. Then, finally, on 29 November he dispatched Filippo Strozzi on a personal mission to establish whether King Ferrante would treat with him directly.

Having established that Ferrante would not be unwilling to receive him, Lorenzo, accompanied by Niccolò Michelozzi, left Florence en route for Naples on 6 December 1479. The care of his immediate family and of his business interests he entrusted to Antonio Pucci. Over the ensuing weeks Pucci visited Lorenzo's children daily, acted as a co-ordinator of the Medicean party, and kept Lorenzo informed of all developments in Florence. Before leaving, Lorenzo confided in a group of leading citizens whom he told that, since the Pope and the King of Naples continued to hold him alone responsible for the war, he would, by going to Naples, either help to bring about peace or else would find out if there were some other reason for the continuation of the hostilities. He was convinced that once it became apparent that he, personally, was not the sole obstacle to peace, Florence would prosecute the war with more enthusiasm, 'and more unity than we have seen up until now'.[51] The *Signoria* he let know of his intentions only when he had reached San Miniato, when it was already too late to stop him. He explained that he felt a personal obligation to undertake this risky mission, because, 'having a greater position and stake in our city, not only than I deserve, but probably more than any citizen in our days, I am more bound than any other man to give up all for my country, even my life.'[52]

One should not underestimate Lorenzo's courage at this point. By choosing to take independent action and without even an official mandate until one was granted by the Ten on 12 December, he was taking a major risk. His position in Florence would become totally untenable were he to fail. His departure gravely displeased the ever suspicious Venetians who were convinced it was all a put-up job, designed to harm their interests. It equally annoyed the Milanese who had not been advised of his intentions. In addition, by leaving the city he was leaving the Medici party without its head, during a period of grave strain, and it was by no means certain that the regime would survive his absence were it to become prolonged. Many Florentines immediately suggested that Lorenzo was going to Naples not to bring about peace, but to make some secret deal with Ferrante over Medici assets in Naples. Further, it would be wrong to suppose that Lorenzo had much confidence in the double-dealing Ferrante; the King might well imprison or kill him, or might arrest him and dispatch him to Rome. Once again, fatalism alone seemed to impel him forward, a hope that 'God will assist my good plan and allow me to return safely, with honour.'[53] As the war had begun with the shedding of Medici blood, so, logically, God must permit Lorenzo to be the means of ending it.

On 10 December Lorenzo was at Pisa, when the Neapolitan galleys which had been sent to convey him to Naples and which had been delayed by contrary winds, finally arrived. Lorenzo was heartened to discover on board Gian Tomaso Carafa, the son of an old friend, Diomede Carafa, one of the most influential men at the Neapolitan court. Also on board was Prinzivalle di Gennaro, a close adviser of the Duke of Calabria's. It was a hopeful sign, in Lorenzo's view, 'for their status is such as would honour a greater man than myself'.[54] Entrusting his future and that of his mission entirely to God, he set sail on 14 December.

Four days later he reached Naples where, according to the Milanese ambassadors he was received, 'with as much honour and dignity as possible'[55] and was lodged in the Medici bank, which, on Ferrante's instructions and at his expense, had been completely refurbished. The King himself was away hunting but returned on the following day. Lorenzo rode out to meet him about a mile from the city, to be received with a great outward display of cordiality and friendliness.

Ferrante, in fact, was anxious to negotiate. His own financial position was very weak, he had trouble with his major feudatories, and he recognised that the recent resolution of the internal political crisis of Milan meant that she would now be in a position to offer more help to her old ally. Furthermore, there were worrying signs that France was about to give more than moral support to Florence and might actively intervene in the affairs of Italy. René of Lorraine was already threatening to revive the Angevin claim to Naples. On Monday, 20 December, the King received Lorenzo in the presence of Diomede Carafa and Antonello Petrucci. After a few brief introductory remarks, Ferrante referred Lorenzo to a written document which was read aloud by Petrucci. This document stated Ferrante's earnest desire for peace but explained that he was unable to break agreements which he had entered into with the Pope and the Sienese. Lorenzo suggested that, in order not to waste time, the King should be more specific about what terms he was actually offering. It was agreed that negotiation would proceed on this basis.

Progress, however, was agonisingly slow. The King continued to treat Lorenzo with every possible sign of honour and spoke of his affection for Florence and his desire for peace. Lorenzo's old friend, Ippolita Maria, Duchess of Calabria, with whom he spent many happy hours, brought all her influence to bear on Florence's behalf. The Pope, however, remained obstinately hostile to any idea of a peace which did not involve the public humiliation of Lorenzo, and Lorenzo's conception of his own honour forbade any such possibility. Florence also, through Lorenzo, made difficulties by insisting on the complete restoration of all territories seized from her during the war.

Lorenzo endured many anxious weeks. His friends in Florence served him well and kept him regularly informed of all that occurred but their letters did not make comfortable reading. With the exception of the commendably phlegmatic Antonio Pucci who refused to panic without cause and told Lorenzo to 'stay happy because our affairs could not go better, just as you would like',[56] they were all preoccupied by the danger which Lorenzo's continued absence was causing the regime. Thus, Angelo della Stufa spoke for them all when, at the end of January, he admitted that, 'the length of these negotiations means that I am constantly worried. I long for your return. I do not know what to do . . .'[57]

Criticism of the regime was widespread, these friends told Lorenzo. Two citizens were arrested and exiled for publicly attacking the government. Pucci made light of the incident. 'Our affairs are very fine', he told Lorenzo, 'and we are more united than we have ever been. . . . your family are all well. Never a day passes without my seeing Piero and Giovanni. . . . I am enclosing a letter from Piero; he makes good use of his time. Giovanni goes readily to bed at an early hour, and he says he never moves all night. He is fat and looks well. . . . Our friends are all well.'[58] Cheerful letters of this nature were, however, few and far between. More frequently Lorenzo was warned that, by staying away, he was daily losing influence and friends. Although Florence remained outwardly calm, Scala told him, 'many different thoughts and words are being expressed both by your friends and by all manner of people'.[59]

By February matters were critical, as even Pucci admitted. Lorenzo was now being pressurised by his home government to accept peace on virtually any terms, and by his friends to return to Florence without delay. On 5 February Pucci warned that Bembo was actively intriguing for the election of an anti-Milanese, pro-Venetian *Signoria* which, inevitably, would be anti-Medicean. Pucci himself was convinced 'that without your personal intervention nothing would have been done and no progress

A portrait medallion by Niccolò Fiorentino depicts Lorenzo. The reverse shows the figure of Florence holding a lily – the symbol of the city – and protected by a laurel tree

made in this affair, since things were in such a bad way',[60] and was certain there were others who agreed with him. 'However', he concluded grimly, 'there are few of them.'[61] Now he advised Lorenzo to return to Florence immediately. Scala also advised Lorenzo that few in Florence believed he could secure an honourable peace and that those opposed to the Medicean regime had taken heart from the situation. In his opinion, he told Lorenzo bluntly, 'it is essential that you should be here, lest by making peace there, you raise a worse war here'.[62]

Despite these warnings, it was not until he was certain of peace terms which were not totally to Florence's disadvantage, and which did not include the demand that he go in person to Rome, that Lorenzo would leave Naples. It was the night of 27–28 February when he finally slipped away to board ship at Gaeta. He endured a stormy and dangerous return journey and was in genuine fear for his life before his ship touched Pisa on 13 March where he said: 'I was received with such great joy and kindness that I was amazed. I hope the same will be true at Florence and I will be welcome to all.'[63]

He need not have worried. The Florentine longing for peace was such that Lorenzo was given a hero's welcome. More than 150 men, including the Venetian, Milanese, Bolognese and Ferrarese ambassadors, the chancellors of Roberto Malatesta, Constanzo Sforza, and Antonello da Forli, 'as well as all the rest of us citizens', according to Angelo della Stufa, rode out from Florence to meet him, honouring him as a prince, 'so that you never saw in Florence a finer squadron nor a greater honour than this of his Magnificence'.[64]

Despite the fact that the peace which was actually concluded at Naples on 13 March was, in fact, more favourable to Milan than to Florence, it was still regarded as a triumph for Lorenzo's personal diplomacy. The restoration of the occupied Florentine territories was to be arbitrated by the King of Naples, a *condotta* was to be paid to the Duke of Calabria, and the Pazzi imprisoned at Volterra were to be released. No mention was made in the peace treaty of Florence's claim to Sarzana, which had been seized by the Genoese. Nevertheless, the Florentines were too war-weary to do other than rejoice at the absence of hostilities. Convinced anti-Mediceans might grumble in private and mutter about secret clauses and Florentine dishonour; but the Ten reported that the news of the peace was received in Florence, 'with incredible joy and both in public and in private there have been quite unprecedented celebrations'.[65]

Lorenzo, for his part, rejoiced to be home among his family and friends. When he heard that Luigi Guicciardini, Florentine ambassador to Venice, was anxious to return to Florence, he told him:

I, also, have had the same desire to come home and I was not away as long as you. I will do all that I can with the Ten to arrange for your return and I expect a speedy success. I long to see you for many reasons and you will find me the same Lorenzo you left, indeed even more loving to you since I daily learn to esteem more and to love better friends of your calibre.[66]

All that he longed for now was for the lifting of the ecclesiastical censures against himself and the city. He hoped against hope to be permitted to make his confession and take communion at Easter, but the Pope continued to refuse. The excommunication and interdict remained, although partially suspended in April. Assistance, when it arrived, came from an unexpected source. In August the Ottomans captured Otranto and Sixtus IV, faced with the possibility of a Muslim invasion of Italy, suddenly remembered his responsibilities as the head of Christendom. He urged all the Italian powers to join together to resist the infidel, and informed the Florentines that, were a delegation to be sent from the city to sue for pardon, that pardon would be granted, even if Lorenzo were not a member of it.

In December, therefore, seated before St Peter's, in purple robes and wearing the papal tiara, Sixtus IV received twelve Florentine commissioners. Touching each of them with his staff, he symbolically cleansed them and, by implication, the whole Florentine population, including Lorenzo. Only now, after more than two years of anguish and struggle, had Lorenzo achieved a personal peace with both God and man.

6

LORENZO AS PATRON OF ART AND LETTERS

The tendency of modern historians to emphasise the difficulties encountered by the Medici bank in the years after 1468, sometimes obscures one of the basic facts about Lorenzo de' Medici. He was an immensely wealthy man and, from birth, was surrounded by every luxury known to his contemporaries. Deprivation was simply never a part of his experience and nor was asceticism. Although he projected an image of himself as a man who led a life of sobriety and simplicity, the fact remains that he always enjoyed the good things of life: wine, food, music, books and beautiful surroundings, and that he positively delighted in spending money.

Such sentiments his humanist tutors would have applauded. The new learning – in fifteenth-century Italy at least – had little sympathy for medieval values based on a contempt for money and on the exaltation of poverty. Wealth, on the contrary, was now seen as a desirable thing, the rich as people to be courted. For more than a generation, humanists, like the Neapolitan, Giovanni Pontano, who held Cosimo de' Medici to be the model of the perfect citizen, had taught that those who possessed wealth should not despise, but use it, cultivating the virtues of generosity, magnificence, liberality and splendour, using their money to build large and luxurious houses, offering open hospitality to friends, clients and dependants. The humanists thus elaborated their paradigm of Renaissance patronage, providing the ideology required to justify the vast system of relief which maintained the indigent scholars, the aspiring artists, the musicians, and the creative intellectuals, whose activities, together, produced that cultural shift which we call the Renaissance. This was also a pattern of behaviour which, along with the rest of the Medici patrimony, Lorenzo simply inherited since, as we have seen, the Medici party was bound together through a series of patron-client relationships.

Inherently, that is, the relationship of the Medici with artists and writers was no different from their relationship with other clients but, whereas Lorenzo might find more purely political clients an irksome burden, he always revelled in the role of patron of the arts. For him it was a pleasant means of consolidating and increasing political power, and he is unlikely to have seen any incongruity in a system which used the arts to achieve political ends. Much of the success of the early Renaissance had depended on the fact that, throughout Italy, men of Cosimo de' Medici's generation came to see that their political reputations might be considerably enhanced, and their power correspondingly increased, by a judicious patronage of scholars, writers and artists. It was also commonly acknowledged that fame of an enduring nature could be purchased only by such patronage, and, in his childhood, Lorenzo had been brought up on stories such as that of Alexander the Great who was reputed to have declared before the tomb of Achilles, 'Fortunate art thou to have so glorious a sepulchre and to have been sung by such a pen.'[1] Lorenzo quickly learned to draw the appropriate moral that, 'without the divine poet Homer, Achilles' body and fame would have been buried in one tomb together'.[2]

Although Lorenzo's role as patron of art and letters was to some degree simply an inherited one, differences in the style of their patronage do exist between Lorenzo and his father and grandfather and these may be identified by the different quality of the relationship which each enjoyed, as an individual, with Marsilio Ficino. Lorenzo, as we have seen, had been exposed to the experience of Neo-Platonism from birth, whereas for both Cosimo and for Piero di Cosimo a knowledge of Neo-Platonic philosophy was acquired later in their lives. Ficino had been a Medici client ever since 1456 when Cosimo first read his *Institutiones ad Platonicam Disciplinam* and advised the young author to perfect his knowledge of Greek. He gave Ficino a villa at Careggi and ordered him to devote all his energies to the study of Plato. Piero proved an equally beneficent patron but neither he nor Cosimo had the inner understanding of Platonic philosophy which Lorenzo developed as a vital source of his own creativity.

Thus, while Ficino was an inheritance from the Medici past, he became for Lorenzo much more – a friend, a fellow-scholar, a man who could share his most passionate interests. Throughout his life, Lorenzo would maintain Ficino, pay him deference, acquire books and manuscripts for him and protect him from every enemy and detractor, particularly those of the ecclesiastical establishment. But, at the same time, he would always treat Ficino with the warmth and generosity of true friendship. Such comradeship added a new dimension to the patron's role.

Ficino, therefore, was emotionally essential to Lorenzo, his companionship an intellectual necessity, and similar relationships existed between Lorenzo and other writers and artists. Yet this new element in a patronage relationship should not blind us to the fact that a traditional structure also remained. Ficino, for instance, was a useful political tool for he played a considerable part in creating the image of Lorenzo as a great patron which, while in general terms true, also contained a large element of artifice. Ficino was no fool when it came to providing for the practical necessities of life and enjoyed his comforts as much as the next man. He was, therefore, always meticulously fulsome in his praise of Lorenzo whom he addressed with such adulatory phrases as, 'restorer of the Platonic discipline' and 'hope of the fatherland'.[3] Visions, created by Ficino, of Lorenzo, the hope of learning, creator of a golden age in which the arts could flourish, conveyed immense prestige on his patron, coming as it did from a man of international standing, cynosure for the eyes of all learned Europe.

Here, then, we come face-to-face with the central problem posed by Lorenzo's role as art-patron, for, in this role, he may be regarded in two contradictory lights. He may be seen either as sincerely preoccupied with the arts and with learning, or as using them as part of the process of political management by means of which he dominated Florence. Thus, we know that, when it was a question of organising tournaments, carnival tableaux, or other public festivities, Lorenzo regularly employed distinguished artists of the stature of Antonio Pollaiuolo, Verrocchio and Botticelli, to paint standards, chase armour, design triumphal arches and to create other decorative ephemera. Such employment may be regarded either as an inspired contribution by Lorenzo to a now lost but once genuine and original art-form – the Renaissance public festival – or, as many contemporary critics suggested, it may more properly be viewed as just another means of manipulating the Florentines, diverting them with circuses in order to encourage acquiescence in the Medici regime.

That political considerations did play a major role seems difficult to dispute. At first, as we have seen, Lorenzo had an ambivalent attitude to public festivities since he was afraid that they might become a means of attacking the prestige of the Medici. Such festivities might prove a vehicle for other families, or even the Florentine commune itself, to assert their values and their honour in public; but as his control over Florence grew, so Lorenzo's attitude relaxed. Particularly after 1488, by which time Lorenzo was convinced that no other family could challenge Medicean hegemony, the streets of Florence were, we are invited to believe, always full of happy, festive crowds, devoted to one purpose only, the celebration of the Medici family by an endless chorus of street songs. These songs were performed by new groups. The aristocratic *brigate*, the family celebrations typical of Lorenzo's youth, had given way to lower-class, neighbourhood or occupation groups, often known as Baronies or Principalities. Such, for instance, was the Company of the Star, directly dependent on Lorenzo's patronage, which, during carnival, performed his songs throughout Florence enacting *tableaux* and masques like that of 1490 with its 'seven triumphs, and a thousand beautiful things and inventions'[4] for which Lorenzo composed one of the loveliest of all his carnival songs; the *Canzona dei Sette Pianeti*.

Even the feast of San Giovanni – St John the Baptist – came to be accepted once it had been transformed. Played down in the years immediately after 1478, in the later years of Lorenzo's life it came to be

The frontispiece of the 1497 *Canzone per andare in maschera* may illustrate
Lorenzo during Carnival

stage-managed in such a way that the celebrations ceased to be a traditional communal festival and became instead a Medici triumph. Lorenzo
became willing to lavish expenditure upon it once more. Increasingly, it
became more and more glamorous until it culminated in the success of
1491 when the celebrations included a *Triumph of Aemilius Paulus*, returning victorious from the East. According to a contemporary:

> Lorenzo de' Medici having conceived the idea, he had the Company of
> the Star construct fifteen *triofi* designed by him. They showed Aemilius
> Paulus triumphing in Rome, on returning there from a city with so
> much treasure that Rome's populace never paid taxes for forty or fifty
> years, so much treasure had he conquered. There were fifteen *trionfi*
> with many, many ornaments. As Aemilius Paulus had provided such
> booty at the time of Caesar Augustus, Lorenzo de' Medici provided it
> now.[5]

It was not the subtlest of political messages but at least it was a clear
one.

A similar problem of motivation also arises in connection with Lorenzo's habit of writing songs for performance during carnival. Should we
say that he did so because he was genuinely interested in the verse forms
of popular poetry? His own writing on the vernacular certainly suggests
that this was the case. No one would dispute Lorenzo's passionate
commitment to the Tuscan tongue and this commitment is reflected in his
activities as a patron. In this area, at least he was confident enough to give
specific instructions to clients as, for instance, in 1480, when he ordered
Landino to write a commentary on Dante's *Divine Comedy* which would
serve for a defence of the use of the vernacular.

On the other hand, there is evidence which indicates that what was
involved in Lorenzo's own writing of carnival songs was a subtle form of
political management of the Florentine masses. The content of such songs
in many cases, certainly suggests that they were a powerful vehicle for
Medici propaganda, and they must, logically, be connected with that
tendency, which we have already noted on Lorenzo's part, to encourage
actively the development of popular brotherhoods, confraternities and
social clubs, based upon neighbourhood allegiance. These organisations
were directly dependent on Lorenzo's patronage and linked with the
Medici name. In 1489, for instance, he lent his support to the wool-
workers of Oltrarno, which, significantly enough, was traditionally an
anti-Medicean area of the city, in their celebration of May Day, loaning
them silver and plate from the Medici collection.

The significance of such loans is that they acted directly as an advertise-
ment of Medici power for each item, of course, prominently displayed the
Medici arms. It was important to Lorenzo to make the Medici *palle*
synonymous with the idea of Florence; to replace, in the popular imagina-

tion, the traditional communal symbols of the lily and the lion with the Medici roundels. That this was a deliberate act of policy is indicated by the number of requests which were made to Lorenzo, particularly from outside Florence, for money for the upkeep of buildings on which the Medici arms were displayed, or the repair of chapels or altar-cloths which also boasted the Medici *palle*. Such petitions for favours often suggest that the Medici arms are invested with a semi-mystical protective quality. Thus, for instance, the priors of a hospital at Empoli assured Lorenzo that the prominent display of the Medici arms throughout their buildings 'has been so useful that without them we should certainly have come to harm, to the detriment, damage and shame of our company and hospital'.[6]

The issue of motivation arises again in the context of Lorenzo's patronage of practitioners of the visual arts. He certainly assisted Florentine painters, sculptors and architects to find commissions outside Florence. Giuliano da San Gallo, for instance, he recommended to the King of Naples, Filippino Lippi to Matthias Corvinus, and Andrea Sansovino to the King of Portugal. He sent Antonio Pollaiuolo to work for Innocent VIII on the tomb of Sixtus IV and Benedetto da Maiano on a number of artistic missions. It was probably as a result of his advice that, in 1481, Botticelli was invited to Rome to decorate the Sistine chapel. How important a recommendation from Lorenzo might be in the career of an artist was unconsciously revealed by Cardinal Carafa, to whom Lorenzo had recommended Filippino Lippi, for Carafa told a colleague, 'Even had Master Filippo not been as sufficient as he is, having been commended by the Magnificent Lorenzo, we would have placed him above an Apelles, or all Italy.'[7]

Lorenzo, was, therefore, important in promoting artists' careers and many had good reason to be grateful to him. What, however, is not clear is why he chose to assist them in this particular way. Was he displaying a genuine interest in their well-being or was he merely engaged in cultural propaganda on behalf of Florence? He would certainly have liked the world at large to think of Florence as the centre of the civilised world, and of himself as the leading promoter of arts and letters. Like many contemporary Florentines, he believed that the age of Rome was ended and that her role would be taken over by a Florence which would become in the words of Benedetto Dei 'a new Rome'.[8] As ancient Rome's greatness had been reflected in and created by the honour she paid to artists and writers since 'the nutriment of every art is honour, and by the desire of glory alone are men's minds spurred to produce admirable works',[9] so should Florence's new greatness be reflected in and created by the esteem in which her artists and writers were held. According to the testimony of Benedetto da Maiano, Lorenzo even had a scheme to bring this about. Benedetto records that:

In 1490 I completed a commission for the Magnificent for the bust of Giotto in the church of Santa Maria del Fiore, and, at the same time, a more perfectly modelled bust of the Medici organist, Antonio Squarcialupi. According to the Magnificent, the cathedral which housed, among others, the remains of Brunelleschi, Giotto and Landino ought to become the Pantheon of Florence.[10]

But the artistic interests of Florence were not always uppermost in Lorenzo's mind. Political considerations often weighed very heavily indeed in his behaviour towards artists. Thus, for instance, on 21 April 1487 Filippo Strozzi commissioned from Filippino Lippi certain frescoes for Santa Maria Novella which Filippino undertook to complete before 1 March 1490. Long before this date, however, Lorenzo had intervened to persuade Strozzi to release Filippino Lippi from his engagement. The reason was a straightforward political one. Lippi was wanted in Rome by Cardinal Carafa to decorate his chapel in Santa Maria della Minerva, and Carafa was a person of considerable influence with the reigning pontiff, Innocent VIII, with whom Lorenzo was anxious to remain on cordial terms.

The same problem is raised if we look at the question of the assistance which Lorenzo gave to artists, musicians and scholars from abroad. When, as in the case of Master Stephen the Organist, he came equipped with commendatory letters from the King and Queen of Hungary, one is certainly justified in suspecting that Lorenzo's assistance owed less to Stephen's musical abilities – although they were genuine enough – than to the status of his patron. On the other hand, it is significant that foreign rulers were convinced that Lorenzo was both sufficiently discerning and sufficiently powerful to be able to put pressure on contemporary artists and musicians. Thus, for instance, as early as 1473, when King Ferrante wished a young Neapolitan to train as a musician under Antonio Squarcialupi, he addressed himself directly to Lorenzo, 'because we know the said Master Antonio is entirely a creature of yours'.[11]

Ultimately the answer to all the problems raised here, and to the overriding problem of the contribution made by Lorenzo to the development of the Florentine Renaissance, will remain a question of interpretation. Our view of what Lorenzo was about as a patron of the arts and of learning will depend on the way in which we interpret his personality, or assess the role that he played in Florentine social and political life. But the area of debate and disagreement can be narrowed. First, we should admit that, on every occasion, Lorenzo's patronage was likely to be more than a purely disinterested support of art for art's sake. In addition, we may come to understand more about the nature of Lorenzo's patronage and the effect of that on the evolution of Florentine culture, by analysing, in more detail, the specific forms which his patronage took.

It used to be assumed that Lorenzo was personally responsible for creating, single-handed, the golden age of the Florentine Renaissance. To him was credited the commissioning of virtually every major work of art produced in Florence during his lifetime. According to this view it was his discerning eye alone which was responsible for the discovery of Botticelli, Michelangelo and Leonardo. Subsequently, it was demonstrated how little, in fact, Lorenzo could be shown, conclusively, to have commissioned, and opinion swung so far in the opposite direction that, in the recent past, some critics have even seemed to believe that the Florentine Renaissance happened despite rather than because of Lorenzo.

It has been argued, in this context, that whereas the patronage of his grandfather and his father was directed largely to public ends, Lorenzo's patronage was designed to satisfy only his personal interests and desires; that, in essence, their patronage was communal, his aristocratic. That this was by no means the whole story can be demonstrated by looking at those areas in which we know Lorenzo to have had an unfeigned personal interest: architecture, book-collecting, music, vernacular writing and the collection of ancient gems, cameos and *objets d'art*.

Lorenzo did not build on the scale of his grandfather although towards the end of his life he appears to have been planning to do so. He was hampered by a lack of money and a fear of alienating public opinion within Florence by too ostentatious a display of Medici power before that power had become generally acceptable. What he did build – like his villa at Poggio   lay largely outside the city of Florence. This does not, however, mean that Lorenzo did not have an effect on the development of Florentine Renaissance architecture.

His own interest in the subject was profound, his knowledge such as to make him an acknowledged expert. As early as 1468 he was invited by the Board of Works of the Cathedral, along with other 'venerable citizens and the best and most skilled masters'[12] to advise on the placing of the ball on the cupola of Santa Maria del Fiore. The group of advisers, which included Luca della Robbia, Andrea Verrocchio and Antonio Pollaiuolo, can hardly be described as artistically undistinguished and it says something about Lorenzo's early interest in architecture that he was invited to participate in their deliberations.

That interest never left him. He himself submitted a design for the uncompleted façade of Florence's cathedral in 1491, was consulted about the design for the new sacristy of Santo Spirito, was deeply involved in the design of the fortress at Volterra, and even more deeply involved in the design of the church of Santa Maria delle Carceri at Prato in 1485. The choice of a design for the latter was determined by open competition which gave rise to prolonged discussion among the citizens of Prato. So heated did tempers become that the question was referred to Lorenzo for resolution. Twice he had to travel to Prato to see the plans and to listen to the views of all the interested parties. Finally, he summoned representatives of the citizenry of Prato to Florence to resolve the matter and, when they left the decision to him, he chose the plan of his own favoured architect, Giuliano da San Gallo.

He was as interested in the theory of architecture as in the practice. New buildings fascinated him. In 1481 he asked the Florentine architect, Baccio Pontelli, to send him detailed plans of the Duke of Urbino's new palace and, in August 1485, he asked for a model of Alberti's new church of San Sebastiano in Mantua to be sent to him. During the following month he was at the baths of San Filippo but still much interested in architectural problems. He was having Alberti's *Architecture* read aloud to him with a view to supporting its publication. At first only a part of the manuscript was available, but so absorbed did Lorenzo become in it that the rest had to be hurriedly copied in Florence and sent on to him at San Filippo. The importance of this particular manuscript to Lorenzo is confirmed by the fact that, when, in 1484, he agreed to lend it to Ercole d'Este, he did so only on condition of a quick return, 'because I hold it very dear and read it often'.[13] Lorenzo's intense interest in architectural theory at this particular period must, of course, be related to the building of Poggio a Caiano, a project in which he had become both so emotionally and intellectually involved that, as he told Michelozzi, 'I think of nothing else by day or night'.[14]

Given Lorenzo's political position, his passionate interest in the new forms of architecture could only encourage others to employ them. When he could not afford to build, others, like Filippo Strozzi, could and did. Those who did so took the sensible precaution of consulting with Lorenzo about their projects and, as he was not slow to proffer advice, it would be foolish to deny that he had a profound influence on shaping the urban face of Florence.

Equally, his prominent role in government ensured that Lorenzo's views would specifically influence communal projects. Giuliano da San Gallo, as we have seen, was Lorenzo's favourite architect and it was this which determined the choice of San Gallo as architect for the building of the fortress of Poggio Imperiale. Lorenzo's influence must also be seen in the choice of San Gallo as architect for the cloister and convent of the Cestello, paid for by his son-in-law Iacopo Salviati and for the church and convent of the Augustinians whose head was Lorenzo's favourite preacher, Mariano da Genezzano.

A natural development of Lorenzo's interest in architecture was his fascination with urbanism, one of the most fashionable and characteristic of Renaissance concerns. His contemporaries were well aware of this particular interest and Machiavelli commented on Lorenzo's wish to build new streets in the unoccupied part of Florence, which he believed to be part of a more general plan 'to make the city greater and more beautiful'.[15] It seems highly likely that he would indeed have liked to remodel the street plan of Florence to make it conform to fashionable theories about the necessity for regularity and uniformity. Here, however, he was faced with a major political difficulty, for the Italian experience suggests that, to impose such urbanistic plans, it was essential to have a political situation such as that which existed at Rome and Ferrara, where power was concentrated in the hands of one individual. The communal and corporate values of cities such as Florence were always a hindrance to such schemes and projects.

What he could do, however, Lorenzo did. At the time of his death, he was planning to build a villa, designed by Giuliano and Antonio da San Gallo, situated in the north-east part of Florence and of a scale that anticipated the grandiose projects executed by the later Medici grand-dukes. As conceived it would have occupied an area about as large as the Pitti palace and the Boboli gardens and would have marked, in concrete form, the reality of Medicean domination over Florence. Although never executed, the project was, in a sense, begun, in that a complete reworking of the urban fabric of Florence was undertaken in the Via Laura and Borgo Pitti area and this, in turn, acted as a stimulus to private building in the area. New streets were laid out and constructed on Lorenzo's instructions, and at his expense. By the end of July 1491, he had ordered 'the construction of a new street from the church of the Servites to that of the Cestello, along the house and garden of the Innocenti, in order to furnish it with houses'.[16] This was the Via Laura on which, by the end of the year, four new houses were already being erected, Lorenzo's intention being to hand them over to the Bankers' Guild in exchange for certain properties which Giovanni di Cosimo de' Medici had left them for charitable purposes. The record of this agreement is quite explicit about Lorenzo's motivations in pursuing this project for it records that Lorenzo, 'in the manner of his ancestors, decided to make the city larger and more beautiful and to have many houses built in it for rent'.[17] Once again, we find Lorenzo acting in conscious imitation of his grandfather, Cosimo.

A similar desire to behave like Cosimo – father of the fatherland – no doubt influenced Lorenzo in his activities as a book-collector, but a strong personal interest probably played a greater role. At the time of Piero di Cosimo's death the Medici library already contained more than two hundred volumes. In adding to this collection Lorenzo who, even as an adolescent, used to ask his friends for copies of rare manuscripts, did far more than either Piero or Cosimo. Already, in 1472, he was toying with the idea of building a completely new library to house his growing collection which, at the time of his death, contained more than a thousand books and manuscripts. He was a discriminating and purposeful purchaser. Books figure prominently in his correspondence which provides ample evidence that Lorenzo had specific interests and projects and was not just interested in acquiring works indiscriminately.

Neither Cosimo nor Piero, for instance, had purchased Greek manuscripts and Lorenzo thought that, in consequence, there was a serious *lacuna* in the Medici collection. He, therefore, employed several agents to purchase manuscripts in the eastern Mediterranean, including Lascaris who acquired more than two hundred codices of which at least eighty were previously unknown in western Europe. His sense of the value of specific collections meant that Lorenzo was particularly disappointed when he failed to purchase the unique collection which Andronicus Callistos was forced to sell.

As well as agents in the eastern Mediterranean, Lorenzo paid calligraphers in Venice, Naples, Ferrara, Padua and Rome to copy particularly rare manuscripts and especially ones of which no other copy existed in Florence. Poliziano and other humanists were paid to seek out such works, and Lorenzo's enthusiasm in this area remained undimmed by the passage of time. He was even more active in his later years than he had been in his youth and, on his death-bed, one of his few expressed regrets was that his library was still not as good as he had intended it to be.

Many of Lorenzo's books and manuscripts were exquisitely illustrated and decorated by the leading exponents of what was, increasingly, to become a dying art, that of the miniaturist. For someone as myopic as Lorenzo the attractions of this art-form are obvious and it is interesting that he began his activities as a patron of miniaturists very early when, in 1466, he commissioned Antonio del Chierico and his son Francesco to illustrate several manuscripts for him. One of his most favoured miniaturists, thereafter, Francesco d'Antonio, produced many works for Lorenzo of which one of the most attractive is an Office of the Virgin whose precious binding is decorated by a frieze made up of Lorenzo's motto, 'Le tens [sic] revient'. Another favoured miniaturist was Attavante degli Attavanti whose illuminated manuscripts were frequently gifts to Lorenzo from his friends. They included Ficino's famous *Life of Plato*, illuminated by Attavante with all the emblems and symbols beloved of Lorenzo and presented to him as a Christmas gift in 1477, and Ficino's *De Triplici Vita*, illustrated by Attavante and given to Lorenzo by Francesco Valori in 1489.

In his book-collecting, therefore, Lorenzo was certainly pursuing a private interest and passion but there was, nevertheless, once again a public dimension to his activities. Thus, he was always generous to scholars and the Medici library was put at the disposal of humanists like Ficino, Lascaris and Poliziano, who wished to study there. Their increasingly erudite scholarship, on which so much of Florentine Renaissance culture was built was, thus, to a great extent, dependent on the Medici library.

Yet, problems remain in assessing the significance of Lorenzo's un-doubted generosity towards scholars and writers. Certainly, he main-tained and protected men like Poliziano, Ficino, Matteo Franco, Luigi Pulci, Girolamo Benivieni and Pico della Mirandola but, with the excep-tion of Ficino and Pico, it is not clear that they were maintained or befriended because they were writers and scholars. Indeed, Lorenzo seems rather to have regarded them as men-of-all-work about the Medici household, clients who could fill in as secretaries, tutors, messengers, baby-sitters and political servants as the need arose. They were employed because they were literate and congenial company rather than from some altruistic desire to promote their writings. Indeed, the demands which Lorenzo made on their time must have hampered their writing as often as his provision of free board and lodging encouraged it. Poliziano was describing the situation of all the Medici clients and not just his own when, in 1479, he remarked that:

> I shall always be at the beck and call of Lorenzo as I am sure he knows better than I, and that he will put me in an honourable position as he always has done and as my fidelity and good services merit.[18]

Another example of a client-friend upon whom Lorenzo often made conflicting demands was the poet Matteo Franco who entered Medici service in about 1474. An excellent vernacular poet and true rival to Luigi Pulci, for the rest of his life Franco was to find his experience interwoven with that of the Medici family. It was he who taught Lorenzo's children to read, he who was adept at soothing Clarice, he who was a preferred companion for journeys or trips into the country. So valued was he that Lorenzo even entrusted his daughter Maddalena into his care when she left for Rome to marry Franceschotto Cibo. As far as Lorenzo was concerned, Franco was, 'one of the first and dearest creatures of my household'[19] but one suspects that it was Franco's domestic rather than his poetic gifts which earned him that honoured place near his 'sacred laurel' and the benefice after benefice which Lorenzo heaped upon him by way of reward.

A more serious criticism which has been made of Lorenzo is that his increasingly autocratic policies stifled rather than encouraged Florentine humanism, that the decline in the active and relatively democratic parti-cipation in Florentine politics, associated with the consolidation of Medici power, led directly to a decline in that civic humanism which had been the triumph of Florence's early Renaissance. This is reflected not only in a notable reduction in the number of humanists and *literati* holding impor-tant political office in Florence, but also in changing attitudes towards politics and government. Later fifteenth-century humanists, it has been argued, came more and more to praise the contemplative rather than the active life, as Petrarch had done a century earlier, and to admire the things of the mind and the spirit before the things of this world. One example of this trend which is always given, is the case of Matteo Palmieri who began his literary career by writing the *Vita Civile*, recommending all citizens to engage actively in politics, but who about the time that he entered the Medici circle, composed his *Città di Vita*, a panegyric of the virtues of the contemplative life. Nor was Palmieri alone; in Florence many humanists became increasingly concerned with philosophical matters and their active involvement in government declined.

This is an accurate description of a cultural change which did occur in Florence. Lorenzo's lifetime coincided with a period in which the serene faith in 'The Earthly Republic', which had been preached by Salutati, Bruni and Alberti, gave way to a different state of mind, one characterised by unease and by a desire to escape from the realities of earthly life. Escapism took different forms; the Neo-Platonism of Ficino, Pico, Landino and Palmieri, the asceticism of Savonarola, the fantasy of Pulci and the imaginings of Poliziano. Lorenzo, himself, as his *Altercazione* reveals, shared in this intellectual and spiritual crisis, but whether that crisis was brought about by his increasingly autocratic style of political management is open to question. It was a crisis which was an Italian, never a purely Florentine, phenomenon, and not even the most convinced Lorenzo-hater has yet suggested that the dead hand of his disapproval could reach far beyond the confines of Florence's borders. Nor is an ambivalence in attitude towards the active and the contemplative life confined to the Laurentian age. It had been present, for instance, in the work of Boccaccio a century earlier and would recur in the future. Indeed, it is probable that in any age a belief in the superiority of the contemplative to the active life, and that of the active to the contemplative, is held simultaneously not sequentially. In the age of Lorenzo it created a kind of cultural tension which appears to have been creative rather than destructive since it was out of such tensions that some of the greatest Renaissance works were to flow.

Music also played a vital part in this Renaissance culture. It had, of course, always been one of the most important public arts in Florence where music played a large part in the life of the commune. As we have seen, from childhood Lorenzo had always delighted in music which he was probably taught by Antonio Squarcialupi, the organist at Florence's cathedral. As early as 1467 Squarcialupi spoke with affection and admiration of Lorenzo who 'takes a passionate delight in music as he does in all the other arts'.[20] In that same year Lorenzo's career as a patron of musicians appears to have begun for, on his behalf, Squarcialupi sent Dufay the song, 'Amor chai visto ciascun mio pensiero' asking him to set it to music.

A gift for music was, fortunately, an hereditary trait in the Medici family for it was a gift which was essential for a man absorbed, as Lorenzo was, in the problem of vernacular writing. Contemporary Florentine poetry was inextricably bound up with music. Ballads, carnival songs, madrigals, *rispetti* and *strambotti* were all designed for performance to musical accompaniment. Thus Lorenzo, simply by being a writer of vernacular poetry, inevitably gave employment to contemporary musicians for, although he could write and perform his own accompaniments, it was usual for him to hand his poems to other composers to work on. His favoured lutanist, at first, was Squarcialupi, but he normally kept with him other improvisers like Antonio di Guido or Ser Mezzante.

Apart from his natural talent and taste, Lorenzo was bound by his commitment to Neo-Platonism to encourage music and musicians, for the Platonists held that musical harmony was a reflexion of divine harmony and that there was a moral obligation to replicate that divine harmony on earth. Music was thus another central, personal interest in Lorenzo's life. But, as always, his personal interests could not fail to touch the public world of Florence. When, for instance, Squarcialupi died in 1473, it fell to Lorenzo to find a substitute for the post of cathedral organist. To find a successor of equal musical ability required knowledge, power and skill in the arts of persuasion. Ultimately, Lorenzo was successful. In 1480 it was he who summoned the famous composer and ex-pupil of Squarcialupi, Heinrich Isaac, from Ferrara to Florence to serve as master of the chapel of San Giovanni and cathedral organist. It was an inspired choice which ensured that Florence would win international fame as an advanced centre of music. Again, however, the public and the private blended as Isaac rapidly became more of a Medici client than an employee of the Florentine state. A close intimate of the Medici family, he taught Lorenzo's children music and was entrusted by him with the task of writing music to accompany the performance of his *San Giovanni and Paolo*. Faithful to the end, it was Isaac who set to music the lament, written by Poliziano, on the death of Lorenzo with its haunting last lines:

> Heu! miser! miser!
> O dolor, dolor

which remains the most touching of all memorials to Lorenzo's activities as a patron of the arts.

Another genuine passion of Lorenzo's was his love of antiquities, particularly cameos and engraved stones and Greek and Roman coins. As we have seen, he had inherited an important collection of such antiques to which he constantly added. Already, in 1465, Francesco Tornabuoni was sending him antique medals from Rome. Then, in 1471, Sixtus IV gave him the busts of Agrippa and Augustus which so delighted him, and during that same visit to Rome, Lorenzo purchased the best of the treasures of Paul II, including the famous Farnese dish which in 1492 was valued at 10,000 ducats. Francesco Valori ingratiated himself with Lorenzo by bringing him antiquities from North Africa, while in 1491 Baccio Ugolini was purchasing antique medals and statues in Naples on Lorenzo's behalf. For years, Lorenzo's dearest wish was to acquire a genuine bust of Plato, and when he finally bought one, reputedly discovered in the ruins of Plato's academy, his delight knew no bounds.

The public value which these antiquities had for Florence is obvious. Gathered together as a collection and cared for in the Medici palace, by the sculptor, Bertoldo, they were a semi-public reference source for all those interested in classical antiquity. Although they were not available for all to see, in that the Medici palace remained a private dwelling, access was freely given to any genuinely interested scholar or artist. The collection, therefore, acted as a further stimulus to the already very strong classicising impulses in Florentine art.

It is when we come to consider the question of Lorenzo as patron of painting or sculpture that doubts arise both about the nature of his role as patron and about his capacity for genuine connoisseurship. That either painting or sculpture were matters of vital concern to him, in the way that architecture, music and literature were, seems unlikely. Certainly such concern is not reflected in his surviving correspondence, although the nature of the correspondence which has survived – largely commercial, diplomatic and political – may be an issue here. The actual works he is known to have commissioned were few in number; the only large-scale paintings executed for Lorenzo were for a set of frescoes in his villa at Spedaletto. On that occasion, he certainly employed the best living artists: Perugino, Botticelli, Ghirlandaio and Filippino Lippi, but his choice, except in the case of the last, was probably determined by their already established reputations and not by a personal preference for their style. But Filippino Lippi he does appear to have liked, since he also employed him at Poggio a Caiano, where he executed a fresco on the subject of *The Sacrifice of Laocoon*.

In so far as Lorenzo had a chief artist at all, it was Verrocchio who executed the tomb of Piero and Giovanni de' Medici in San Lorenzo as well as a number of other commissions for Lorenzo. These included his famous *Putto with a Fish*, orginally executed for a fountain at Careggi, and the portrait busts of Lorenzo and Giuliano, now in the Washington National Gallery. At one time or another, Lorenzo is also known to have employed Antonio Pollaiuolo, Benedetto da Maiano and Signorelli whom he invited to help judge the projects for the cathedral façade. Signorelli's *Education of Pan**, was a mythological painting which was probably executed for Lorenzo about 1490. In this painting Pan, the nature-God – identified by the Mediceans with Cosmos, symbol of the world, and so, inevitably with Cosimo – gazed at the nymph who escaped his advances

* Destroyed during the Second World War.

by turning into a reed. In his loss the young god could be consoled neither by music, represented by a young man on his left, nor by philosophy, represented by an old man on his right. Love is all-powerful, but love is also unattainable. The contemplation of love thus leads inexorably to melancholy, the natural temperament of the poet. It was the closest possible visual interpretation of the inner workings of Lorenzo's mind, and the best evidence we possess of his world-view.

Botticelli was another painter who Lorenzo almost certainly admired and whose poetic vision he must have shared. While Botticelli's *Pallas and the Centaur* cannot be shown to have been directly commissioned by Lorenzo it is highly likely that it was, for it alludes directly to the wisdom with which Lorenzo calmed the political passions of Florence after the Pazzi conspiracy. In the painting Pallas Athene, the goddess of wisdom, whose dress is adorned by intertwined diamond rings – an heraldic symbol of the Medici – and is bound by fronds of olive, the symbol of peace, tames a Centaur, traditionally held to be a symbol of violence and disorder.

Apart from Verrocchio, Bertoldo was Lorenzo's favoured sculptor, although it was probably his personality which really appealed to Lorenzo, not his work. Bertoldo enjoyed good food, wine and company, was an inmate of the Medici palace, and was a frequent companion of Lorenzo's at the baths. As we have seen, he was placed in charge of Lorenzo's collection of antiquities and his own work is, to a large extent, a commentary upon that collection. Like his patron, his preference was for the production of imitations of antiquities and of miniature bronzes whose inspiration was classical. Here, Lorenzo's interest is unambiguous, for he commissioned similar works from Antonio Pollaiuolo, the most famous being *Hercules and Anteus*, now in the Bargello museum. Of Pollaiuolo, Lorenzo remarked to Lanfredini, 'He is the leading master of this city, and perhaps greater than any there has ever been: this is the common opinion of all those who understand these matters.'[21] This judgment suggests that, in the area of sculpture, Lorenzo was not lacking in vision or understanding, for Pollaiuolo was a key figure in laying the foundations of High Renaissance sculpture and, in particular, the triumphs of Michelangelo. He was one of the first artists to undertake dissections in order to reveal the underlying structures that control the appearance of the human form. In him Lorenzo was patronising the future.

A balanced view of Lorenzo's role as a patron of the arts must, therefore, reinstate him in a primary position as a major contributor to the development of the Florentine Renaissance. He cannot sensibly be relegated to the sidelines simply because he failed to commission work in quantity from the leading painters and sculptors of his day. Indeed, such considerations are largely irrelevant in that Lorenzo's major contribution to stimulating learning and the arts in Florence was that he made both the

Pallas and the Centaur by Botticelli, probably alludes to the wisdom by which
Lorenzo calmed the passions of Florence after the Pazzi conspiracy

Hercules and Anteus sculpted for Lorenzo by Pollaiuolo

patronage and the practice of the arts fashionable. As a creative artist himself, Lorenzo fully understood that the ideal patron did not merely provide a livelihood, but conveyed distinction and honour to his clients, for, in the symbiotic relationship which was ideally sought for between patron and client, art, literature and learning brought fame and glory both to artist and to patron alike.

As the leader of Florentine society, Lorenzo was able to foster similar attitudes in other wealthy patrons who, through him, were encouraged to maintain scholars, artists and musicians. Equally, Lorenzo's attitude towards learning, literature and the arts encouraged others to take them seriously. Ficino could think of no better way to encourage Antonio de' Pazzi to apply himself to serious study than to suggest that this would find favour with Lorenzo. Thus, the essentially serious approach taken by Lorenzo towards learning helped to create a whole wealthy class of patrician patrons who shared his intellectual, literary and artistic interests.

In addition, Lorenzo's dominance in government meant that he was able to create a framework within which the arts could flourish. He was, for instance, instrumental in 1474 in obtaining the passage of a law granting tax relief for twenty years to every house erected on virgin land within Florence, legislation which was re-enacted in 1489. His relations with the papacy and with Rome were also instrumental in obtaining papal permission for the release of ecclesiastically owned land when it was needed for building purposes. This, in turn, led to what has been termed the Florentine building-boom of the late fifteenth century when, in the words of Luca Landucci, 'the men . . . were so overworked with building walls that there was a shortage of men and materials'.[22]

Like his Sienese counterpart, Pandolfo Petrucci, Lorenzo, as we have seen, sat frequently on government boards connected with patronage of the arts. Thus, for instance, when in September 1485 the *Signoria* commissioned from Filippino Lippi a *Madonna* for the *Sala del Consiglio* in their palace, it was to Lorenzo that they delegated the responsibility for fixing the price. Again, in May 1491, when he served on the Board of Works of the Cathedral, Lorenzo was able to arrange that the new mosaic for the chapel of San Zenobius should be entrusted to Botticelli, Gherardo and Monte di Giovanni and Domenico and Davide Ghirlandaio.

By his very presence on such boards and his more intimate contact with friends and clients, Lorenzo initiated debate, discussion and interest which bore fruit in outstanding works of art, architecture and literature. Within Florence, he managed to create a kind of hothouse of aesthetic interest which was culturally fruitful. In this context, two of the better-known Medicean clients provide evidence suggestive of the central role which Lorenzo played in the development of the Florentine Renaissance. One is Gentile Becchi whose letters, after his appointment as Bishop of Arezzo, are full of complaints that he is out of touch with events in Florence, and, particularly, with Lorenzo and his *brigata* of friends, poets, scholars and artists. For him Florence was a cultural paradise, Arezzo a stultifying backwater. The other is Pico della Mirandola who, in his restless search for ultimate truth, first arrived in Florence in 1479, and immediately found himself at home as he discussed love, philosophy and poetry with Poliziano and Lorenzo. Writing subsequently to his beloved master, Ermolao Barbaro, Pico spoke of his joy in finding in Florence an incomparable fount of wisdom and intellectual energy. At the heart of this vital circle of culture, within which Pico flourished, existed Lorenzo, patron of the arts, just as at the heart of the Florentine state existed Lorenzo the politician.

7

LORENZO AS WRITER

The circumstances of Lorenzo's life, the nature of his role as head of the Medici power structure and his position as effective, if unacknowledged, ruler of Florence meant that, as he himself pointed out, his most private acts, his most intimate experiences, inevitably became public property. Thus, even the brutal murder of his brother could not be an occasion for private grief for, as we have seen, the circumstances in which it occurred ensured that all of Lorenzo's mourning was done in the full blaze of the public eye. Yet we know that his own deepest interests were ones that are best nourished in privacy: poetry and philosophy.

It was these twin interests which, ultimately distinguished Lorenzo from the ablest of contemporary politicians. He is a figure of importance in world history because his life demonstrates that experience is not divisible; poetry and philosophy were not relegated to some inner compartment of Lorenzo's mind nor unrelated to his political or social activities. On the contrary, the wisdom and clarity of vision which men most admired in him and which, in the end, led them to see him as a great statesman, were part and parcel of that same creativity which made him among the most gifted of vernacular writers and one of the very few men of letters in fifteenth-century Italy who managed to combine theory and practice, translating the somewhat arid concepts of Neo-Platonism into a living, relevant and enduring reality, informing every area of life.

This is not, perhaps, a fashionable viewpoint. It has become customary to disparage Lorenzo's literary work, to argue that he created no new forms nor discovered any original themes and it is easy to demonstrate that, among others, Pulci and Poliziano were better poets. Lorenzo even provides his critics with ammunition to use against him since he was never satisfied with his own work. In consequence, he tended to rewrite it throughout his life, thus creating, incidentally, a whole industry of critical scholarship which has devoted itself to discovering the exact date of his compositions. Nevertheless, Lorenzo *was* a great writer and some of his best works, such as the *Bacchus and Ariadne*, have a lyrical quality which would ensure them a place in any anthology of Italian poetry no matter who their author had been. Lorenzo wrote good poetry both of necessity and for enjoyment. He wrote prose equally effortlessly and wrote it to good effect. In addition, in his own way and within his own terms, he was a highly original thinker.

It is normal to divide Lorenzo's literary work into three periods. The first is that of the youthful writings – *Nencia*, the *Uccellazione*, the *Altercazione*, his imitations of Petrarch and the *Capitoli*. The second period, between 1472 and 1484, is seen as that of his mature work, notably the *Comento*, and the third the period until his death during which he wrote *Corinto*, *Ambra*, *Selva* and the *Rappresentazione di San Giovanni e Paolo*. The first period is characterised by a dazzling display of Lorenzo's erudition, the second by an understanding of the major philosophical, linguistic and literary problems of his age, coupled with a propensity to treat more aristocratic themes, and his final years by a return to the pastoral tradition, a reorientation towards classical themes and an expressed desire for personal and public peace. Such a division of Lorenzo's work is, of course, artificial since, as we have seen, he was constantly reworking it. Nevertheless, it is also a helpful way of looking at his literary career for it does indicate, in general terms, the way in which his mind developed and his ideas changed over time.

In essence, Lorenzo's gift was for recreativity. He neither lived nor thought nor wrote in a vacuum, but made use of every experience, brought to bear all that he read, heard or thought, upon whatever he was doing. His writings do not take the form of philosophic discourse, pushing human knowledge to the limit, although he well knew where that limit lay. It is not here that one finds originality and creativity, not even in the *Altercazione*, but rather in his ability to take the ideas of others and to remould them into a vision which is, characteristically, his own. His work is, thus, always eclectic in the extreme but, in him, eclecticism becomes, paradoxically, orginality, for, while Lorenzo imitated, he also adapted using the models of others to make sense of concrete personal experience. He himself described this process when he talked of the meaning of wisdom, mulling over in his mind and bringing together both what he had read in Cicero and what he had talked about with Ficino, concluding that:

> We see also that difficulties over deciding what course to adopt in our civic and private actions derive from the fact that virtually any course of action will bring some kind of inconvenience, nor is it possible to choose from a thousand possibilities, one true course to be followed, which has nothing to be said against it. For that reason, those who are the most prudent delay the longest in making a decision, and because of such delays they are known as 'wise men'. And time is called 'most wise' because true wisdom consists in waiting for the right occasion and then seizing it . . .[1]

Laurentian recreativity is at its most obvious in the use which he made of language, for his vernacular writings – both prose and poetry – are composed of a remarkable blend in which popular, street Tuscan is married to the elevated language of the ruling class. This, indeed, is the most notable feature of his carnival songs whose innovatory qualities all admired and in which allegorical-mythological themes, fashionable among humanists, are successfully blended with popular traditions. An equally innovatory aspect of Lorenzo's use of language was his deliberate return to the age of Dante and the *stilnovisti* in order to create for the Florentines and, ultimately, for all Italians, a vernacular which would be a perfect medium for the expression of all human sentiment and experience.

This originality which was Lorenzo's ultimate legacy to civilisation was, of course, partially born out of qualities which were innate. He was, without doubt, marked out from other men by being possessed of exceptional intellectual gifts. The way in which he chose to exercise those gifts, however, was determined by personal preferences and external events. Most important, in this context, was the characteristic which, as we have seen, his very position appeared to deny him – a capacity for intense personal feeling. In all of Lorenzo's writing this is expressed through a tendency to shy away from the collective and to emphasise personal experience. Having a rare ability to analyse his own emotions rationally, Lorenzo was able to express such experience in his *Comento ad alcuni sonetti*. Here he described how, when emotionally disturbed or feeling 'the bitterness of remembrance' he would seek out some 'solitary and shady place, or the beauties of some green meadow'.[2] And, indeed, much of Lorenzo's life was spent both in an actual and in a metaphorical search for solitary or shady places or green meadows where he might recreate himself.

It is, of course, possible to argue that, in doing so, Lorenzo was merely following a common contemporary literary convention. According to Landino's *Disputationes Camaldulenses*, Alberti had expatiated at length on the value to the statesman and the scholar of retirement and meditation, and this view was also one often expressed by Ficino. Seen in such a light, Lorenzo's retreats to Careggi or Poggio a Caiano might be regarded as little more than window-dressing, yet another prop to the public image of Lorenzo, the wise statesman.

In Lorenzo's case, however, there is much evidence to suggest that his retreats to the country fulfilled a deep need and were essential if he was to function as a person. He did not, as some contemporaries were already beginning to do, deliberately seek a more aristocratic, princely life-style, or wish to ape the customs of hereditary rulers. Rather, he was engaged in a process of emotional survival. No feeling comes through more strongly in his writing than his love of the countryside, as, for example, in the famous lines in which, Florentine though he was, he expressed his contempt for the city and his delight in the relaxing qualities of the Tuscan landscape:

Let who will, seek grandeur and fame:
Piazzas, temples and magnificent buildings,
Enjoyments, treasures, always following
A thousand cruel thoughts, a thousand pains.
A green meadow with beautiful flowers
A flowing stream circling the growing grass,
A little bird, sadly singing of love,
Will far better appease every desire;
The shady woods, the rocks and high mountains,
The dark caverns and fugitive wild beasts,
Maybe a charming, fearful nymph . . .

Lorenzo's poetry never degenerates into academic pastoralism but is full of the sights, sounds and smells of the countryside and accurate observations of the natural world. The novelty of *Nencia*, for instance, derives from direct observations of rustic life, while Lorenzo's famed capacity for setting a scene, describing the seasons or the time of day, comes from a constant involvement in and observation of the natural world. In this sense, his writing is immediately accessible in the same way that Leonardo's paintings are, for both are firmly rooted in reality. It is worth recalling precisely how unusual this is, and that it is the norm, in any age, for writers or artists to be subject to the influence of other works, rather than going directly to nature in order to obtain their impressions.

Recreation in the solitude of the country, whether in an actual place or a metaphorical retreat was, thus, not a self-indulgence but a means by which to return refreshed to the social world. Poetry provided for Lorenzo the necessary link between the individual and society. From the 'delightful places' one must always return to the 'hurry and hurly-burly of civic life' with its 'thousand cares'.[3] In the loneliness of his own experience which, as he pointed out, 'it is impossible that anyone but myself can understand',[4] his poetry provides a bridge to other human beings. Thus he could argue that, if his writing served no other purpose, 'at least some will find a little pleasure in it, because they will, perhaps, find some idea similar and identical to their own'.[5]

A way back to human contact had to be found for Lorenzo was vividly aware that withdrawals from city life laid him open to criticism. He was equally aware that the expression of creativity, through writing, could lead to the objection that he cared little for public affairs, since:

some might think it unwise to have wasted time composing and commenting on poems whose subject matter is largely the passion of love. It might also be seen as more blameworthy in me because there are continual concerns, both public and private, which ought to keep me from such thoughts, which in the eyes of some, are not just frivolous and of little matter but actually pernicious and even dangerous both to my soul and to my reputation.[6]

Such criticism was particularly likely in the latter half of Lorenzo's life, a period of mounting introspection in Florentine cultural life, associated with the emergent asceticism and mysticism which found their ultimate flowering in the Savonarolan movement, and its explicit criticism of all that the Laurentian circle stood for.

Lorenzo gave various answers to his critics. Of these the first was that, for him, poetry was not the luxury of an aristocratic dilettante, anxious to keep up with the prevailing fashions of the day. For him, rather, it was a necessity which he had earned a right to, 'having been in my youth much persecuted both by men and by fortune, a little relaxation ought not to be denied me, relaxation which I have found only by falling passionately in love and by commenting upon my own poems.'[7]

His second line of defence was a philosophical one, that justification of the emotion of love which Lorenzo had learned from Ficino and from his own reading and meditation. It was a position of which he was always a rigorous defender, so rigorous, indeed, that it is obvious that it was, for him, a central obsession. Neo-Platonic doctrines, which ultimately derived from the writings of philosophers working in Alexandria in the early

Cristoforo Landino, Marsilio Ficino, Angelo Poliziano and Gentile Becchi as they appear in Ghirlandaio's *Apparition of the Angel to Zacharias*

years of the Christian era, were based on the central tenet of the identity of God, Creativity and Love. The force which impelled God to create was Love. Man, therefore, loving or creating, was participating in the divine essence. Thus, both the pursuit of the arts and love were justified, for love ruled the Universe and placed on each individual soul the obligation to find its way back to God, the only true Good. Such love was not, of course, to be confused with animal love, inherent in the senses and the flesh, for this was an evil to be subdued and conquered.

Ficino's teaching impressed Lorenzo, in particular, where it appeared to explain experience, and to offer the possibility of breaking down the barriers which the existence of corporeal nature placed between individuals. Love, for Ficino, was the basis of all experience and was available to all. To all men, love offered the means to participate in the divine but, he argued, it was also the means by which men attained what was most human in themselves since it was only through love that divisions between men could be transcended.

A person is first attracted to another through corporeal beauty, normally symbolised in the eye. This, as Lorenzo explained, following Ficino's teaching:

> . . . is the first step on the staircase of love, and, naturally, the most imperfect, since Platonism holds that corporeal beauty is a sort of shadow of true beauty or the idea of true beauty, which, in the body is seen only under a veil.[8]

From this contemplation of the beauty of the body a person would be inexorably drawn on to the next stage on the ladder of love that is contemplation of the soul of the beloved and, finally to the highest stage of all, the love of the divine. On this earth, this must be a journey without end and a journey through paradoxes since the nature of the corrupt world ensures that 'there exist perennially possession and non-possession, sadness and joy, hope and fear'.[9] It is, however, the essential spiritual journey which all must make.

The care with which Lorenzo followed and commented on Ficino's writings shows how important his intellectual life was to his creative writing. His writings are dependent on nature but on nature interpreted through wisdom derived from extensive studying and reading. Studying and creativity, indeed, went hand in hand for Lorenzo. Thus, for instance, we have seen how one of his most intense periods of studying philosophy – 1473–4 – was also one of the most successful in terms of poetic production, for he produced the first *Selva*, numerous songs and sonnets of love as well as his verse translation of Ficino's *Oratio ad deum theologica*. His life was continually punctuated both by the discovery of new books and by the rediscovery of old ones, and books were, thus, a part of the essential furniture of his daily life. The width of his interests is remarkable. His writings show a considerable familiarity with the Latin poets, particularly Virgil, Ovid and Horace, a deep knowledge of Cicero, a mastery of hermetic literature, contemporary medical and architectural theory, and an interest in magic and astrology, both of which were also, of course, matters of great concern to Ficino and Pico. To this formidable burden of knowledge must be added Lorenzo's total familiarity with Italian and, particularly, Tuscan vernacular literature.

Looking at this wide-ranging taste in reading matter, one can begin to understand the source of creativity within Lorenzo, both the writer and the politician, lying as it does in that constant tension, found in all great masters of the Renaissance, and deriving from an attempt to reconcile two incompatible world-views which could not, in reality, be married together outside the work of art. In this Lorenzo was entirely representative of his generation, a typical 'Renaissance man', inhabitant of that world so accurately described by Chastel who pointed out that, 'Regarded from close to, Florence, at the time of Lorenzo de' Medici, provides the spectacle of a city in which there were many more problems than there were certainties.'[10] Lorenzo, that is, was one among many who found their love of the newly-discovered classical world in conflict with their traditional ideas.

Previous generations of Florentines had also admired antiquity and more recently an interest in Platonism had become widespread in the ruling class. Yet members of that élite had grown up in older traditions, solidly rooted in Aristotelianism, and had subsequently grafted onto this still healthy stock their new interest in Plato. But, although they thought about Plato, they never thought like him. Lorenzo, on the contrary, had been taught to think like Plato, to think with Plato. That he was successful we know from his own writings whose effortless borrowings from, and commentary on, Plato show that Lorenzo did not just know his works at second-hand. His familiarity with *The Republic* is particularly striking. Lorenzo had been taught to admire the ancients before the moderns, to believe in the superiority of the classical to the medieval Christian world. Yet, at the same time, in total contradiction, he had been brought up within the framework of traditional Christian ideas which, because of the history of the western intellectual tradition, were suffused with Aristotelianism. Nor was this part of his education in any way superficial. On the contrary, Lorenzo's *Altercazione* and his *Laudi* suggest that he was a profoundly religious man.

It was, in fact, in reflecting on religion that Lorenzo expressed most clearly the problems inherent in his contradictory intellectual inheritance. This is the significance of his heartfelt:

> O Dio, o summo bene, or come fai
> Che te sol cerco e non ti truovo mai?

and of the contrast which he draws throughout the *Comento* between the 'passion' which inevitably accompanies human experience and the peace of death, so that 'we may say that our life is made up of opposition, contradiction and different ills, and that only death brings peace'.[11] A similar reflection of contradictions may be seen in another characteristic of Lorenzo's writing, which is the way in which the divine and the human spheres are constantly confused as, for instance, when speaking of the woman he loves and his physical separation from her, he argues that she was not, herself, alone 'even though she was far from my sorrowing and weeping eyes, since, in her company, were Love, Hope and Faith, together with all my thoughts'.[12] A similar commingling of the sacred and the profane can be seen in Lorenzo's *Laudi* sung to the accompaniment of tunes immediately familiar to all Florentines as those of popular songs.

Mention has already been made of another source of Lorenzo's creative approach to the vernacular – his return to the great Tuscan masters at a time when they were out of fashion. As far as the leading intellectuals of the day were concerned, Ciceronian Latin and Latin verse forms were the only satisfactory modes of communication among the ruling classes. The vernacular was the language of the people and there was something innately shocking in the fact that Dante, Petrarch and Boccaccio were familiar and accessible to all Florentines. Landino, it is true, had endeavoured to rehabilitate the *trecento* writers and particularly Dante. His influence directed Lorenzo towards a close study of Dante's language, the ultimate fruit of which was a commitment to Dante on Lorenzo's part so intense that he tried, albeit without success, to have the poet's body returned to Florence from Ravenna.

The cynical might suggest that this was merely another aspect of Lorenzo's policy of promoting Florentine cultural hegemony. Equally, the fact that more than two-thirds of the poems in the *Raccolta Aragonese* were either by Dante or by other *stilnovisti* poets might be explained in the same way. Here was a public assertion that Tuscan poetry was superior to all other Italian vernacular poetry. On the other hand, a policy of Florentine cultural imperialism does not, of itself, explain why Lorenzo's language should have so consistently reflected that of Dante, nor why his *Comento* should have been so closely modelled on that of Dante's *Convivio*. The *Comento* even reveals Lorenzo reverting to Dantesque modes of thought for his assertion that: 'no one is more suited to comment on a work than the man who wrote it', while it would have been totally acceptable to Dante's contemporaries, was completely at variance with normal practice in the *quattrocento*. Equally, it was not just from the philosophers of Neo-Platonism but also from the *dolce stil nuovo* tradition, that Lorenzo took his concept of the nature, quality and purpose of love between man and woman seen not as something base and reprehensible, 'but almost as something necessary and proof enough of gentility and of greatness of mind' for 'love and gentility are one thing'.[13]

It was not only Dante who, among earlier Florentine poets, proved important in determining the content and the style of Lorenzo's writing. His knowledge of 'our Florentine',[14] Petrarch, was also profound, and it was the Petrarchan model that he took for his own sonnets. Petrarch also provided the model for the ruthless self-analysis and the self-consciousness of those sonnets where every feeling is carefully dissected and every moment of shift in sensibility is atomised. The ambience in which Lorenzo had been educated was, of course, still dominated by Petrarchan modes and ideas, which provided all writers in the vernacular with a shared vocabulary, a common repertory of situations, expressions and terms, which could be used to express various equally common themes: the sorrows of love, the fickleness of fortune, the vanity of hope, the fleetingness of time. These were all common currency but Lorenzo was perhaps unique among the intellectuals of Florence in according as much value to Petrarch as an author of vernacular poetry, as of a master of Latin prose and verse.

The influence of other masters on Lorenzo was, therefore, considerable, but this does not mean that his verse was merely derivative. He was never uncritical even of those he most admired. Thus Dante's poetry, in his view, was 'not altogether free' from 'antique ruggedness'[15] and he surprisingly criticised Dante for his failure to define gentility accurately. Dante had merely equated gentility and nobility, but this did not satisfy Lorenzo who preferred to define gentility, in his own way, as that which 'is well suited and perfectly adapted to do that office which belongs to it, accompanied by gracefulness, which is a gift of God'.[16] Lorenzo was not subservient to convention but was tending to build on traditions. Thus, even in the treatment of the well-worn theme of love, what he had to say was new. He entirely lacked the passionate spirituality which informed Dante's devotion to Beatrice, or the otherworldliness of Petrarch's for Laura. For Lorenzo the rewards of love do not come in another world. On the contrary, the moving quality of his love poetry lies precisely in that tension we have already noted: his longing for physical fulfilment and his consciousness that it can never be permanently achieved.

Lorenzo did not, of course, write only in the vernacular. He also wrote about it. His views were first expressed in the famous letter to Federico of Aragon extolling Tuscan poetry which accompanied the *Raccolta Aragonese*. When the letter was actually penned and whether it was written by Lorenzo, or by some Medicean client close to him, are largely immaterial questions. Since the letter bore Lorenzo's name it is not unreasonable to assume that it also expressed his views, particularly as the same views are expressed and amplified in the *Comento*.

Essentially Lorenzo's arguments on behalf of Tuscan as a literary language boiled down to three main points which need to be considered if we are to understand Lorenzo's life and work. The first and, perhaps, the most significant, is that Tuscan is a language which can express any idea or emotion and which can be adapted to any mood. Lorenzo, himself, was a model illustration of this. His true sense of decorum provided him with a vernacular style which could be adapted to any mood or situation. Thus, for instance, the style of his letters ranges from the most refined, elegant and elevated, to the lively style he used with intimates like Girolamo Morelli, to whom we find him writing in October 1478: 'You'll say my letters are like mushrooms; you either find a whole lot together or none at all.'[17]

This point about adaptability has to be borne in mind, also, when considering the range of Lorenzo's poetic output. He appears to have experimented with every possible style and mode, not so much from choice, as in order actually to demonstrate the very facility with which he had argued that Tuscan could be used. He was, for instance, perfectly capable of writing a sonnet as if the author were a betrayed young girl. Thus, many have argued that, in trying to come to terms with Lorenzo as a person, we may not take the evidence of his lyrics into account since they are not necessarily expressive of his own personal feeling. They can be read, rather, as clever literary exercises by a man determined to make a point. Yet this is too negative a position to take. Some things we may legitimately deduce about Lorenzo from his lyrics for throughout them run persistent themes which are quintessentially Laurentian. Such, for instance, as we have noted, is the sense of the inevitable passage of time and the sadness associated with it: 'time waits not, but flies away'. Such too is the sense of the vanity of human wishes. Such, finally, is the value placed upon wit and humour, qualities which Lorenzo deeply valued, as he explained in a typically paradoxical letter addressed to Ficino in January 1474:

> What makes me so long for your letters is that, in them, humour appears so mixed with gravity that, if considered lightheartedly, everything seems full of humour, if seriously, then they appear more serious than anything else.[18]

The second major point Lorenzo made, on behalf of Tuscan, was that it was a language which possessed the unique quality of having been created by philosophers who were, at the same time, poets. The third was the constant need for language to change, adapt and develop if it was to remain alive.

In arguing that language was always alive and always changing Lorenzo was making a major cultural advance, almost in defiance of the contemporary wisdom of other scholars and the Florentine humanists. As far as Lorenzo was concerned, the uses which might be made of Latin as a literary medium were essentially limited ones. Latin was admirable and worthy of study and use, but was recognised for what it was – the language of an historical, dead civilisation. As such, it could never hope to express contemporary reality. This insight of Lorenzo's was important for he was not alone among Florentines in finding himself essentially tongue-tied by a fashionable insistence on the use of Ciceronian Latin to express elevated ideas. One illustration of the problem concerns the writing of history. Commenting on the indubitable fact that little good historical writing was produced during Lorenzo's lifetime, detractors of Lorenzo and latter-day opponents of the so-called Medici 'tyranny', have reasoned that this lack arose because of the stranglehold which Lorenzo had over Florence's political and cultural life. Thus, the major developments in historical writing which occurred during the fourteenth century could not be built on in the fifteenth. But a more realistic assessment of this phenomenon might suggest that it was the straitjacket of Latin that was the problem. The language of Cicero and Livy, even that of Tacitus, simply could not be employed if an historian wished to give an accurate portrayal of Florentine history. For good history to be written in Florence again, as it would be by the generation which included Vettori, Machiavelli and Guicciardini, it had to become respectable to write in the vernacular. This respectability Lorenzo was able to provide largely because of his prominent role in Florentine life.

Thus we may see Lorenzo as a 'typical Renaissance man', if we seek such a figure, because his works clearly reflect the fact that, in many ways, what the Renaissance was about was a crisis over language. There was a widespread concern, not limited to Lorenzo's circle nor, indeed, to Florence, that human vocabulary was no longer mirroring external reality, that words no longer corresponded to things. Neo-Platonism merely reinforced this anxiety in that many of its central concerns were to do with the problem of language, with the fact that language cannot describe the process of thought, but only the thought once it has passed through the brain. Thus the Neo-Platonists began to emphasise the importance of the image; believing that images rather than words might better convey truth, they placed great value on music and frequently resorted to word-play. As we have seen, Lorenzo shared all these interests and concerns. In addition, in expressing his support for the vernacular, he also came to understand that language was only a tool, that it was susceptible to change, and could become the means whereby people consciously shaped and reshaped their world into something new.

It was this realisation by Lorenzo that led on to something else for which he had been attacked: his conscious use of the Tuscan language as an agent of Florentine imperialism. Tuscan, he argued, expressing all the hopes and aspirations of his Florentine contemporaries, would be perfected, 'should the dominion of Florence be extended, a thing not merely to be hoped for but striven for by our gallant citizens with all their energies of body and mind'.[19] In Lorenzo's thinking the 'Three Crowns of Florence' – Dante, Petrarch and Boccaccio – were to become models of good writing not only for the citizens of Florence, but for those of Tuscany and, ultimately, for all Italy. Lorenzo's celebration of these poets was Florentine cultural imperialism, demonstrating the primacy of Tuscan over all other vernaculars and, by implication, the supremacy of Florence over all other Italian states.

This 'political programme' for the Tuscan vernacular derived yet again from one of Lorenzo's most original insights and one which, paradoxically, depended on his knowledge of Latin. It was the study of the latter which led him to understand the crucial role which language played in the development of the Roman empire: Latin was the supreme means by which Roman culture was disseminated. Hence, language, he came to understand, was the true foundation of the Roman empire and explained the length of its duration. This understanding then led, inescapably, to another conclusion, which was also a further justification for Lorenzo's writings. The pursuit of literature was not a matter of personal choice, but was a political duty. Thus, we return to what can be seen as the central fact about Lorenzo's life, that his activities cannot be separated out but are all part of the same expression of a single man, whose supreme achievement lay in holding all parts of his life in balance intimately related to and depending upon each other.

8

LORENZO'S ASCENDANCY

The ambivalences and contradictions in Lorenzo's behaviour became even more striking in the decade after 1478 and frequently occasioned comment among his contemporaries. On the one hand they encountered a man who wished to escape completely from the world of diplomacy, politics and intrigue in order to concentrate on his private pursuits, but, on the other, they saw a Lorenzo whose power and prestige increased daily as he began to play a truly central role in Italian politics. In the case of the modern historian, a sense of contradiction also stems from the fact that this was a period of hiatus, of grey and confused years sandwiched between what can be regarded as the golden periods of Laurentian management. Giuliano's charm and good looks had, as we have seen, added lustre to the Medicean regime and there could be no replacement for him while Lorenzo's own children were still too young to play a part in the life of the city. Not only was Lorenzo himself now reluctant to engage in public show or display but he also discouraged such activities on the part of others. Even the public festivities of Florence became more subdued and, in a decade which saw both famine and plague, life there took on a more serious, a grimmer aspect, matters not being improved by the way in which, as Lorenzo's health deteriorated, his tendency to melancholia increased.

While, after the Pazzi conspiracy, Lorenzo became much more of a public figure in the sense that his every action became a matter of comment for diary and letter writers, this growth in interest does not necessarily indicate an increased popularity. The spontaneous support manifested at the time of the conspiracy had not entirely evaporated during the subsequent war but, as Lorenzo knew full well, the affections of the Florentines were proverbially fickle, especially when their pockets were threatened. Consequently, as we have seen, the depressing and financially disastrous war years brought a steady erosion of support both within the political nation and at a popular level.

Lorenzo is recorded as having acknowledged that the best protection of any regime was not soldiers or guards, but the goodwill of the populace. His problem, therefore, was how to win and keep such goodwill. As a result of the Pazzi conspiracy, he now saw factionalism, nourished by Florence's powerful family structures, as an open threat to the Medici and he therefore consciously directed his energies towards the twin goals of destroying the power of the old family clans of Florence, and building up a city-wide support for the Medici, drawn from all classes. In pursuit of these aims marriage alliances, for instance, were made into a powerful political weapon, being used, according to Guicciardini, as a potent instrument of Medicean control. A very large number of patrician marriages were actually celebrated in the Medici palace and witnessed by Lorenzo who sometimes also provided the dowry. In such cases we may safely assume that what was at stake was a political alliance of which he approved.

Old wounds were, as far as possible, healed. The marriage of Lorenzo's daughter, Lucrezia, into the Salviati family in August 1481, said to have given Lorenzo 'singular satisfaction and content' and 'great joy and contentment'[1] to all Florence, was a part of this policy. So was the deliberate building up of Medicean support in the district of Oltrarno, for previously that had been a centre of opposition to the Medici. Friends continued to be wooed, flattered and cajoled, as Lorenzo became over-meticulous in fulfilling promises and obligations. Meanwhile the poor were purchased by a cheap food policy. Lorenzo regularly sold them grain at below market-price, especially during periods of acute shortages such as the autumn and winter of 1483 when he used all his diplomatic contacts to facilitate grain imports into Florence.

These policies all involved the expenditure of money at a time when Lorenzo's financial affairs remained embarrassed despite the fact that he had begun to appropriate public funds to his own uses. As we have seen, he had also been misappropriating funds belonging to his own family, above all his two wards, Lorenzo and Giovanni de' Medici. In the critical months between May and September 1478 he had taken a total of 58,643 florins from their estate in order to remain solvent. The consequent legal dispute dragged on until 1485 when an arbitration award forced Lorenzo to surrender the villa at Cafaggiolo along with sixty-six farms, twenty houses, three mills and three ovens as well as jewels valued at over 16,000 florins. Two years later, in order to repay yet another debt, he was forced to give up his last holdings in the Mugello.

The Medici bank continued its steady decline and gave endless trouble, particularly the Milan branch. The irresponsible activities of the Portinari brothers regularly provoked outbursts of violent rage in Lorenzo who held them mainly responsible for his difficulties and for creating the situation he described when making his tax return of 1481 when he explained that he could not:

> follow the same procedure as my father in 1469 because there is a great difference between that time and the present, with the consequence I have suffered many losses, as is well-known not only to your Lordships but to the whole world.[2]

Lorenzo's financial difficulties were, inevitably, well-known to the Florentine establishment and the reaction of that establishment to his problems illustrates how central the position which he occupied in Florentine government was. When, in 1482, he was granted substantial tax concessions, this was not done by means of public appeals to the city's councils, as would have been normal, but by a special financial commission:

> since the health of the present regime depends largely on the preservation of the said Lorenzo both in fact and in appearance, and the good state of the *Monte** depends on the preservation of the regime.[3]

Such, then, is the context in which the decision taken to create new safeguards for that regime must be placed. No doubt, the collective feeling of insecurity which the Mediceans experienced between 1478 and 1480 explains the timing of the constitutional changes which occurred: it was in April 1480 that a new *Balìa* was created to draft proposals for constitutional reform. The reason given was the city's economic difficulties, and a promise was made that, among its other tasks, the *Balìa* would consider the tax burden, but, although some financial reforms were undertaken, most of the *Balìa's* time was taken up with devising means by which power could be further concentrated in the hands of the Medici *parte*. By the simple expedient of having the *Signoria* choose a group of thirty prominent Florentines, who then co-opted a further forty, a Medici-dominated council was to be created to replace the *Accoppiatori*, and this Council of Seventy was empowered to fill all future vacancies by co-option.

It should be stressed that the Seventy were to prove more than mere Medici time-servers. Many distinguished Florentines served on the Council and all its members had to be over forty and to have already held major office. Nevertheless, it was universally regarded as the instrument of Lorenzo and the heart of the Medici regime. In addition, simultaneously, the powers of the traditional communal councils were drastically reduced because the Seventy was given the right to appoint to the *Signoria*. The powers of the *Signoria*, in turn, were reduced by the creation of two new bodies; the *Otto di Pratica* – the Eight – who replaced the Ten and thus assumed control of all military and foreign affairs, and the Twelve – the *Dodici Procuratori* – who were the supreme body in charge of the city's security, jurisdiction, finance and commerce. Membership of these bodies changed every six months but, since they were nominated by the Seventy from their own number, this also represented a substantial narrowing of the constitution.

Lorenzo had deliberately distanced himself from the *Balìa's* proceed-

---

* i.e. the public funded debt.

ings, and its recommendations must be seen as representing the views of the Medici *parte* as a whole, and not of Lorenzo personally. However, the implications of the changes were not lost on his political opponents who argued that this new constitution marked a water-shed in Florentine political life. Although it did little more than recognise what was already true – that only supporters of Lorenzo might hope to become part of the political establishment – yet a change had occurred. 'The decree', Alamanno Rinuccini said, 'contained many things dishonourable and opposed to citizen-life and to the freedom of the people; and, indeed, from that day their freedom seemed to me dead and buried.'[4] And to the historian, Giovanni Cambi, it appeared that it was only after these changes that sycophancy and servility became the dominant features of Florentine political life:

> for the members of the new . . . body cared for nothing but to keep their own position and assented to everything. Thus a servile feeling gained ground; the citizens sacrificed their freedom to obtain office. Yet what they did obtain was not enough to satisfy them; for all looked enviously on the inner council, to which each thought himself worthy to belong.[5]

Lorenzo might continually insist that he was no more than 'a private citizen, equal with other citizens and in no way superior'[6] but it was accepted that, to get on in the world or to get on with the Florentine government, it was essential to ingratiate oneself with Lorenzo who must be proffered gifts, done favours, publicly deferred to. One must even give up one's own honour – that most prized Florentine possession – in order to enhance that of Lorenzo, as happened in the case of Costanzo Landucci:

> when he went to race at Siena, there was a tie between his horse and one belonging to Lorenzo . . . called *La Lucciola*, that of Costanzo being in reality one head's length in advance of the other. And the people who were present declared that he had won and told him to go to the magistrate and they would bear witness. Costanzo, however, refused to do this out of respect for Lorenzo . . .[7]

Whether such developments were inevitable, whether Lorenzo actively sought them, or was merely a victim of the insecurities of his close familial and political associates who escaped the opprobrium of later historians and, unlike Lorenzo, have never been branded as tyrants, must remain a matter of debate. What is certain is that, throughout the 1480s, Lorenzo frequently expressed a desire to retire from public affairs in order to lead a life of scholarship and quiet in some rural retreat, and that the expression of such sentiments was quite genuine. He wanted more time for his writing which had entered a period of intense creativity, while these, of course, were also the years in which Poggio a Caiano was being built and landscaped. His correspondence shows that he was still actively involved in all the rural experiences which had delighted him since adolescence – creating water-meadows at Poggio, hunting, fishing and intensive stock-breeding. His race-horses were an unfailing source of interest although it was now a matter of regret that Lorenzo usually had to hear of their exploits from others as, for instance, in April 1483, when his servant Andrea Malfatti was instructed to go and watch a race at Ferrara, 'and to return with as much information as possible',[8] or again in September 1485 when Amerigo Corsini gave Lorenzo a graphic report of a race in Lucca where the victory was disputed between Lorenzo's horse and that of the Marquess of Mantua.[9]

Lorenzo, therefore, continued to be happiest, it appears, when away from the political world of Florence, and his ill-health obviously increased the attractions of retirement. On the other hand, as we have seen, the central role which he played in Florentine government was no longer disguised. The situation was complicated, particularly after 1485, in that Lorenzo was often so ill that he could not leave his palace even when he was in Florence. This meant that much business had to be transacted twice over, once in the Palazzo della Signoria and once in the Medici palace, as foreign ambassadors who had to trudge backwards and forwards between the two found to their cost. But Lorenzo's official position, at least, was never ambiguous. He was a member of both the Seventy and the Eight, and kept in touch with both daily when he was away from Florence. He was also elected as one of the officials of the *Monte* to which the 1480 *Balìa* delegated control of Florence's financial affairs. He was not a member of the Twelve, but, as it turned out this did not matter, since, simply because Lorenzo was not a member, that body never assumed the important role in government which had been intended.

Within Florence, then, the firm hand of Medici control was always evident, while in Florence's subject territories that control was even more obvious. Lorenzo's habit of dealing directly with local communities – instructing them on which officials, priests, law-officers or school-masters to appoint, interfering with the course of justice – increased. Even the most trivial matter might involve him as, for instance, in April 1481, when he asked the authorities of San Gimignano to excuse payment of a fine, incurred by the daughter of a Medici client, as a result of offending against the sumptuary laws. Naturally, Lorenzo was by no means the only Florentine to interfere with local communities in this way. He was, however, more successful in getting his own way as the Medici patronage web spread; as a result more and more local officials were dragged into the web and a whole generation grew up which was accustomed to obeying Lorenzo without ever questioning the source of his authority. Thus, in many towns and villages, Florentine rule was effectively replaced by Medici rule, and a direct relationship was built up between 'subject' and 'prince' which paved the way for the absolutist regimes of the Medici grand-dukes of Tuscany.

As far as foreign policy was concerned, it is technically true that policy decisions were never made by Lorenzo personally but by Lorenzo in consultation with the Eight or, in times of war, the Ten. It is also true that, on occasion, he faced opposition within these bodies, particularly in relation to his pro-Neapolitan policies and his irritating habit of dealing directly with official ambassadors. Yet both these offices were normally occupied by close friends and associates of Lorenzo who tended to leave all major decisions to him, even when he would have genuinely preferred to be uninvolved. They were no doubt right to do so. Objectively speaking, Lorenzo was probably the best diplomat in Florence. As a negotiator he had a gift for putting people at their ease, disarming them with charm. Equally effective was his ability to switch suddenly to a stern manner and the expression of displeasure. While he himself gave little away, 'because it [was] his habit and custom to keep things to himself and not to open his mouth much',[10] his command of all the rhetorical skills and his eloquence, so often praised by contemporaries, were often put to very effective diplomatic use. Additionally, of course, Lorenzo was the best-informed of all Florentines in matters of foreign policy. He saw all the official correspondence; Iacopo Guicciardini was quite right to assume in December 1485 that Lorenzo would see 'all that I write to the office of the Ten'.[11] Ambassadors were usually Lorenzo's nominees and, in consequence, tended to look to him for instructions. It is significant that, in 1486, Bernardo Rucellai spoke of having a 'commission' from the Ten but an 'order' from Lorenzo.[12] Such men as Rucellai wrote regularly and fully to Lorenzo, but did not think they needed 'to inform the Ten of every little detail'.[13]

Sometimes the very position of ambassador was as ambiguous as Lorenzo's general position in Florence. The kind of confusion expressed by Rucellai similarly emerges in Francesco Gaddi's *Libro di Ricordi* where he describes how, in May 1480, he was sent from Florence to France, 'by order of Lorenzo with a public commission'.[14] But, in fact, the position was even more confused than Gaddi remembered for he was not officially nominated as an ambassador until December and, even then, the Florentine government assumed that there would be no need to send him official dispatches since Lorenzo would be sending him any necessary information.

All this explains why, after 1480, foreign governments made few bones about treating Lorenzo as the effective ruler of Florence. Lorenzo himself might insist that he was merely an ordinary citizen, but no one believed him. Rather they recognised the accuracy of the view, expressed by the Sienese ambassador, Tommaso Biringucci, that in Florence, 'No one so much as moves a piece of paper without the consent of the Master.'[15]

A detail from Ghirlandaio's fresco in the Church of the S. Trinità showing
Lorenzo with members of the Sassetti family

Lorenzo, therefore, in the early 1480s, was emerging as the undisputed, if unofficial, ruler of Florence, a position underlined by the panic which always afflicted the regime at even the hint of a threat to his life. Thus, in 1481:

A certain hermit came to the house of Lorenzo de' Medici at Poggio a Caiano; and the servants declared that he intended to murder Lorenzo, so they took him and sent him to the *Bargello*.[16]

Here he was tortured to death. The same jittery response was evident later in the year when a new plot was uncovered. The conspirators subsequently confessed that, after assassinating Lorenzo, they planned:

> to take refuge in some safe house until part of the people had risen. Then, with a banner taken from a church with the arms of the Commune, to parade the streets crying, 'Long live the People' . . . and in the lower parts of the city to broach casks of wine for the poor.[17]

In the evening of 2 June 1481 Amoretto Baldivonetti, the illegitimate son of an ancient but impoverished Florentine family, was arrested and, on the following morning, his arrest was followed by that of Battista Frescobaldi who, while consul at Constantinople, had been responsible for apprehending Bernardo Bandini and subsequently felt that he had been inadequately rewarded. The conspirators were all duly sentenced to death; when an appeal against sentence was lodged on the correct legal grounds that what was in question was merely a criminal project, not an actual crime, the *Signoria* and the Seventy declared that the conspirators' act had been one of high treason since they had tried to 'curtail liberty and change the government which depended upon Lorenzo'.[18] They further decreed that any act which in the future injured or threatened Lorenzo would be punished in the same way, 'thus giving him great honour'.[19] On 6 June, the conspirators, who appear to have been motivated at least in part by genuine republican zeal, were executed, the Ferrarese ambassador commenting that while this had increased both Lorenzo's position and his authority, it had also increased the number of his enemies.

Lorenzo was convinced that the conspirators had had a large number of sympathisers within Florence, and he took the opportunity to arrange a series of pro-Medicean demonstrations both in the city and in the subject-towns. Effective though such demonstrations might be in terms of propaganda, they did nothing to alleviate Lorenzo's sense of unease about the security of his family. That family lay at the heart of his thinking; it remained the well-spring of all his actions. It was there, at the core of his life, a close-knit unit bound together by genuine affection and shared interests. It even had a new member, for after Giuliano's death, it was discovered that he had left an illegitimate son, Giulio, who was welcomed into the Medici nursery and was regarded by Lorenzo as almost his own son.

This family was a source of boundless pleasure and joy. Lorenzo took undisguised delight in the progress his sons made with their studies, particularly the brilliant Giovanni. His daughters' company also gave him many hours of unalloyed pleasure. His sisters remained close to him; even Bianca and her children remained a constant source of interest and objects of support. In the spring of 1482, however, the family circle was shaken by an event from which Lorenzo found it difficult to recover – the death of his mother on 25 March. Lucrezia had always been his best adviser and counsellor, and he was forced to confess that while 'It is true that we ought to submit patiently to the will of God . . . in this case my heart refuses to be comforted.'[20]

He felt the loss particularly since it occurred at a time when he most needed sustained good advice. This was a critical period in Italian affairs when mounting tensions within the peninsula were accompanied by a manifest and growing interest in Italy on the part of other powers, notably the French, the Aragonese, and the Ottomans. Everywhere it seemed there were minor incidents which threatened to escalate into major conflicts, and each month brought new invasion scares. Since Lorenzo knew that his own position was most vulnerable when Florence faced a period of protracted warfare, he could not be indifferent to these crises. In order to protect his family he was forced, therefore, to do all that was humanly possible to secure the conditions and the framework within which a general Italian peace could become a reality.

Lorenzo's consequent diplomatic activities earned him a formidable reputation among contemporaries who spoke frequently of his prudence as a statesman. Subsequent historians built upon this image and argued that Lorenzo was responsible for creating in Italy a balance of power which he maintained by wise and subtle political deliberation. But this is not a true picture: the truth is that if any balance was created in Italy between 1480 and 1492 it was a balance of weakness and not a balance of power. The Italian states, with the possible exception of Venice, were all in a state of crisis. Throughout Italy and especially in Florence, rapid administrative developments of the type encouraged by Lorenzo, coupled with vast military expenditure, had led to economic decline and fiscal chaos. Virtually every state was bankrupt and it was this simple fact more than any other that forced them back, on occasion, from the brink of warfare, or brought wars to an end rapidly when they did break out. While Lorenzo played an important part in creating the diplomatic conditions to bring about peace, he did not do so because Florence was strong, but because of his accurate assessment of how weak the position of his family and the Medici regime would be, were the gradual but inexorable economic decline of Florence to be accelerated by long and expensive periods of warfare.

What is more, Lorenzo could not always avoid warfare, for as other Italian powers were in the habit of pointing out, his own position sometimes made it difficult for him to promote the peace of Italy. Lorenzo simply could not afford to ignore the popular prejudices and the imperialistic ambitions of the Florentines who were embittered by their loss of territory during the Pazzi war and incensed by the continued occupation of Sarzana by the Genoese. This was, indeed, a matter on which Florence as a whole could be said to have suffered from a generalised paranoia. Every action by another power, however insignificant, was immediately assumed to have the sole purpose of preventing Florence retaking Sarzana. The Medici regime would never have survived if it had not consistently pursued Florentine interests, and, when those interests were involved, the best that Lorenzo could hope for was to satisfy Florentine ambition more by diplomacy and compromise than by force.

He was not always unsuccessful. In the case of Siena, for instance, he succeeded remarkably well. There was no Florentine, including Lorenzo, who did not nourish an almost primitive ambition to conquer the city's ancient rival which, in decline, now offered a perpetual threat to the peace of Italy. Scarcely a year passed without the instability of the succession of weak regimes which professed to govern Siena creating a dangerous diplomatic or military situation. These always threatened the peace of Tuscany and created the possibility of intervention by any one of the numerous mercenary captains who dreamed of becoming rulers of Siena. From a Medicean standpoint it would obviously be preferable for Siena to be under Lorenzo's control than ruled by Roberto da San Severino, the Count of Pitigliano, or Virginio Orsini. Yet, in public, Lorenzo gave no hint of this but maintained a conciliatory attitude towards the Sienese. He continued to prevent the interminable frontier disputes, which still plagued the border communities, from getting out of hand, assisted the Sienese government when it was threatened by exiles, used independent arbitration when quarrels arose between Florence and Siena, and, in 1483, was instrumental in drawing up a league of friendship between the two cities. Thereafter, he spoke of his intention to make no distinction between Florentines and Sienese since 'both the one state and the other are indissolubly linked'.[21] Yet, at the same time, employing his customary methods of patronage, bribery and management, he was able to build up within Siena a very large Medicean following which, by its very existence, could only contribute to the instability of that city.

As it turned out, however, it was not Siena which once more plunged Italy into a general war but Venice, in alliance with the ever restless Girolamo Riario who began hostilities by declaring war on Ferrara. Since Milan, Florence and Naples were united in objecting to the possibility of any territorial expansion on the part of either the papacy or Venice, they sent troops to assist Ferrara and attack the army which Sixtus IV was gathering near Rome to send to his nephew's aid. The successful destruction of the papal army, and the equally successful Florentine occupation of Città di Castello, so alarmed Sixtus who was now faced with the possibility of Venice seizing Ferrara for herself, that he agreed to enter into peace negotiations at Cremona.

Lorenzo was determined to participate in person in these deliberations, for he hoped to use the occasion to make tangible gains for Florence. He believed that Lodovico Sforza, now the effective ruler of Milan, had already shown a limitless capacity for dissimulation, and he had little reason to trust Sixtus IV. It was therefore essential to be among the diplomats at Cremona and he would not be put off from going even though the French warned that Girolamo Riario would certainly try to take advantage of the opportunity to assassinate Lorenzo. Whether Lorenzo's insistence on going should be regarded as an act of courage or simply obstinacy is not certain. What is known is that it was highly unpopular in Florence where, as Scala subsequently reminded him, 'it was very difficult to obtain an agreement to your going . . . the difficulty deriving from the fact that your presence is very necessary here'.[22] And, even when Lorenzo had convinced his colleagues and friends that he must go, they would only agree on his assuring them that his absence would be as brief as possible since they had argued that it was absolutely impossible for any decision about the raising of money or defence to be made without him. Speed was therefore essential. Lorenzo left Florence on 12 February, reached Cremona five days later – followed by the usual crop of panic-stricken letters from leading Mediceans urging his return – and was back in Florence on 8 March.

By the treaty of Cremona the signatories bound themselves into an alliance – which Sixtus IV insisted on calling a 'Holy League' – designed to compel Venice to abandon her attack on Ferrara. Venice, herself, was placed under interdict and, although she responded by inviting the French Dukes of Lorraine and Orleans to reactivate their dormant claims to Naples and Milan, she was economically exhausted and militarily defeated by the end of the year. Yet the war dragged on, as wars in Italy were wont to do, and it was not until 8 August 1484, when Sixtus IV was already on his deathbed, that the Peace of Bagnolo was finally signed.

It was not a peace which was popular with the Florentines who had committed considerable resources to a struggle from which they gained nothing. Lorenzo was particularly irritated by the fact that Sarzana, which the Florentines had made several unsuccessful attempts to recapture during the war, was not even mentioned in the peace treaty. His response reflects less the mature statesman of balanced judgement than the young and impetuous Lorenzo at the time of the Volterra incident. Once again, he made a rash decision with potentially far-reaching consequences: he encouraged the Florentines to seize the Genoese fortress of Pietrasanta on the grounds that the garrison there had plundered a Florentine convoy which had been taking supplies to the troops attacking Sarzana. Although far from well, he insisted on being personally present when Pietrasanta surrendered.

Lorenzo had correctly judged the Florentine mood. The capture of Pietrasanta was celebrated amid scenes of wild rejoicing. Lorenzo's 'Florentiness' had triumphed, but he had shown less wisdom in an 'Italian' context. The capture of Pietrasanta further alienated Lodovico

Sforza and led in the long run to the return of Genoa to Milanese overlordship while, even within Florence, it subjected the economy and the republic's creaking tax structure to such a strain that by April 1485 Florence's finances could be described as 'exhausted'.[23]

It was also unfortunate, in the circumstances, that the new pope, Innocent VIII, was a Genoese who therefore looked unfavourably on Florentine ambitions in Liguria. His election alarmed Lorenzo, for from the outset Innocent made clear his feelings of hostility both towards Ferrante of Naples and towards Lorenzo's relatives, the Orsini. Lorenzo therefore would have liked to form part of the customary delegation sent from Florence to congratulate the new pope on his election, but the precarious state of his health made this impossible. In his stead, therefore, he sent Piero, under the tutelage of Poliziano.

Now fourteen years old and, by all accounts, extremely good-looking, Piero showed serious defects of character which were not lost on his father who once remarked with his usual perspicacity that he had three sons of whom one, Piero, was foolish, one, Giovanni, was clever, and one, Giuliano, was kind. Piero did have some good qualities; he was always anxious to please his father, was a tolerably good scholar, and was not above taking pains if it was in his interest to do so. Matteo Franco, indeed, was of the opinion that his manners were so captivating that they enchanted all who encountered him. Inevitably, perhaps, he was nevertheless being progressively spoiled by the role into which the Florentines cast him as a substitute for Giuliano, the young prince of the Medici family. It was said that, 'he couldn't go outside the door without all Florence running after him',[24] and such public adulation did little to encourage Piero to control his hot temper or to moderate his overweening pride. Lorenzo, therefore, rightly experienced serious misgivings about the future. Recognising how he himself had been disadvantaged by his inexperience of business affairs and public life when he succeeded to the Medici inheritance, he was making deliberate efforts to involve Piero in the day to day business of managing the Medicean empire. This visit to Rome was thus to be Piero's initiation into foreign affairs, but the anxious and detailed letter which Lorenzo sent with his son clearly indicated that he had serious doubts about Piero's ability to act either with social tact or with political good sense.

Taking it all in all, Lorenzo would probably have done better to go to Rome in person, but the complications of his health made it impossible. All his old illnesses had returned and he was frequently incapacitated by asthma, gout or a combination of the two. In February 1485 he suffered his first complete collapse and retired with Clarice, herself ill with tuberculosis, his doctors, and a number of intimate friends, to Morba. He was unable to concentrate on business because of frequent bouts of acute pain and could not even reply to the most urgent letters. Often he could not sleep. When Michelozzi rode out from Florence to consult him he was sharply rebuked. Lorenzo remarked, with acerbity, that he had come to the baths, 'in order to cure himself and to restore his health and neither could nor would attend to any other matter'.[25]

So began a new period in Lorenzo's life in which his health enforced long absences from Florence and therefore set a new pattern of existence. As soon as spring came, or autumn put an end to the suffocating heats of a Tuscan summer, he would leave Florence for the baths, travelling either via Pisa if he was going to Morba, or by Castellina and Poggibonsi if he were going to San Filippo. These were characteristically leisurely journeys with frequent halts – at Poggio a Caiano, Pisa, Spedaletto, Badia di Passignano, Siena, San Casciano or Poggibonsi. He was always accompanied by one or other of his secretaries, by some of the *brigata* of his household, family, friends and clients, for, while he was at the baths, he liked to be surrounded by those who could entertain him and lighten the atmosphere. Piero da Bibbiena, for example, would read aloud to him whenever Lorenzo felt unable to read himself.

Apart from taking the waters, Lorenzo liked to relax by walking and talking, or by fishing, but, if the pain was severe, he would remain indoors playing games, watching others play, or talking with old friends who would deliberately seek him out. These holidays did bring some improvement, although the good they did was largely psychological for during the first few days he would always feel better. Then, however, would come a relapse and his resident doctors would be called in to make one of their optimistic diagnoses which did not really fool anyone. After 1485 Lorenzo himself recognised that his illnesses were incurable.

It is possible that, if he had been able to retire from business entirely, his life might have been prolonged. He himself thought so. Throughout that diffiult spring of 1485 he regularly expressed his irritation at having to deal with matters of business, whether the hiring of mercenaries, or nominations to the new *Signoria*. On the latter question his annoyance flowed out in an extremely bitter letter to the long-suffering Michelozzi to whom he wrote:

> About the priors I don't want you to tell me anything, since I don't yet want this burden. . . . Let the others do what they want. Get all these suitors off my back, because I have more letters from those who want to be members of the *Signoria* than there are days in the year. I have decided not to want everything my way, and to live this time which I have left as quietly as I can for that is what all our ancestors did and they were old and healthy.[26]

He blamed the Mediceans in Florence for betraying him behind his back as well as creating unnecessary extra work, at a time when he could least put his mind to political affairs, and warned that, 'I don't know whether on my return I will recognise our friends, for they seem so changed and corrupted.'[27]

This was less than fair. The ambiguous position which Lorenzo held in the government of Florence inevitably made for problems over communication if he was away from the city, but the Sienese ambassador, for example, was certain at this time that the Florentine government, 'on their own and without the opinion and wishes of [Lorenzo] do not want to make any decision'.[28] On the one hand there was Lorenzo complaining about being overburdened by business, and on the other suggesting that decisions were taken without consulting him. Yet if he were consulted on every minor matter the delays in conducting government business would become intolerable. As it was, all diplomatic business was being conducted in a complicated three-way process by which letters which came to Florence were then dispatched to Lorenzo. He would send a draft reply back to Florence, and only then could an official reply be sent out from the Florentine government.

Many matters were too complicated or too secret to be dealt with by correspondence so it was essential to have a go-between. This was usually the task of Michelozzi, who was the mediator between Lorenzo and Pierfilippo Pandolfini, who appears to have been Lorenzo's anchor man in Florence at this time. The role played by Pandolfini illustrates the way in which a new problem had arisen in Lorenzo's life. As his health deteriorated, he became far more dependent on the total loyalty of leading Mediceans like Iacopo Guicciardini and Pandolfini, yet, often, his suspicious nature led him to distrust even those closest to him and to accuse them of disloyalty and lack of affection. Circumstances dictated that he depend upon them, but he obviously disliked having to do so.

Meanwhile, Piero's behaviour did nothing to improve Lorenzo's temper. At a time when he would have wished to be able to depend upon his eldest son, he learned that Piero, who had returned from Rome with a new sense of his own importance, had appeared in public so splendidly dressed that he had offended against the city's statutes, and that there had been considerable ill-talk in consequence. When questioned, Michelozzi was forced to confess that this was indeed the case, adding, for good measure, the information that since his return from Rome 'Piero has not seemed to me the person he was before his departure. He has need of your authority and it is time that you returned to Florence.'[29]

Retreat and retirement were, therefore, impossible, and there could be no escape from the constant round of decision-making, for, as the Council of One Hundred remarked gloomily on 19 April, 'The affairs of Italy have not quietened down. Everywhere many new threats to peace are only too obvious.'[30] There was, for instance, renewed trouble in Siena. Lorenzo, like the majority of leading Florentines, was convinced that an attack

PIERO DI LORENZO DI PIERO DE MEDICI

Piero di Lorenzo by Bronzino

launched on Siena by her exiles and supported by Virginio Orsini, had papal backing and was designed to force the Florentines to reach an agreement with Genoa over Pietrasanta and Sarzana. Once again it appeared as if the whole of Italy must be plunged into war so that the Sienese might change their government. Lorenzo laboured incessantly and successfully to persuade the reluctant Florentines, who resented the expense, to succour the Sienese, to dissuade Virginio Orsini from becoming involved, and also to bolster the confidence of Siena's rulers. The characteristic mixture of flattery, firmness and calculated ambiguity he used in dealing with the Sienese is well illustrated in one of his many letters of advice, sent from Morba on 4 May, in which he explained that:

> It is my intention to find out from time to time about every move made by these exiles of yours. Both because it is my duty and because I know it is the wish of my government, as soon as I have any news I will inform your lordships, for I know that you are well aware that, even if I lack prudence, I will never lack in sincerity and faith towards your state. I will, lovingly, tell your lordships what I think you should do in this situation.[31]

On 9 May 1485 Lorenzo was finally well enough to leave Morba and return, by easy stages, to Florence, travelling via Poggio and Pisa, and confident that, 'by the grace of God, I am restored to my former health.'[32] He was being over-optimistic. The autumn found him as bad as ever and he retreated to San Filippo in Sienese territory with the twin purpose of taking the curative waters there and keeping an eye on the Sienese crisis. He gained little benefit in terms of his health and, after his return to Florence, was for months too ill even to leave the Medici palace where the large fires which were kept constantly burning could not keep out the chill of what was an unusually cold, wet and windy winter.

It was in this condition that he had to cope with a crisis which, in one way or another, was to keep him occupied for the rest of his life, and which was provoked by, on the one hand, the breakdown in relations between the Pope and King Ferrante and, on the other, the appallingly bad relationship between the King and his barons, who now broke out in open rebellion. Innocent VIII immediately took the barons under his protection, persuaded Venice to release the mercenary leader Roberto da San Severino from her sevice and made him Captain-General of the Church, issued a bull of excommunication against any who should come to the aid of Ferrante, and urged the Duke of Lorraine to assert his claim to the throne of Naples.

Hungary and Milan both declared their support for Ferrante who also turned directly to Lorenzo, 'as we turn to the best friend we have in Italy and one for whom, in case of need, we would risk our state, our children and our person'.[33] Meanwhile, French ambassadors arrived in Florence to remind the city both of its traditional devotion to the Church and of the injuries which had been visited on Florence by the Neapolitans.

So the familiar dilemma was presented. Whose interests were at stake now? Were they those of the Medici family, of Lorenzo personally, of all Florence, or of Italy? Was it any longer possible to distinguish between them? Lorenzo was able to satisfy his conscience by his conviction that 'the interests of the house of Medici are united with those of Florence – La casa ne va con la città'[34] and that 'both our state and that of all Italy'[35] were dependent on a victory for Ferrante. None knew better than Lorenzo how chronically impoverished was the crown of Naples and he was genuinely concerned that the Pope might succeed in conquering Naples. He repeatedly pointed out that success for Innocent would mean that the Church would control two-thirds of Italy, since the Pope would immediately be in a position to become 'effective ruler of Bologna, Perugia and the other lands of the Church'.[36] Lorenzo also hoped that support for Ferrante at this juncture would mean that the King would subsequently assist in the recapture of Sarzana, and he recognised the importance of Florentine economic interests in Naples. Yet he was also heavily influenced by two personal considerations which had little to do with the general well-being of Florence. One was the fact that valuable benefices in the Kingdom of Naples might come Giovanni's way, and the other that there would be little hope of a repayment of massive Medici loans to Ferrante in the event of his defeat.

It was thus easy enough for Lorenzo to decide on a policy. The difficulty came in persuading the Florentines that he was right. The financial situation in the city, which continued to limp from one fiscal crisis to another, had not improved. What was described as the 'money difficulty' had been a constant theme of Lorenzo's correspondence for at least twelve months. The ruling élite of Florence remembered only too clearly the damage done to their banking and mercantile interests during the Pazzi war. They also believed that the revolt of the Neapolitan barons was entirely justified in that it had been provoked by the cruelties of Alfonso Duke of Calabria who was loathed by the Florentine community in Naples who, for months, had been complaining that the Duke refused to meet his obligations to them.

Lorenzo's difficulties at this juncture are particularly well-documented because he was at San Filippo, and the letters sent to him there have been preserved. From these it is apparent that many prominent Florentines hoped that they could get away with giving only verbal support to Ferrante. Indeed, so general was the opposition, at all levels of society, to becoming involved in the Neapolitan war, that it even extended to the Seventy, a fact which Pierfilippo Pandolfini found sufficiently alarming to suggest new constitutional safeguards to protect the Medici ascendancy.

Lorenzo wavered between rage and irritation at attitudes which he found 'idiotic'[37] and irrational, and a desire to wash his hands of the whole business. 'Do what you like', he told the Florentine government, 'and I will give way to your prudence, and may God illumine you.'[38] Although convinced that he was right, and as always ill-disposed towards not getting his own way, he yet persisted throughout September in his determination not to get involved for, as he told Michelozzi:

> As you know . . . I have always acted as seemed best for the needs and honour of the city; so I am determined to do in the future, and, above all, have come to this conclusion, that what seems best to our citizens will always seem best to me.[39]

On the grounds that he did not want to fight both his friends and his enemies at the same time, and that he did not want to have to cope with business as well, he implored Michelozzi 'to send as few letters as you can, because, since I have been here, I have done nothing but read and write letters'.[40]

It is obvious that Lorenzo was deeply hurt to find some of his closest friends among his opponents. So disillusioned was he that he suggested that their loyalty to him lasted only until he was ten miles from Florence. Yet, his actions to some extent belied his words. He was so convinced that he would get his own way in the end that he arranged to meet with the Orsini leaders while he was at San Filippo. On 30 September he concluded an agreement with them that they would support Ferrante and serve as Florentine mercenaries during the coming conflict.

In the middle of October he returned to Florence to take control of the increasingly confused situation by asserting the need for Florence to succour Ferrante. As he had anticipated, he was faced with considerable opposition but, according to Niccolò Valori, 'notwithstanding, Lorenzo urged the necessity of taking a side with so much eloquence that those who doubted were encouraged and at last all were brought over to his view'.[41] Naples was to be supported by every possible means and money provided, 'without respect or regard to anything, *Monte*, gabelles, taxation of the citizens' even if it meant raiding the dowry fund.[42]

It had been a remarkable achievement by a sick man. Throughout that winter, 'what with rain and cold so intense as to be unbelievable',[43] he was often incarcerated in the Medici palace as, for example, in early January when for several days the pains in his feet and stomach were so bad that, 'no one [could] speak to him and he [had] no interest in anything except baths and medicine'.[44] On other occasions he retreated to Poggio or to Careggi causing further hiccups in the smooth running of the conduct of the war and diplomacy. His pain made him ill-tempered and his irritation was often visited on devoted friends and associates like Francesco Gaddi who, replying to one of these outbursts, wrote defensively, 'because, in your letter, you say that I never send you anything . . . but ice and snow, I reply that it is necessary to write the truth of things so that you know on what to base your plans'.[45]

Despite his physical condition, throughout the ensuing conflict Lorenzo was the central director of all Florence's policies which aimed at avoiding an escalation of the conflict and preventing either side winning a decisive victory. His position was that Florence was fighting to 'defend the public good and liberty of Italy from the dominion of priests who are moved by an ambition and desire to conquer'.[46] Lorenzo was, from the beginning, convinced that the Pope did not have the financial resources to pursue a long conflict, and he was proved right when a decisive defeat of the papal forces forced Innocent to negotiate. Lorenzo's efforts were then directed towards bringing about a rapid peace settlement.

Lorenzo's demands, on behalf of Florence, were extremely moderate. He told Lodovico Sforza he wanted only four things: the reservation of Florence's claims against Genoa, a pledge of assistance in any Florentine attempt to recover Sarzana, the maintenance of the pro-Medici regime in Siena, and permission from the Pope for Florence to levy a tax on her clergy. Yet modest as these demands were, there was from the beginning a fear that they would not be met, for, as Piero Capponi told Lorenzo in June 1486, 'These Milanese have such a desire for peace . . . that I fear our interests will not be favoured. Already there are those who say about the peace of Bagnolo – "they are not satisfied with Pietrasanta." '[47]

These suspicions proved justified. News of the signing of peace on 11 August took Lorenzo by surprise and outraged the Florentines. Despite promises which had been repeatedly made both by Milan and by Naples no mention at all was made of Florentine claims to Sarzana, nor had the Pope granted their request to be allowed to tax their clergy.

On both counts Lorenzo made a considerable public display of dissatisfaction while, in private, he put pressure on Ferrante to repay his loan. The recovery of Sarzana had now become a matter of personal prestige and it was thus to redeem Medicean honour and, with it, that of Florence, that immediate preparations were made to attack it. Meanwhile, the Genoese took pre-emptive action by launching a surprise attack on Sarzanello, a Florentine fort which lay to the east of Sarzana. Florence immediately dispatched a relieving force which defeated the Genoese on 15 April 1487.

The recapture of Sarzana itself proved altogether more difficult and costly. Lorenzo's commitment to the campaign was evident. Essentially he became the director of the whole affair which bore the clear imprint of his interests. Thus, it was Orsini troops who were used as mercenary forces and it was obviously Lorenzo's personal pressure which extracted some naval assistance from the reluctant Ferrante who finally ran out of excuses in June and dispatched the best of his galleys to Liguria. Lorenzo was, in fact, so involved that he could not bear to stay away from the scene of the operations and, although unwell, he travelled via Pisa to the Florentine camp which he reached on 8 June. He immediately ordered an even closer investment effectively blockading Sarzana which finally capitulated on 21 June.

The recapture of Sarzana was probably the greatest public triumph of Lorenzo's life. The Florentines considered that he had personally vindicated their honour before all Italy, and they praised him accordingly. 'Never', wrote the Ferrarese ambassador of Lorenzo's return to Florence, 'was he received with such acclamations by the people who attribute the recapture of Sarzana to him above all others.'[48]

Among the Florentines, therefore, the reputation of the Medicean regime had never stood so high. Yet all the old haunting insecurities remained and intensified with each new bout of illness. Knowing his eldest son so well, Lorenzo felt unable to put any faith in his ability to meet any threat to the regime, and, after 1487, he knew that his own death could not be far away. Thus, much of his life became bound up with erecting defensive bulwarks to serve as a protection for his family and to ensure their status within Florence.

Remembering his own early difficulties, he first set about providing Piero with available troops for use in emergency. For some time he had been strengthening his family's ties with the Orsini who were, by now, among the most important clients of the Medici bank. Lorenzo became particularly close to the great *condottiere* Virginio Orsini, to whom he declared himself bound by the closest ties 'of family and friendship'.[49] Finally he forged one further familial bond. After lengthy negotiations conducted, interestingly enough, as much through the office of the Ten as through Lorenzo's personal chancellery, in a proxy ceremony at Naples, Piero was betrothed to Alfonsina Orsini in February 1487. The Medici family were now twice related to the Orsini clan and a tie of obligation had been created on which Piero could depend in the future.

A second source of protection for the Medici family was found by gaining closer access to the power and the patronage of the Curia, and here it was Giovanni who was the key figure in Lorenzo's plans. Destined as he was for an ecclesiastical career, he was already a pluralist on a remarkable scale even judging by the somewhat lax standards of the fifteenth century. One of the main activities of the Lyons branch of the Medici bank had become the search for benefices for Giovanni. The Rome branch, likewise, was bombarded with letters concerning the furtherance of Giovanni's career. Prominent Florentines abroad could also rely on being requested to keep an eye open for good benefices or moribund clerics, while Florentine diplomats devoted increasing amounts of time to the same question. Even at the height of the Papal–Neapolitan war, for instance, Lanfredini, ambassador successively at Naples and at Rome, spent as much time on Giovanni's concerns as he did on regular diplomacy.

The results were impressive. Louis XI gave Giovanni the abbey of Fontdouce and promised him the see of Aix until it was discovered that the incumbent was unfortunately still alive. Sixtus IV had granted him the convent of Passignano, the Duke of Milan the abbey of Miramondo, and Ferrante of Naples Monte Cassino. Within Tuscany Giovanni held a canonry in every single cathedral. *In toto* he held some twenty-seven separate benefices but, while these certainly provided him with the income of a prince of the Church, he yet lacked that crowning glory which would make him such a prince – the gift of a cardinal's hat. True, Giovanni was still very young but Lorenzo was now a man in a hurry and began vigorously promoting his son's claims at Rome.

Success, however, would be absolutely dependent on mending relations with Innocent VIII. Although, in doing so, Lorenzo was obviously mainly compelled by family interests, improved relations with Rome could only benefit Florence. It would certainly reduce fears of papal expansion into Tuscany, for instance, and there were also important business interests at stake. Rome, which was the quintessential example of a purely service city whose citizens could neither feed nor clothe themselves and depended entirely on imports, offered important banking and mercantile opportunities to Florentines.

So Lorenzo set out to woo Innocent VIII. No trouble was seen as being too great in this particular cause. It was not just a question of lending Innocent large sums of money, although this was certainly done. Infinitely more trouble was taken almost daily in order to flatter the Pope. Learning, for instance, of a papal taste for ortolans, Lorenzo ensured that every courier who left Florence took with him a gift of this rare delicacy. On one occasion he dispatched eighteen flasks of a kind of red wine which the Pope was known to enjoy, together with some of the much-prized Tuscan *vernaccia*; on others, a piece of pink cloth and 'damask of matchless beauty'.[50]

Then, in 1487, Lorenzo had the good fortune to place the Pope under an even greater obligation. The *condottiere* Boccolino Guzzoni rebelled against Innocent, seized the papal town of Osimo, and appealed to Sultan Bajazet for aid. When Giuliano della Rovere failed to capture Osimo by force, it was Lorenzo who provided the solution, persuading Boccolino to surrender Osimo on payment of 8,000 ducats and promising him a safe refuge in Florence.

Such stratagems were successful. Innocent began to turn to Lorenzo for advice on all issues until, eventually, he was a captive of Lorenzo's political judgement. The Ferrarese ambassador complained that, 'the Pope sleeps with the eyes of the Magnificent Lorenzo',[51] while the Florentine ambassador in Naples assured Lorenzo that, 'it is recognised perfectly well all over Italy what influence you have with the Pope and that the Florentine ambassador *quodammodo* governs the policies of Rome'.[52] As far as the troubled world of Italy was concerned, the influence which Lorenzo could exercise over Innocent can only be regarded as beneficial. Equally clearly, the Medici family and the Medici party made considerable gains from the connection. It brought Lorenzo personal gain, for the Medici were reinstated as papal bankers, it enhanced his prestige, and increased his honour. Thus, he had provided yet another defence against hard times for the Medici.

Suitably, perhaps, therefore, it was Lorenzo's immediate family who paid the necessary price with the marriage of Clarice's favourite daughter, Maddalena, to Franceschotto Cibo, Innocent's unprepossessing and brutal son. Negotiations for the alliance began in 1487 and faced Lorenzo with agonising dilemmas. Not least important were personal considerations. He was very fond of his daughter, knew that her sick mother needed her, and was well aware that a marriage to the much older Cibo could never bring her any personal happiness or the kind of domestic comfort in which she had always lived. The proposed bridegroom was over forty, fat, boring, perpetually drunk, and was said never to have made an interesting remark in his life.

The marriage also brought political difficulty. Lorenzo was aware of the fact that, in marrying above themselves, the Medici courted jealousy among the Florentine ruling class. There had always been trouble over the Orsini connection and now because of 'local unease'[53] he was forced to promise that he would not marry any other of his daughters to a foreign potentate.

Equally serious was the possibility that the marriage would lead to an estrangement with Naples, for a marriage between Ferrante's daughter and Cibo had also been mooted. Fortunately, Ferrante's need of Lorenzo, at this moment, was great enough for him to make no difficulties and on 4 November 1487, Maddalena, accompanied by her mother, left Florence for Rome where in January her formal marriage-contract was signed. Her dowry of 4,000 ducats was not large, by contemporary standards, but even so Lorenzo found it difficult to pay, there being, as he admitted, so many other 'holes to fill up';[54] in place of the money, he gave Cibo the Pazzi palace in Florence, their villa at Montughi, and an estate at Spedaletto.

Lorenzo continued to experience misgivings about this marriage, fearing that it could bring neither political profit nor personal happiness, and indeed the day would come when Cibo's name would be infamous throughout Italy. For the moment, however, Lorenzo surrendered to the fatalism which, as we have seen, was always his recourse at the most critical periods of his life. Seeking to set this marriage in the context of the rest of his life he commented:

Now may God guide all for the best and give me grace that the thing may benefit ourselves and others, and be for our personal and the general advantage. Such things are wont to be judged by their results more than by the rule of reason . . . I have never been so exclusively and passionately interested in my own private affairs as to forget public honour or that which becomes a straightforward and honest man . . . I know where to seek the fountain of things and what differences arise from the daily events which go on gradually evolving themselves.[55]

9

THE LAST YEARS

On 17 February 1491 the Company of St John the Evangelist, a confraternity of young boys, performed a sacred drama written by Lorenzo – *La Rappresentazione di San Giovanni e Paolo* – in order to celebrate the election of Lorenzo's youngest son, Giuliano, as Lord of their company. In the course of the play, the Emperor Constantine is represented as delivering a speech on the subject of power which may well express some of Lorenzo's conclusions concerning the troubled years he had spent manipulating the unruly Florentines. The Emperor claims that:

> Often he who calls Constantine happy
> Is better off than I, and does not speak the truth,

and argues that there are no genuine delights in power, only the appearance of such, for all that a ruler can anticipate is trouble and fatigue both of body and spirit. In order to maintain his authority, he must be constantly on the alert, never considering his own advantage but only the common good, ever aware of the importance of public opinion, shunning all luxury and avoiding avarice. He must be always kind and gracious, setting a good example since all eyes are perpetually trained on him, and he can never cease his labours by day or night. The drama ended with a final despairing prayer: 'Lord, I am tired, call me to thee.'

It is a picture of a life that is neither happy nor peaceful. And yet, after the turmoil and constant hard work of the decade which followed the Pazzi conspiracy, Lorenzo at last began to find some of the personal peace that had always eluded him. The careful nurturing of his children, his care for their education and upbringing, the endless cultivation of the papacy, the perpetual search for friends and allies, the hours given over to writing business letters, stolen from more enjoyable pursuits, began to bring some tangible rewards.

The last four years of Lorenzo's life thus have a bitter-sweet quality when great personal suffering and considerable personal achievement were brought together in a quintessentially Laurentian harmony. In retrospect Francesco Guicciardini would see them as a golden period when Lorenzo was at last secure in Florence and was acknowledged to be so powerful that not only did none dare to challenge his authority, few even desired to do so. For Florence it was a period of relative prosperity. Although the woollen industry was suffering from a lack of good imported raw material, and from a trade war with Venice, its relative decline was compensated for by a growth in silk production. In addition, the tax concessions which, at Lorenzo's instigation, had been granted to new buildings produced a building boom and offered welcome employment to the poorer classes who also continued to benefit from Lorenzo's cheap food policy. It was a period of cultural efflorescence, of the youth of Michelangelo, when Florence was perpetually caught up in a round of Medici-inspired festivals and celebrations. Even the festival of San Giovanni was revived in 1488 to celebrate the marriage of Maddalena and Franceschotto Cibo.

These were not, however, years of ease for Lorenzo. There was the growing menace of a French invasion of Italy, which Lorenzo alone seems to have taken seriously. Scarcely a month passed without some warning of just such an invasion reaching him from the Medici bank in Lyons or from some other source. Nor did the problem of Ferrante, the Neapolitan barons, and the Pope end in 1487. Their interminable quarrels continued to reverberate throughout the peninsula causing countless mini-crises which demanded Lorenzo's attention and whose complexities few but he understood. He was determined to prevent a complete breakdown in relations between King and Pope and even those historians most critical of Lorenzo have been forced to acknowledge that it was his tact and hard work which prevented the rashness of Innocent VIII, and the obstinacy of Ferrante, precipitating a general Italian conflagration. The activities of his Orsini relatives also created permanent tensions in central and southern Italy, 'their brains', according to Lorenzo, 'being so contrary and of such a nature, that they are incomprehensible . . . they are greedy and ambitious and if they are not forced by necessity to stick to one course, they are very unstable.'[1] The strain of maintaining good relations with Lodovico Sforza, who while complaining about the Florentine seizure of Sarzana had himself taken Genoa, was often intolerable, while Lorenzo had still to play an active role in managing both the Medici *parte* and the Medici bank.

To add to such perennial problems, the year 1488 brought a new series of diplomatic problems in the wake of a number of assassinations and assassination attempts. The first victim was Lorenzo's old adversary Girolamo Riario. Although Riario's death caused him little personal regret, Lorenzo was forced to take quick action to prevent moves from both Milan and Rome to take possession of Forlì and Imola which he wanted left in the hands of Girolamo's young heir, Ottaviano, since he believed that it was in the best interests of Florence that those two cities should be in the hands of, 'small lords rather than those of a great potentate'.[2] Florentine interests were also served by the prompt reoccupation of Piancaldoli which Riario had taken from her in 1478.

A month later, Galeotto Manfredi of Faenza was murdered by assassins

This page from the dedication copy of Niccolò Valori's *Life of Lorenzo de' Medici* is lavishly decorated with Medicean symbols and a portrait medallion of Lorenzo

hired by his wife. She was the daughter of Giovanni Bentivoglio of Bologna with whom she had clearly plotted her husband's death since it was with suspicious promptitude that Giovanni arrived at the gates of Faenza together with a troop of Milanese soldiers. Since Faenza had long been an area of strong Florentine influence and Manfredi essentially a Medici client, Lorenzo again reacted quickly. His position was made clear in a letter of Paoloantonio Soderini's which asserted that, 'the city of Florence and Lorenzo would not take less care to preserve the independence of Bologna, of Perugia, of Città di Castello, of Faenza and of Siena than they would to preserve their own. . . .'[3]

It was thus with the support of the Florentines that the citizens of Faenza took up arms and, with the help of peasants from the *contado*, overpowered the Bolognese and Milanese troops and took Giovanni Bentivoglio prisoner. It was also Lorenzo's agent in Faenza who persuaded the victorious citizens to hand Giovanni to the Florentines for safe-keeping and Lorenzo himself who, in a lengthy meeting at Cafaggiolo, negotiated a solution. In return for a guarantee of Faenza's 'independence' which, essentially, meant her retaining the status of a Florentine client-state, Giovanni, along with other Bolognese who had been captured, was released. A few months later, a plot to assassinate Giovanni was, in its turn, foiled, largely because of Lorenzo's refusal to take an active part in it, although it must be admitted that he failed to warn Giovanni of the project.

So crisis followed crisis and the pressure of business grew, reaching a peak in June 1488 when Lorenzo was so preoccupied that, let alone leave the city, he was quite unable to leave his office. It is, therefore, scarcely to be wondered at that about this time he was heard to remark that he wished he could go away and bury himself in some inaccessible place where no rumour of Italian events could ever penetrate.

Lorenzo's diplomatic achievements are the more remarkable when they are set in their proper context of his own physical and mental suffering. Plagued continually by gout and arthritis this was the worst year he had yet endured in terms of his health. He was constantly surrounded by doctors. In May they forced him to retreat to Spedaletto for treatment, and in the same month he suffered a severe attack of renal colic. In July he suffered another attack and in October his gout was so bad that he could not write, while, in December, the Ferrarese ambassador reported that he was in such pain that no one could even talk with him. To add to this physical pain there was the mental anguish of losing two of those dearest to him. In an effort to heal the breach between the two branches of the Medici family, he betrothed his daughter, Luisa, to his cousin Giovanni, but she died soon after at the age of only twelve and her death was followed, a few weeks later, by that of her mother.

Clarice had, of course, been ailing for some time and her disease was known to be mortal but, nevertheless, when her death came it was a grave blow. She had seemed to be better, comforted by an extended visit to Florence by Maddalena who had always been her favourite daughter, and this improvement had encouraged Lorenzo's doctors to urge him to take the waters at Filetta in Sienese territory in an attempt to relieve his own pain. He was still there when Clarice died on 30 July, much sooner than had been expected. Lorenzo, whose doctors would not allow him to return to Florence for Clarice's requiem mass, was shattered by the loss of his wife. His intense reaction gives the lie to those who have argued that the marriage of the two was little more than mere form. He told the Pope how the death

> of Clarice . . . my most dear and beloved wife, has been and is so prejudicial, so great a loss, and such a grief to me for many reasons, that it has exhausted my patience and my power of enduring anguish, and the persecution of fortune, which I did not think would have made me suffer thus. The deprivation of such habitual and such sweet company has filled my cup and has made me so miserable that I can find no peace . . .[4]

Nor was he able to work, always a sure sign that Lorenzo was deeply upset, and it was not until several weeks later that he was able to write to Lanfredini in Rome, apologising for his failure to answer important business questions and explaining, 'You know the cause; when my mind is occupied with one thing it can think of little else.'[5]

Clarice may appear unimportant to historians, as she often appeared to contemporaries, but she was not so to Lorenzo for whom she had created an ambience within which he could flourish. She provided a happy and secure domestic retreat where he could relax when the burdens of his political life became intolerable. In latter years she had played an increasingly large part in dealing with Medici clients, and Lorenzo had come to respect her judgment in these and other matters. She had, for instance, played a major and crucial role in arranging the marriages of both Piero and Maddalena. While she had never been Lorenzo's intellectual equal, she had fulfilled to perfection that role which in the fifteenth century was traditionally allotted to women of the upper classes, that of a dutiful wife and a good mother. Interestingly, therefore, one consequence of her death seems to have been that Lorenzo was drawn closer to his children and, particularly, to his remaining daughters. He felt Maddalena's absence and worried over her constantly. He was afraid that Innocent VIII would die before he could make proper provision for his son and urged the Pope 'to begin and act as a Pope with regard to the family of Your Holiness and not to trust so much in posterity and good health'.[6] Maddalena, herself, he bombarded with letters, gifts and good advice.

Lorenzo was always at his most human in the company of children whom he invariably treated with consideration and tenderness. Thus, even when he was ill at Spedaletto, hearing that his youngest daughter Contessina was hourly asking after him and about his return, he hastened to promise that he would soon return to her. In the meantime, he urged her to be kind to Piero's wife, 'and keep her company: tell her from me to take great care of the baby'.[7] That baby was his grandchild in whom he took such pleasure that he would carry it around in his arms for hours at a time. But it was not only his own family who captured his affection and engaged his interest. One day, for instance, when he was confined to the Medici palace and saw Michelozzi's wife and children in the Via Larga, he summoned them up so that he could caress and play with the children.

It was as if their company helped him to cope with the almost continuous pain which he now endured, and for which a typical prophylactic suggested by his doctors was the wearing of a sapphire ring on the third finger of the left hand. Ill on and off throughout 1489, and frequently driven to take refuge at the baths, he suffered an extremely serious attack of gout in March 1490 when his foot swelled up to elephantine proportions. He was similarly prostrated in the following February and unable to walk until the beginning of March, but that appears to have been the final serious attack before the one that killed him.

It was perhaps the knowledge of the seriousness of his illnesses which now drove Lorenzo back to scholarship and to writing. The sense of the flight of time and the vanity of human life became ever more dominant in his writing, as if he was recognizing how little of life was left to him to enjoy. He was also now composing far more religious poetry. There was, however, a further stimulus to such activities in the presence in Florence of Pico della Mirandola to whom Lorenzo had generously offered protection against the Inquisition, of which he had fallen foul. Lorenzo gave Pico his Fiesolan villa of Querceto and informed Innocent VIII that he was living a most saintly and Christian life. So Pico indubitably was, but he was also continuing to think and to write, dedicating to Lorenzo his *Heptaplus* in which he expounded the seven aspects of creation. Since Pico was congenitally incapable of ceasing to philosophise, to study, or to think, and since Lorenzo was frequently in his company, he could not fail to influence Lorenzo and encourage him to return to the scholarly and philosophical pursuits of his youth.

One intellectual pursuit which gave Lorenzo great pleasure at this time was, no doubt, linked to his renewed interest in philosophy. Assisted by Poliziano and Piero, he began a complete reorganisation of the Medici library. His interest in the project is confirmed by the fact that, during Lorenzo's many absences from Florence, Piero would send progress reports on the project. At the same time Lorenzo was buying, and having copied, books on a large scale, as the process of reorganisation revealed gaps in his collection.

Other pursuits also absorbed him. He was buying antiques and jewels on a regular basis but, above all, his interest in architecture was now given full rein. A large part of his time was taken up with town-planning, palace-building, and the design of gunpowder fortifications for the *contado*. He sat on a number of committees concerned with the redecoration of the Palazzo della Signoria, the building of the Sapienza at Pisa, and other group projects, and advised other prominent Florentines about their building plans.

Lorenzo was also, without doubt, a prime move in the project to complete the cathedral of Santa Maria de Fiore which still lacked a façade. On 12 February 1490 the consuls of the wool guild issued a decree which acknowledged that a number of leading citizens, 'have repeatedly called to mind what a great dishonour it is to this city that the front of the cathedral church should remain in its present condition, to wit, unfinished, and also that the parts already executed in no wise correspond to the rules of architecture',[8] and expressed their determination to complete the building. A competition was arranged to find the best architectural resolution to the problem and on 5 January 1491 a commission, under the presidency of two master-masons, Maso degli Albizzi and Tommaso Minerbetti, met to pass judgment on the twenty-nine designs and models which had been submitted and which included one from Lorenzo. Although he was not officially on the judging panel the dominant role which Lorenzo now played in all Florentine affairs, cultural as well as political, is suggested by subsequent events.

After Minerbetti had examined and reported on the designs, one of the canons of the cathedral, who was also a competitor, Carlo Benci, rose to his feet and suggested that no decision could be taken without Lorenzo's opinion since he was a man so well-versed in architecture that, if they followed his advice, they would be less likely to fall into error. In such a situation Lorenzo could hardly press the claims of his own design, and so tactfully suggested a delay saying that:

> All who had sent in models or designs were deserving of praise; but as the work in question was of lasting importance, long and grave deliberation was needful, and it was advisable to postpone a decision in order to consider the matter further.[9]

In consequence, no further progress was made on the cathedral during Lorenzo's lifetime.

These pursuits were all enjoyable but one event caused him satisfaction above all others. At long last, in March 1489, came the news that Giovanni had been formally nominated Cardinal Deacon of Santa Maria in Domenica. The Pope had stipulated, however, that because of the lad's extreme youth the nomination should remain a secret for three years. But Lorenzo wanted none of that. Sensible that this was, 'the greatest honour that has ever befallen our house'[10] he could scarcely wait to get his secretaries to send off letters announcing the good news to all and sundry. Visitors thronged the Medici palace with messages of congratulation while Florence went wild with joy. Bonfires illumined the whole city as if it were day, and processions wound through streets where, from every window, were hung the Medici arms. 'Thank God!' Landucci exclaimed. 'It is a great honour to our city in general and, in particular, to his father and his house,'[11] while Lorenzo commented that, 'Never have I seen more general and true rejoicing.'[12] The elevation of Giovanni to the dignity of a prince of the Church meant that the Medici family could finally be said to have achieved that respectability they had so long sought.

Innocent VIII, it is true, was irate to discover that his specific request that the news should remain secret had been openly flouted, and can scarcely have been mollified by Lorenzo's rather lame explanation that, since Giovanni's elevation was public knowledge in Rome 'the people here can hardly be blamed for following the example set there, and I could not refuse to accept the congratulations of all these citizens, down to the very poorest.'[13]

Still the Pope's anger was but a temporary and minor irritation at what was a moment of great triumph for Lorenzo. He had succeeded in achieving both his own most deeply cherished ambition and in doing something which was universally popular in Florence. Here, at last, it seemed that he could do no wrong. Although the trend towards a narrower government continued when, in 1490, the right to elect to the *Signoria* was removed from the Seventy and transferred back to *Accoppiatori* who were arbitrarily hand-picked by a committee of seventeen which included Lorenzo, this change passed scarcely without comment.

The style of Lorenzo's management now seemed to suit the Florentines who were also being seduced by the constant round of public festivities in which Lorenzo took considerable pleasure – not least in Carnival for which he was once again writing songs which his intimates were convinced were 'marvellous . . . and of a new and wonderful invention'.[14] Few activities earned him greater credit or better demonstrated his ability to respond to Florentine public opinion. Being by their very nature ephemeral, it is difficult for us now to understand the impact of these cavalcades, processions and theatrical spectacles, but they both met a public need and earned Florence a reputation for splendour throughout Europe. In addition, for Lorenzo they were a means of binding the population of Florence into a harmonious whole as the learned mingled with artisans, the nobility participated alongside the merchants and the poor in celebrations which popular memory always asserted had been stage-managed and orchestrated by Lorenzo. That he was able to play this role is probably related to the fact that he was beginning to have more time to himself as he shed some of the burdens of routine work onto the shoulders of the not always willing Piero.

The only clouds on the horizon were the activities and the preaching of the uncompromising friar, Girolamo Savonarola who, in these years, managed to achieve the apparently impossible, and created an open opposition to Lorenzo. A charismatic preacher of extreme puritanical views who first came to Florence from Ferrara in 1482, remaining initially for five years, Savonarola was opposed to all that Lorenzo and his circle stood for. His interest was not in the enjoyment of life as it was but in the creation of the Kingdom of God on earth. His message was of the need for repentance and public atonement, and he had no time for Neo-Platonic speculation which he attacked for its attempt to synthesize Christian and pagan thought. Both in his writings and in his preaching he attacked what he saw as the paganising tendencies of humanistic thought. He thundered against profane poetry from the pulpit. He condemned astrology in the full knowledge that this was Ficino's peculiar area of expertise, and he was equally free in his condemnation of those who acted as patrons of astrologers. He was given the title of 'Preacher of the Despairing' because of his defence of the poor and his attacks on social injustice. In front of a packed crowd in the cathedral, he pointedly attacked the excesses of the rich and made reference to tyrants who, he said, like Nebuchadnezzar, Nero and Domitian, must all come to a bad end. He condemned those who spent large sums on buildings, in order to render their names immortal, while the poor went hungry. So absorbed, he argued, were the ruling class of Florence in thier own sensual pleasures and diversions that they now no longer even remembered the obligations of charity.

It says much for Lorenzo's tolerance that he bore with Savonarola's attacks and did not have him expelled from the city as, in 1488, he had expelled a similar fanatic, Bernardino da Feltre. In so far as he spoke disapprovingly of Savonarola, it was on the grounds that the friar was sometimes guilty of a lapse in taste or good manners. Ironically, of course, even Savonarola was, in a sense, Lorenzo's protégé, for it was entirely due to Lorenzo that he was invited to return to Florence to preach the Lenten sermons in 1490. In addition, as we have seen, Savonarola's convent of San Marco was essentially a Medici foundation, for it was Cosimo who had been most instrumental in arranging its transfer to the Observant Franciscans in 1436, Cosimo who had paid for the rebuilding of its cloister in 1442, and Cosimo who had enriched it with paintings by Fra Angelico and the library of Niccolò Niccoli.

It was, therefore, customary for the newly-elected Prior of San Marco to pay a courtesy visit to the Medici but when Savonarola was elected to the office, he refused to visit Lorenzo. Sadly, and a shade bitterly, Lorenzo commented, 'Here is a stranger come into my house who will not even deign to visit me.'[15]

It is, however, easy to make too much of the antagonism between Lorenzo and Savonarola, an antagonism which was subsequently embroidered upon by Savonarolan hagiographers. It is true that where Lorenzo saw uncertainty, Savonarola saw only certainty, that where Savonarola was most intransigent, Lorenzo was most tolerant. Savonarola was always a man of faith while Lorenzo's faith was tinged with not a little scepticism. Doubt did not enter into Savonarola's world-view, whereas Lorenzo had an intellectual commitment to doubting everything. The man who in his *De Summo Bono* could assert that:

> . . . Our mortal vision is so limited
> That it gives us no true knowledge of God,

was speaking in a language quite alien to the Thomist tradition in which Savonarola had been trained. Lorenzo was always a deeply religious man, but the basis of his belief was his conviction that there was an unbridgeable gulf between heaven and earth. Savonarola, by contrast, was convinced that perfection not only could but must be achieved on this earth. The truth is that Savonarola was a religious fanatic and Lorenzo essentially a man of balance and moderation who would advise his son to 'avoid the Scylla of sanctimoniousness and the Charybdis of profanity . . . to be moderate in all things . . . and especially not to make a parade of austerities or strict life.'[16]

Yet, for all their differences, the two men were not poles apart. Savonarola was not an unfamiliar type in Florence which had always welcomed fiery preachers, particularly during Lorenzo's lifetime, and there was enough in Savonarola's messages to appeal to several prominent Mediceans like the poets Ugolino Verino, Alessandro Braccesi, Girolamo Benivieni and his brother, Domenico, the philosopher Oliviero Arduini, and Pico della Mirandola who is reputed to have been responsible for persuading Lorenzo to recall Savonarola to Florence in 1490. Even the friar's reiterated message that Christianity stood at a turning-point found many echoes in Landino's teaching at this time.

In addition, a major explanation of Savonarola's appeal to the Florentines was his proclamation of Florence – admittedly a reformed Florence – as the new Jerusalem, destined to inherit the mantle of imperial Rome; such sentiments were not so very different from those which, as we have seen, were being expressed in the Laurentian-inspired festivals of these years with their constant theme of an Italy united under Florentine rule. Both Savonarola and Lorenzo offered future greatness to the citizens of Florence, although they differed in their vision of what the nature of that greatness might be.

Both were of course wrong. Florence was destined neither to become a city of saints nor the unifier of Italy, but history, perhaps, accords Lorenzo the best of the argument, for, if Florence is remembered in terms of greatness today, it is because of the cultural achievements of the Renaissance which Lorenzo may have done little to create, but something to foster, and to whose values he remained true to the last. Throughout the last two years of his life he was restating that commitment as he revised the *Comento* to his own sonnets as a kind of answer to the attacks of Savonarola. There was, however, now little time left to do more, for he was, finally, losing his battle against disease.

On 29 December 1491 Lorenzo was once more stricken by gout, the pain greater than ever before. He had always suffered in cold weather and this was an excessively hard and long winter with heavy snowfalls. On 19 January it was reported that Lorenzo had not left the Medici palace for twenty-two days, and although, on 4 February, his gout had improved, he was still weak, unable to eat, and complaining of the cold. A week later he was again worse, his entire body so wracked by pain that he was unable to attend to any business. It was, said the Ferrarese ambassador, surprising that he could continue to live. According to one of his secretaries, for three weeks he would not look at a single letter.

Although concerned by Lorenzo's deep depression and great weakness, his physicians remained optimistic and seemed to be justified when on 17 February he was sufficiently improved to be able to attend to business again. He was even well enough to descend to the courtyard to inspect some new horses of Giovanni's. He spoke of going to Poggio for a change of air but, on 28 February, his pains returned with renewed severity, causing general concern throughout Florence, and preventing him from doing any business.

Lorenzo, himself, was bitterly disappointed in that he had hoped to participate fully in an event to which he had long been looking forward – the official consecration of Giovanni as a cardinal. On 3 March Giovanni, now aged sixteen years and three months, left Florence with a small retinue to ride up to the Badia – an ancient abbey, long patronised by the Medici, which stood on the slopes below Fiesole – where he spent a night's vigil in solitary prayer. On the following day his solemn consecration took place and Giovanni then returned to the city where he was met by a deputation of leading citizens, by the whole body of the Florentine clergy, and a host of ordinary Florentines. He paid a courtesy visit to the *Signoria* before returning to the Medici palace. On the following day he celebrated High Mass in the cathedral in the presence of eight bishops and the *Signoria*. Lorenzo was unable to take part in any of these ceremonies although he did manage to come into the hall of the Medici palace to watch Giovanni entertaining the leading citizens of Florence, and a number of foreign ambassadors, at a formal banquet.

This was Lorenzo's last public appearance. Indeed public affairs seemed of little importance now, and much of his mind remained fixed solely on his family, on their probable future, and on the problems which

Vasari's *Lorenzo receiving the gifts of various princes* is a posthumous piece of image-building. It includes a picture of Lorenzo's famous pet giraffe

the defects in their characters might bring. He could always leave them good advice and, indeed, one of the last letters he wrote was to Giovanni exhorting him to lead a virtuous life in his new position, and to avoid the company of those who would 'endeavour to drag you down into the abyss into which they have fallen . . . . to be guarded and reserved, so as to keep your judgments cool and unswayed by the passions of others'. Speaking out of his own lifelong experience, he advised his son to adopt the life-style which had served him well:

> Let it be your rule to rise early. Setting aside the advantage of the practice to your health, it gives you time to get through the business of the day and to fulfil your various obligations, the recitation of the office, study, audiences and whatever else has to be done . . . call to mind in the evening what will be the work of the day following, so that you may never be unprepared for your business.

The advice ended on a characteristic Medicean note, 'Take care of your health.'[17]

In the second week of March Lorenzo's pains became less severe and more intermittent, although still bad enough at night to prevent him from sleeping. He was able to walk about the Medici palace and was even well enough on 12 March to ride to Careggi and back. In his condition the journey to his beloved Poggio was out of the question, and it was, accordingly, to Careggi that he returned when he left Florence for the last time on 18 March, accompanied by his sister Bianca, his daughter Lucrezia, by Piero, Poliziano and other close friends, as well as his doctor, Piero Leoni. His doctors continued to be hopeful that a change of air would be beneficial, and in the first few days in the country he did, indeed, seem to improve. His fever left him, the pains diminished, and Lorenzo took pleasure in the warm spring air.

It was, however, but a temporary respite and, for the last time, Lorenzo took to his bed. His companions sat beside him, talking or reading aloud. Once Lorenzo remarked to Poliziano that, if his life were spared, he would dedicate the rest of it to studying and to writing poetry, but Poliziano bluntly pointed out that the Florentines would never let him.

All expected the worst and read a dire message in a number of portents reported at this time. Lightning struck the cupola of the cathedral with such force that one of the marble balls on its summit crashed into the piazza. When Lorenzo heard that it had fallen towards the Medici palace he cried out, 'Alas! Then I am a dead man.' In the gardens at Careggi it was said that grotesque and gigantic shapes could be seen and heard groaning while two of Florence's public lions were killed in a fight in their cage. A new comet heralded some great event.

A clearer message could be read in Lorenzo's rapid deterioration. By 5 April he was in continuous pain with a perpetual fever and a throat so swollen that he could barely swallow. One of his companions reported that, 'He is very depressed and can scarcely bear company, and, in conclusion, these symptoms of his disease do not look good to us. . . . we are all in suspense and utterly miserable.'[18] The next twenty-four hours brought no improvement and on 7 April all, including Lorenzo, acknowledged that the end could not be far away. The family priest came to hear his final confession. Towards midnight another priest arrived to administer communion. Lorenzo insisted on rising from his bed saying, 'It shall never be said that my Lord who created and saved me shall come to me – in my room – raise me, I beg you, raise me quickly so that I may go and meet Him.'[19] His servants supported him to the next room, where he knelt to pray in tears, but he was soon overcome by pain and had to be carried back to bed. He retained all of his mental faculties, and used these last hours to talk with Piero about the future, urging him to fear God and to live as a good Christian. In his son's presence, according to Poliziano, Lorenzo deliberately held back his tears in order not to distress Piero further. He told his son that he anticipated that the Florentines would recognise him as his successor – as, indeed, they did – but offered a final word of warning: 'Since', he said, 'the collective state is a body with many heads, remember always to follow that course which appears to be most honourable, and study rather the general welfare than individual and private interests.' Meanwhile the famous physician, Lazaro da Ficino, who had been sent by Lodovico Sforza, arrived and prescribed a concoction of pulverized pearls and precious stones merely for the sake of something to do, for he saw that the case was hopeless. Lorenzo now asked for Pico and Poliziano explained that he had remained behind in Florence lest his presence might be troublesome. 'And I,' said Lorenzo, 'but for the fear that the journey here might be irksome to him would be most glad to see him and speak to him for the last time before I leave you all.'[20] So Pico was sent for and stayed for some time talking with Lorenzo and Poliziano. They even managed to joke with each other, Lorenzo telling Pico that his one major regret was that death had not spared him enough time to complete his library or to see the manuscripts which Lascaris was bringing back from Greece.

Soon after Pico had left the room, Savonarola arrived. Contradictory accounts exist of what passed between the two men. Subsequently it became a part of the Savonarola legend to say that the friar had refused to give Lorenzo absolution because he would not promise to restore the city's liberties. But this story finds no confirmation in other eye-witness accounts nor is it historically likely. In the first place Lorenzo had no need to ask Savonarola for absolution for, as we have seen, this was given by the family priest. And, in the second place, as Savonarola knew full well, Lorenzo was in no position to restore the city's liberties which had been eroded, not just by Lorenzo, but by the whole of the ruling oligarchy of Florence. Poliziano's account of the meeting is altogether more plausible, and Poliziano is quite clear that Lorenzo received Savonarola's benediction.

On 8 April Lorenzo lapsed for a while into unconsciousness and was presumed dead until a Camaldolesian friar held the lens of his spectacles to his mouth. He received extreme unction and the story of the Passion was read aloud to him. Although he could not speak he moved his lips to show that he understood what was being read while, occasionally, he kissed a silver crucifix which was held in front of him. Finally in the early hours of the night his breathing ceased.

His body was taken immediately to the convent of San Marco. On 9 April it was carried by the Company of the Magi to the ancestral church of San Lorenzo where, on the following day, in a simple ceremony, it was laid to rest in the old sacristy beside that of Giuliano. His contemporary Florentine, Lucca Landucci, by no means a mere Medici time-server, recorded in his diary that:

> This man, in the eyes of the world, was the most illustrious, the richest, the most stately, and the most renowned among men. Everyone declared that he ruled Italy; and in very truth he was possessed of great wisdom and all his undertakings prospered.[21]

LIST OF ABBREVIATIONS

AS Mi SPE : Archivio di Stato Milano. Archivio Sforzesco, Carteggio
Potenze Estere.
ASS   : Archivio di Stato di Siena.
Comento : Lorenzo de' Medici, 'Comento ad alcuni sonetti d'amore' in
ed. E. Bigi, *Lorenzo de' Medici: Scritti Scelti* (Turin 1965).
Lettere   : Lorenzo de' Medici, *Lettere* ed. N. Rubinstein *et al.* (Florence
1977–).
MAP   : Archivio di Stato di Firenze, Mediceo avanti il Principato.
Protocolli : *Protocolli del carteggio di Lorenzo il Magnifico per gli anni
1473–74, 1474–92* ed. M. del Piazzo (Florence 1956).
Ross, *Lives* : J. Ross, *Lives of the Early Medici as told in their Correspondence*
(London 1910).

NOTES

Chapter 1

1 A. Perosa, ed., *Giovanni Rucellai ed il suo Zibaldone: I. Il Zibaldone Quaresimale* (London 1960), 4.
2 MAP. XVII c. 150.
3 A. Rochon, *La Jeunesse de Laurent de Medicis (1449–1478)* (Paris 1963), 22.
4 MAP. XVII c. 341.
5 Ross, *Lives*, 144.
6 The phrase is Poliziano's. See A. Poliziano, 'The Pazzi Conspiracy' in eds B. G. Kohl and R. G. Witt, *The Earthly Republic: Italian Humanists on Government and Society* (Manchester 1978), 317.
7 Ross, *Lives*, 77.
8 See, e.g. the *Comento*, 319.
9 H. Acton, *The Pazzi Conspiracy: the Plot against the Medici* (London 1979), 15.
10 Ross, *Lives*, 74.
11 C. Ady, *Lorenzo de' Medici and Renaissance Italy* (London 1955), 21.
12 Ross, *Lives*, 93–4.
13 *Lettere*, ii. 31.
14 Ross, *Lives*, 128.
15 Ibid.
16 N. Rubinstein, 'Lorenzo de' Medici: the Formation of his Statecraft', *Proceedings of the British Academy*, lxiii (1977), 74, Lorenzo, *Lettere*, i. 41.

Chapter 2

1 Ross, *Lives*, 154.
2 R. de Roover, *The Rise and Decline of the Medici Bank* (London 1968), 348.
3 *Lettere*, i. 191.
4 E. Barfucci, *Lorenzo de' Medici e la Società Artistica del suo Tempo* (Florence 1964), 279.
5 R. Hatfield, 'Some unknown descriptions of the Medici palace in 1459', *Art Bulletin*, lii (1970), 283.
6 *Lettere*, i. 60 n. 8.
7 C. Ady, *Lorenzo dei Medici and Renaissance Italy* (London 1955), 143.
8 R. Trexler, *Public Life in Renaissance Florence* (London 1980), 226–8.
9 R. Hatfield, 'The *Compagnia de' Magi*', *Journal of the Warburg and Courtauld Institutes*, xxxiii (1970), 122.
10 *Lettere*, i. 82.
11 U. Dorini, *I Medici e il Loro Tempo* (Florence n.d.), 93.
12 Perosa, op. cit. 39–40.
13 *Protocolli*, xv.
14 Ibid.
15 Ibid.
16 Ibid. 45.
17 *Lettere*, i. 226.
18 *Protocolli*, 221.
19 MAP XXVI, c. 45.
20 See R. Trexler, *Public Life in Renaissance Florence* (London 1980), 293.
21 MAP XXI c. 351.

22 *Protocolli*, 30.
23 Ibid. 46.
24 *Lettere*, i. 28.
25 Ibid. 33.
26 Ibid. 335.
27 Ross, *Lives*, 154.
28 A. Poliziano, 'The Pazzi Conspiracy', transl. E. B. Welles, in ed. B. G. Kohl and R. G. Witt. *The Earthly Republic: Italian Humanists in Government and Society* (Pennsylvania 1979), 311.
29 R. Trexler, *Public Life in Renaissance Florence* (London 1980), 279.
30 E.g. MAP XLVII c. 58.
31 Ibid XXVI c. 413.
32 Ibid. c. 527.

Chapter 3

1 R. Trexler, *Public Life in Renaissance Florence* (London 1980), 448.
2 E.g. *Lettere*, i. 487.
3 A. Brown, *Bartolomeo Scala 1430–1497: Chancellor of Florence* (Princeton 1979), 61.
4 *Lettere*, i. 350.
5 *The Letters of Marsilio Ficino*, transl. Language Department of the School of Economic Science, i. (London 1975), 61.
6 *Comento*, 318–9.
7 MAP XXVI c. 286. See, also, *Lettere*, i. 267.
8 See J. R. Hale, *Florence and the Medici: the Pattern of Control* (London 1977), 54.
9 *Comento*, 327.
10 *Lettere*, i. 391.
11 *Protocolli*, 16.
12 Ibid. 29–30.
13 *Lettere*, iv. 61.
14 Ficino, *Letters*, op. cit. 130.
15 Ibid. 131.
16 N. Rubinstein, 'Lorenzo de' Medici: the Formation of his Statecraft', *Proceedings of the British Academy*, lxiii (1977), 71.
17 Ross, *Lives*, 154.
18 *Lettere*, i. 51.
19 Ibid. 52.
20 N. Rubinstein, 'Lorenzo de' Medici' op. cit. 73.
21 Ibid.
22 *Lettere*, i. 59.
23 Ibid. 61.
24 Ibid. ii. 405.
25 N. Rubinstein, 'Lorenzo de' Medici' op. cit. 76.
26 This was the view of Gianozzo Pitti and Domenico Martelli, according to the Ferrarese ambassador. A. von Reumont, *Lorenzo de' Medici, the Magnificent*, transl. R. Harrison, i. (London 1876), 246.
27 *Lettere*, i. 54.
28 A. Brown, *Bartolomeo Scala*, op. cit. 60.
29 R. Trexler, *Public Life*, op. cit. 409.
30 Ibid.
31 A. Brown, *Bartolomeo Scala*, op. cit. 56.
32 Ibid.
33 Ibid. 72.
34 Ibid. 74.
35 Ibid. 96.
36 Ficino, *Lettere*, op. cit. 56.
37 *Lettere*, ii. 387.
38 Ibid. i. 207.

39 Ibid. 206.
40 Ibid. 172.
41 Ibid. 188.
42 H. Acton, *The Pazzi Conspiracy: the Plot against the Medici* (London 1979), 20.
43 N. Rubinstein, 'Lorenzo de' Medici' op. cit. 79.
44 A. Brown, *Bartolomeo Scala*, op. cit. 68.
45 R. Trexler, *Public Life*, op. cit. 410.
46 *Lettere*, i. 67.
47 Ibid. 336.
48 R. Trexler, *Public Life*, op. cit. 439.
49 *Lettere*, i. 353.
50 MAP XXVI c. 29.
51 N. Machiavelli, *The Florentine History*, Book VII.
52 *Lettere*, i. 376.
53 Ibid.

Chapter 4

1 Ross, *Lives*, 154–5.
2 M. Martelli, *Studii Laurenziani* (Florence 1965), 185.
3 Ibid. 187.
4 *Comento*, 323–4.
5 MAP XXVI c. 146.
6 See R. Trexler, *Public Life in Renaissance Florence* (London 1980), 400.
7 *Lettere*, i. 399.
8 Ibid. 129.
9 Ibid.
10 Ibid. 400–401.
11 Ibid. 425.
12 Ibid. 126.
13 Ibid. 392.
14 Ross, *Lives*, 219–220.
15 MAP XXI c. 231.
16 Ross, *Lives*, 220–3.
17 MAP XXVI c. 99.
18 *Lettere*, i. 129.
19 Ibid. ii. 482.
20 Ibid. 481.
21 V. Ilardi, 'The Assassination of Galeazzo Maria Sforza and the reaction of Italian diplomacy,' in L. Martines ed., *Violence and Civil Disorder in Italian Cities, 1200–1500* (London 1972), 97.
22 *Lettere*, ii. 421.
23 Ibid. 391.

Chapter 5

1 *Lettere*, iii. 253.
2 Ibid. ii. 392.
3 MAP XLVII c. 149.
4 *Lettere*, ii. 430.
5 Ibid.
6 Ross, *Lives*, 188.
7 Ibid.
8 *Lettere*, ii. 412.
9 H. Acton, *The Pazzi Conspiracy: the Plot against the Medici* (London 1979), 55.
10 *Lettere*, ii. 413.
11 H. Acton, op. cit. 60.
12 Report of the Milanese ambassadors, written on 28 April 1478 and printed in L. von

Pastor, *The History of the Popes from the Close of the Middle Ages* (London 1910), iv. 513.
13 A. Poliziano, 'The Pazzi Conspiracy', transl. E. B. Welles in eds. B. G. Kohl and R. G. Witt, *The Earthly Republic: Italian Humanists on Government and Society* (Pennsylvania 1978), 311.
14 N. Machiavelli, *The History of Florence*, Book viii. cap 5.
15 Ibid.
16 Pastor, op. cit. 513.
17 H. Acton, op. cit. 71.
18 Machiavelli, op. cit. Book viii. cap 8.
19 Ibid. cap 9.
20 AS Mi. SPE 295 f. 32.
21 Poliziano, op. cit. 321.
22 *Protocolli*, 48.
23 J. R. Hale, *Florence and the Medici* (London 1977), 67.
24 *Protocolli*, 48.
25 AS Mi. SPE 295 f. 32.
26 Ibid. f. 219.
27 N. Rubinstein, 'Lorenzo de' Medici: the Formation of his Statecraft', *Proceedings of the British Academy*, lxiii. (1977), 86. See, also, AS Mi SPE 295 f. 42.
28 Rubinstein, op. cit. 86.
29 AS Mi SPE 295 f. 32.
30 Ibid. f. 220.
31 Ibid. f. 230.
32 Ross, *Lives*, 203.
33 *Lettere*, iv. 92.
34 MAP XXXI cap 231.
35 *Lettere*, iv. 80.
36 AS Mi SPE 295 f. 231.
37 Ibid. f. 162.
38 Ibid. f. 295.
39 Ibid. f. 239.
40 Ross, *Lives*, 198.
41 *Lettere*, iv. 122.
42 Ross, *Lives*, 198. See, also *Lettere*, iii. 368.
43 *Lettere*, iii. 81.
44 Ibid. 133.
45 Ibid. 403–4.
46 Ibid. 404.
47 Ibid. iv. 126.
48 Ibid. 151.
49 Ibid. 204.
50 Ibid. 233.
51 Ibid. 260.
52 Ibid. 264–9.
53 Ibid. 264. See, also, ibid. 272.
54 Ibid. 272.
55 Ibid.
56 MAP CXXVIII c. 66.
57 MAP XXI c. 399.
58 MAP CXXVIII c. 68.
59 A. Brown, *Bartolomeo Scala 1430–1497* (Princeton 1979), 95.
60 MAP CXXVIII c. 71.
61 Ibid.
62 *Lettere*, iv. 323.
63 Ibid. 333–4.
64 Ibid. 337.
65 Ibid. 342.
66 Ibid. 344–5.

Chapter 6

1 Ross, *Lives*, 89.
2 Ibid.
3 A. Rochon, *La Jeunesse de Laurent de Medicis (1449–1478)* (Paris 1963), 295.
4 M. Martelli, *Studii Laurenziani* (Florence 1965), 39.
5 R. Trexler, *Public Life in Renaissance Florence* (London 1980), 451.
6 MAP XXVI c. 174.
7 E. Barfucci, *Lorenzo de' Medici e la Società Artistica del suo Tempo* (Florence 1964), 143.
8 F. W. Kent, *Household and Lineage in Renaissance Florence* (Princeton 1977), 101.
9 Ross, *Lives*, 89.
10 Barfucci, op. cit. 174.
11 MAP XLV c. 98.
12 Barfucci, op. cit. 13.
13 Ibid. 226–7.
14 Martelli, op. cit. 203.
15 C. Elam, 'Lorenzo de' Medici and the Urban Development of Renaissance Florence', *Art History*, I. 1 (March 1978), 44.
16 Ibid. 46.
17 Ibid. 47.
18 G. Pottinger, *The Court of the Medici* (London 1977), 76.
19 Barfucci, op. cit. 40.
20 Ibid. 78.
21 Ibid. 151.
22 L. Landucci, *A Florentine Diary from 1450 to 1516* (New York 1969), 49.

Chapter 7

1 See T. Zanato, *Saggio sul 'Comento' di Lorenzo de' Medici* (Florence 1979).
2 *Comento*, 323–4.
3 *Comento*, 324, 325.
4 *Comento*, 324, 325.
5 Ibid. 299.
6 Ibid. 323–4.
7 Ibid. 305–6.
8 M. Martelli, *Studii Laurenziani* (Florence 1965), 73.
9 Ibid.
10 A. Chastel, *Art et Humanisme à Florence au Temps de Laurent le Magnifique: Etudes sur la Renaissance et l'Humanisme Platonicien* (Paris 1961), 3.
11 Zanato, op. cit. 81.
12 Zanato, op. cit. 72.
13 *Comento*, op. cit. 300.
14 Ibid. 303.
15 Ross, op. cit. 91–2.
16 *Comento*, op. cit. 353.
17 *Lettere*, iii. 271.
18 *Lettere*, i. 115.
19 A. von Reumont, *Lorenzo de' Medici the Magnificent*, transl. R. Harrison, ii. (London 1876), 7.

Chapter 8

1 MAP XLV c. 362.
2 J. R. Hale, *Florence and the Medici: the Pattern of Control* (London 1977), 77.
3 A. Brown, *Bartolomeo Scala 1430–1497: Chancellor of Florence* (Princeton 1979), 333.
4 A. von Reumont, *Lorenzo de' Medici, the Magnificent*, transl. R. Harrison, ii. (London 1876), 190.

5 *Ibid*. 191.
6 ASS. Balìa n. 525 c. 23.
7 L. Landucci, *A Florentine Diary from 1450–1516* (New York 1969), 42.
8 *Protocolli*, 238.
9 MAP XXVI c. 439.
10 ASS. Balìa n. 526 c. 15.
11 MAP XXVI c. 509.
12 E. Pontieri, *La Politica Mediceo-Fiorentina nella Congiura dei Baroni Napoletani contro Ferrante d'Aragona (1485–1492)* (Naples 1977), 222.
13 MAP XXVII c. 497.
14 L. Sozzi, 'Lettere inedite di Philippe de Commynes a Francesco Gaddi', *Studi di Bibliografia e di Storia in Onore di Tammaro de Marinis*, iv. (1964), 216.
15 L. Landucci, op. cit. 31.
16 Ross, *Lives*, 242–3.
17 Ibid. 244.
18 Ibid.
19 Ibid.
20 Ibid.
21 ASS. Balìa n. 526 c. 50.
22 MAP XLV c. 311.
23 ASS. Balìa n. 522 f. 16.
24 Ross, *Lives*, 273.
25 ASS. Balìa n. 522 f. 16.
26 M. Martelli, *Studi Laurenziani* (Florence 1965), 198.
27 Ibid.
28 ASS. Balìa n. 522 c. 18. See also cc. 23, 49.
29 Martelli, op. cit. 200.
30 R. Palmarocchi, *La Politica Italiana di Lorenzo de' Medici: Firenze nella Guerra contro Innocenzo VIII* (Florence 1933), 1.
31 ASS. Balìa n. 522 c. 40.
32 Ibid.
33 von Reumont, op. cit. 238.
34 C. Ady, *Lorenzo dei Medici and Renaissance Italy* (London 1955), 104.
35 Martelli, op. cit. 201.
36 Ibid. 203.
37 Ibid. 201.
38 Ibid.
39 Ibid. 203.
40 Ibid. 205.
41 von Reumont, op. cit. 241.
42 ASS. Balìa n. 526 c. 50.
43 Ibid. c. 7.
44 Ibid. c. 35.
45 MAP XXVI c. 475.
46 ASS. Balìa n. 526 c. 11.
47 Pontieri, op. cit. 193.
48 von Reumont, op. cit. 257.
49 ASS. Balìa n. 522 c. 37.
50 Ady, op. cit. 97.
51 C. Hibbert, *The Rise and Fall of the House of Medici* (London 1974), 161.
52 Ibid.
53 R. Trexler, *Public Life in Renaissance Florence* (London 1980), 455.
54 Hibbert, op. cit. 162.
55 von Reumont, op. cit. 265–6.

Chapter 9

1 R. Palmarocchi, *Lorenzo de' Medici* (Turin 1941), 161.

2 Ibid. 157.
3 Ibid.
4 Ross, *Lives*, 296–7.
5 Von Reumont, op. cit. ii. 289.
6 Ross, *Lives*, 308.
7 Ibid.
8 von Reumont, op. cit. ii. 157.
9 Ibid. 158.
10 Ross, *Lives*, 303.
11 L. Landucci, *A Florentine Diary from 1450–1516* (New York 1969), 47.
12 Ross, *Lives*, 303.
13 Ibid.
14 M. Martelli, *Studi Laurenziani* (Florence 1965), 38.
15 G. Pottinger, *The Court of the Medici* (London 1977), 63–4.
16 Ross, *Lives*, 333–4.
17 Ibid. 332–5.
18 Martelli, op. cit. 221.
19 Ross, *Lives*, 337.
20 Ibid. 338.
21 Landucci, op. cit. 54.

SELECT BIBLIOGRAPHY

I PRINTED SOURCES

The Letters of Marsilio Ficino, transl. Language Department of the School of Economic Science (London 1975).

B. G. Kohl and R. G. Witt, *The Earthly Republic: Italian Humanists on Government and Society* (Manchester 1978). Includes Poliziano's account of 'The Pazzi Conspiracy'.

L. Landucci, *A Florentine Diary from 1450 to 1516* (New York 1969).

Lorenzo de' Medici, *Lettere*, ed. N. Rubinstein (Florence 1977 –   ).

Lorenzo de' Medici, *Scritti Scelti*, ed. E. Bigi (Turin 1955).

G. Pampaloni, 'Fermenti di riforme democratiche nella Firenze medicea del quattrocento.' *Archivio Storico Italiano* (1961), 11–61, 241–81.

A. Perosa ed.: *Giovanni Rucellai ed il suo zibaldone: I.ll Zibaldone Quaresimale* (London 1960).

E. Pontieri, *La Politica Mediceo – Fiorentina nella Congiura dei Baroni Napoletani contro Ferrante d'Aragona (1485–1492)* (Naples 1977).

Protocolli del carteggio di Lorenzo il Magnifico per gli anni 1473–74, 1477–92 ed. M. de Piazzo (Florence 1956).

J. Ross, *Lives of the Early Medici as shown in their correspondence* (Boston 1911).

L. Sozzi, 'Lettere inedite di Philippe de Commynes a Francesco Gaddi', *Studi di Bibliografia e di Storia in Onore di Tammaro de Marinis*, iv (1964).

II SECONDARY WORKS

H. Acton, *The Pazzi Conspiracy: the Plot against the Medici* (London 1979). A pro-Medicean straightforward narrative account.

C. Ady, *Lorenzo de' Medici and Renaissance Italy* (London 1955). This has been, for too long, the only short, readily available scholarly biography in English.

E. Barfucci, *Lorenzo de' Medici e la Società Artistica del suo Tempo* (Florence 1964). Encyclopaedic and enthusiastic rather than critical in its approach.

C. Bec, *L'Umanesimo Letterario* (Turin 1976).

C. Bonello Uricchio, 'I rapporti tra Lorenzo il Magnifico e Galeazzo Maria Sforza', *Archivio Storico Lombardo* (1964–5), 33–49.

A. Brown, *Bartolomeo Scala 1430–1497: Chancellor of Florence* (Princeton 1979).

Giovanni Cecchini, 'La guerra della congiura dei Pazzi e l'andata di Lorenzo de' Medici a Napoli', *Bullettino Senese di Storia Patria* (1965), 291–301.

A. Chastel, *Art et Humanisme à Florence au Temps de Laurent le Magnifique: Etudes sur la Renaissance et l'Humanisme Platonicien* (Paris 1961). Less informative about Lorenzo than its title suggests.

U. Dorini, *I Medici e il loro Tempo* (Florence n.d.).

C. Elam, 'Lorenzo de' Medici and the Urban Development of Renaissance Florence', *Art History* I.1 (March 1978).

R. A. Goldthwaite, *Private Wealth in Renaissance Florence; a study of Four Families* (Princeton 1968).

J. R. Hale, *Florence and the Medici: the Pattern of Control* (London 1977). The best introduction to the subject.

R. Hatfield, 'The Compagnia de' Magi', *Journal of the Warburg and Courtauld Institutes*, xxxiii (1970).

C. Hibbert, *The Rise and Fall of the House of Medici* (London 1974). A popular and rather highly-coloured introduction.

V. Ilardi, 'The Assassination of Galeazzo Maria Sforza and the reaction of Italian diplomacy' in L. Martines ed. *Violence and Civil Disorder in Italian Cities 1200–1500* (London 1972).

D. Kent, *The Rise of the Medici; faction in Florence 1426–1434* (Oxford 1978). Essentially deals with the emergence of Cosimo but useful background for the understanding of the later fifteenth century.

D. Kent, 'The Florentine *reggimento* in the fifteenth century', *Renaissance Quarterly*, 28 (1975), 575–638.

F. W. Kent, *Household and Lineage in Renaissance Florence* (Princeton 1977).

D. Koenigsberger, *Renaissance Man and Creative Thinking* (London 1979). A difficult but rewarding book.

M. Martelli, *Studii Laurenziani* (Florence 1965). A collection of essays, meticulously researched. Pro-Lorenzo but, nonetheless, critically objective.

L. Martines, *Lawyers and Statecraft in Renaissance Florence* (Princeton 1968).

R. Palmarocchi, *Lorenzo de' Medici* (Turin 1941).

R. Palmarocchi, *La Politica Italiana di Lorenzo de' Medici: Firenze nella Guerra centro Innocenzo VIII* (Florence 1933).

A. van Reumont, *Lorenzo de' Medici, the Magnificent* transl. R. Harrison (London 1876). A monumental nineteenth century work, inevitably out-of-date, it still contains much useful material.

R. Ridolfi, *The Life of Girolamo Savanarola* (Connecticut 1959).

A. Rochan, *La Jeunesse de Laurent de Medicis (1449–1478)* (Paris 1963). Although covering only the period up to the Pazzi conspiracy, this is the most successful attempt to see Lorenzo as a whole person, rather than categorised as 'statesman' 'poet' 'artist' etc.

R. de Roover, *The Rise and Decline of the Medici Bank* (London 1968). An immensely influential work whose repercussions on scholarship are still being felt.

N. Rubinstein, *The Government of Florence under the Medici* (Oxford 1966).

N. Rubinstein, 'Florentine Constitutionalism and Medici ascendancy in the Fifteenth Century', in ed. N. Rubinstein, *Florentine Studies Politics and Society in Renaissance Florence* (London 1968).

N. Rubinstein, 'Lorenzo de' Medici: the Formation of his Statecraft', *Proceedings of the British Academy* lxiii (1977). A brilliant reconstruction of the political events in Florence in the years immediately following Piero's death, written by a scholar who knows more about the subject than anyone else alive.

J. E. Seigel, *Rhetoric and Philosophy in Renaissance Humanism* (Turin 1976).

G. Soranzo, 'Lorenzo il Magnifico alla morte del padre e il suo primo balzo verso la signoria', *Archivio Storico Italiano* (1953) 42–77.

R. Trexler, *Public Life in Renaissance Florence* (London 1980). Stimulating and exciting, this is likely to become a very influential work.

D. Weinstein, *Savonarola and Florence; prophecy and patriotism in the Renaissance* (Princeton 1970).

C. Weissmann, *Ritual Brotherhood in Renaissance Florence* (New York 1981).

T. Zanato, *Saggio sul 'Comento' di Lorenzo de' Medici* (Florence 1979).

INDEX